PRAISE FOR MARY WILLIS WALKER'S

All the Dead Lie Down

BANTAM BOOKS

New York
Toronto
London
Sydney
Auckland

ALL THE DEAD LIE DOWN

Mary

Willis

Walker

This edition contains the complete text of the original hardcover
edition.
NOT ONE WORD HAS BEEN OMITTED.

ALL THE DEAD LIE DOWN

A Bantam Book

PUBLISHING HISTORY
Doubleday edition published May 1998
Bantam mass market edition / March 2002

Library of Congress Catalog Card Number: 97-24131

ISBN: 0-553-57822-7

Published simultaneously in the United States and Canada

Bantam Books are published by Bantam Books, a division of
Random House, Inc. Its trademark, consisting of the words
"Bantam Books" and the portrayal of a rooster, is Registered in
U.S. Patent and Trademark Office and in other countries. Marca
Registrada. Bantam Books, 1540 Broadway, New York, New
York 10036.

PRINTED IN THE UNITED STATES OF AMERICA

OPM 10 9 8 7 6 5 4 3 2 1

For Holly Willis Darby and
Susan Willis Devening.
Sisters are forever—
thank heaven!

Acknowledgments

My favorite part of writing a book is the research. It gives me license to pick up the phone and call people, out of the blue, and ask them to tell me what they know about a certain subject. And, to my delight, they do tell me! Here are just a few of the people who have shared their time and expertise with me. I am very grateful to them all.

Fred Askew, Robert Barnstone, Jodi Berls, Bill Cryer, Dinah Chenven, Norman Chenven, Gary Cohen, Frank Groves, Joe Hairston, James L. Haley, Jeff Hartman, Sandy Levinson, Kristy Ozmun, Peter Pincoffs, Carl Reynolds, Elaine Salazar, Susan Wade, Amanda Walker, Suzanna Walker, Alison Wetzel, Ralph Willis, and Bryan Wyatt.

All the
Dead
Lie
Down

1

THE MAN IN THE MOON LOOKED OUT OF THE
   MOON,
LOOKED OUT OF THE MOON AND SAID,
" 'TIS TIME FOR ALL CHILDREN ON THE EARTH
TO THINK ABOUT GETTING TO BED!"
                                        —*MOTHER GOOSE*

Sarah Jane Hurley wakes with a wetness on her fingertips.
She raises her hand to her eyes and tilts it to catch the narrow ribbon of moonlight shining through the slats of the
deck above. Blood. Yes, it's blood. *Fee, fi, fo, fum.* On her
fingertips and under her nails. Fresh blood, shiny and new.
Her own blood. Must've been scratching her bites in her
sleep. She's pulled some scabs off and they've bled again. It's
happened so often she doesn't feel it anymore. It doesn't
even hurt.

She brings her hand closer to her face and studies the
blood, surprised: it's so *beautiful*—bright and shiny as a
brand-new red Crayola—the same as when she was a girl.
Way back then, lying in the hammock in her gramma's backyard in Galveston, she'd hold very still and let a mosquito
land on her arm. Barely breathing, she'd watch its stinger
pierce her skin, her perfect, smooth ten-year-old skin—
summer-tanned, stretched tight over thin arms. She'd hold
her breath and watch the insect fatten itself. She'd wait until
it was full, and then she'd raise a hand and slap down hard—
splat. And, wonder of wonders, she would see her own bright
blood smeared on her skin next to the squashed mosquito.

Sarah Jane sticks her tongue out and touches it to a bloody fingertip. Salty, rusty taste. Just like back then. But it should taste different now. It should taste like cheap wine and stale cigarette smoke and day-old pizza scrounged from Dumpsters and cold, scummy coffee—all those snips and snails that make up her body now.

But, somehow, she still has the same blood as that young girl in the hammock, that smooth-skinned, sugar-and-spice child. Even though now her skin is ruined—reddened and weathered, and even though she's covered with insect bites and scabs and scars and cuts and bruises she can't even remember how she got.

Yes, her blood should look different. But it doesn't. It is still bright red and wet and hopeful. As though she might be the same inside—Sarah Jane Hurley, good girl. *"There was a little girl who had a little curl,"* Gramma would say, stroking Sarah Jane's curly hair, *"right in the middle of her forehead. And when she was good, she was very, very good."* That was when Sarah Jane talked proper English and behaved in the ladylike way Gramma wanted her to. And when she held on to her temper and didn't let people make her mad all the time.

Sarah Jane screws her face up in disgust. Ladylike? What a joke! If Gramma were alive now, she'd cross the street to avoid her, such a filthy, hopeless old hag she's become. *"But when she was bad she was horrid."* Gramma said that too—when Sarah Jane acted just like her no-good mother and got into all that trouble as a teenager. But even Gramma didn't imagine just *how* horrid Sarah Jane could be, that she would end up like this—a homeless old drunk. And that wasn't even the worst of it. She had far worse to account for than just ending up a bum.

She shakes her head to stop this train of thought; she's letting herself get sucked into that old rearview-mirror trap. She won't think about what's done and can't be changed. She wipes her bloody fingers off on the dirty black and white coat that's wrapped around her and tries to go back to sleep. She is just drifting off when she hears noises—some sharp bangs and thuds above her. Thunder? No. Footsteps. Well, damn! There's not supposed to be anyone up there. At lunchtime, sure, they let people eat out there, but then the deck closes and it belongs to her. After dark, it's all hers.

A bright light comes on, chasing away the moonlight.

Sarah Jane looks up at the wooden deck, at the thin stripes of harsh floodlight between the slats. Carefully she turns over on her back, keeping her big canvas bag under her head. She tries not to make any noise, not to rustle the flattened cardboard refrigerator carton she is lying on. She stares up at the deck, three feet above. Black forms break up the yellow stripes. The lines of light flicker. A clopping right over her head makes her blink. Then a scraping noise.

Someone's sitting down. Damn. This has never happened, in the ... how long has it been? More than a year. No one has ever sat down on the deck after dark. Occasionally someone would wander out, but they would see it was closed and leave.

Now there are voices overhead, male voices. A smooth, phony-type voice is droning. She catches some words. "Full moon tonight, sir. Real pretty. Sure it's not too cool for you out here? Technically, the deck is closed, but since your friend needs to smoke—"

A loud laugh barks out. "Fine. Real fine. You just be sure and tell Mr. Vogel I'm out here when he comes. And, pardner—let's keep it private out here, know what I'm saying?" This voice is one of those bossy, king-of-the-world voices Sarah Jane hates the most. It's the kind of voice that tells you to get off the bench, get out of the park, leave the library, move along, 'cause he owns the world and you don't.

"Would you like something to drink while you're waiting?" the smooth voice overhead croons.

Oh, my. Sarah Jane lets her eyes close. A drink—that's the ticket. That's the way you keep your eyes off that old rearview mirror. That's how you get beyond pain.

A set of footsteps retreats and a door closes.

It's quiet, except for the tapping of a quick, nervous toe above. This makes the light dance in a jittery pattern and jangles Sarah Jane's nerves. Now she can't go back to sleep, but she's afraid to move around, or the toe-tapper up there will hear her. She'll have to keep real quiet or they'll call the cops on her like they threatened to do last time. And that would be the end. They'd find out her real name and put it in their computer and come up with what happened in Houston, and they would lock her up for sure. Then she'd be kaput, done in. God, she couldn't even manage school, or working steady, or being married or any of those closed-in things people are supposed to do. She'd never survive jail.

So she waits without making a sound. She's pretty good at waiting; it's the one thing she's been practicing for years—waiting for fate to come along and tell her what to do next. It's quiet now except for a faint buzz of voices and dishes clinking inside the Creekside Grill and, of course, the toe tapping, which never lets up—tappety, tap, tap. That's one nervous dude up there. His edginess vibrates her body, speaks to her own skittish nervous system. Like Morse code, it tells her his skin feels too tight, his blood too thick, his veins too narrow, his hair follicles too full of living roots. It makes him tic and tap and itch.

Sarah Jane itches too—her bites are driving her crazy. Goddamn fire ants. Buggers act like they own the world, too. Maybe they do. Or will. When people destroy everything else, those mean little red ants will inherit the earth. She pictures it—a round planet still spinning, but barren, no lakes or trees or buildings, nothing but millions and millions of those dirt mounds that fire ants push up. When all is said and done, concentrated meanness will inherit the earth.

Finally the deck shudders with more footsteps. One set sounds like a giant wearing jackboots. "Here he is, sir," says the phony, suck-up voice. "You gentlemen make yourselves comfortable out here. Your waiter will be right out."

The wimpy footsteps retreat and the door closes. "Well, pardner," Toe-tapper says, "it's getting to be—"

"Wait!" says a new voice. "I want to look around." This voice is low and growly, much older, with some kind of foreign accent. It matches the heavy footsteps that rattle the deck. The guy must weigh a ton. Clumpety, clump. The noise reminds Sarah Jane of something—a nursery rhyme, maybe—where someone goes tramp, tramp over a bridge and someone else is hiding under that bridge. Now how did that one go? Gramma read it to her and she used to read it to Tom and Ellie back in the good days of stories and nursery rhymes, when she was still trying to be a real mother, before everything went wrong. It had to do with goats.

"Looks all right," says the guttural voice. A memory zings her: Gruff! Billy Goat Gruff! And the biggest goat had a threatening, kick-butt voice like this guy's. She can't quite recall how the story went. She'll look it up at the library—if she can sneak back in.

Overhead a chair scrapes on wood.

"Glad to see you're a careful professional," Toe-tapper says. "You ready, pardner?"

"Ready to get paid," the guttural voice growls. "I've incurred expenses."

"Hey, Mr. V., we agreed. For the cause—half up front, half on completion. We're good for it. The posse's got real deep pockets."

"So I hear."

Sarah Jane wishes they'd pipe down or move indoors so she can go back to sleep.

"You got the stuff all ready?" Toe-tapper asks.

"Yah." Old Billy Goat Gruff is a man of few words.

"It's time for you to take a tour of the Capitol, Mr. V. Free public tours every fifteen minutes. See how your tax dollar's been spent."

Sarah Jane tunes in here. The Capitol—she passes it on her rounds every day. She's wondered if it would be a good place to cop some A/C on hot days.

"They've done a real pretty job of renovating the old girl," Toe-tapper is saying, "but for a hundred and eighty-seven mil, they ought to, huh? Follow the guide and look real good at the Senate chamber."

"The Senate chamber?"

"Yessir. That's where you're gonna do your thing. You're going to turn that Senate chamber into a gas chamber. Being a Kraut, you know all about—"

"Stop right there, mister!" The gruff voice is dead mean. It makes Sarah Jane suck in her breath. Anyone talked to her that way, she'd reach for her knife real quick. "I'm a citizen of the United States," he says, cold as ice, "just like you."

"Okay. Okay," Toe-tapper says. "Keep your powder dry." He laughs. "You like art, pardner?"

"If it's naked."

"Well, hate to disappoint you, but this is art with no tits. Take a long look at *Dawn at the Alamo*—the guide will point it out—an old oil painting with lots of blue in it, real pretty, my personal favorite. Right above it, in the public gallery, is where you'll probably want to set up shop.

"Hang around awhile after the tour. But if you see me, don't say howdy 'cause we never met. Get the layout of the chamber in your head. Sit up in the gallery a spell and ponder the security. Know what I'm saying, pardner?"

There is silence, then the flick of a cigarette lighter. Sarah Jane holds very still. She is close enough to smell the cigarette smoke. Public gallery? Sounds like a place you could sleep and no one would notice. If it's public like he says, they have to let you in or you can make a big stink about being discriminated against. Sarah Jane decides she's going to take that tour. She needs a new place to hang out during the day after what happened at the library.

"When do you want the service delivered?" This is the big billy goat talking.

Toe-tapper laughs his high horse laugh. "Why? Your dance card getting filled up?"

"I asked you when." The voice drips with menace.

Toe-tapper says, "Now, pardner, we agreed you'd be on call, ready to deliver between now and sine die, the end of the term." He laughs, a nervous laugh that tells Sarah Jane he is scared of this dude but is trying not to show it. "I'm gonna let you know in plenty of time, just like I said. See, we won't know until the bill gets scheduled. But I'm there watching every day. When it's set for a vote, I'll call you just like we agreed. In about a week, we figure."

"I been reading the paper. They say it's a done deal."

"Sure," says Toe-tapper. "If it ever comes to a vote, but

we're not gonna let that happen. Know what I'm saying, pardner?"

"Yah. I know what you're saying," growls Billy Goat Gruff.

"We let them pass this bill and we're saying so long to our God-given rights. Once they get us to sign up for licenses, the Feds got their lists ready for the big confiscation, sure as shooting." He chuckles as if he's made some joke. "The four L's of gun control, pardner. Licenses lead to lists. Lists lead to loss. Loss leads to lamenting. Know what I'm saying, pardner?"

"Yah, I know. You're preaching to the choir," Billy Goat says, "but does the posse understand how lethal this soman is?"

"Meanest-ass gas around. Sure, we know. You aren't going mushy on me, are you, Mr. V.? Tell you what: you sit in the gallery like I do every day, up there above the chamber, and you look down at your state senators scurrying around. Know what they are? Cockroaches. Traitors. In league with the Feds, trying to take away our constitutional right to defend ourselves. That's what they are—cockroaches, and they deserve exterminating. Think about Waco and Ruby Ridge."

Suddenly Sarah Jane tenses in panic. A hand is clamped over her mouth. It has come out of the darkness with no sound to warn her. Someone has crept under the deck, into her space. She reaches up to grab her bag, her knife, but a hand pins her arm down and a heavy shoulder leans on the other arm. The hands feel horny and rough. He crawls on top of her, his lanky body weighing her down, settling into hers. His breath smells of deep sewer rot. His beard, pressing against her cheek, feels like sandpaper and wire. He doesn't make a sound.

He lets go of her arm, reaches down, and hikes her long coat up around her hips. He keeps one hand pressed over her mouth.

Very slowly, Sarah Jane lifts her free arm and raises it toward his face. She extends her index finger and lays it gently against his lips. "Shhhhh," she whispers into the hand covering her mouth.

He lifts his hand.

She breathes into his ear, "Not now."

"Fair lady," he whispers, "I got wine."

Wine! She loses all interest in the conversation overhead. "How much?"

"Enough." He is inching his zipper down. "Plenty."

"Lufkin, shhh. They'll hear," she whispers. She is torn. She wants the wine but, even more, she wants to keep this space she's staked out. The earth is powdery and soft here under the cardboard where she's cleared away all the rocks. It's near the creek and mostly protected from the rain. She likes it here. It's home. "Just wait," she whispers.

He holds still for a few seconds, listening to the conversation on the deck above. The two men are talking about baseball now. Sarah Jane wraps her arms around Lufkin's thin body and holds him tight to keep him quiet. They lie like that for a few minutes, and soon they are rewarded for their patience. Chairs scrape the deck and the light flickers. There's some stomping around, some more talk. And, finally, the beautiful sound of the invaders leaving—trip-trap, trip-trap. Yes, that's the noise the goats make on the bridge, she thinks—trip-trap. And under the bridge is someone who wants to eat the goats up. It's a troll, an ugly troll, and he says...something. What is it the troll says? She's gotten so she can't remember a damn thing, even when she wants to. Maybe that's what happens when you block out the past— you lose the knack of remembering anything at all.

Overhead, the footsteps beat a retreat—trip-trap. Oh, yes! The troll says—*Who's that tripping over my bridge?* That's *it.* She's so pleased to remember it she whispers it in Lufkin's ear: *"Who's that tripping over my bridge?"*

"Huh?" he says, finally inching his zipper all the way down.

She feels like calling it out loud: *Who's that tripping over* MY *bridge?* That'd shake 'em up for a second or two—those goats up there—show them maybe they don't own the world after all.

The door closes, muffling the distant clink of knives and forks, the chatter and laughter from inside the grill. The harsh floodlight flicks off. Now it is peaceful again, with just the soft moonlight drifting through the cracks in the deck, making everything look nice and dreamy, exactly the way Sarah Jane likes it.

"Now," she croons, "let's take a look at that wine."

2

AN ARMED NATION IS A POLITE NATION.

—NRA SLOGAN

"Stars everywhere you look," Molly Cates said with her head resting on the back of the seat. She was gazing up at the constellation of glass stars etched on the skylight panels that made up the ornate ceiling of the Texas Senate chamber. "Stars on the ceiling, stars in the chandeliers, stars on the doorknobs, even the hinges."

"Texans do not scrimp on stars. Maybe that's why I put stars in this new design," Rose Morrisey said, studying the needlepoint in her lap. Molly looked down at the half-completed piece—a mostly floral design with pansies on a royal blue background, but scattered throughout were tiny white stars.

Wanda Lavoy, the handgun expert with the big hair, who was sitting on Molly's other side, leaned across her to look. "That's real pretty, Miz Morrisey."

"You can't overdo stars." Molly rolled her head from side to side, trying to relax the kinks in her neck. Every day she spent in the legislature watching her state government at work made her neck stiffer and her current project less interesting, like a term paper whose subject has turned sour.

Everybody agreed that the concealed handgun bill was a

slam dunk, a done deal from the start. It had whizzed through the House and showed every indication of doing the same in the Senate. The new governor was on the record with a campaign promise to sign it into law. After several weeks of following it, Molly had concluded there was no real drama and, ultimately, very little importance. Texans would most likely continue to shoot one another in record numbers whether they could get licensed to carry concealed handguns or not.

"Rose, you remember those star cookie cutters Aunt Harriet had?" Molly asked. "And those fabulous butter cookies she'd make at Christmas with the shiny colored sprinkles on top? She'd put them in baskets on the table and they'd twinkle in the candlelight—like baskets of real stars."

Rose looked up from her needlepoint. "Harriet sure knew how to bake and how to make a house pretty at Christmas."

The memory made Molly's stomach lurch with a sudden dip, like when an airplane hits an air pocket. Now her Aunt Harriet, that opinionated, cookie-baking bane of Molly's adolescence, was in a nursing home and didn't know a star from a bedpan.

Molly had been experiencing more than the usual number of memory air pockets lately. Family was on her mind. It wasn't just the stars. It was spending so much time with Rose and Parnell Morrisey that was doing it. Rose, her godmother, sitting next to her in her elegant navy knit suit and silk blouse, still wore her long hair French-braided in one thick plait, though it was pure white now, and she still smelled coolly of the same tea rose perfume she had always used. The scent recalled vividly the summer evenings of Molly's childhood, when they had all sat on the Cateses' front porch and told stories.

Parnell, especially, had a way of opening Molly's old wounds—and old delights as well. All it took was his physical presence: his whiskey-and-tobacco smell, his raspy drawl and booming laugh. The way he said, "Molly, sweetheart, you just sit your pretty self right down here and let me worry about that," made her feel like a girl again, taken care of in a way she hadn't felt since her daddy died—her daddy, who had been dead and buried these twenty-eight years. But not forgotten, no, never forgotten.

She looked for Parnell amid the chaos down on the Senate floor. There he was, sitting at his desk, talking with several legislative aides. The old senator's bald pate gleaming in the lights looked vulnerable as a bird's egg, and his doleful mud slide of a face droopier and more creased than usual, as if it were threatening to slip right off his skull. He's getting old for this circus, Molly thought, seventy-three now, the same age her daddy would be. He'd had a heart bypass last year and had never fully recovered, it seemed to her. The powerful men of her childhood were now either dead or decrepit versions of what they had been, and she hated it.

They'd been best friends from the third grade on—Parnell Morrisey and Vernon Cates. They'd gone to grade school and high school together out west in Crosbyton, near Lubbock, run track together, worked on the school newspaper together, and gone to Texas Tech together. Parnell and his wife Rose were Molly's godparents; her earliest memories included Parnell and Rose at family birthdays and picnics and holidays. And funerals, of course. The Morriseys had been at all the Cates funerals. When her mother died, it was Parnell and Rose and Molly's Aunt Harriet who filled in to help her and her daddy cope with the loss. Molly had been nine. And then when her daddy was killed, when Molly was sixteen, the same three people were there to console and support her, even though she was inconsolable and her Aunt Harriet always maintained she was insupportable.

"When's he going to retire from this circus?" Molly asked.

Rose looked down at her husband of more than fifty years. "When he loses an election, or when they bury him—whichever one comes first."

Down on the floor, the pastor from the First Baptist Church of Waco was finishing a long-winded invocation, thanking God for just about everything he could think of, including the bicameral body of the Texas legislature, the lieutenant governor, the pages, the new governor, the visitors up in the gallery, the spring weather, and the renovations to the Capitol. The lieutenant governor then introduced the first speaker for Bill 98—the honorable Senator Garland Rauther from Schulenburg.

Senator Rauther, the cosponsor of the concealed handgun bill, a large man in a pinstripe suit and lots of French cuff at the wrist to show off gold cufflinks in the shape of pistols, stood at his desk and picked up his microphone. "Folks, today I could recite to you the many polls that show how strongly the citizens of Texas support this bill, but I'm not gonna do that. And I could tell you how successful and trouble-free such carry laws have proved to be in states like Florida which have been pioneering the way for us, but I'm not gonna do that either. Instead, I want to tell you a story. It is a story that will break your heart and it will also explain why I am cosponsoring Bill 98 that will allow any law-abiding citizen of our state to obtain a license to carry a handgun for personal protection. Now this story may be familiar to you, but I believe it warrants being told today."

"Oh, no," Molly groaned, "the Pizza Parlor again."

"Shhh," Wanda said.

Rose leaned her shoulder against Molly's. "Behave yourself."

"But, Rose, there can't be a single person in the state who hasn't heard this story twenty times," Molly said. She had a sudden rebellious urge to take off and go home. She'd much rather be working on her other project—the stories of five homeless women she'd been interviewing for several months. She could just declare her research in the legislature finished and leave. True, she had a lunch date with the Morriseys, but Rose would understand if she decided to leave now. She had enough information to write her handgun article right now. The problem was, once she got started on research, she found it difficult to stop, even when she was disenchanted with a subject, as she was now. She was afraid if she stopped she'd miss the one perfect detail or the one quote that would make the story.

"Folks," Senator Rauther was saying, "you've all read

about Elizabeth Shoemaker in the newspaper. She is a remarkable woman, a fifth-generation Texan, a loyal wife, a loving mother and grandmother, who never once, in thirty-five years, missed teaching her Sunday school class at First Lutheran in Houston. She is also a lifetime member of the National Rifle Association, a crack shot with a pistol," he intoned, "the daughter of a Beaumont police officer who taught all his children the fine points of gun safety and marksmanship. Before she was twelve this lady could shoot off a gnat's eyebrow at twenty yards."

Wanda leaned over and whispered, "You're coming tomorrow, right? You and your daughter?"

Molly nodded. She had committed to the course of handgun training as part of the research for her article on the bill and there was no getting out of it now.

"You can stay after the lesson," Wanda said, "and watch my WIC gals shoot."

Molly nodded again. She was entertaining herself by letting her gaze range around the gallery, looking for more stars, like the children's game of finding Waldo. She spotted a group of elementary school children wearing matching gimme caps with little Texas flags on the front—more stars. Then her eyes stopped on a glittery silver star she hadn't noticed before—a man's belt buckle proudly displayed just below his prominent paunch. "And star-spangled bellies," she muttered.

"Say what?" Wanda said.

"Why is it, Wanda, that Texas men wear their belts so low?"

"Is this a joke?"

"No. A quest for enlightenment. That one standing over there with the belt buckle, for example." She pointed at the man across the gallery who was talking with one of the security guards, his hands in his pockets, his head turned away from them.

Wanda studied the man. "Don't it beat all? The way men'll flaunt their big guts like that? A woman would be doing her best to hide it."

"Yeah," Molly said, "it's a dominance thing, I think. Like

baboons raising their hackles and jumping up and down to make themselves look bigger."

As though he sensed he was being talked about, the man turned in their direction.

The second she glimpsed his face, Molly stopped breathing. She couldn't believe what she was seeing. It was a face she hadn't seen in twenty-five years, but she remembered every detail of it: the weak chin, the lumpy cheeks, the slightly off-center nose, the mean-spirited slit of mouth. His hair had grayed and thinned to a few strands combed over the top, but otherwise he looked pretty much the same.

Molly felt her cheeks flush with heat. It was as if her recent dwelling on family memories had conjured up this nightmare from the past, this demon that had lain dormant for twenty-five years.

"Wanda," she said when she had caught her breath, "Wanda, do you know that man?"

Wanda got her glasses out of her purse and put them on. "The one with the star on his gut?"

"Yeah. Him." She could barely squeeze the words out.

"I think he's one of the lobbyists for TEXRA, but darned if I can remember his name."

"Olin Crocker." The name tasted like acid on Molly's lips.

"Crocker, yeah. That sounds right. You know him?"

"A long time ago. He used to be Travis County sheriff."

"Was he?" Wanda said with no interest. "Must've been before my time." Her attention had clearly shifted to the floor where Senator Rauther, finished extolling Elizabeth Shoemaker's virtues, was launching into the Pizza Parlor horror. "It was a Friday night," he said, "two years ago—a rainy Friday night in November, and Miz Shoemaker, her daughter Jessica, and Jessica's three young children happened to stop for dinner at the Pizza Parlor in Liberty. They'd put their order in and were sitting at the table waiting for their food, innocent of the fact that the worst kind of bad luck was about to befall them—the kind of random bad luck that could just as easily happen to any of us."

Molly found the story too painful to hear again and she

couldn't take her eyes off Olin Crocker. "Rose," she said, leaning over to whisper in her ear, "that's Olin Crocker over there."

Rose looked where Molly was pointing. "The sheriff, you mean? Is that him? I don't believe I ever met him, Molly."

The guard had moved back to his station in the corner of the gallery and Crocker was standing alone now, his hands still in his pockets, looking down at the speaker on the Senate floor.

"If I could raise my finger right now," Molly said to Rose, "and smite him with Pharaoh's plagues—all ten of them—I would do it." She raised her index finger in front of her eyes and lined it up so it rested on Olin Crocker's belt buckle. "Pow."

Senator Rauther was saying, "The bad luck came in the form of Randall Carpenter, a drifter with a long history of mental problems. Randall Carpenter had just been fired that morning from his job as dishwasher and floor sweeper at the Pizza Parlor and he was angry, real angry, so angry he decided to get even. He still had a set of keys and the first thing he did this November night when he got to the Pizza Parlor was lock the front door so no one inside would be able to escape his wrath. Miz Shoemaker says she looked up and saw him standing there at the door all wild-eyed, with his rifle at his side, and she knew he was fixing to go on a shooting spree."

Molly kept her finger lined up on Olin Crocker. "You owe me something," she whispered to herself. "You vicious, corrupt, lecherous son of a bitch, you still owe me something, and I still want it."

Senator Rauther's voice got lower. "And she was right, folks. Randall Carpenter raised that rifle and commenced to shoot. First he shot the manager who'd fired him. Then he shot a pretty seventeen-year-old waitress who'd refused to go out on a date with him. Then he shot the cook and the new dishwasher who'd replaced him. And then he started in on the customers. There were twenty-seven of them, including a kids' soccer team; see, Friday night in Liberty lots of folks like to go out for pizza. You can imagine the scene, can't you? Everyone screaming, running for the door, hiding under tables and behind chairs, trying to shield their loved ones. But it didn't do them any good. The shooter went about his business real slow and deliberate, Miz Shoemaker says, walking around the room calmly, shooting them, one by one, those people who were unlucky enough to have gone out for pizza that night. Fish in a barrel." He shook his big head. "Fish in a barrel. The Shoemakers were the last ones. Before he got around to them he'd already shot the twenty-two other customers and reloaded his gun twice."

He paused for dramatic effect, his head hanging as if in mourning. Then he looked up at the gallery and said, "Now, folks, Miz Shoemaker happens to be the owner of several guns. One of them is a .38 police special her daddy gave her when he retired from the force. When she travels she carries that revolver in the glove compartment of her vehicle for personal protection. She would of liked to bring it with her in her handbag into the restaurant that Friday night, but she didn't because it is against the law to carry a concealed weapon in the state of Texas and Elizabeth Shoemaker is a law-abiding citizen who has never gotten so much as a parking ticket."

Molly was barely listening; she knew the story all too well and had noticed Elizabeth Shoemaker sitting stoically on the other side of the gallery, listening to the retelling of her tragedy. But right now Molly had eyes only for Olin Crocker. He moved down to the front row and sat. Since she was in the front row too, directly across the gallery, they were separated only by space, empty air. If she were Elizabeth Shoemaker, in possession of that .38 police special, and if she could shoot like Mrs. Shoemaker, and if she had the gumption, which she probably didn't, she could blow Crocker to kingdom come right here and now. Maybe carrying a handgun wasn't such a bad idea: once or twice in a lifetime you just might need it.

Would Crocker recognize her after twenty-five years? And if he did, how would he react? She kept her eyes fixed on him and willed him to look in her direction, but he seemed to be totally engrossed in the scene down on the Senate floor.

Molly shifted her gaze back to Senator Rauther, who was saying, "Miz Shoemaker had plenty of opportunity to think about that .38 police special of her daddy's sitting in the glove compartment of her car that was parked outside, just a few yards from where she and her daughter and her three young grandkids were hiding under the table. She says if she'd had it she knows she could have stopped the massacre because the shooter was taking his time, enjoying his work. She could have slipped the gun out of her bag and aimed it in that two-handed police grip her daddy always favored." He acted this out using the microphone as the gun.

He brought the mike back to his mouth. "But, of course, she didn't have the gun. So she was helpless. She and her daughter were huddled under the table in front of the young-sters, trying to shield them. But Randall Carpenter was a re-lentless killing machine that Friday night. He worked his way around the room until he got to the Shoemakers and first he shot Jessica, who was begging for mercy for her three babies. Then he shot Miz Shoemaker, then the older boy, Kevin, who was eight, then the girl, Lizzy, who was four, and the other boy, John, who was five."

The back of Molly's neck prickled. Across the gallery, Olin Crocker was staring at her. When she met his eyes, he raised his hand and, with two fingers extended, pointed right at her. Then he narrowed his eyes and looked down the fin-ger, as though he were aiming a gun.

Molly looked back at him with what she hoped was an icy stare, but her stomach was roiling with fury and loathing.

After a minute he stood up and stuck his hands in his pockets. Then, looking directly at Molly, he made a move-ment so tiny no one else would have noticed—a quick ob-scene little thrust with his belly. The silver star on his belt winked once in the lights. He turned away and headed toward the door to the lobby. Molly felt as violated and victimized and cheated as she had after their last encounter twenty-five years earlier.

She looked around her to see if anyone else had noticed the interplay. But everyone, including Wanda and Rose, seemed utterly caught up in Senator Rauther's story, which ended with twenty-nine dead. Thirty, counting Randall Carpenter himself; before he could leave the Pizza Parlor, he was shot dead by an off-duty policeman who'd heard the shots from the bowling alley next door. Only two people survived the massacre: a twelve-year-old soccer player and Elizabeth Shoemaker, who spent two months in the hospital recovering from her wound.

"Now, folks, here's a fact I don't like any better than y'all do—we live in a violent world and we need to protect ourselves because nobody else is gonna do it. This bill will allow our aunts, our daughters, and our wives to protect themselves when they must be out in this violent world alone. Let's do our duty and get this bill passed." Senator Rauther sat down, finally, and a break for lunch was declared.

Wanda stood up immediately. "Can't argue with that." She fished in her bag and pulled out a hand-drawn map. "I've got to run, Molly, but this'll get you out to Clem's. Tomorrow, four o'clock. We'll start with safety basics, then we'll go out on the range and shoot the living bejesus out of a target. It'll be fun. You'll be surprised." She disappeared into the stream of people leaving the gallery.

Molly made plans with Rose to meet in ten minutes down in the lobby. She felt uneasy about letting the old woman, who was nearly crippled with arthritis, navigate the stairs on her own, but she couldn't wait to find out what she could about Olin Crocker. She made a beeline against the traffic, to the west end of the gallery where she'd seen Cullen Shoemaker sitting with his mother. Young Cullen, who served as Senator Rauther's aide for the handgun bill, had his fingers glued to the pulse of the legislature. A leader in the university chapter of the Texas Rifle Association, Cullen had started as a student intern for the senator right after his mother and his sister and her three children had been shot in the Liberty Pizza Parlor. He'd shown such energy and zeal, the senator had hired him to help shepherd the handgun bill. If Olin Crocker was lobbying for Bill 98, then Cullen Shoemaker would know all about him.

Mother and son were deep in what looked like an argument, but when they caught sight of Molly approaching they fell silent. Molly had interviewed Elizabeth Shoemaker for a piece she did a year before on victims' rights. She was a large, somber, gray-haired woman whom Molly had found to be a sensible and effective advocate for her causes, even though Molly disagreed with her zealous advocacy of the right of citizens to carry guns.

But the son was a different kettle of fish—intense and officious, with a forced hearty voice and swaggering macho bearing. His blue eyes were magnified behind round wire-rimmed glasses and his pale hair was cut so short you could see the pink of his scalp. Molly couldn't shake her uncomfortable feeling that Cullen was a young man who derived a great deal of self-importance from the tragedy his family had suffered, that he was using it, capitalizing on it for his own purposes.

"Miz Cates," he said, "I bet you're checking up on me, to see if I remembered to put you on the senator's calendar for your little chat."

"Oh." Molly had forgotten she'd requested an interview. "No. I wanted to ask you something else, Cullen. Hello, Elizabeth." She shook hands with the mother, who was then swept away by a group of lobbyists.

"The problem is the senator's so busy this week," Cullen said, "he may not be able to squeeze you in."

"That's all right. That's not what I wanted to ask." She took a step closer to him so the people standing around them would not hear. "Cullen, is Olin Crocker working for TEXRA?"

"Crocker?" He pursed his lips, pretending to think about it. "Yes, ma'am. He surely is."

"What's he doing?"

"Coordinating things with law enforcement groups around the state, I believe. Why do you ask?"

"What do you know about him?" Molly asked.

"Crocker? He was Travis County sheriff back in the late sixties, wasn't he? In the farming business up in Williamson County now, I believe. Supporter of the Second Amendment. Wanted to help the cause. That's about it."

"You know he left office under a real cloud," Molly said.

"Corruption in the jails. Sexual harassment charges out the kazoo."

Cullen shrugged. "I believe the senator heard that talk, but we feel it's just talk. Crocker was never indicted for anything. As the senator always says, find me a politician who doesn't have any dirt talked about him and I'll show you a corpse." He smiled his humorless smile. "And those charges came from inmates, didn't they? Trailer trash, all of them. Some folks'll say anything to get themselves some attention."

"In Crocker's case there may be some truth in it," Molly said, unable to stop herself. "Maybe you folks at TEXRA should be more careful about the company you keep."

"Funny you should say that, Miz Cates, when I was just noticing that you're none too fussy about the company *you* keep."

"Huh?"

"Consorting with outlaws."

"Outlaws?"

"I saw you sitting with Wanda Lavoy."

"Wanda!"

"Yes, ma'am. You liberal media folks—always writing about the NRA and TEXRA as gun nuts and extremists, but then you look right past the real nuts out there."

"You're saying Wanda is a real nut?"

"The scuttlebutt is that she's turning those angry harridans of hers into feminist vigilantes."

"WIC? Oh, c'mon. They're not angry harridans, they're victims of violent crimes."

"If you say so, ma'am. But that's where you ought to be looking, not at a good ol' boy like Olin Crocker. And if you want to talk to a real gun nut . . ." His eyes panned the gallery until he spotted what he was looking for. "Over there. See that tall man in camouflage fatigues and yellow beret? He's part of a militia group up in the panhandle. Keeps a copy of *The Turner Diaries* in his pocket and a .22 strapped to his ankle." He tapped his temple with his index finger. "If there are any plans for violence around here, he's the guy to look at."

"Violence!" Molly looked at him in surprise. *"Are* there plans for violence?"

"Well, the Feds must think so 'cause they're out in force. I know you don't—" The phone in his jacket pocket buzzed. "Excuse me a minute," he said, putting the phone to his ear and sitting down to talk. The interruption was a relief; Molly had had more than enough of Cullen Shoemaker. She waved at him and mouthed a good-bye.

As she walked away he was tapping his toe nervously and saying into the phone, "You heard right. He says the vote's set for Monday, and he ought to know. Know what I'm saying, pardner?" He laughed. "You got it, pardner. An armed state *is* a polite state."

IF AN ARMED NATION WERE A POLITE NATION,
AMERICA WOULD BE PARADISE. WE HAVE MORE
THAN 200 MILLION GUNS IN PRIVATE OWNERSHIP
HERE, BUT OUR MANNERS ARE NOT GETTING
BETTER.

—MOLLY IVINS

Molly Cates stood on the edge of the boisterous crowd of legislators, aides, lobbyists, and reporters. She was looking for Parnell and Rose, to keep her lunch date, but she was also keeping an anxious eye peeled for Olin Crocker, as if he were an evil spirit she needed to keep tabs on. She searched the lobby crowd, mostly men milling around, laughing and slapping one another on the back. This, Molly had learned over the past four weeks, was where the real legislative business got done; what happened out on the floor was just for the record, and for the local papers back home.

After a minute of surveying the crowd, she didn't see Crocker, but she spotted Parnell's bald head. He was standing near the stairs talking with several aides. Rose held her husband's arm, looking so frail and shaky a sneeze could knock her over.

Molly started working her way through the crowd. Parnell, always alert in a crowd, caught sight of her immediately. His eyes lighted up and he waved her over. Then he bent down and said something to Rose. Rose looked toward Molly and smiled, but it seemed to Molly a feeble replica of what had once been Rose Harwood Morrisey's world-class, thousand-watt, Texas beauty queen smile.

Molly could barely wait to talk to the Morriseys about Olin Crocker, but Parnell was involved in giving instructions to his aides. She waited, barely able to contain her impatience, until he finished and sent the aides off to do his bidding. But before she could ask, Cullen Shoemaker called to her. "Miz Cates, good." He arrived a little breathless. "I just talked with Senator Rauther and he's agreed to the interview. His schedule is real complicated. But don't worry," he intoned. "I'll arrange a good time and let you know."

"Thanks." She had asked for the interview two weeks ago; she'd lost interest since then. She couldn't imagine the senator had anything new to say. "Cullen, do you know Parnell and Rose Morrisey?"

Cullen shook Parnell's hand. "Cullen Shoemaker, sir, legislative aide to Senator Rauther."

"I know who you are, young man," Parnell replied.

"It's a real privilege to meet you." Cullen nodded his head to Rose. "And you, ma'am."

"Congratulations to you and your senator on your victory in the House," Parnell said, "and your inevitable victory to come in the Senate. I believe Texas is poorly served by this bad piece of public policy, very poorly served, but as one politician to another, I salute your skills." He put a hand to his forehead in a smart military salute. "And your resources, Mr. Shoemaker. I envy your resources something fierce."

A small smile of satisfaction pulled at Cullen's lips. "It's true the groups who support us are blessed by members who believe so strongly in protecting our Second Amendment rights that they give generously to our cause. But this bill is being passed because the public supports it, sir, not because the Texas Rifle Association has a bank account."

"So you folks don't buy votes?" Parnell said pleasantly.

"No, sir. We don't have to."

"How about the nine uncommitted representatives your senator took on that hunting trip?"

"Hunting trip?"

"Ashburn Hill, Georgia—best quail hunting in the world. You remember. The trip where you sent all nine of them back home with brand-new Holland & Holland side-by-side double-barrel shotguns as party favors. That trip."

"Oh, Senator, that was just a bunch of ol' boys getting together to walk in the woods and discuss public policy."

"Must've been a good talk, Cullen," Molly threw in, "since all nine of the representatives who went on the trip ended up voting in favor of the bill."

"They voted for it because their constituents want it."

Parnell nodded. "You're close, Mr. Shoemaker. The bill is being passed because most of the members of this legislature *believe* the public wants it. But I think, if we had a referendum, the public would vote it down—by a slim margin, but down it would go."

Molly had always loved listening to Parnell's full-blown, Texas-flavored prose. It reminded her of the way her daddy used to talk.

"Well, sir, it would depend on how the referendum was worded."

Parnell smiled, clearly surprised by the agreement. "And here I thought you and I would never agree on so much as the color of shit."

Rose Morrisey, never comfortable with discord, in spite of having been a politician's wife for fifty years, changed the subject. "How is your dear mother, Mr. Shoemaker? I grieve for your family's losses." She spoke with such warmth and sincerity it made Molly feel guilty for disliking a young man who had suffered so much. Rose had always had in great abundance what Aunt Harriet called "Southern charm." It was a trait that, in other women, Molly often found gushy and shrill, but in Rose she found it comforting and irresistible. When Rose Morrisey focused her attention on you, it felt like soaking in a warm bath.

"She's as well as can be expected, ma'am. Thank you for asking."

"A fine lady, your mother," Parnell said. "A fine lady and a brave one."

Garland Rauther appeared from the crowd with an entourage in tow and called out to his aide. "Cully, you coming, boy?"

"Yessir," he called. "I've got to run," he said to Molly and the Morriseys. "Good seeing y'all." He turned to leave, then paused and turned back to them. "Oh, Miz Cates." He pulled a folded sheaf of papers from his pocket. "I've got a favor to ask, ma'am. I've written a little something." His face colored slightly. "I'd be real obliged if you'd read this and let me know if you think I might could get it published somewhere. Your magazine might like a different point of view."

Molly didn't reach for it. She was all too accustomed to this occupational hazard of being a writer: everyone in the world had something they'd written and would like to publish. In self-defense, she had developed a policy of not reading manuscripts.

"Cullen, I'm not a good one to—"

"Well," he interrupted, "I wish you'd take this anyway." He reached out and tucked it into her big bag, which was hanging open on her shoulder. She vowed next time to remember to zip it.

He hurried off in his senator's wake.

The crowd had thinned out in the few minutes they'd been talking; the legislature took lunch very seriously. Finally Molly had Parnell and Rose alone. "You know who I just saw?" she said, unable to keep the agitation out of her voice. "Olin Crocker. In the gallery just now, bold as brass. He's lobbying for TEXRA. Did you know that, Parnell?"

"I've seen him around. I reckon I knew he was lobbying."

"And you didn't tell me?"

"Sweetheart, it just never occurred to me."

"So you let me run into him and nearly faint from the shock? Rose, did you know this?"

Rose looked hurt and confused, but Molly was not about to back off this one. Finally Rose said, "Franny may have mentioned it at the funeral, but I—"

"Franny?" Molly interrupted. "Franny *Lawrence?*" She hadn't heard that name in many years. Even after all this time, it made her feel as it always had—a touch queasy.

"Yes." Rose glanced up at Parnell. "Franny Lawrence . . . well, Quinlan, now, of course."

"Quinlan? She's married?"

Rose nodded, looking miserable. "She married Frank Quinlan last year, Molly."

"Frank Quinlan of the Lubbock Quinlans?"

Rose nodded again.

Molly was stunned. Now it wasn't just Crocker, but a whole host of demons from the past swirling around her. "Let me get this straight. Franny Lawrence has married Frank Quinlan of the oil family? The Jasper Quinlan family? Quinlan Oil? She couldn't have."

"Molly, calm down." Parnell put a hand on her shoulder.

"Sorry, but this seems so . . . bizarre. Tell me about it."

"Not much to tell," Parnell said. "Frank's wife was ailing for years. When she died last year, he married Franny. They'd known each other forever out at Lakeway. Franny sold him his lot on the lake when he built his house, maybe fifteen years ago."

"Doesn't it seem strange to you," Molly demanded, "that Franny would marry someone from that family?"

Parnell shrugged.

Molly looked at Rose. "Rose, *you* never mentioned this to me either."

Rose raised her eyes slowly to meet Molly's. "Why, Molly, it never occurred to me you would be interested in Franny. As I recall, you were never real fond of her."

Fond of her? From the past zoomed an image of Franny Lawrence clinging possessively to Vernon Cates's arm, pushing a tendril of curly red hair away from her eyes and laughing up at him. That was the day they'd announced they were going to be married. Molly had been sixteen then. She'd detested the woman and never made any bones about it. Franny Lawrence must be over sixty. That bright hair must be gray by now, the pale skin covered in liver spots, the slender waist thickened by menopause.

Rose was studying her with a worried expression. "Well, it's true," Molly said, "I was no fan of hers, but Frank Quinlan!" Her heart was beating fast. "He was a vice-president of the company back then and—" She stopped mid-sentence when she saw that Rose's face was screwed up with misery. She had been going to say that the Quinlans were responsible for her daddy's death, that the Quinlans were killers. She believed it still, but it was an allegation she should not make in a public place. Especially here.

Anyway, she needed to find out more about this. "So," she said with an attempt at lightening up, "Franny. How is she? What funeral was this?"

Rose said, "Well, she seems fine, but Frank is taking his son's death awful hard. The funeral was for his son Willie—from his first marriage, you know. The saddest thing—the boy committed suicide right after graduating from the Yale Law School. First in his class. Such a smart boy."

"He killed himself?" Molly asked.

"Yes. And that got Franny to talking about your daddy."

Molly tensed, feeling more pain on its way. "Why?"

"Well, because—"

"Ladies, enough!" Parnell said, interrupting his wife. "Let's go to lunch. I'm a workingman."

"Wait a minute," Molly insisted. "Let her finish." She turned to Rose. "Why would that remind Franny of my father?"

Rose looked up at Parnell again and sighed. "Well, it got her to speculating that maybe being too smart tended a person toward depression. Maybe it was hazardous to life and limb. Like your daddy, she said."

"Franny said that?" Molly tried to keep her voice level, but her face felt hot.

Parnell put an arm around Molly's shoulders. "Molly, sweetheart. You know there were people who thought that at the time. Give us a break here. Rose has bumbled into a hornet's nest, all innocent."

"But Franny didn't think my daddy committed suicide."

She was met with silence.

"Did she?"

Rose said, "Now, Molly, I don't believe she actually said that. And, honey, it was such a long time ago—twenty-five years or so—"

"Twenty-*eight*," Molly said. "Twenty-eight years, and"—
she thought for a moment—"six days."

"Oh, Molly, my dear," Rose said, her dark eyes moist
with sympathy, "so long ago. Why worry yourself?"

Molly knew she should stop pushing, but she couldn't.
"Does Franny really think that, Parnell?"

"Molly—" But he didn't finish; instead he shook his head
in exasperation. Then he glanced at his watch. "Ladies, we
were going to have lunch. Let's do it." He steered Molly
firmly by the arm. "Come on."

They headed toward the elevators, but very slowly to accommodate Rose's pace.

"We'll go to the cafeteria, if that's all right with y'all," he
said. "It's easiest."

"The cafeteria. Sure." Molly was feeling an inner turmoil
way out of proportion to the news. She hadn't even thought
about Franny Lawrence in years. Why should she care what
that woman thought? Or who she'd married?

She said, "Just tell me. *Does* she think my daddy committed suicide?"

"Molly, let it go," Parnell said, giving her arm a squeeze.

"Let it *go?*" The shrillness in her own voice surprised her.

"What's the woman *supposed* to think? The medical examiner, the sheriff, the newspaper, and public opinion all
said it was suicide."

"But I can't—"

"Franny always believed it was suicide. If you'd given the
poor woman the time of day back then, you'd have known
that. She thought it was suicide, just like everyone else." His
voice was full of exasperation.

Molly stopped in her tracks, even though they hadn't
made it to the elevators yet. "Everyone else *didn't* think that.
I didn't. *You* didn't. *Rose* didn't."

She searched his face, waiting for confirmation, but he
didn't say anything. Her throat felt dry and narrow. "Did
you? Parnell, you didn't think that, did you?"

"Molly, please. Rose needs to sit down. Let's talk about
this later."

They walked in silence until they reached the elevator.

After he pushed the button he said, "Everybody has always been afraid to talk to you about this because you were so...emotional about it. Now this is upsetting Rose, and it's upsetting me. Let's go have a nice lunch and some iced tea."

"Iced tea, yes." He was right: she was overreacting. But she needed a minute or two alone to collect herself, to absorb everything. It had been too much all at once—seeing Olin Crocker and then getting hit with this news—a triple whammy from the past. "I need to stop at the ladies' room first," she told them. "I'll meet you in the cafeteria, okay?"

"Sure," he said. "Rosie, you want to go along with Molly?"

Rose shook her head. Molly was relieved; she wanted to be alone.

"Okay," Parnell said. "We'll meet you in the cafeteria." He looked into her face. "You all right, Molly? You look a little peaked, sweetheart. I hope I haven't—"

"No. I'm okay." She turned and walked away, picking up speed once she'd turned the corner and they couldn't see her. She had no idea where the ladies' room was on this floor and she didn't want to ask anyone. She walked part way around the rotunda and turned into the first corridor she came to. At the end of it was a men's room. But no corresponding ladies' room. Damn. This building probably had ten men's rooms for every ladies' room—some sort of toilet-per-capita formula to keep the female population in check.

She backtracked, nearly circling the rotunda this time. Why, of all the people in the world, would Franny Lawrence marry Frank Quinlan? She turned into an area she'd never been in, walked past some offices and around the corner to a dark corridor. Off the beaten track. At the end was a ladies' room. Good. She just needed to sit down and be alone for a minute to absorb this. Had Franny *really* always believed Vernon Cates killed himself?

Molly shoved the door open and entered. A large naked woman whirled around to face her. Before she could stop herself, Molly let out a squeal of surprise. The woman was totally naked, tall, and wild-looking, with a tangle of frizzy gray hair. She had been standing at the sink, one arm lifted, washing her armpit with a paper towel.

The woman lowered her arm and glowered, her dark eyes full of outrage.

Molly's throat constricted. "Sorry. You surprised me."

"This your private rest room or something?"

"No, I just wasn't expecting it." Keeping her eyes averted from the woman's nakedness, Molly hurried past her and into one of the stalls. She closed and bolted the door, and sat down. Oh, to be alone—it was such a relief. Just a minute or two and she could collect herself. She leaned forward and closed her eyes. Franny Lawrence. The woman who would have married Vernon Cates. The woman who would have been Molly's stepmother if her father had lived two more weeks.

Outside the door, the naked woman was muttering something under her breath. Molly didn't want to listen, but she couldn't help it. *"Little Bopeep,"* the woman was saying, *"has lost her sheep, and can't tell where to find them."*

Oh, God—a crazy woman. She should have known. She should have walked out the second she saw her. Well, now she'd just wait until the woman was gone so she wouldn't have to deal with her.

She sat quietly, breathing deeply, trying to calm herself, but it was difficult with the noises outside—the splashing and sputtering and angry mumbling: *"Leave them alone and they'll come home and bring their tails behind them."*

Parnell and Rose would worry if she took too long. After the scene she'd made, they'd probably worry anyway. Who could blame them? For a few minutes there Molly had felt something terrifying—a stirring of the old madness from that bad time of her life after her father was killed—that crazy, obsessional, grief-filled time. She had thought she was long past that; it was scary to discover how close to the surface it all still was.

She sat up and pushed her hair back, surprised to find that her forehead was clammy with sweat. Lord, there was no fooling your body, was there? No pretending to your sweat glands that everything was just fine when your world was in upheaval.

Outside the door, the water had stopped, but the woman was still muttering in a voice that sounded like the angry buzzing of bees, or like a pot of fury boiling over and sizzling onto the burner.

Suddenly the woman's voice rose to a conversational level: "Don't happen to know the second verse, do you?"

Oh, God.

The woman mumbled a little, then said clearly, "It starts *Little Bopeep fell fast asleep and dreamt*... she dreamt some damn thing." There was a moment of silence before the voice came louder, more aggressive: "Didn't really have to pee, huh? False alarm."

"Are you talking to me?" Molly said.

"Who else is here?"

"I'm okay."

"I know who you are," the woman said.

"Oh?"

"You don't recognize me."

Recognize her? Oh, no, not this again. Lately it happened all the time. Molly ran into people who seemed to know her, but she would have sworn she'd never seen them before. It terrified her because it reminded her of Aunt Harriet's Alzheimer's, but she rationalized her own lapses as simple overload, a lifetime's accumulation of more names and faces than the human brain was designed to hold. "No," she said through the door, "I'm afraid I don't."

"I'm Tin Can's friend."

"Tin Can?" Of course—Tin Can, the bag lady. One of the homeless women she'd interviewed. "Oh, you're a friend of Emily Bickerstaff."

"Is that her name?"

"Yeah. You don't know her name?"

"On the street, we use street names."

Molly looked at her watch. She'd been gone ten minutes. Parnell and Rose would be waiting for her to get there before they went through the cafeteria line; she needed to go. She stood and zipped her pants, buckled her belt. There was no avoiding this woman. She unbolted the door and stepped out.

The woman was standing at one of the two sinks, getting dressed. She had put on black high-top tennis shoes, jeans, and an undershirt. Now she was pulling on a dirty plaid flannel shirt. Without looking at Molly, she said, "If a half-wit can be a friend."

Molly stood in front of the other sink to wash her hands. If she did it quickly maybe she could escape without any more talk.

"You knew she was retarded, didn't you?" the woman demanded. "Why'd you want to talk with a retard?"

Molly said, "I like Emily. I worry about her."

"But not enough to do something about it, huh?" the woman said.

It was a direct hit, a guided missile right to the center of what Molly hated most about herself. She looked at herself in the mirror and liked nothing she saw there—the thin, pale face, the dark hair, which looked flat and lifeless, except for the alarming new white hairs that were springing up every day—curly and coarse and unwelcome among the smooth black strands. She was tempted to strike back at this crazy woman, to say, *What about you? You doing anything about it?* Instead, she turned on the water and pushed the lever on the soap container. Nothing came out. She felt like weeping. "No soap."

"There never is."

Molly rinsed her hands under the cold water and then leaned down to splash some water on her face. When she lifted her dripping head, the water ran into her eyes and broke up her reflection, refracting it into pulsing, kaleidoscopic astral shapes that slowly drained away and materialized, inevitably, back into the same pale face.

She dried her face and hands with a paper towel, then rummaged in her bag to find a lipstick.

The woman was buttoning her shirt, but it was going to turn out unevenly, Molly could see.

"Has that thing come out in the paper?" the woman asked. "What you were writing about Tin Can."

"No. It's not for the paper. It's for my magazine, and it's not finished. I'm doing several interviews over a year."

"Oh, yeah. To see what happens to them, huh? Who lives, who dies, who wins the lottery, who finds a job, who gets AIDS, who gets sober—all that?"

Molly didn't answer; she was running the lipstick over her mouth.

"And these 'interviews' make you some sort of expert, huh?"

Molly paused, her mouth half painted. "No. But the women tell me about their experience and I write about what they tell me."

"Well, la-ti-da. Their *experience,* huh?" Finished dressing now, the woman looked Molly over with a mocking grin. "So your heart bleeds for them and you think you understand the *experience.*" She uttered the last word with more bitterness than Molly had ever heard packed into one word.

Stung by the woman's contempt, Molly didn't respond. She took a paper towel and blotted her lipstick.

The woman moved closer. "Lady, you don't know diddly squat about Tin Can's life." She flicked her hand against the purse dangling from Molly's shoulder. "You got your expensive leather handbag stuffed with credit cards, and you got your gold watch and your lipstick." She smacked her lips together in a parody of Molly blotting her lipstick. "You don't know shit!"

Molly felt a wave of fear; the woman was invading her space, touching her. She resisted the urge to move away. "I do the best I can. I listen and I think I do understand. If you're worried I won't get it right, why don't you talk to me? Tell me what I should know."

"Some things you can't *tell* anyone." The woman looked at Molly with disgust and shook her head in dismissal of the whole subject. Then she leaned down and pulled out of her bag a long white cloth coat with black spots on it—a cow design.

In a flash of recognition, Molly remembered the coat and the big, hostile woman who was with Tin Can when Molly first approached her at the Salvation Army. "You're Cow Lady," she said. "Tin Can talks about you all the time."

In the mirror Molly saw the woman's face reflect a small smile.

"Yeah. You remember the coat, not me. You didn't look at my face, just what I was wearing. When you're on the street people don't look you in the eye."

Molly nodded into the mirror, watching the woman button her coat.

"When you first come in here," the woman said, "you looked like Little Bopeep just lost your sheep, or your best friend."

"Yeah. I'd just gotten some . . . news. Something from the past that upset me."

The woman picked up her big bag and slung it over her shoulder. "Here's something I know for sure: don't look in that rearview mirror. Ever. You do it, you'll be sorry."

Molly was still watching her in the mirror. "That's probably good advice, but I don't know how to stop myself from doing it."

The woman shrugged and headed toward the door, muttering, *"Little Bopeep fell fast asleep and dreamt . . .* oh, shit, what was it she dreamt?"

Molly turned around quickly, wanting, for some reason, to stop her. "I'm Molly Cates. What's your name? Your real name."

The big woman paused with her hand on the door. "I don't want to be in the paper," she said.

"No. I just wondered what your name is."

The woman stood there, her chin stuck out pugnaciously. "Why? What's it to you?"

"Well, we have a friend in common. When I see her again I'd like to say, 'Hey, I ran into your friend.' But I don't like calling you Cow Lady. Just like I don't like calling her Tin Can."

"Well, that's what I want to be called, and you ought to call people what they want," the woman said.

Surprised by hearing from this woman a sentiment she

often expressed herself, Molly looked at her with new respect. "I agree. I'm sorry." She leaned down and pulled a card from her bag. "Here's my name and phone number in case you change your mind and want to talk sometime."

"Talk? Why?"

"Because I'm interested."

"Well, I'm not."

"Okay." Molly held the card closer to her, trying to tempt her. "But take it. Just in case." Molly looked her in the eye for the first time and was not surprised by the anger she saw there, but she was surprised by the glitter of intelligence and defiance.

The woman took the card and, without glancing at it, dropped it into her big bag. Her body seemed to relax, as though her erect quills had suddenly flattened. "Well, then." She pushed the door open and walked out.

Molly turned back to the mirror. She still didn't like what she saw there. "Don't look in that rearview mirror," she whispered to her reflection. "You'll be sorry if you do." But she knew she was going to look. Come hell or high water, she was going to talk to Franny Lawrence. After twenty-eight years of avoiding her. "Twenty-eight years," she whispered into the mirror, "twenty-eight fucking years." Oh, God, here she was mumbling to herself, raving just like any other old bag lady.

She sounded every bit as crazy as Cow Lady, and every bit as angry; she was just better at concealing it in public.

4

> IF WISHES WERE HORSES, BEGGARS WOULD RIDE.
> IF TURNIPS WERE WATCHES, I WOULD WEAR ONE BY
>   MY SIDE.
> AND IF "IFS" AND "ANDS"
> WERE POTS AND PANS,
> THERE'D BE NO WORK FOR TINKERS!
>
> —MOTHER GOOSE

It has been a quiet Monday evening under the deck at the Creekside Grill. Sarah Jane Hurley is wide awake when Lufkin sticks his head under the deck just after the Grill has closed. She crawls out, dragging her bag behind her. She is pleased to see him because he is carrying a brown paper grocery bag with some heft to it.

Together they head down the bank toward Waller Creek. They can see where they are going very well because the moon is full. The bank is dangerously steep and overgrown, but just south of the deck a muddy rut of a path descends to the creek. Lufkin, hugging the grocery bag to his chest, runs down it, his boots slipping and sliding in the muck. Sarah Jane takes it slower. She is wearing old high-top tennis shoes with the tread worn off and no heels to dig in, so she inches her way down, grabbing on to bushes as she goes, trying to avoid the debris scattered along the path: filthy, stiffened old blankets, broken glass, crushed Styrofoam containers, brown paper bags with empty liquor bottles inside, piles of human feces.

At the bottom the limestone rocks, flat and white, reflect what little of the moonlight filters down to the creek bed. It feels colder down here so she buttons her long black and white coat all the way up to her neck. The night is unusually damp and chilly for May.

They walk along the creek to the base of the Fourth Street Bridge where Tin Can stands over the rusty oil drum she uses to cook on, poking at the fire inside with a stick. She is humming tunelessly and smoking a cigarette. Her dry, mouse-colored hair hangs in clumps around her face. The fire illuminates her flat-features—the scarred upper lip and nose, which she claims were joined together when she was born. She wears only a T-shirt and baggy jeans rolled up on her stubby bowed legs. She starts to smile as they approach, but stops just short of opening her lips. The calico cat she is cradling in one arm looks up; his eyes are flat yellow disks, each one reflecting a single miniature fire.

"Got a good fire going here," Tin Can says in a singsong voice, "but Silky and me, we got nothing to cook. Y'all got something?" She looks at Lufkin because he is a likelier source of handouts and because he is carrying a grocery bag.

Lufkin sets his bag down on the ground in front of her. "Fair maiden," he says, "inscrutable feline, I brung home the bacon—four T-bone steaks and the finest French wine—Le Thunder Chicken. What say you, me pretties?"

Wine again! Sarah Jane brightens up. It'll be a good night for forgetting.

Tin Can quickly puts a hand over her mouth and giggles. Sarah Jane knows she covers her mouth because she is sensitive about her two missing front teeth. Even when Tin Can had pneumonia last winter and nearly died, the first thing she did when she came to in the Emergency Room was to cover her mouth. This vanity in a retarded old hag amazes Sarah Jane. Three years on the streets has erased all remaining shreds of her own vanity. She is a hopeless crone, past redemption, and she knows it.

Sarah Jane holds her hands out toward the fire. The heat feels good; it eases the tension that has been building up inside her. She pictures the bottle of wine in Lufkin's bag. She imagines the warmth of it sliding along her tongue and down her throat. She anticipates the flush in her skin, the glow in her blood, the numbing buzz in her brain as it begins to work its magic. She hopes there is enough of it—two bottles or three—and that they won't have to share it with Tin Can, who doesn't care much about drinking anyway.

Lufkin pulls from the bag a cellophane-wrapped package with a steak in it. He shows it to the women. It's a T-bone, thin, but with lots of marbly fat running through it. Sarah Jane's stomach flutters in anticipation and she tries to remember when she ate last. "You been Dumpster-diving?" she asks Lufkin, who is pulling another steak out of the bag.

"Paid for 'em," he snaps. "See, date's right here on the package, woman—not even close to the expiration." He is annoyed because she has broken his mood. He likes to play roles and pretend they are all something they are not. Sometimes she goes along with it, and sometimes she doesn't.

Sarah Jane takes a step back and from lowered eyes watches Lufkin's profile, his long, bony nose and thin red mouth just visible in the nest of his long black beard, which is streaked with gray. She is checking to see if he is more than annoyed. Not that he's ever done more than speak sharply to her, but she's wary. You have to be on your guard around men. She's seen this one beat up other tramps who did nothing more than walk too close to his bottle. But that happened when he was drunk. And drunk or sober, he's never turned that anger on her. She pictures her carving knife, all sharp and shiny, wrapped in a black sweatshirt at the bottom of her canvas bag, the bag she always carries with her. He has never tried to do her any harm. And he better not.

"Win the lottery?" she asks him.

"Yeah, the labor pool lottery. Prize was I got to dig post holes for eight hours, no break. This yahoo carried me out to a farm in East Bum-fuck in the back of his pickup. Dog sat up front with him in the air conditioning."

Sarah Jane smiles. "Dog probably smells better."

Lufkin tears the wrapping off the steaks and hands them to Tin Can, who receives each one with a look of reverence and sets it carefully on the grate across the top of the barrel. "Pay was all right," he says, "eight bucks a hour. Course, that fuckin' Squint takes the first ten bucks."

"Squint," Tin Can says, hugging the cat in close to her

chest. She always closes her eyes and scrunches her face up at the mention of his name. Sarah Jane is not sure what happened, but it must've been bad. When Tin Can was released from the State Hospital, she stayed at Squint's camp, the Patchwork Pit, for a while. Now she refuses to set foot south of the river for fear she might get too close to the camp.

"I don't like him," Tin Can says. "You stay away from him, Lufkin."

"Can't avoid him," Lufkin says through tight lips, "if you need day gigs. You want to score in the day labor cage and stay alive, you pay Squint. That's the way it is."

"It isn't fair," Sarah Jane says. She has reason to hate Squint, too, and to know you can't cross him. "It pisses me off—him making money off you digging post holes."

Lufkin turns away from her. "Pisses me off too. But you don't give Squint his cut, Roylee and them'll slice you a new asshole for sure." He pulls a newspaper out of the grocery sack and hunkers down next to the barrel so he can use the firelight to read by. Somehow he manages to get a newspaper every day and he reads it all, even the obituaries. Such a waste of time. The paper looks the same every day, year in and year out—the same old crap—big headlines that don't make a rat's ass of difference to anyone. Like those endless football games passive old slack-jawed Harold used to watch on TV. He never noticed they were just showing the same plays year after year. Never noticed much of anything.

Sarah Jane rummages in her bag for her Camels. Thinking about Harold ruins the good mood she was feeling. That's what happens when you look in the rearview mirror. She shakes a cigarette part way out and grabs it with her lips, putting the pack away quickly so she won't have to offer it around. She leans over the fire to light it, takes a deep first drag way deep down in her lungs, and looks down at the shallow water in the creek. Near the bridge a spiky red reflection in the water looks like a spill of crimson paint, or her own bright blood.

She blows the smoke out.

The blood she's lost over the years, she thinks—buckets of it, gallons of it, rivers of it. The red reflection shimmies at her. Every major event of her life was marked by spilled blood. Good lord, if you added it all up—that endless bleeding during her "curse," as Gramma always called it, and from cut knees and nosebleeds and childbirth, and the blood she's sold these last three years—if you captured all that blood in one place, it would fill up Waller Creek and maybe even Town Lake. Like those rivers in Egypt that turned to blood in the Bible.

It's amazing, really, that she has any blood left at all. Somehow, it just keeps renewing itself.

Wondering what is making that red reflection in the water, she glances up to find the source. She studies the city lights twinkling all around them until she settles on the red Sheraton sign high above. She takes another long pull on the cigarette, holding the burn in her lungs as long as possible, trying to sear away the memory of that other blood, not hers, but the Howler's blood that spurted out from Sarah Jane's knife onto the filthy cement floor in that Houston shelter. It was so easy, like sticking a pin in a balloon, as if that old crazy woman was just a bag of blood, asking for someone to prick her and let it all gush out. To get rid of that ugly image Sarah Jane blows the smoke out and says, "Hey, Tin Can, I ran into a friend of yours today."

Tin Can looks up from the steaks. "A friend of *mine?*" Her big popeyes open wider.

"Little Bopeep," Sarah Jane snorts.

"Who?"

"That woman, the one who talked to you for her magazine. Molly someone."

"Oh, she's so nice."

Sarah Jane shrugs. Tin Can is such a simpleton. She thinks everyone who so much as smiles at her is nice.

"Where did you see her?" Tin Can asks.

"At the Big Lady. I was in the can and she came in."

Lufkin looks up from his newspaper. *"Where* was this?"

Sarah Jane jerks a thumb in the direction of the huge lighted dome ten blocks to the north. "The Capitol. I been hanging out there, copping some A/C. They got this public gallery. Good rest room, too."

"What about the library?" Lufkin says. "I thought you was hanging there days."

Sarah Jane has just sucked in a lungful of smoke and it fuels her furies, those shriekers and howlers that live inside her chest. They flare up suddenly with a whoosh, like a gas burner; blue flames lick at her ribs and make sweat pop out on her forehead. "Fuckers kicked me out! Said I was sleeping but I wasn't. Just closed my eyes for a minute." She leans over and scratches furiously at the scabs on her legs, ripping them open again, making blood ooze down her leg. "Wasn't hurting anything. Think they own the world."

"I know," Lufkin says. "Those signs that say, "No bedrolls, no blankets, no drinking, no eating, no loitering, no smoking, no camping, no soliciting.' "

"No sleeping," Tin Can adds.

"No sneezing," says Sarah Jane, feeling the furies calm down, "no breathing, no farting."

Tin Can giggles. "No peeing."

"They said I couldn't come back—ever," Sarah Jane says. "Who cares? I'll go to the Big Lady now."

"For *sleeping* they said you couldn't come back?" Lufkin says with surprise.

"Well, that. And..." She lets her voice trail off, not wanting to remember the scene.

"And what?" Lufkin asks.

"Oh, they hassled me, pushed me around," Sarah Jane says.

Tin Can shakes her head. "Fighting again. Cow Lady, you gotta count to ten. I been telling you. You gotta start countin' to ten. You been kicked out of almost ever place in town now. Even the Sally."

Sarah Jane hates being nagged by this retarded hag. "That writer person," she says to Tin Can. "I hope she's paying you for those interviews."

"Paying me? No."

"Tell her you want to be paid. She looks like she can afford it."

"We just *talk,* Cow Lady. An interview is talking. And a man come and took some pictures, that's all."

"You're getting ripped off," Sarah Jane says. "Why do it if you don't get paid?"

Tin Can wrinkles her brow with the difficulty of the question. "See, people don't know how our life is," she says slowly. "They don't know."

Sarah Jane blows out a long stream of smoke. "You think anyone gives a rat's ass how your life is?"

Tin Can's mouth turns downward. "Oh, I don't know," she whines.

"So what do you tell her?" Sarah Jane asks.

"About how I got to be homeless and all. About collecting cans and selling blood. How MHMR don't take cats, and the Sally neither." She looks down at Silky in her arms. "Molly asks about all that. She cares."

"If she cares so much, why isn't she paying you? I bet *she's* gonna get paid."

Tin Can is quiet for several seconds, thinking it over. "Maybe it'll help for people to know what it's like."

Sarah Jane knows she should drop it, but she can't stop herself. "Tin Can, you're such a dummy. No one who hasn't been out here can know what it's like. You're wasting your time."

Tin Can quickly lowers her head and pretends to be examining Silky's fur. A tear runs down her cheek.

Lufkin rolls his newspaper up and slaps it down on his knee. "Now stop that!" He stands up. "Know something, Cow Lady? You are a *real* negative person. And I dump on all that negative shit."

"Negative? I'm just saying no one cares about her problems. Or yours. Or mine. So we got to take care of our-*selves*—that's all I'm telling her. She's wasting her time with this interview stuff."

Tin Can lifts her head. Her eyes are shiny with tears.

Lufkin drums the rolled-up newspaper against his skinny thigh. He is about to make a speech. Sarah Jane can see it coming. He says, "What goes around comes around, Cow Lady. Don't you know that yet?"

"You say that all the time, and it doesn't mean shit."

"It means you do something to help someone, and later

on the universe does something good for you. But it happens in some way that's a surprise." He slaps the newspaper hard against his thigh again. *"That's* what it means."

Sarah Jane lets out a long raspberry. "Fairy tale *crap.*"

"See. That's what I mean—negative, negative," he says.

"If wishes were horses, beggars would ride." Sarah Jane is surprised she has actually spoken this; she usually keeps Mother Goose echoing inside to calm herself, but lately the rhymes seem to be spilling over.

"Huh?" says Lufkin, looking at her hard. *"Who's* a god-damn beggar?"

She dismisses his anger with a wave of her hand. "What happens to you in this life has got nothing to do with what you did or didn't do. It's like..." She searches for the right comparison. "You know that game over at Dirty's where you've got a glass box with all those stuffed toys and you try to pick one up with the claw thing? The toy that gets picked up just happens to be in the way. That's life. Fate. You get in the way of the claw thing, you get picked up and you got no choice but to go with it."

"No, no, no." He slaps the paper into his palm with each word. "You're wrong."

She didn't mean to get into this conversation, but now she's really steaming up. "Like me. Old Harold took up with his secretary, divorced me. Then he took my children away, even though they wanted to be with me. I lost my job at the Chevy dealership. I think I told you—I was overqualified, really—high school graduate, a year of business college. Then I lost my room at the boardinghouse. So I ended up on the street. See, I just happened to be in the way of the claw."

"Well, yeah," Lufkin says. "What I mean—"

"And you. Look at you, for Christ's sake. Nine years on the street and you haven't learned squat. You worked hard as a carpenter, right? Then you had an accident and you hurt your knee really bad and they fired you, right? You got no family and no one else cares, right? So you're out on the street. Is this because you put *bad* things into the universe?"

"I'm just down on my luck right now, but that's got to change. Look at me." He thumps the newspaper on his chest. "I got my health. I got friends. I got a trade I used to make twenty bucks an hour at."

Sarah Jane opens her mouth to question this but thinks better of it. On the street it's best not to question people's lies, especially if you don't want them to question yours.

Lufkin is going on: "I've been in a slump, sure, but it ain't gonna last forever. I'm gonna find a job and get me a little apartment."

"Maybe. But it doesn't have anything to do with whether you do good stuff or not."

Lufkin is agitated now; he is twisting the newspaper in his hands, rolling it tighter. "I see we need to do a little experiment here." He points the paper at Tin Can. "Look at your friend there. She's shivering. You see that."

Sarah Jane takes a drag on her cigarette and looks down into the creek. She doesn't like the direction this is taking.

"I said look at Tin Can," Lufkin says in a hard voice she's never heard from him before.

Sarah Jane keeps looking down at the water.

"Oh," he says, "you gonna be like that, huh? Okay, then. You want one of them steaks I bought?"

She glances up at him in surprise. This really sucks. She's sorry she let herself be drawn into this bullshit argument.

"You want some of the wine I got?" he says.

She nods.

"Okay then, you gotta participate in this experiment. This is important. You're real attached to your cow coat, ain't you?"

Reflexively she wraps her arms around herself, holding on to the coat she never takes off, the black and white spotted coat that has given her her street name, the name everyone here knows her by. It is part of who she is now.

Lufkin nods at her. "Yeah," he says, "and Tin Can's just wearing that thin little skimpy shirt, and last winter she got bad pneumonia. Remember that? Well, you got on a sweater under your coat and I know you got some more warm clothes in your bag. So what you need to do here is give Tin Can your cow coat."

"Oh, no!" Tin Can says. "That's *her* coat. I *never* seen her without that coat."

"That's what makes it so good," he says. "She's gonna give you this coat offa her back, the coat she wears all the time." He fixes his beady eyes on Sarah Jane and waits.

Sarah Jane takes a last drag on her cigarette and tosses it into the creek. "That's nuts. I'm down to the clothes on my back. I got nothing to give."

He points a long finger at her. "Yes, you do. And it means more when you ain't got much. The universe knows it's more important than some rich guy giving millions."

Sarah Jane hates it when men point at her, and, even more, she hates being preached at. Shades of old Harold, always pointing and preaching, holier than thou. "No," she says.

"Now come on, Cow Lady. I hate to do this, but if you don't give her the coat, there's not gonna be no more wine from me. No steaks neither."

The cigarette butt's floating on the ripply red reflection. "This is so stupid."

"Well, maybe it is and maybe it ain't, but that's the deal."

He reaches down into the grocery bag with both hands and pulls out two bottles by the necks. He holds them out so she can see them. "Thunder Chicken. Fourteen percent alcohol. You wanna share it, you gotta do this good deed. Take your coat off and give it to Tin Can and say, 'Wear it in good health.'"

Sarah Jane sighs; he's got his teeth into this and he's not going to back off. She decides to compromise. "Tell you what—I got a nice black sweatshirt in my bag. It would fit her better. The coat's gonna be way too long for her."

"How're them steaks doing?" Lufkin says over his shoulder to Tin Can. "They're smelling mighty tasty."

"Almost done," says Tin Can, poking one of them with her stick.

Lufkin keeps his eyes on Sarah Jane. "The coat for Tin Can," he says. "And for me, one of them Camels you got in your bag. I don't believe you've ever offered me a smoke."

Sarah Jane unbuttons the coat, slowly. It's best just to go along. She'll get it back from Tin Can later when Lufkin's not around. It'll just be a loan. *Hey, diddle, diddle! The cat and the fiddle.* She takes the coat off, wads it up, and tosses it toward Tin Can's feet. *The cow jumped over the moon.*

Tin Can bends over to pick it up.

Lufkin is nodding. "Now say, 'Wear it in good health.' "

"Jesus," Sarah Jane mutters. "Wear it in good health." She already feels naked.

"And don't forget the smoke for me," he says. "Then we'll watch to see what the universe does for you."

"Fuck-all," Sarah Jane says as she rummages furiously in her bag for the pack of Camels. Out of the corner of her eye she sees Tin Can putting on the coat, which is so long it nearly covers her feet. *The little dog laughed to see such sport.* "Fuck-bloody-all," she says under her breath. "Same thing the universe always does for me."

5

LITTLE BOPEEP FELL FAST ASLEEP,
AND DREAMT SHE HEARD THEM BLEATING;
BUT WHEN SHE AWOKE, SHE FOUND IT A JOKE,
FOR STILL THEY ALL WERE FLEETING.
—"LITTLE BOPEEP," VERSE 2, *MOTHER GOOSE*

Grady had turned his back and was pretending to be asleep, but it didn't fool her. Even in the dark, Molly could see the tension between his bare shoulder blades. There was a question she wanted to ask him. It was a question she had wanted to ask for a quarter century but had been afraid to. She wanted to ask it now more than ever, but she didn't feel quite ready. If she could keep him awake, maybe she could work her way up to it.

"Grady, stop playing possum," she said. "I know you're not asleep."

Without moving he muttered into the pillow, "How could I be asleep with you lying there grinding your teeth?"

"I'm not grinding my teeth."

"Must be your mental gears, then. You're grinding them so hard it's going to wake the neighbors."

"You can stop the racket real easy. Just say you'll do that tiny favor for me. Then I'll leave you alone."

"I don't want you to leave me alone. What I want is for you to drop this thing. I want it so much, I'm begging you. Please drop it." His voice was thick with fatigue or emotion. She wasn't sure which.

The favor would be a piece of cake for him; he was an

Austin police lieutenant with contacts all over the state. All it would take was a phone call. She rested her hand on his shoulder. "I can't drop it, Grady. Do this one thing to help and I won't ask for any more."

He let out a bitter laugh. "You always say that, and I hate it because you make it sound like I keep score on things I do for you. I'd love to help, but plowing up this old soil is not going to do you any good."

"This is not about what might or might not be good for me."

"That's for *damn* sure."

"Grady, you're making a mountain out of a molehill. I can find an unlisted address myself, but it might take a few days. It's so much easier for you to do it. Please."

He rolled over to face her. In the soft glow from her night light, his pale eyes looked silvery, the skin under them creased with worry. "You promised me you were finished with this."

"I know, but you have to admit that this new development is interesting—Franny Lawrence marrying *Frank Quinlan.*"

"Only if you believe he or someone in his family killed your father. And you've never come up with a shred of evidence that they did. And it sure as hell wasn't for lack of trying."

He reached out and stroked her cheek. "Let me give you some advice?"

She hated advice, and she didn't like the direction this conversation was taking: it could easily end up in the forbidden zone—that time, twenty-five years ago, when they had been married. Their four-year marriage had crashed in flames, mainly—she accepted it now—because of her craziness after her father's murder. By mutual agreement they never talked about it, and she was afraid this conversation was going to goad one of them into breaking the pact. "No," she said, "don't give me advice."

He closed his eyes and she could see he was trying to subdue his exasperation. In the silence, she thought about asking him the question. It had been on the tip of her tongue all evening, through dinner and her long rehash of the whole situation. But this was probably a bad time to ask it. So instead she skirted it by saying, "It's not just this thing about Franny and Frank Quinlan that's bothering me. It's the suicide thing and Rose and Parnell. All along they've let me believe they agreed with me that my daddy was murdered. Sure, they tried to convince me to let it go and get back to my life. But that was because they thought it was impossible to prove anything. That's what I *thought* they thought, anyway. But now, suddenly I get the feeling that they never agreed with me. This huge chasm opened up."

"I can see that."

There was a silence, in which the only sound was the heavy breathing of the dog stretched out next to the bed. She could ask him the question now. He was an honest man. He'd give her an honest answer. But she couldn't quite bring herself to do it yet. She said, "How could Franny possibly think he committed suicide? I mean here's a man who's forty-five years old, in good health, everything to live for. He's about to have a big article published in a national magazine. He's finally gotten away from Lubbock. He's going to get married again. And he's got a daughter who adores him, friends—everything. Everything to live for."

"Uh-huh." Grady's eyes were still closed. She wasn't sure if it was because he was bored with her repeating some variant of this all evening, or because he really was sleepy.

"I mean, I guess I understand why the medical examiner would call it suicide. It did look like that. But people who *knew* him, like Aunt Harriet and his old friends in Lubbock—for them to even consider the idea of suicide always seemed so unreasonable to me."

"Uh-huh."

"I just want to go see Franny. I never really talked to her alone after my daddy was killed. And I should have. This would give it closure."

"What worries me, Molly, is your getting caught up in it again." He lowered his voice to a whisper. "Last time it got so...out of control."

He was being cautious, just skirting the forbidden topic,

using euphemisms. She didn't respond right away. The subject was so emotionally loaded for them, it was like walking barefoot on broken glass. She hadn't been able to bring herself to mention that she had seen Olin Crocker today. Even a quarter of a century later, just thinking about her excesses during that frenzied time gave her hot flashes.

When Vernon Cates had been pulled from Lake Travis on May 25, 1970, with a gunshot wound in his temple, she had been sixteen, just finishing her junior year in high school. She had dropped out and spent the following year desperately trying to find out what had happened to him. She had followed every possible lead as far as it would go, no matter what it required of her. It was a nightmare time. A year later, while she was pursuing one of those leads, she'd met Grady Traynor, fallen in love with him, got pregnant and married—in that order. She settled briefly into contentment, but when new information came her way, she'd started up the quest again. During that time she had neglected her daughter, betrayed her husband, and alienated everyone who tried to talk reason to her. There had been no limits to her obsession with trying to prove that Vernon Cates had not killed himself and with finding the person who did kill him. Even Grady didn't know the worst of it.

"Out of control?" she said. "More like berserk. Demented." She had left baby Jo Beth with Aunt Harriet for months while she spent every waking moment following one hunch or another. At one point, when Jo Beth was two and a half, Molly had returned to a child who didn't recognize her and cried when she came near. The memory was so painful she shook her head to chase it away. All that had happened when she was very young. Now Jo Beth was older than Molly had been in that bad time. "Don't worry, Grady. It could never happen again. I just want to talk to Franny—for the record."

"But, Molly, that's how it starts with you. Just one thing. Then one more. And pretty soon it takes over your life. And mine. And Jo Beth's. Keep away from this. It'll suck you down again."

Her head began to throb. "What is this, Grady? You think you know better than I do what's right for me? And Jo Beth, for God's sake—you're bringing her into this?"

"Of course. She's suffered more than anyone."

Molly was so angry her jaw felt locked. "You think I'd do anything that might hurt her?"

"Not deliberately, but I think you've got a blind spot here."

"Oh, *I've* got a blind spot, but *you*, on the other hand, are perfectly balanced about it, carrying no grudges from the past."

"No, I'm not saying—"

"Yes, you are. You're saying you don't trust me to look back at this without going berserk."

"No. I'm just trying to remind—"

"Oh, here it comes! You're going to throw all that ancient history at me. You're going to dredge up the Olin Crocker shit. You're going to tell me what I did when I was twenty and you're going to—"

"Stop!" he shouted. "Stop it right there. Let me finish just one goddamned sentence, will you?"

In the lowest and most reasonable voice she could muster, she said, "Sure. Go ahead."

"I just want you to think over what is to be gained by pursuing this."

"I have thought it over. It's a very normal thing for me to pay a call on Franny. After all, she was almost my stepmother."

"It might have been normal to do it twenty-eight years ago. It's not normal now."

"Suddenly you're an expert on normal?"

"You're the one who used the word." He rolled over again, turning his back to her. "Give it a rest."

"Rest? Who the hell can rest?" She threw back the covers and slid out of bed.

She landed with both feet on top of the dog. He exploded to his feet, snarling.

"Oh, God!" She jumped back onto the bed. The dog stood stiff-legged, growling, his narrow eyes glowing amber in his black wolfish face. He looked like some nightmare vision of a family pet gone mad.

Trembling, she moved back from the mattress edge.

Grady said, "Molly, there's no reason for us to—"

"Listen, Grady. If you don't like what I do, you can leave. Go home." She pointed at the growling dog. "And take that hellhound with you."

Grady leaned across the bed. "Shhh, Copper, it's okay, sweetie, that's a good dog." He reached out and rubbed the dog's head. "You startled him."

The growling subsided and then stopped.

"That's right. Good Copper," Grady cooed. Still lying across the bed, he looked at Molly, who sat propped up against the headboard. "See," he said, "Copper doesn't believe you should ever get out of bed mad. He thinks it's important to embrace forgiveness." He stopped petting the dog and reached his hand out toward Molly.

The dog resumed his growling, louder and more menacing than before.

Molly said, "Copper also doesn't believe you should touch anyone, so maybe *you* need to embrace chastity."

Grady laughed. The sound was so pleasing to her, so full of affection and good will, that her anger lost its edge. "Molly," he said in a low voice, "Molly, my darling, forgive my clumsiness about all this. I love you. There is nothing in this world I wouldn't do for you. I just hate to see you invite misery."

He reached out to touch her but stopped short and glanced down at the dog still staring at them. "Here." He stretched out on the bed, reached down for the covers, and pulled them up over himself. Then he lifted them high over his head, inviting her to come under the tent with him. Molly accepted the invitation, and the apology. She crawled in and stretched out next to him. Grady drew the covers over their heads.

Molly was still in a turmoil, but it did feel comforting to be together inside this cocoon of blankets. She decided it was time to ask him. "Grady?"

"Yes?"

"I have to ask you something." Her voice sounded forced and unnatural to her.

"I know."

"You know what?"

"What you have to ask me."

"Oh."

"Uh-huh. But I wish—" He stopped.

"What do you wish?"

"I wish you wouldn't ask. I wish you would let it go and never talk about it again. I wish you'd put your arms around me and press up against my back, real tight, and run your toes up the inside of my leg. I wish—"

"Whoa! Some of this we could arrange, Grady. But you know I can't just let this go."

"Yes, I do know." His voice sounded defeated. That was a good sign, she decided.

"So tell me," she said. "And no matter what you say, I'll still do lascivious things to you with my toes. Tell me the truth."

"I will."

She took a little time to fortify herself. Finally she said, "Okay, here it is: do you think my father committed suicide?"

"There was so much about it that didn't make sense. If it had been my case, it would've been one of the ones that haunt me."

She nodded in the dark. It wasn't the total agreement she wanted, but at least he understood how bothersome the loose ends were. He was a very smart man, a good homicide detective, and he knew almost as much about it as she did.

"But," he said, "I also think you should declare this twenty-eight-year-old case closed. Stamp it unsolved and closed. Weep over it one last time. Then walk away from it."

"Maybe I'll do that. Maybe I will. But I need to do just this one last thing. Then I'll walk away from it."

"Frank Quinlan in Lakeway?" he said.

Bingo. She lowered her head to the pillow and began to relax. "And Frances Lawrence. I wonder why they're unlisted." She snuggled up against his back. "Just for fun, see if

he has a sheet, or anyone in his family back in Lubbock."
She pressed her body tight along the length of his.

"That's a good start," he murmured.

She inched her toes up the inside of his leg. "Grady?"

"Hmmm?"

"Do you know the second verse of 'Little Bopeep'?"

"I don't even know the first verse."

"It's bothering me. She fell fast asleep and dreamt something."

"Molly," he moaned, "no more words. Concentrate on what you're doing. Live in the moment. Mmmm, yes, just like that."

Grady had fallen asleep, but Molly was still wide awake and edgy. She got out of bed, careful this time not to step on the dog, and walked quietly downstairs. In her dark office the only light came from her new computer monitor. From the dark screen a shower of brilliant stars hurtled toward her: her current favorite screen-saver. She sat down and stared into it, letting herself be swept into space, carried through galaxies of multicolored stars and planets. They zoomed toward her and flowed around her as she headed to the center of the universe.

Stars again. The same color and luminosity as the sprinkles on Aunt Harriet's star cookies. She tapped the space bar. The star shower vanished and the screen appeared, with some notes she'd made for an essay she'd been trying to write, an essay that wasn't working out.

She read from the screen:

Next month I will have (celebrate?) my forty-fifth birthday, which will make me the same age (!) my father was when he died. This birthday looms in front of me as a major milestone, one I both fear and welcome.

I have noticed that women in midlife who are fortunate enough to have living fathers seem to grow increasingly close to their fathers as the years pass. More than they ever could when they were younger, they come to savor and embrace the ways in which they are like their fathers. Father and daughter become peers, easy companions, intimate friends. Maybe the reason for this is women's waning estrogen levels, or having gotten child care out of the way; or maybe, having finally discovered that being our mothers hasn't served us well, we decide to try living the second half of life more like a man; or maybe age just confers the freedom to be more ourselves and to get in touch with our male side. I'm not sure of the reason for it, but I have observed with interest and with more than a little envy the increasing rapport between middle-aged women and their fathers.

My own father was murdered when I was sixteen, so this experience is denied me. But as I get older, I certainly recognize the many ways I am growing more like him.

There are of course the obvious things: Vernon Cates was a writer. I am a writer. He had one daughter whom he loved unconditionally. I do too. He loved to drive the back roads of Texas with no itinerary and no set destination. He loved to read in bed, to do crossword puzzles, to sit and talk and drink on the front porch long into the night, to explore an interest to the point of obsession. I love doing those things too. He liked seedy old hotels and coastlines and dusty town squares and honky-tonk bars with neon signs and the moment when the sun drops behind the horizon. I like those things too.

And there's more: he was at heart a loner. So am I. He was given to bleak moods; me too. He had no desire to accumulate possessions; what little desire I once had is withering away.

I don't know—???

Here it ended. It had just been an experiment, one of those many writing ideas that seem like a good idea at first and then just peter out. She thought about deleting the text but couldn't quite bring herself to do it, so she saved it to her hard disk, calling the file "Fathers and Daughters."

She got up and wheeled her desk chair toward the storage

closet. She turned on the light and looked up at the stacks of dusty boxes crammed together on the top shelf. Like the rest of the Cates family, she was a pack rat who never threw away anything that could be put in a box and stored in a closet or a garage. Her father, her Aunt Harriet, her grandmother—they had all been prodigious, lifelong letter writers and they all kept every piece of paper, every memento that came into their lives.

The top shelf was an inaccessible place, where she stored things she didn't think she'd need very often—or ever: old tax returns and receipts, years of bank records, Jo Beth's school projects from grade school, computer paper for a long-abandoned printer. Up there, alongside an old rolled-up sleeping bag, was the carton she was seeking. In her own scrawly handwriting, it was marked, "H. Cates photos."

She pulled the chair into the closet, climbed up on it—carefully, since it was on casters—and reached up. The box was heavy; Aunt Harriet had been the family's alpha pack rat, a born archivist. She carried it to the middle of the floor, set it down with a thump, and sat cross-legged in front of it. Immediately she heard quick light footsteps on the stairs and, a few seconds later, the jingle of Copper's tags. The dog burst into the room with his ears erect—even the ear he'd lost half of in the line of duty with the APD K-9 Unit. He was retired, but still on patrol.

"It's okay, Copper. It's just me." The dog came to her and Molly scratched under his chin. "Sorry about stepping on you before, buddy." She pressed her cheek to his muzzle. "And the name-calling. All forgiven?"

The dog circled a few times and plunked down next to her.

Molly used a letter opener to cut the tape sealing the box. Three years ago when Aunt Harriet moved—or, more accurately, when Molly had moved her—from the house she'd lived in for fifty-four years to the Regency Oaks Senior Care Center in Lubbock, Molly had been overwhelmed by the amount of stuff in the old frame house. It had been a battle royal to get Harriet to agree to the move in the first place. The addled old woman had been frantic about losing her home and her possessions, especially her file cabinets and boxes of accumulated Cates memorabilia. She was sure that Molly would throw something away, anxious not so much about the move to the nursing home as about keeping her archives intact.

Molly had calmed her by striking a deal: Harriet would go peacefully to the nursing home in return for Molly's vow to keep the archives in a safe place. Harriet had watched in high anxiety as Molly had the movers take it all away, and then she had gone to her fate so meekly that Molly had been overcome with regret.

From all the items put in storage, Molly had brought home with her only one thing: a boxful of family photographs. She had intended to go through and label them and put them in albums. But she hadn't done it, and now, in the cold shivery light of 3 A.M., she acknowledged to herself that she probably never would. It was one of those many chores, like cleaning out the garage, that she fully intended to do, but in the brutal triage of her work schedule, they simply didn't have sufficient appeal to make the cut. When she died, or when, like Aunt Harriet, she was hauled off to some nursing home, those things would still be undone.

The box was filled to the top with old albums and loose photos. Molly pulled them out in handfuls. She stretched out on her stomach and went through them one by one.

An hour later, her eyelids beginning to droop, Molly had gone through them all and put them back in the carton—all except the two she had decided to keep out. Those she laid out in front of her on the rug. One, a crystal-clear black and white snapshot, showed the two Cates siblings, Harriet and Vernon, standing on the porch of the old ranch house near Lubbock, the house in which they had grown up, the house in which Molly had grown up for her first fourteen years. Written in faded blue ink on the back was the year— 1943. Harriet Cates at twenty-two was raven-haired and slender, the sharpness of her wit and temper evident in the pointed chin and high arched eyebrows. Molly studied her aunt's face with the mixture of love and resentment that baffled her as much now as it had when she was seventeen.

This slip of a girl had grown into the formidable woman who had taken Molly on when her mother died, who had nurtured her and nagged her, doted on her and disapproved of her. She had tried her damnedest to impose on Molly her value system of churchgoing and white gloves and thank-you notes and gracious Southern behavior, but Molly had been the most unpromising raw material: a tomboy determined to live life on her own terms, a teenager bent on adventure and independence. They had clashed constantly and bitterly, but Molly had always known that when she was in trouble—and that had happened often enough—Harriet Cates was there to help. She had been present and involved, front and center, for all the joys and disasters of Molly's life. And she had been a forceful, nurturing presence in Jo Beth's life as well. The only one of Molly's ancestors still above ground, the only one from that older generation still standing guard between Molly and eternity. Harriet wasn't dead, but she wasn't really alive either. She had been diagnosed five years ago with Alzheimer's, and now she spent her days sitting in a wheelchair staring into space. Molly missed her like fury.

Molly looked back at the photo. Slouching against the porch post next to his older sister, his long legs crossed, was Vernon Cates, Molly's daddy, at eighteen. His dark hair was slicked back and his black almond-shaped eyes looked down his long straight arrogant nose at the camera with the assurance of a young princeling convinced of his own immortality.

The other picture she'd selected was of a group of family and friends sitting on blankets, a lavish picnic spread out in front of them. There was no date written on it, but it must have been taken around 1958 because Molly, leaning against her father, looked to be around four. Her mother, Josephine, was smiling into the camera, unaware she had only five more years to live, only three more years before the lump growing in her breast made her life a misery. Molly's Grandma Cates looked severe, as might be expected of a basically dour woman who had recently lost a husband. Harriet sat with her hands folded in her lap, next to her big, blond, cheerful husband, Donald Cavanaugh. Parnell, already in the state legislature by then, looked prosperous, as befitting a man who'd just inherited the Morrisey family ranch and fortune from his father. He looked on top of the world. Rose, leaning back against him, her face shaded by a wide-brimmed straw hat, was laughing and knitting. She had daisies stuck into her long, thick braid, which hung over one shoulder.

Molly looked at the child she had been, her eyes closed against the sun, her head pressed against her father's shoulder. You could see the faint half-moons of sweat under the arms of his white shirt. Lying here now, forty years later, the smell of him infused the air—that suggestion of sweat mixed with the bay rum aftershave he used and just a touch of whiskey.

Daddy.

Molly rested her head on the carpet and allowed the old litany to play through her head. A man does not kill himself when he's just finishing the revisions on an article he has hopes of selling to a big national magazine, an article he's spent two years investigating. A man does not kill himself when he's two weeks away from getting married. And a man does not kill himself when he has a date the next day with his daughter, to watch her be inducted into the National Honor Society. She closed her eyes. It didn't make any more sense now than it had twenty-eight years ago.

Molly woke with the carpet rough against her cheek. Grady Traynor was standing in the office door, dressed and ready for work even though it was still dark outside. She looked up at him. "It can't be six already?"

"Yes, ma'am." He nodded toward where the dog was sleeping with his nose pressed against her hip. "I see you two made it up."

Molly patted the dog's head. "He decided not to kill me after all. And I promised not to call him names."

"How about me?"

"I won't call you names either."

He hunkered down and kissed her cheek. "Good. Want me to feed him before I go?"

"No, it's okay. I'll do it." She reached out and took Grady's head in her hands, burrowing her fingers deep into his thick white hair, restraining him from getting up. "And, Grady, the favor. Do it as soon as you get there and call me. Okay?"

"Yes, ma'am." His eyes shut for a moment. "At your service."

6

IF CHARNEL HOUSES AND OUR GRAVES MUST SEND
THOSE THAT WE BURY BACK, OUR MONUMENTS
SHALL BE THE MAWS OF KITES.

—MACBETH

Just as she'd suspected, the Quinlan house was one of the imposing mansions perched high above Lake Travis, its multi-levels dug into the bank like talons. Though she couldn't see it as she pulled into the circular driveway, she knew there would be a dock with a power boat behind the house. It was exactly what a rich retired oil man from Lubbock would crave: a house high on a hill overlooking an expanse of blue water and green rolling hills—those things that couldn't be bought in Lubbock for all the money in the world.

She understood that craving for water and hills. When she and her father had moved from Lubbock, they, too, had settled on Lake Travis, but in a far lower rent district—at the seedier, wilder north end. Her daddy, after forty-five years in Lubbock, during which he always maintained he was meant to have been born on the Maine seacoast, adored everything about the lake. Not only did he rent them a small house right on the water, but he established his office in a houseboat docked at Old Gun Hollow just past Volente. Even now, whenever Molly made the half-hour drive from Austin to the lake, she felt her spirits rising with the same lilt of holiday excitement she'd felt during the year they'd lived out here, the year before her daddy was killed and her life changed forever.

But this trip to the lake had been different. Her stomach was roiling with apprehension as she parked in front of the pink brick mansion with the Palladian windows. It had taken Grady forty seconds to get Franny Lawrence Quinlan's unlisted phone number and address, but it had taken Molly an hour to work up the nerve to make the call. She kept picking up the phone and putting it down without dialing, remembering each time how abysmally she had always treated Franny Lawrence, who had tried so sweetly and doggedly to befriend the teenaged Molly. Also, there was the issue of the Quinlan family and the accusations Molly had once made against them. She was afraid Franny would refuse to see her. And what if Frank Quinlan answered the phone and she had to identify herself? He would remember the name Molly Cates even though they had never met. No one ever forgot the kind of accusations she had made against the Quinlans.

But eventually she'd dialed and a maid had answered and called Mrs. Quinlan to the phone. Franny had expressed delight to hear from her. Molly had said she'd like to come out right away. To Molly's amazement, Franny had agreed with seeming enthusiasm and no awkward questions.

From their first meeting twenty-nine years ago, when Franny Lawrence had taken Molly and her father to see the house they leased in Volente, Molly had loathed the woman. It was clear immediately, from the flush in Franny's cheeks and the gleam in her eye when she looked at Vernon Cates, that her interest in him went way beyond renting him a house. Franny had been thirty-three then, a brand-new real estate broker, a divorcee with an eleven-year-old son. She had been a vivacious, sensual redhead, a vision right out of a Renoir painting.

Molly was used to women looking at her daddy that way. Long before Franny came along, Molly had had to accept that her father, a handsome young widower, loved the company of women, and that women loved him back—fervently. But Franny Lawrence was different from the others because

Molly could see that, for the first time, her father was emotionally swept away. There was no mistaking it: he was totally, joyously in love. Molly's response had been to withdraw and be as sullen and uncommunicative and disapproving as possible. She had spoken to Franny only when absolutely necessary.

And after her father was killed, she had rebuffed all Franny's attempts to comfort her and to maintain contact with her. The last time she'd seen Franny had been at Vernon Cates's funeral. Franny had put her arm around Molly's shoulders and said she'd like to have some private time to talk, but Molly had disengaged herself as quickly as possible. Now, twenty-eight years later, it seemed that they were finally going to have that private conversation.

Molly sat in the truck for a few moments to collect herself, then checked her face in the rearview mirror. Her bad night had etched itself into the skin around her eyes. She wondered if her nearly forty-five-year-old face would still be recognizable to someone who hadn't seen her since she was sixteen. Slowly, she got out of the truck and walked up the stone path to the front door and rang the bell. A Hispanic-looking woman answered the door. She was holding the hand of a towheaded toddler who was wearing only a diaper.

"Hi, I'm Molly Cates. I'm here to see Mrs. Quinlan."

"*Sí. Sí.* Come. I get her. One minute." Pulling the child behind her, the woman walked off.

The house was cool and airy with pale Saltillo tile floors and high vaulted ceilings. She wandered into the huge living room, where the simple furniture and lack of clutter seemed designed to focus attention on the view. She walked to the window that framed the lake and its grand white limestone cliffs. Today Travis was at its best: a sparkling Mediterranean blue, dotted with white sails.

But under that blue water lay the consecrated ground of an old graveyard. They had cleared it away when the lake was made fifty-five years ago with the completion of the Mansfield dam. And in that same shining water every year people drowned while at play, snagged in the branches of old trees that reached up and pulled them to their watery deaths. In

girls don't use profanity or carry a drink in public," Franny said. "What are you working on now, Molly?"

"I've been doing some research at the legislature on the concealed handgun bill. But my main thing right now is a piece on homeless women."

"Bag ladies?" Franny raised her eyebrows.

"Yeah. I've done some interviews and we'll talk with them over the course of a year and photograph them and see how their lives change. Or don't change. It's something I've been wanting to do for a long time."

"Why?"

Molly shrugged. "They fascinate me."

"Me too. Bag ladies appear in my nightmares."

"Yeah," Molly said, "I'm discovering that's pretty common among women."

Franny pulled her slender ankles up under her, as though settling in for some serious conversation. "When I was first divorced from Kevin's father, I'd have these nightmares about being a bag lady and then I'd see them on the street and I couldn't take my eyes off them."

"Same with me," Molly said. "But I tend to be more extreme. I always wanted to follow them around and see what they do during the day, where they sleep, how they're treated. And I wanted to look through their bags and find out all their secrets."

Franny smiled. "And now you get to do that."

"And get paid for it," Molly said with enthusiasm. "It's such a scam."

"You know, we don't think about them as having anything to do with us until we go through some crisis. Then we see how easily it could happen to us."

"I'm still just two paychecks away from it," Molly said.

"So was I till I married Frank." Franny surveyed her opulent living room. "I guess it could still happen since he's got the money and I gave up my business when we got married." She looked at Molly, and her full lips curved slowly upward into a rueful smile. The corners of her luminous hazel eyes crinkled good-naturedly. This was the woman her father had loved, had wanted to marry. And for the first time Molly allowed herself to see why.

The maid came in with a tray and set it down on the massive coffee table in front of Franny. Behind her toddled the baby, now dressed in overalls and a striped T-shirt. He was clutching a nursing bottle.

"Thanks, Juanita," Franny said. "Come here, Alex, and meet a friend."

The baby grinned and toddled toward her, holding his bottle aloft. He teetered as he neared the table and Franny reached out to steady him. "Say hello to Molly, sweet boy."

Alex lowered his head and started to suck on his bottle.

"Hello, Alex," Molly said.

Juanita scooped him up and carried him off.

Molly watched him go with regret, thinking it might not be so bad being a grandmother if she could look as good as Franny and have a maid to do the work.

Franny poured the coffee into a delicate bone china cup. "How do you take yours, Molly?"

"Black. Thanks."

Franny poured herself a cup. "I wonder what the bag ladies have nightmares about."

"Being us. Having to go to work and wear pantyhose."

Franny laughed. "Do they say that?"

"No, but they *do* say that after you've been on the street a few years it's too late to go back to the working world and its constraints. Even though their existence is miserable." The coffee was vanilla-flavored and delicious. "Great coffee. But, even though we know that, there's still a little twinge of attraction to them, isn't there?"

Franny looked up, surprised for a second, then murmured, "Yes. Yes. Maybe it's the temptation to just stop all the struggling and give in. Just let it all go. Such a relief."

"Sweet surrender," Molly said. "Freedom's just another word for nothing left to lose."

They looked at one another and nodded.

Now was the time, Molly decided. She took a sip of coffee for courage. "Franny, yesterday at the legislature I saw Olin Crocker. I didn't talk to him, just caught a glimpse of him."

Franny sipped her coffee. "Yes. I know he's been doing some lobbying. I ran into him at a fund raiser out here for Jim Renkert. About a month ago. Hadn't seen him since . . . back then, when it happened."

"Same with me. Did you talk to him?"

"No." Her lips were tight, as though she were stopping herself from saying more.

Molly went on. "Right after I saw him, I was having lunch with Rose and Parnell. They talked about the funeral—I'm so sorry to hear about that."

Franny nodded. "Poor Frank. Willie was the apple of his eye."

"Rose said you said it reminded you of my daddy. That he committed suicide too." She watched Franny's face drain of animation. "Did you say that? Do you think it?"

"Oh, Molly. So that's why you've come."

Molly nodded.

"You haven't laid him to rest, have you?"

"No."

"Well, I'm sorry something thoughtless I said got back to you and upset you."

"But you did say it?"

"Yes. We were talking about brilliant people being more . . . prone to depression and suicide."

Molly leaned forward. "Franny, you *really* believe my daddy killed himself?"

Franny's cup rattled on its saucer. She set it down on the table. "I know he did."

It was a body blow. When she caught her breath, Molly said, "You *know* he did?"

Franny nodded.

"How?"

"Oh, Molly, this is still so hard for you. Do you really want to go into this?"

Molly looked out at the lake, which seemed to be sending off golden sparks now as the sun approached its midday intensity. "I have to. Tell me."

"All right." Franny closed her eyes. "God." She leaned back into the corner of the sofa. "I know he committed suicide because I worried the whole week before it happened that he might do exactly that."

Molly was short of breath. "You did? Why?"

"The week before his death, Vern was"—she held her hands out as if begging for the right word to fall into them—"depressed doesn't even approach it. He was distraught, tormented. It was so extreme I thought he ought to be in a hospital, but I couldn't even get him to see a doctor. I've never seen anyone in worse shape."

Molly was stunned. She didn't believe it. It couldn't be true that this had been going on without her knowing it. "Is this *true?*" she whispered.

Franny nodded. "He was in crisis, total agony, for a week before it happened."

"I never saw any of this."

"Of course not. You were a teenager and you were busy with your own life, just as you should have been. And he didn't *want* you to see it."

Could it be true that her daddy was despondent, even suicidal, that last week and she hadn't noticed? Hot guilt squeezed at her. Where had she been that week? On Mars? No, she'd been having her first romance, with a senior baseball player, Sam Gardner, Sam of the long sinewy arms and the smooth back, Sam who had introduced her to baseball and sex. She'd been seeing him at every opportunity, and she'd been getting ready for exams. She'd been worrying about getting pregnant, she'd been playing on the tennis team, she'd been resenting the growing closeness between Franny and her daddy. They'd just told her they were getting married and she'd been hoping it wouldn't happen. But she had not been paying any attention to her daddy.

"So," Molly said, "he was depressed. Why? What was the problem?"

"Darling, I wish I knew. It seemed to come out of the blue. One day he was happy, riding high. The next day he just crashed. I asked him, *begged* him, to tell me what it was. All he said was he was sorry but he couldn't marry me and he wanted me to go away and leave him alone."

Molly's heart stopped dead with surprise. "He broke your engagement?"

"That was the least of it. He said he was unfit for marrying anyone, that he should never have gone this far with me, he should have known it was impossible."

"But *why?*"

"Molly, if I knew the answer to that, my life the past twenty-eight years would have been easier. There isn't a day I haven't asked myself why." She leaned forward so she was inches from Molly and spoke in a voice so low Molly had to strain to hear. "Vernon Cates was the love of my life, my other half, the man I was born to love. And in spite of what he said to me that last week, I believe I was the love of his life too. That may sound corny to you, but it's true."

"I can't believe this. That whole year he was courting you, he was giddy with happiness. Why this all of a sudden?"

"I don't know." Franny sat back into the corner of the sofa. "Something happened. We were together on the houseboat one afternoon, and it was wonderful. He got a phone call, just before dinner. It was Harriet calling from Lubbock. He was clearly upset after he talked to her. We'd been planning on going out for barbecue, but after the call he said he'd have to beg off. Some old business acquaintance was coming in from Lubbock and he needed to take care of it alone. I didn't mind, I had some paperwork to do on a closing, and I wanted to spend time with Kevin. When I saw Vern the next night he was a different man. He said our wedding was off, and I needed to leave him alone."

Her voice cracked on the last word. She picked up her cup and took a sip of coffee, looking at Molly over the rim. "I had no pride, Molly. I refused to go away. I wouldn't accept it. I begged him to go to a counselor with me, to see a doctor, to elope with me, anything I could think of. All week, I kept at him. I said I'd never let him go.

"Then, a week after all this started, he disappeared.... And five days later he turned up dead in the lake."

"You sure it was Harriet who called?"

"Yes."

"Did you ask her about it later?"

"Oh, yes. Many times."

"And—?" Molly prompted.

"And she'd never discuss it. She said it was nothing, that she was just checking in with her brother. Molly, his face after that phone call—he looked like he'd just heard the world was ending."

"When did you see him last?" Molly asked.

"The night before he disappeared. I stopped by the houseboat to see him. He was sitting on the deck in the dark, drunk, flipping one of those gold Mexican coins he loved, and drinking straight bourbon. I told him I loved him and he told me to get off his property. Actually, he shouted it at me."

"To get off his property!" Molly was shocked. "I never heard about any of this. Did you tell Crocker this?"

Her lips got tight again. "Sure, but Crocker wasn't worth a damn."

"That's the kindest thing you could say about him. But you agreed with his ruling of suicide."

"Yes, but if there had been foul play, Crocker would never have figured it out. He was too busy trying to cop a feel."

Molly was stunned. "You too?"

"Crocker was a dirty old man even though he wasn't old then."

For a split second Molly felt like telling her about what had happened with Crocker, but it was something she'd never talked about. She didn't want to bring up the feelings. It was like resisting throwing up: you knew you would feel better afterward if you went ahead and did it, but the violent upheaval and the foul taste in your mouth were too unpleasant. She simply agreed: "He definitely was a dirty old man."

"Molly, if I had it to do over again, I still wouldn't know what to do. I saw Vern needed help, but can you get a man committed because he's decided not to marry you? I don't think so."

Molly was in turmoil. To calm herself, she felt compelled to lay out her case against suicide, simply and forcefully, as she had done for herself hundreds of times. She started in the usual place: "Franny, the man didn't own a gun."

"I know."

"And there's no record of his buying one. I checked every gun store in Texas."

"Did you? That must have taken awhile."

"About six months. Daddy hated guns."

"I know."

"He was coming to see me inducted into the National Honor Society the next night. And we'd invited some of my friends to go to dinner in Austin afterward."

Franny was nodding.

"He never, ever broke a promise to me, not once. He would have written me a note, something."

"Honey, I know it's hard to accept."

"His writing career was finally taking off."

"Yes, I think maybe it was."

"As much as I hated it at the time, he was madly in love with you."

"Yes."

"Franny, someone killed him, then sank the houseboat to destroy all his notes and papers. Someone did that because he was writing something dangerous to them. I'm sure of it."

Franny reached out and picked up Molly's hand. "Maybe Vern destroyed those things himself."

"Franny, no." Molly withdrew her hand. "He was a man who kept everything. He had my mother's poems in those files, his parents' love letters, my school projects, every essay I ever wrote. Even if he *were* going to kill himself, he'd have left those things for me."

Franny responded with a sigh.

"And what about the houseboat?" Molly said. "Did he sink his own houseboat that he loved?"

"Yes."

"Why would he do that?"

"To clean up, get things tidy. People who commit suicide often destroy their journals and other files first. Willie did it too. He'd gotten rid of everything. There wasn't a scrap of paper in his room."

Molly sat back in the big chair. The plushness of the cushion sucked her in, made her feel that she would never be able to get up. Suicide. She had never, not for a moment, accepted the medical examiner's suicide ruling. Now, for the first time in all these years, she was shaken in her conviction. Should she believe all this? Was Franny telling the truth or did she have some ax to grind here? Was she covering up for somebody?

"What's your best guess?" Molly asked. "About that phone call?"

"Molly, I don't have one. I've gone through all the possibilities—financial ruin, paternity suits, old crimes. I just don't know what could be so devastating, so bad, that we couldn't have worked it out."

"And Harriet wouldn't say?"

"No. You know how close they were."

Molly nodded. They had been lifelong confidants, Vernon and Harriet, and she had often felt deprived at not having a brother or sister to share that kind of relationship with.

"Harriet knew Daddy had broken off your engagement?"

"Yes. I talked to her, too, that week. She had already heard it from Vern and she was worried about his depression. We discussed it. She talked it over with Parnell Morrisey in Austin. There was lots of phone calling going on. She was trying to get him to a psychiatrist."

"A psychiatrist! Aunt Harriet was doing that?"

"Yes."

"But she always said psychiatry was a hoax."

"That's what people say when they haven't needed it yet."

Molly pushed her hair back from her face. It was starting to get hot in here with the noon sun beating in the window. "Well, whatever Harriet knows is gone forever," Molly said.

"Alzheimer's. Rose told me. Such a shame."

"Yeah, sometimes she recognizes me and sometimes she doesn't."

"So unfair."

They stopped talking because they heard the front door open and slam shut. Molly put her hands on the chair arms to brace herself. She had dreaded this. It must be Frank Quinlan home from the golf course. She had never met

Quinlan, although she had had a stormy interview with his father and older brother many years ago. It was getting really hot in here now; she wished Franny would turn up the air conditioning.

A small, fit man with white hair and a sunburned face burst into the room. He wore a turquoise Ralph Lauren shirt, white shorts, and deck shoes with no socks. "Hi, darling." He strode over and leaned down to give his wife a kiss. Molly watched him closely. It had been two and a half decades since she had made her accusations against Quinlan's family and the oil company they owned. She had tried to have charges brought against them and had been quoted in the newspaper as saying that they had murdered Vernon Cates. It had happened a long time ago, but it was not the sort of thing anyone forgot.

Frank straightened up and looked at Molly. "Miz Cates?" His mouth tried to smile, but it seemed afraid to, as though someone had told him the best way to treat a cobra was to smile at it and he was doing his damnedest. He tried the smile again and this time it worked.

Molly extended her hand to him. "Hello, Frank. I'm Molly. Nice day for golf."

Looking relieved, he took her hand and pumped it. "Yes, yes. Beautiful day on the course. Franny said you were coming out. She was so pleased you called. Sure is nice to have you here at our home." Frank Quinlan looked more like a kindly retired coach than a murderer, but Molly had seen too many sweet-faced murderers to believe that these things were written in the flesh.

He looked at Franny. "Can I get you pretty ladies anything from the kitchen?"

"I don't think so, dear," Franny said. "Thanks."

"Well, that being the case, I think I'll go round up old Alex for a boat ride."

"He'd love that," Franny said. "Don't forget his pre-server—on the hook at the back door."

"Yes, ma'am," he said. "Pleasure to meet you, Molly." He backed away in evident relief, a man exiting a snake pit.

"Good to see you, Frank," Molly said, thinking what a blessed relief social conventions were in a situation like this.

The women were silent until they heard a door close at the other end of the house.

Franny leaned forward and smiled to defang what she was about to say. "Surely it can't be true that you think that man killed your daddy?"

"Oh, Franny, I don't know. I *do* know Quinlan Oil was trying to keep Daddy from publishing his story on the white oil scam. I *know* they tried to pay him off. I *know* the article never got published because my father was killed and the backup material destroyed."

Franny appeared to be listening carefully. "Jasper Quinlan was not a nice man. Frank will be the first to admit it. But I don't believe Jasper would have killed anyone. Frank I've known for twenty years, and I've never seen or heard of him doing an unkind thing. I knew him during his wife's long illness, when I would happily have become his mistress, but he doesn't believe in infidelity even under extreme conditions. I know how much he loves children. He would never kill anyone. Find some other tree to bark up."

"Franny, I never said *he* did it. It's a big family."

"True. But he was active in the company then. He would have known about this, Molly. He says he is certain no one involved with Quinlan Oil had anything to do with your father's death. I've never known him to lie." Franny's cheeks pinkened with the fervor of her belief.

"What did he say when you told him I was coming out this morning?"

Franny hesitated. "When I told Frank you'd called and that you were coming out, he said that, back at the time you were going around making wild accusations, you got them all upset. *Real* upset. He thought you were a crazy woman. But after what happened with our poor Willie, he understands how you would do anything in the world to avoid believing that someone you love has committed suicide. He said if there were any other possibility for Willie, he'd go to the ends of the earth to find out."

The ends of the earth, Molly thought, leaning back into the plush chair. At the very least.

Molly was invited to stay for lunch, but she declined. She wanted only to get in her truck and drive. She needed time and solitude to think this over. She headed back toward Austin, intending to go straight home, but when she came to Four Corners, to her surprise, her truck turned left onto Bullick Hollow instead of right onto 2222. Apparently she was headed to Volente.

Their old cottage had been torn down several years before by the current owners, in favor of a big new two-story colonial, so she drove instead to Old Gun Hollow, where her daddy's houseboat had been moored, with his little fishing boat tied up behind it. The dock, rickety even back then, was a ruin now, with just a few slats remaining. She parked right next to it and opened the windows. The lake water lapped the shore with a faint sucking sound. She leaned her head back and closed her eyes to picture the scene Franny had described: her father sitting on the deck that last night, drunk. What was it that he was thinking about in the dark? What was bedeviling him? Was it something bad enough to make him kill himself, to leave her behind without a word of good-bye?

One of the cornerstones of her life for nearly three decades had been her conviction that her father had been murdered. She still believed it, but this morning a fault line had cracked through the foundation of her belief. Her whole body felt shaky and weak.

That belief had shaped her character and directed her life. She drove a Chevy truck because her daddy had loved his and had left it behind for her—her first vehicle, which she drove for eleven years until it broke down past all repair, when she replaced it with another. She was a professional writer because he had died before he could be the writer he wanted to be. She wrote about crime because she had developed a passion for the subject while looking into his death.

She was an indefatigable worker who never gave up because she had cut her teeth on an impossible quest. She lived alone because she needed to be unencumbered to follow her obsessions.

What if all this time she had been wrong? What if Vernon Cates had killed himself in a state of despair over God knew what? Had so much of her life been built on a fiction?

She opened her eyes and was dazzled by the glittering water and the glare of the Texas sun. A sailboat with a red and white striped spinnaker scutted by. A lone turkey vulture cruised the air current along the high western bank. The water kept up its steady low lapping at the shore. About a month before his death, she and her daddy had gone out on the lake in his little fishing boat after a heavy rain. On the shore they saw a dead tree with scores of vultures perched in it, their immense black wings spread out wide to dry. Her daddy had shut off the outboard motor so they could just drift and watch it in silence. The current had lapped against the boat's hull with that same soothing rhythm she was hearing now. After a while, awed by the scene, Molly had said, "It's like catching a glimpse of death waiting for us."

Her father had nodded and said, "A good reminder to live while we can."

She felt so confused now. So exhausted.

She reached down for the lever and lowered the seat back. Her eyes closed. If there were anything more to do for him, anything in the world, she would do it. But she didn't know what that would be. Maybe Grady was right and she needed to declare the case closed. Unsolved and closed. Could she do that?

Yes. For now, for this minute, she thought she could. She would let it all go, just let herself float. The plush fabric of the seat buoyed her. The sun on her face warmed her. The lapping of the water lulled her.

She did something she hadn't done during the daylight hours since she was a small child: she took a nap.

Clem's was the sort of hot, dusty, redneck place Molly Cates
had spent her life trying to avoid. The driveway consisted of
two gravel ruts, the buildings were ramshackle wood affairs
with layers of red paint laid on thick in hopes of holding
them together for a few more years. At the front, closest to
the road, stood several towers for skeet shooting and a small
office. A crooked, hand-lettered sign said, CLEM'S SKEET
AND SHOOTING RANGE. It was the last place on earth Molly
wanted to be right now. It had been her editor's idea: two
women who had never before fired guns, a mother and
daughter—Molly and Jo Beth—would be in the first group
to go through the training to get licensed to carry a handgun.
And Molly would write about the experience as part of the
coverage of the new law. At the time he proposed it to her, in
the air-conditioned tranquility of the *Lone Star Monthly* offices, it had seemed like a good idea. But the hot sticky reality
was far less appealing.

Jo Beth Traynor coughed and rolled up her window
against the dust. "Mom, I can't believe I let you talk me into
this."

"You ought to know better by now." Molly parked her
truck next to Wanda's in front of the office. Wanda was

pulling a bulging duffel bag out of her truck. She slung it over her shoulder and headed toward the office. She wore a pink and white checked Western-style shirt with pearly snap buttons, skin-tight Levi's, boots, and a wide leather belt with an enormous buckle that had engraved on it "Central Texas Women's Handgun Champion." Her black hair was teased and sprayed into immobility.

They'd just spent an hour and a half across the highway in the trailer-classroom learning about the safe handling of firearms, the difference between a revolver and a semiautomatic, the anatomy of a round of ammunition, and how the damn things worked. And they'd been exposed to a hefty dose of Wanda Lavoy's philosophy, a paranoid brew of *Dirty Harry* mixed with *Thelma and Louise:* the world was full of bad guys and they were all out to get you, so a woman needed to know how to blow them away. She also played a really frightening tape recording of a woman talking with a 911 dispatcher for sixteen minutes while she listened to a man breaking into her house and waited for the police to arrive. The bad guy got to her first and raped her before the good guys got there to arrest him. Molly was impressed; it was an effective illustration of the need to be able to defend yourself.

Inside the office they paid their fees and asked for thirty rounds of ammunition apiece for Molly and Jo Beth. "Clem, give my gals those reloaded wadcutters, will ya? And, honey, they want your best price," Wanda said with a wink at the thin-lipped proprietor. Without smiling, he handed each of them a box of cartridges.

During the classroom session, Wanda had let them select guns from her own arsenal—a Rossi .38 special with a small frame for Jo Beth, and a Ruger .38 special for Molly. They had amused themselves by playing with the guns and dry-firing while Wanda lectured.

As they walked to the shooting range at the back of the property, Wanda said, "How have you two gals managed to make it to your ages without ever shooting off a gun?"

Jo Beth said, "Everybody thinks because my dad is a cop I must be an old hand. But he's probably the only cop on the planet who's not interested in guns. When I was little I used to beg him to teach me to shoot. But he never did."

"Probably a good thing, sweetie," Molly said, "since he's the worst shot in the history of the APD."

"How about you, Molly?" Wanda asked.

"Oh, same thing, I guess. My daddy grew up in a West Texas hunting family, but he hated guns and the whole scene, so we never had any around the house and I just never had the opportunity."

Wanda said, "Well, my stepdaddy taught me to shoot when I was six. It came in real handy when I was thirteen and needed to get him the hell out of my bedroom, the sumbitch." She patted the gun case she carried under her arm. "Amazin' how much behavior modification you can accomplish with a handgun applied in just the right place."

Behind Wanda's back Jo Beth rolled her eyes at Molly.

The shooting range stretched from a rough wood shelter at one end to a grass-covered berm at the other. Wood frames with tattered paper targets attached to them stood at various distances.

The only other customer this hot weekday afternoon was a man wearing a pair of striped boxer shorts and a set of hearing protectors that looked like immense earphones. He was shooting a revolver while three barefoot, dirty children in swimsuits sat on the rickety table and watched.

As they entered the shooting area, there was a crunch under her feet that Molly took for gravel at first, but when she looked down she realized they were walking on shell casings. The brass and aluminum casings were so thick you couldn't see the dirt below.

Wanda handed each of them a pair of hearing protectors from her bag. "You'll need 'em," she said. She set the bag on the table and pulled the guns out, unzipped each from its case, and leaned her bag against the greasy sandbag on the table. "Now let's see you load these babies up. Just like I showed you. Keep 'em pointing down with your trigger finger straight along the frame and you won't get into trouble."

Molly had chosen the Ruger because the rubber grip

seemed to fit her hand perfectly. She held it in her left hand and pressed the cylinder release as she'd practiced and tipped the gun muzzle down so she could see through the six empty chambers. She dropped a cartridge into each chamber, surprised by the way they clicked into place so precisely. She had to admit these revolvers were beautifully made objects, sensual even, the shape and solidity pleasing to her hand. And the design fitted the function perfectly. There was no denying the appeal.

Wanda waited until the man two stations down had stopped firing. She went to talk with him, then walked out onto the range. She stopped at the target frame closest to Jo Beth and unrolled the targets she had brought with her. She stapled one onto the frame. Molly smiled when she saw it. The target was a picture of a stubble-faced man in an undershirt and jeans. He held a pistol pointed at the viewer. One of Wanda's bad guys.

"I bring my own," Wanda called back to them. "More realistic than those bull's-eye things they use here." She stuck a round red Day-Glo sticker smack in the middle of the man's chest. Then she stapled a second picture-target to the stake in front of Molly and put a sticker in the same place.

She walked back to them. "Seven yards today. It's the most likely scenario. Elizabeth, why don't you go first, darlin'." It still gave Molly a start to hear her daughter called Elizabeth. Growing up, she had been Jo Beth, but during law school she'd decided to use just her middle name—Elizabeth. Everybody but Molly and Grady seemed to have adjusted to it.

"Shoot for the center of the mass," Wanda was saying, "where the sticker is." She pointed a long gleaming nail at the target. "Remember, he's a bad guy. He's broken into your house and he's coming at you. Shoot to stop him. None of this disable him crap. This is not the movies, gals, where you shoot someone and he falls down dead. This is the real world where you shoot someone and he just keeps on coming at you." Wanda took the hearing protectors that had been hanging around her neck and fitted them against her ears.

Jo Beth and Molly did the same with theirs.

"Okay, Elizabeth," Wanda shouted to be heard through the protectors, "shoot the crap out of that sumbitch!"

Molly watched her daughter take the gun in the two-handed grip Wanda had taught them. Jo Beth was wearing a white tank top that revealed the full length of her smooth honey-colored arms. Knees bent slightly, she raised the gun until it was straight out in front of her. Her arms were absolutely steady. Molly enjoyed watching her daughter's preparation; it was the cool, deliberate approach she brought to everything she did. From babyhood Jo Beth had had the gift of focus and concentration, and now at twenty-five she lived her life as though the outcome were all within her control.

"Get your sight picture. Make it a lollipop with the red circle right on top. Now squeeze it," Wanda said. "Slow and easy."

Jo Beth's arms tensed as she squeezed the trigger, then jerked up with the recoil. Molly flinched at the noise. She looked at the target and saw daylight through a tiny hole in the man's chest about an inch from the red sticker. Jo Beth let out a snort of delight.

"Real good, darlin'," Wanda said. "An inch to the left this time. He's still coming at you. Stop him."

Jo Beth aimed and fired again. This time the hole was an inch to the other side of the sticker. By the time she'd fired off all six shots, there was a neat circle of holes surrounding the red sticker.

"Darlin', you are a natural," Wanda crowed. "You don't even blink when you fire. Cool as an igloo. If your mama and daddy had brung you up right, you'd of been a state champion today."

Jo Beth smiled at Molly. Her cheeks were flushed with pleasure. "Try it, Mom."

"Your turn, Molly," Wanda said. "Blow that sucker away."

Molly had been holding the revolver in the two-handed grip. Now she brought it up in front of her face and aimed so the front sight nestled neatly inside the notch of the rear sight. How hard could this be? Then she put the red circle right on top of the sights. But she was having trouble holding it steady. It kept bouncing around because her arms were shaking.

"Keep that lollipop steady," Wanda commanded. "And focus on the front sight."

"My arms are wobbling."

"Well, keep it as steady as you can and squeeze."

Molly finally gave up trying to hold still and pulled the trigger to get it over with. The impact on her palms was like a hammer blow that hurt all the way to her elbows. The noise, even with the ear protectors, made her flinch. She opened her eyes and looked at the target. Nothing.

"Oops," Jo Beth said.

Wanda said, "You mashed on the trigger. This time, keep your eyes open and squeeeeze it, nice and slow."

Molly shot five more times. With numbers five and six, she hit the target, but nowhere near the red sticker. Her arms were already aching and her nose was itching with the stench of cordite. This was much harder than it looked in the movies.

"Okay, gals," Wanda said, "free-fire time. Experiment a little. Remember, you *hate* that guy. Shoot his heart out."

By the fifteenth round Molly was getting the feel of it. The jolt every time the gun discharged set her body to humming like a tuning fork. It felt as powerful and momentous as such condensed lethality should feel.

She looked over at Jo Beth and was surprised to see a trancelike smile on her lips as she methodically aimed and fired.

When they were finished with all thirty rounds, Molly's target had one hole that took an edge off the sticker and about twenty sprayed somewhere on the bad guy's body. Jo Beth had thirty holes in her target, all of them in the chest.

Wanda walked out onto the range and retrieved their targets. She handed Jo Beth hers. "You stopped him for sure, Elizabeth." Then she looked at Molly's. "I believe you caused him some discomfort, but I sure hope there were no innocent bystanders."

Wanda glanced back at the office parking lot, where several cars were pulling in, then at her watch. "It's six. The range is closing to the public, but stay awhile. Some of my WICs are here. You'll see some real shooting. We're planning to do some quick draw and point shooting at close range today. It's pretty advanced stuff."

A tall dark-haired woman in jeans was heading toward them. "That's Helen," Wanda said. "She was raped in her big house in Northwest Hills coupla years ago. She's one of my best marksmen, won a combat-shooting competition a few weeks ago."

Another woman, a slender young woman with wispy blonde hair, ran to catch up with Helen. "And that's Gracie. She's the night manager at Kendall's and she makes the 4 A.M. bank deposit. Makes her a little nervous. She started out about like you, Molly, but she's gotten pretty good."

When Helen and Gracie reached them, Helen looked back toward the highway and said, "Wanda, that same car's there, the one from last week. White Camry with one man in it. Across the highway."

"I wonder why he doesn't just come in and say howdy and ask whatever it is he wants to know." Wanda was smiling, but Molly noticed the furrow between her eyebrows that hadn't been there before.

During the next ten minutes seven more women ranging in age from seventeen to seventy walked back to the range carrying boxes of ammunition. Wanda reached into her big duffel and started to pull out identical leather handbags. She gave one to each of the WIC group as they arrived. These handbags looked like regular leather shoulder bags, but they had a special compartment for concealing a handgun. "I ordered these for the WIC group," Wanda said to Molly, "but I got some extras if you gals want to buy one—thirty-nine ninety-five."

Wanda explained the drill. Each woman would start with her gun concealed in her handbag. When Wanda gave the signal, each was to draw and put six shots into the target as quickly as possible with Wanda timing her.

Molly and Jo Beth watched as they did the first drill. Now that she'd discovered how difficult it was, Molly was impressed with their speed and control. Wanda had taught them well. And the women sure didn't look like the angry harridans and vigilantes Cullen Shoemaker had described. Unless it was extremist to want to defend yourself.

"We've got to go, Wanda," Molly said after they'd watched for about twenty minutes.

"Next week," Wanda said, "same time, same place." She handed the Ruger in its carrying case to Molly. "You need to practice. Take this home and dry-fire until it feels comfortable."

Molly hesitated.

"Go on. If you decide you like it, I'll sell it to you cheap."

Molly hadn't considered the idea of buying a gun, but right now the idea was appealing. She took it. "Okay."

"If you're gonna get a license you need a gun. Also, one of these genuine leather shoulder bags."

"Well, I don't—"

She pushed the handbag at Molly. "Borrow it. You can let me know next time." She walked off to examine the targets.

Molly and Jo Beth walked back to the car.

On the way out of the driveway, Molly looked for the white Camry. There it was, about fifty yards from the entrance on the opposite side of the road, pulled off on the shoulder. She could just make out through the dark tinted windows the shape of a man slouched down in the driver's seat.

"Someone's husband?" Jo Beth said. "Checking up."

"Maybe," Molly said.

They drove for a while in silence. "What do you think, honey?" Molly asked finally.

"I hate to say this," Jo Beth said.

"Go ahead."

"I used to think having a gun gave you bad karma, that just having it would attract trouble."

"Yeah. I know what you mean," Molly said.

"You know how often I work late."

"Uh-huh."

"Every time I walk into that parking garage I'm scared shitless. And I stay scared until I'm out of there with my car doors locked."

Molly nodded, keeping her eyes on the road.

"I hate feeling that way. So powerless."

"Yeah."

"If I had a gun and knew how to shoot it, I wouldn't be so scared. I think I'll buy one when we get our licenses," Jo Beth said. "I'll practice regularly so I won't be a menace."

"You won't be a menace."

"No, but you might."

Molly looked over and was glad to see Jo Beth was smiling. "Oh, I'll get better. Just watch."

"I thought I agreed to this to humor you," Jo Beth said, "but maybe I was glad to have an excuse to check it out. And I enjoyed it."

"Me too. Controlling all that power."

"But you're still opposed to it," Jo Beth said.

"Reacting to crime by letting people carry guns seems to me like reacting to the sewers backing up by letting people piss in the streets."

"You're softening though, aren't you?"

"I guess. When we get down to specifics like Gracie and Helen and you, I sure can see the benefits of self-protection."

"And *you*, Mom."

"Yeah. And me."

"So basically you're a WIC. You believe in doing exactly what they've been doing—carrying illegally."

Molly didn't answer right away. There was no way to defend her inconsistency. "I'm not sure," she replied.

"Wow! I love it—something you're not sure about."

Molly glanced over at her daughter. "Am I really so opinionated?"

"Yes."

They rode in silence while Molly considered feeling hurt, but she decided not to be.

Molly hadn't yet told Jo Beth about her conversation with Franny Lawrence, but she needed to now. "Jo Beth, this morning I went out to Lakeway to talk with Franny Lawrence Quinlan, who was engaged to my daddy at the time he died." She glanced sideways at Jo Beth. "She thinks he committed suicide."

"Oh, Mom."

Molly told her Franny's version of Vernon Cates's last week on earth.

When she was done, Jo Beth said, "Mom, would it be so awful if he really did kill himself?"

"But he didn't."

"Okay. But just suppose for a minute that she's right. It wouldn't change how you feel about him, would it? I mean, don't you think everyone has moments when they might do it if the conditions were right?"

"I don't know."

"Did Rose and Parnell say they thought he did?"

"Rose didn't say much of anything. Parnell said everybody thought it, but he never actually said that *he* thought it."

Molly could feel Jo Beth studying her profile. Finally Jo Beth said, "Mom, are you going to take this any further?"

"No. I wouldn't know where to take it."

"Good. It would drive Dad crazy. Last time it drove him away."

Molly was startled by this. She had never told her daughter what had gone wrong with the marriage. "What makes you think that?"

"I'm not stupid, Mom."

"You certainly aren't, but you were too young to remember all that."

"I remember a lot of it."

"Jo Beth, you were only two. You remember what your father told you happened."

"No. He never talks about it. I remember that you were gone all the time. I remember living with Aunt Harriet. I remember it as a bad time."

Molly drove in silence. It had been the worst time of her

life. In trying to be a good daughter, she had been a bad mother and a bad wife. In the end she'd failed at all three. "I'm so sorry," she said.

Jo Beth smiled at her. "I forgive you. Just don't let it happen again."

8

"PUSSY-CAT, PUSSY-CAT,
WHERE HAVE YOU BEEN?"
"I'VE BEEN TO LONDON
TO LOOK AT THE QUEEN."

"PUSSY-CAT, PUSSY-CAT,
WHAT DID YOU THERE?"
"I FRIGHTENED A LITTLE MOUSE
UNDER THE CHAIR."
　　　　　　　—MOTHER GOOSE

Sarah Jane Hurley is in her magic carpet place, that dreamy alcohol-induced drift somewhere between waking and sleeping, between heaven and earth, flesh and spirit. She's lying on a soft oriental carpet gliding through the air, her body light-limbed and cool, in tune with the carpet as it undulates along the contours of the earth below. When she feels herself beginning to come down, she tries to stop the descent. Sometimes she can prolong the sensation by lying still and keeping her eyes closed.

But voices and the clump of feet overhead bring her crashing to earth. She wakes up cold and trembling. Her earth-bound body aches in the worst way. The harsh light shining through the cracks stabs her eyes. The footsteps above pound to a stop right over her head.

Damn. People up there on her deck. Talking. Loud and pushy, thinking they own the world.

"Here, let me just wipe that chair off for you, sir. And this one. You're expecting the other gentleman again?"

"Mr. Vogel. Yeah."

"There you are. I'll let him know you're out here, sir."

"Keep it private, pardner. Here."

"Oh, thank you, sir."

Sarah Jane can tell by the suck-up tone that an exchange of money has just taken place.

One set of footsteps walks away, the door into the Creekside Grill shuts, and the night is quiet again. She closes her eyes. Maybe she can still get back there, to the magic carpet. She has some float time left from Tin Can's pint of scotch. Hard liquor is a rare treat, so she doesn't want to waste a single second of it. *There was an old woman tossed up in a basket, seventeen times as high as the moon.* She starts to feel drifty. It might work. But a noise stops her—a tapping, an infuriating, nervous tapping. It drags her back to earth. She looks up and sees the light flicker. A toe is drumming on the deck. It's him again—that asshole Toe-tapper. She'd nearly forgotten him.

God, that fidgety noise makes her nerves twang. Her bites are stinging, infected maybe from the picking and scratching she can't seem to stop herself from doing. And she's all shivery, even though the air is hot and muggy. She feels like one enormous exposed nerve. She wraps her arms around herself and is alarmed to find she's not wearing her coat. Where is it? She looks around for it in the light leaking through the slats. It's not here. It's gone. Her cow coat with the black and white spots and the shiny black buttons. She's worn it for the whole year she's been in Austin. Got it out of a Dumpster behind a fancy women's store, brand new, with the price tag— two hundred ninety-five bucks—still on it. She likes that coat, depends on it. It's so soft and long and roomy—a cloth coat, just the right light weight for summer. She likes the way it wrapped around her and made her feel better, the way it hid her body. It was comforting, a protective second skin. That's what it was—comforting—and there isn't much left in the world that is comforting anymore. Just the magic carpet, her rhymes, and her coat. And now the coat's gone and her nerves are exposed.

Then she remembers: Tin Can's got it. That fucking

Lufkin made her give it to Tin Can—some stupid experiment, and then Tin Can gave her the pint of scotch whiskey so she could keep it. And Sarah Jane agreed. Now she has no coat and the pint is gone and so is the drift.

Overhead, the deck shakes with heavy footsteps.

"Here he is. Can I get you gentlemen something to drink?"

Two male voices order drinks—a bourbon and branch and a Heineken. The voice ordering the Heineken is the deep, accented voice from before, old Billy Goat Gruff, the one that likes nekkid art.

Just the sound of drinks being ordered makes her body tense with craving. She'd like a beer too. Oh, would she ever! She licks her dry lips. Her throat contracts with desire. Her hand twitches to close around a cold beer bottle, her lips part to suck at it, her tongue waits to feel the liquid flow over it, cold and hot at the same time. Every part of her body desires it, right down to her blood and bones.

The waiter leaves, and it's quiet on the deck.

"Did you—"

"Wait!" It's the deep voice. A heavy thumping moves around the deck. He must weigh a ton and he's got to be wearing boots to make a ruckus like that. She follows with her eyes the flicker of his feet as he walks the perimeter. He stops and starts, seems to be looking over the rail, checking for something. *Fee, fi, fo, fum, I smell the blood of an Englishman.* She holds her breath. Surely she's safe. There's no way he can see her under here.

She hears the distinctive flick of a lighter.

Finally the big man clumps back to the table. A chair scrapes the wood. "Just making sure," he says, his deep voice a raspy whisper.

"We're alone, pardner. Relax."

"In my business, *pardner,* you don't relax—ever. Keep your voice down."

"You do your homework?" Even though Toe-tapper is talking real low, Sarah Jane can still hear every word—unfortunately. She's right underneath them so she can't avoid hearing. She can even smell the smoke from the cigarette Billy Goat Gruff has lit.

"Took the tour, like you said," says Billy Goat.

"Good man."

"Security's fucking pathetic. After Oklahoma City you'd think they'd beef it up, but no. You could bring a howitzer in there. We'll set it up in the gallery, looks just like camera equipment. We'll fire the projectiles with timers. I got them all ready. You got my press badge?"

"Right here. And the date's set, pardner. Monday."

"Monday. Good. I'm ready."

Toe-tapper lowers his voice. "Something I been wondering: how much does it take?"

"What?"

"How much soman to kill a man?"

"A particle of mist will do it."

"How much for the Senate chamber?"

"You could fit it in a beer bottle."

"No shit?"

"No shit. It's a higher form of killing."

"How, exactly, does it kill?"

It's a question she'd expect of Toe-tapper. To know him is to hate him.

The restaurant door opens and footsteps thud across the deck. "Here you go, gentlemen. A Heineken, a bourbon and branch, a bowl of pretzels. Anything else?"

After his footsteps recede, there is silence for a while. Sarah Jane hears the tinkle of ice, a sound that always gives her a little anticipatory shiver. She thinks she can smell the bourbon fumes. She breathes deeply to capture what she can.

Toe-tapper says, "How does it work? I'd like to know."

"Well," the gruff voice says, "inhaled or absorbed through skin—it's deadly either way."

"But how do people die?"

"You don't want to know."

"I do want to know."

"Asphyxiation."

"But what does that look like? Since I don't plan on being there." He chuckles.

"Convulsions. They clench up tight, fall down, get paralyzed. Then they die. From asphyxiation. Can't breathe."

"Goddamn!"

"Yah."

Sarah Jane rolls her eyes. Men are such bullshitters. Who would believe this crap?

"Yah," Billy Goat says again. "You know, even Adolf Hitler wouldn't use this stuff. He had stockpiles of it he could of used in the war, but he was morally offended by it."

"Hitler was morally offended?"

"Yah. He got a taste of mustard gas in the first war, in 1918, when he was a corporal in the 16th Bavarian Reserve Infantry. Blinded him for a few hours."

"Really?"

"Uh-huh. My hobby's military history."

"Yeah, I can see."

"Another thing—there's no treatment. The posse aware of that?"

"Sure. So what?"

"When I was taking that tour, there was kids down on the floor—pages, I think—and up in the gallery there was school groups and tourists all over the place. Makes no difference to me, but those people are gonna get hit too. I just want to make sure you know that."

Ice tinkles in a glass. And some moving shadows right above, a scraping sound. Sarah Jane blinks. Some sparks are drifting down toward her face. Reflexively, she closes her eyes and turns her head. Then something pings her on the cheek, stings, and bounces off. Jesus. His cigarette butt. Still lighted. He's pushed it through the slats. Panic flutters in her chest. Maybe he knows she's here. No, he couldn't. This discussion is making her jumpy.

"So it'll take everyone out?" Toe-tapper says.

"Yah. People down on the floor will get it first. But it rises quick."

"Will people in the gallery be able to get out if they see it?"

"Maybe. But once you get the smallest whiff of it, well, you never recover."

"You ain't worth shooting, huh?" He laughs.

There is a pause. Sarah Jane feels her breathing coming

hard. She doesn't believe any of this bullshit but, still, she wishes she were anyplace else.

Toe-tapper speaks. "Don't worry about it, pardner. Remember, you're the exterminator man. Your job is to kill cockroaches—big ones, little ones—what does it matter? Did they worry about that at Waco? You know what I'm saying, pardner?"

Sarah Jane is trembling. She closes her eyes and rolls the eyeballs back, trying to drift, so she doesn't have to hear it. This is just men big-dogging it like they do, from their balls, not their heads. None of it is true. Anyway, it doesn't have anything to do with her. She's just going to drift off and ignore it all. *To bed, to bed, says Sleepyhead.*

"How about my expenses?" rumbles Billy Goat.

"I can take care of that little matter right now, pardner," says Toe-tapper. A chair scrapes and something rustles. "Compliments of the posse."

There is a long silence. "Looks okay," says Billy Goat. "The rest right after delivery?"

"As agreed, pardner. You do right well for yourself."

Billy Goat grunts. "Big expenses. Special Hastelloy vats from Germany, raw materials cost a fortune. And the risk. In this business, one mistake and pfuut."

"So we hear, pardner. So we hear. But the posse appreciates this. It's gonna be big, pardner. Like Oklahoma City, but better."

Sarah Jane stiffens. Someone is crawling under the deck toward her. Making a swishing noise. Christ, what is this—Grand Central Station? If those two up top hear, she's dog meat. She lifts her head to see. In the light spilling through the cracks, she recognizes Tin Can. She's got that mangy cat Silky in one arm, and she's wearing Sarah Jane's cow coat.

In the dark Sarah Jane gestures to Tin Can to stop.

Above, a harsh voice whispers, "You hear something, man?"

"Where?"

"Down there. Listen."

Tin Can keeps coming, swishing through the dirt. God, she's dumb as a rock.

As soon as Tin Can gets into range, Sarah Jane reaches out and grabs her hair to stop her. Tin Can lets out a whine. Silky leaps out of her arm and darts off.

Sarah Jane sees Tin Can's mouth open to call out. She clamps a hand over the open mouth. Tin Can looks at her with wide, terrified eyes.

Above them, there's a loud thud, like a chair falling over. "Jesus H. Christ. There! Hear that?"

"Yah! Under the deck."

Out of the corner of her eye, Sarah Jane sees a dark blur of motion. It's Silky dashing out and leaping up to the deck.

"Oh, shit! A cat. It's a goddamn cat, a fucking cat." Toe-tapper gives out his braying laugh. "Just a cat. Christ, that gave me a scare. Here, kitty. Come here. Kitty want a nice pretzel?"

Tin Can's big eyes roll upward, showing the whites in panic. She dotes on that dumb beast. Sarah Jane shakes her head in warning.

"Come here." It's Toe-tapper calling in a falsetto. "Nice kitty-witty. Come to Daddy, so I can break your neck for scaring us like that."

Tin Can jerks back from Sarah Jane's hand. "No, don't," she squeals in her high-pitched voice. "Silky! Come to Mama."

Up on the deck, there's a screeching of chairs and a rapid thudding of feet.

Sarah Jane is frozen to her spot. *Be he alive or be he dead, I'll grind his bones to make my bread.*

The men above are on the move, thundering around the deck. "What the hell? Oh, m'God, someone's under the deck!"

Tin Can slithers backward on her stomach, faster than Sarah Jane has ever seen her move. She shrieks, "Silky!" and crawls out from under the deck into the bushes that are in the darkness, just outside the circle of light radiating out from the deck.

"Silky!" Tin Can wails again. Amazingly, the cat comes to her call. Sarah Jane hears him gallop across the deck. He leaps from the deck and races into the bushes. Tin Can scoops him up and, with the cat clutched to her breast, runs toward the bank that leads down to the creek. She can move surprisingly fast for such a retard. The black and white coat flaps behind her.

Sarah Jane wants to run too, but the two men are standing at the edge of the deck. She'd have to run right past them. They'd see her. She flattens herself into the earth and tries to stop breathing. Her heart is pounding so loud that she has to hug her arms to her chest to mute the racket.

On the deck Toe-tapper says, "Christ, the bitch was right under the deck."

"She heard us," Billy Goat growls.

"She *saw* us," Toe-tapper says. "All lighted up here like a goddamn stage. Shit, shit, *shit!*"

The restaurant door squeaks open and the toady voice calls, "Is there a problem out here, sir?"

"Goddamn right there is," Toe-tapper says. "We were attacked by a wild cat and some crazy woman just came bursting out from under the deck."

"Oh, dear. One of the campers probably."

"Campers?"

"Yes, sir. We've had a problem with them. You know, vagrants, homeless people."

"Vagrants under the deck!" Toe-tapper bellows.

"I thought we'd taken care of it, sir. There was this old bag lady used to sleep there. But we ran her off months ago."

"What did she look like, this bag lady?" Billy Goat asks.

"Look like? I don't know, just an old bag lady. But she always wore this crazy coat with black and white spots."

"It was *her,*" Billy Goat says. "I saw that coat when she was running off."

There is a scurry of rapid footsteps and angry words at the door. Then the door slams.

Sarah Jane waits, rocked by her out-of-control heartbeat. When she's sure they're gone, she grabs her bag and crawls out from under the deck. Crouching, she glances around frantically. She shivers and her legs wobble as she stands.

When she decides the coast is clear, she slings her big bag over her shoulder and makes a run for it. She heads up toward the road, the opposite direction from the one Tin Can has taken and away from the parking lot where the men are probably heading.

She trots without looking back at the deck where she's slept for the past year. It's the closest thing to a home she's had. But she doesn't look back. It never pays to look in that goddamned rearview mirror.

It's not until she gets to the Sally, sweating and breathless, still shaking, that she wonders about Tin Can. But she is sure the little twit got away so she's not going to worry about it. And then she spots Lufkin leaning against the brick wall smoking, and he has a brown paper sack tucked under his arm. The shape and size sure do look like a quart bottle of Thunder Chicken. Oh, boy! Her heart quickens. For climbing back onto that flying carpet, there's nothing in all the world so helpful as a bottle of Chicken. She smiles at him and waves. He beckons her to come and she crosses the street.

A few minutes later she catches sight of Tin Can climbing the steps to the Sally. She is panting and clutching Silky in her arms, the long spotted coat flapping around her feet. Sarah Jane doesn't call out to her; if she did, Lufkin might decide to share his bottle three ways instead of keeping it just for the two of them.

She will talk to Tin Can tomorrow, and she'll figure out how to get her coat back then. It shouldn't be too hard to outwit a half-wit.

9

DAME TROT AND HER CAT
LED A PEACEABLE LIFE,
WHEN THEY WERE NOT TROUBLED
WITH OTHER FOLKS' STRIFE.
—MOTHER GOOSE

The photograph sucked Molly's breath away.

Emily Bickerstaff, who was called Tin Can on the street, was sitting on the sidewalk next to a bulky plastic garbage bag. The calico cat was draped across her lap, and she was looking down at it with utter adoration, as if it were the dearest, funniest creature in the world. Her mouth was collapsing inward where the front teeth were missing, and her long stringy hair, stiff with dirt, was standing out from her head. Behind her, the sun had caught some wayward gray strands and gilded them.

Molly said, "Oh, Henry, it's a pietà. No one could look at this without being snagged in the heart. My God, how do you do it?"

He shrugged his meaty shoulders. "Dunno. Sometimes you don't know what you've got at first." He pointed at the glowing aura made by the gilded strands of hair. "When that halo appeared in the developer, it was like some fucking Shroud of Turin vision."

Molly gave it a long last look and then flipped through the rest of the black and white proofs, setting aside the ones she liked best. There were six different photos of each of the five women she'd talked with, and all of them were outstanding.

"This one of Roxie shows how luminous her eyes are and this one of Arlene and the Dumpster is extraordinary."

She looked up at Henry Iglesias sitting on the corner of her desk, idly picking his teeth with a dirty fingernail, and marveled at the unlikely forms artistic genius took. "Let me go with you next round," she said. "I want to watch."

The photographer shrugged. His face remained impassive, though very little face was actually visible. His thick kinky black hair grew down low on his forehead and his jet-black beard seemed to cover much more of his face than beards usually covered. He wore a gold ring through one nostril and a diamond stud in his left ear. "You'd be a pain in the ass," he said.

"No, I wouldn't. I'm just interested in seeing how you work." She spread her favorites out on the desk top. "They're fabulous. It looks like you know these women so well. You must talk with them a lot before you shoot."

Talk to them? Those smelly old bums! No way." As he smiled, Henry's broad nose spread out across his face and his nose ring jiggled. Molly was fascinated. She'd been an enthusiastic fan ever since she first saw his work—an exhibit of black and white photographs of barrio teenagers in San Antonio. She frequently requested that he do the photos for her stories but rarely got him. He was very expensive and didn't seem eager for the work. He was also difficult to work with because, so far as Molly had been able to determine, he was preverbal and didn't tolerate much guidance about the assignment. But these photos he'd taken of her bag ladies far exceeded her expectations, which was amazing since her expectations were unreasonably high.

"Tell me this," she said. "This one with Tin Can—did you pose her like that or did she just happen to sit that way with the cat and the bag and the sun behind her?"

He shrugged. "Don't remember." He stood up and hooked his thumbs in his black suspenders. "When can I get my check?"

Molly's phone rang. It was Andrea from the reception desk. "Molly, there's a Frank Quinlan to see you."

"Frank Quinlan!"

"He says he's sorry he didn't call first, but he was in the area and wants just a few minutes of your time."

"Frank Quinlan?"

"Right. We've already done this, Molly. Can you see him?"

"Hold on." She glanced at Henry. "Are we finished?"

He shrugged. "My check."

"Oh, yeah. Why don't you stop and ask Ron about it." Into the phone she said, "Okay. I'm just finishing up here with Henry. Send Mr. Quinlan back."

She hung up and looked down at the photographs. "Let me keep these for a few days, Henry. So I can discuss them with Richard—all of them."

He shrugged. "Okay by me."

Molly walked him to the door and stood watching as he passed Frank Quinlan in the hall. She wondered how Henry would do if she sent him out to Lakeway to photograph retired millionaires on the golf course. He'd probably come back with character studies that made you look at millionaires in a whole new way.

Frank Quinlan was dressed for business today in a dark suit and tie. His white hair was carefully groomed, swept straight back from his tanned face. He carried a battered leather briefcase, which he set down next to a chair. He held his hand out to Molly. "I hate to disturb you at work, but I do need a few minutes of your time."

She shook his hand, trying to hide the reluctance she felt in touching him. "It's amazing you caught me here. I only come in about once a week." The really amazing thing, she thought, was that here she was shaking hands with a Quinlan and making small talk.

"You work at home then." He looked around her office, which was small and square without a single personal item or hint of décor in it.

"Yeah. Usually. Uh, have a seat?"

"Thanks." He lowered himself into the straight-backed chair and crossed his legs. Then he put his hands on his knees and stared down at them. It looked as if he were saying a silent prayer before doing something he was afraid he might regret later.

If her life depended on it, Molly thought, she could not come up with a theory about what had brought this man here. But every nerve in her body was tingling, telling her it was going to be something of great interest. She sat down across from him and waited.

When he finally looked up, his mouth was set firmly. "My father," he said, shaking his head. "My father is most likely stringing barbed wire in hell right now. Jasper Quinlan was a complete sumbitch."

"I know," Molly said.

"When we six kids were coming up he bullied us in the worst way. He treated my mother shamefully. He was ruthless in business. More than ruthless—Jasper did some shady things, and some downright illegal things. I'm sorry to have to say that, but it isn't news to you, is it?"

Molly held her breath. She had no idea where he was going, but she wanted him to hurry up and get there.

"Jasper started as a roughneck in the West Texas oil fields and he never did get gentled. I'm sorry about two things. I never beat the shit out of him for the way he treated my mother, and I didn't stand up to him sooner about some of his...business practices." He looked up at Molly for a reaction.

She made a cooing noise in her throat—the noise that she had found over the course of hundreds of interviews to be the best way to keep people talking.

"He tried to bribe your father not to publish that article on Quinlan's role in the white oil business. You know that." He uncrossed his legs and shifted in the chair, trying to get comfortable. "I want to say here, Molly—right up front—that I knew about that—the attempted bribe, I mean. I also knew the article was essentially correct, that Jasper *had* been running that oil scam in his panhandle fields. He'd been passing off his natural gas as crude oil and getting the wells classified as oil producers."

"That way he could get more wells in his fields."

"Lord, yes. It was wildly profitable and he was way ahead of his time, before any of the bigger companies were doing it. I didn't approve, and told the old man so, but I didn't have the guts at the time to oppose him beyond just protesting." He looked down at the rug. "When Jasper got wind of Vernon's poking around, he was furious. And he was afraid. Of prosecution and losing his profits. He went to see your father and offered him far more than he would ever make selling that article to forget about it. Your father refused. He said he'd include the bribery attempt in the article."

"I know," Molly said.

"I know you do. But I'm about to get to the part you don't know." He lowered his voice. "The old man was mean enough to suck eggs and cunning enough to hide the shells. I'm not trying to tell you otherwise. He was a bully, an adulterer, and a swindler. I can see why you suspected him. He had a strong motive here, but"—he looked up at Molly and spoke very deliberately—"he did not kill your daddy. He did not *hire* anyone to kill your daddy. He did not steal any papers belonging to your daddy. And no one else in my family did either."

"How can you be so sure?"

"I was the comptroller of the company then. I was involved in everything that happened. I would have known."

"I'm not convinced."

"Let me finish. Remember when you came to Lubbock and did that interview with the *Morning Clarion* where you accused Quinlan Oil and Jasper Quinlan in particular of killing your father to avoid having their illegal drilling practices exposed?"

"Nineteen seventy-five, September," Molly said. "I remember it well."

"I've never seen the old man so mad as when that reporter came to ask him about it. He was spitting nails."

"I know. I met with him and your brother Roger. I thought Jasper was going to have a stroke while I was in his office."

"What you don't know is that, when you left, they hired a private detective to investigate Vernon's death."

Molly stopped breathing. "They did?"

He nodded. *"We* did. I was in on it. The idea was to find out what did happen to your father. To prove Quinlan Oil wasn't involved. And, Molly, we hired a reputable firm to do it. The best. If any one of us had been responsible for his death, we wouldn't have done that."

Molly's phone rang. Without taking her eyes off Frank Quinlan, she reached over and switched it off. "You hired a private investigator?"

"That same day you were there. I wrote the retainer check myself."

"Who did you hire?"

"A retired FBI man who ran his own agency. His name was Julian K. Palmer of Palmer Investigations in Lubbock."

"Was?"

"Yes, ma'am. He died about ten years ago."

"What did Julian K. Palmer find out?"

"Well, now. It's been twenty-five years and my memory is not what it once was."

"Yes, but you—"

Quinlan raised a hand to stop her. "I figured you might want to know this. If you do, you should get it as accurately as possible. From the horse's mouth."

Her heart pounded. "You mean—"

"I talked with Shelby Palmer in Lubbock yesterday. He runs his father's firm now. They've still got the original case file."

"They kept it all this time." She heard the reverence in her voice.

"I've just faxed him an authorization to release that file to you—if you want to go to Lubbock and take a look at it. They won't let their files leave the office, but he'll let you read it there, and he'll help you decipher it." He sat back in the chair. "If you want to."

"If I want to," Molly said. It was like questioning whether she wanted to continue some involuntary function like breathing or digesting. There were some things that took no deciding.

"There are reasons you might *not* want to."

"What reasons?"

"Well, when you hire a private investigator, you want them to find all the dirt."

A ripple of apprehension passed through her. "So?"

"They didn't just investigate your daddy. They investigated you too."

"Me?"

"Yes, ma'am. There's things in that report you won't like one little bit. If you choose to look at it, it will be painful. Part of the plan was to discredit you so your accusations wouldn't carry any weight."

"I see," she said grimly. "Should be interesting reading."

"I can't tell you how sorry I am. That I was part of that."

"What did Julian K. Palmer find out about my daddy's death?"

"I'd rather you went right to the—"

"The horse's mouth, I know. But just give me the gist of it, as you remember it."

"Well, what my father wanted Palmer to come up with was a clear case of suicide. An unbalanced and depressed man shoots himself and his unhinged daughter undertakes a wrongheaded vendetta."

"And did he come up with suicide?"

"Yes, he did. Vernon Cates was depressed, having women problems, money problems. The ME called it suicide. It was all consistent with suicide. But—" He paused, looking down at his hands again.

"But?"

"But Mr. Palmer didn't drop it there. He turned out to be too thorough. Too honest."

"What did he find?"

"Molly, you need to read the report."

"But what—"

"You'll find some indication that the police work was deficient."

"Olin Crocker." Molly surprised herself with the amount of bitterness she managed to squeeze into those four syllables. "He did *no* police work."

"If I'm remembering rightly, you might find some suggestion to that effect in the report."

Molly felt a hot buzzing in her ears. She'd never been able to find a shred of proof, or get anyone else to believe it, but she knew right down to her toenails that Crocker was called off the case by someone.

"Now don't get to thinking this report will give you any definitive answers, because it won't. But it might help some." Quinlan seemed to be studying her face and what he saw there caused his brow to furrow. "I sure hope I'm doing the right thing here, Molly. I hope to hell it's going to be helpful to you."

"Is that why you're doing this—to be helpful?"

"Yes, but it's more complicated than that."

"You feel guilty."

"Of course. Wouldn't you? After you were out at the house, Franny said you were still agonizing over what really happened to your daddy. After all this time. I thought this might help you bring it to some conclusion. But Franny's afraid this will just add to your pain, give you false hopes."

"But you don't agree?"

He was slow in answering. "If this were information about Willie, I would want to have it. Even if it was twenty-eight years late in coming."

"Me too."

"That's the best I can do in explaining myself. You're going to Lubbock?"

Molly looked at her watch. "I wonder how late the Palmer agency is open today."

He smiled. "Shelby's in Houston today. He'll be back in Lubbock tomorrow. But you can call his office to set up an appointment." He reached into his briefcase and pulled out a long envelope. "Here's a copy of the fax I sent him. And a letter introducing you. And the address and phone number of the agency."

She took the envelope from him and set it on her desk.

He stood and held out his hand. "I can't tell you how sorry I am about my role in this. I'm truly ashamed."

Molly took his hand, and this time she wanted to. She held on to it. "Thank you. This must have been hard to do."

He picked up his briefcase. "It surely was."

As he turned to leave, she said, "Frank, I'm so sorry about your son."

He paused for a few seconds, then turned back to face her. His eyes had teared up. "Oh, me too. Me too. Everybody says it'll get easier, but it doesn't seem to." He tried to smile. "Let me hear how this goes. And please keep in touch with Franny."

"I will."

When he'd gone, Molly sat at her desk and opened the envelope. She stared down at the Lubbock phone number of Palmer Investigations. For years she'd had a recurring dream in which her father had sent her a message to call him. She would rush to a phone and try to dial the number—always on an old black wall phone like the one they'd had in Lubbock—but something always interfered: her finger would slip out of the holes in the dial, or some of the numbers on the dial would be missing, or she would forget the number she was trying to call halfway through. Frantically she'd try—again and again—to make the call. But she could never complete it. Each time it turned into a feverish nightmare of frustration.

She picked up the phone and punched in the number.

She got through on the first try.

10

IT WILL HAVE BLOOD THEY SAY: BLOOD WILL HAVE
BLOOD.
STONES HAVE BEEN KNOWN TO MOVE, AND TREES
TO SPEAK.

—MACBETH

The hellish orange fireball is sliced in three angry pieces and
it is burning her away. It's blistered her leg and soon it will
gobble the rest of her. Sarah Jane Hurley has finally hit rock
bottom where she belongs. She's crash-landed in the pit of
torment, just like Gramma always said she would if she
didn't mend her ways.

She smells awful, like there's some dying animal inside
her—ungainly, stinking, oozing—and now it's finally dying.
And she knows why all this is happening. It's because of the
coat. *Lucy Locket lost her pocket.* The coat's what kept her
safe while she's been on the move. Then that fucking Lufkin
made her give it away, and now she is unprotected—just a
mass of raw, terrified animal nerve exposed to that garish
fireball out there.

She's had that coat since the day she arrived in Austin
more than a year ago. She found it with the tags still on it—a
piece of good luck for a change, an omen. The second she
put it on, she became Cow Lady, a brand-new person with
no past whatsoever. *Hey, diddle, diddle!* It always made her
feel there were still possibilities. *The cat and the fiddle/The
cow jumped over the moon.* It's not that she's superstitious,
but if she's going to survive, she's *got* to get it back.

She struggles to a sitting position and gasps to see the orange fireball become whole. She blinks down at the long grasses she has been looking through. It is morning and the sun is rising over this vacant lot where she's been sleeping. There's no part of her that doesn't hurt—the usual aching and nausea that plague her after a binge, plus the pain in her joints and the throbbing, scorching bites on her left leg that are certainly infected.

She looks down at herself. She's got no blanket, and no coat. She's lying on the bare ground, her jeans and sweater damp from the grass. *Diddle, diddle dumpling, my son John went to bed with his britches on.* She struggles to her feet and staggers to the fence at the back of the vacant lot. She pulls her jeans down and squats to pee. Only then does she see the others, those three long cocoons stretched out on the ground. One shape she recognizes as Lufkin and the other two are the tramps they've been drinking with, but she can't remember their names. She doesn't even know how many days they've been at it, or what day it is now.

She picks up her bag, limps toward the street, and slowly makes her way a few blocks to where a newspaper box stands on the corner. She glances at the paper. It's Thursday. They've been drunk since Tuesday night, she thinks. Somewhere she's lost a whole day and a night.

She knows without any doubt what she has to do: she has to find Tin Can and get the coat back.

Thursday is Tin Can's blood day. If she walks up to Twenty-ninth Street she might find her at the Plasma Center. She starts trudging north on Red River, resigning herself to the long walk, limping because of the shooting pains in her left leg.

A block away from the Plasma Center, she finally stops to rest. She leans against the side of Hub's Donuts and watches the bums wandering into the Center. The smell of fresh doughnuts and coffee drifting from Hub's makes her wish she had some money. Four of those soft, sugary, glazed doughnuts washed down with a cup of coffee might help. But she has no money—except for the hundred-dollar bill safety-pinned inside her flannel shirt, and, of course, she can't use that. It is a sacred object, the last thing Ellie gave her. She has vowed never to spend it. Sarah Jane refuses to let herself think about that parting scene when Ellie gave it to her and told her to stay away. When she quits drinking one of these days and gets back on her feet, Sarah Jane plans to give that hundred-dollar bill right back to Ellie. And she's worked out exactly what she'll say to her. She'll hug her and say, "You're a good daughter, honey, but you need this for yourself. I can take care of myself now."

Across the intersection she spots Squint and Roylee talking with Zippo, a mongrel-skinny addict who always has an unlit cigarette butt hanging from his lips. Zippo seems harmless, but Squint and Roylee are dudes Sarah Jane tries to stay away from—predators, bottom feeders always on the lookout for a way to cash in on other homeless people. Squint is the boss and Roylee serves as his Seeing Eye dog because Squint is said to be legally blind, able to see only shapes and colors. Sarah Jane doesn't know whether she believes that or not; it might just be one more of Squint's scams. Today she is actually glad to run into him because he knows all the homeless people in town and he's got his nose in everybody's business.

She crosses the intersection. Squint turns his head and seems to watch her approach. He is a tall, well-built man in his thirties, with long black hair and high cheekbones. His eyes, which are mere slits, are set close together and very deep into his skull under jutting brows. Roylee is short and square and hairless. His massive arms are covered with blurry blue tattoos. Roylee says something into Squint's ear, and Squint smiles in Sarah Jane's direction.

"Hey, Zippo," Sarah Jane says to the addict. She nods at Squint and Roylee.

"Long time, Cow Lady," Squint says, studying her through his slits with an intensity that surprises her.

"Cow Lady?" Zippo says. "Where's your coat?"

"Tin Can's got it. I'm looking for her. You seen her?"

Zippo's head bobs on his scrawny, wattled, chicken neck. "Tin Can? That the lil gal carries a pussy cat around? She was here last week, I believe. We was next to each other inside. Makes us blood brothers or some such thing." He laughs at his joke, managing to keep the butt between his lips unmoving.

"You seen her this week?"

He shakes his head.

Squint says, "When'd you give her your coat?"

"*Lent* it. Coupla days ago," Sarah Jane says. "Why? You see her?"

"No. Just wondering. You don't come see us at Patchwork no more. Got digs now?" Squint asks.

"Do me a favor," Sarah Jane says. "If you see Tin Can, tell her I'm looking for her. It's real important."

"You didn't answer me," Squint says, not smiling now. "Where you hanging these days?"

"Oh, here and there. With friends," Sarah Jane says.

"Who? Lufkin?" Squint asks.

"Sometimes," she says, puzzled at his interest. He's certainly never shown this much interest in her before.

"Y'all still camp down by the crick? Behind the Grill?"

"No," she says.

"I bet you still hang at the library days."

"What's it to you?" Sarah Jane asks.

"I just like to keep track of friends," Squint says with a broad smile that looks to Sarah Jane like a bear trap opening up.

"Sure," she says. "See you around." She enters the Plasma Center, passing right by the nurse at reception, who is busy with some paperwork. She stands at the door and surveys the big room with the rows of black couches. She knows this room well, comes twice a week to sell plasma at nine bucks a shot. This morning about half the couches have people lying on them. They are hooked up to the big white machines that take blood and spin it to separate out the plasma and put the red blood cells back in you. It's just another way of selling your body, but the money's regular, and you probably won't get a disease from it.

There's a very young black girl she recognizes from the lunch line at Caritas and a skinny guy she's seen flying a sign on one of the traffic islands, but no Tin Can. She manages to get out the door again without talking to the nurse, which is a relief because she's afraid if they see what bad shape she's in they might not let her donate next time. Even here they have some standards.

Stepping out of the air conditioning, she really feels the heat. It's only May, but at this rate summer will be a scorcher.

Zippo has gone, but Squint and Roylee are still there. "Hey, Cow Lady," Squint says, "why you so unfriendly? Don't you like me no more?" He reaches out and takes hold of her arm.

"I gotta go," she says.

"Where?" he asks, tightening his grip on her.

"We been through this already, Squint."

He squeezes her arm. "But you ain't answered yet."

She jerks away, breaking his grip, and walks off.

"Hey!" Squint calls out. "Come see us. Come on over to Patchwork. I'll make it worth your while."

She glances back at Squint and Roylee, remembering the one night she spent there when she first came to Austin. "Never. I wouldn't come back there if you were giving away winning lottery tickets." She turns and walks on, troubled by why Squint thinks she's worth bothering with. She decides it must be because of Lufkin. Squint's been making money off Lufkin's day-labor gigs and he wants to butter up the old lady. But, still, it worries her. Squint is not someone whose attentions you want to attract.

She figures that Tin Can's probably back at her old place along the creek. That's the place to look. She starts walking south on Trinity, but after a block she decides to take a detour, go wake Lufkin up. She's mad at him about the coat, but she needs someone to talk to. She needs the company.

She turns east toward the vacant lot off Red River. The soles of her high-tops are worn so thin that her feet feel the red-hot pavement and every piece of gravel. *Hot cross buns. One a penny, two a penny.* Her bag feels heavier than usual, the strap cuts into her shoulder, but she has no safe place to leave it, and even if she did, she can't be separated from it. Everything else she once owned has disappeared because she let herself get separated from it. This bag she's got to hold on to for dear life. It's part of her.

The lot is a jungly overgrown patch between a junk store and an abandoned bar, mostly concealed from the road by a rickety wood fence. Sarah Jane shuffles through the long grass. Two blanket-covered lumps show no signs of life, but Lufkin is awake and sitting propped against the fence, staring into space. He looks up at Sarah Jane as she approaches.

"Ah," he says, "the damsel cometh, bearing in her bag doughnuts and coffee for her lord and master, I hope." He presses his hands together in a praying gesture. He once saw a movie called *The Scarlet Pimpernel* and he likes to try to copy the way the hero talked in it.

She looks down at him—a tall, emaciated tramp sitting on a filthy bedroll. His streaky black and gray beard has pieces of grass and loose tobacco in it. He's so pathetic with that silly talk from an old movie when he's sitting here on a dung heap, hungry and hung over. And he's so ridiculous—she's never once brought him anything, and here he is thinking maybe she's brought him doughnuts.

"If I had any money for doughnuts, you think I'd bring 'em back here?" she says.

"Ah. A fiery wench, proud and spirited. No man's servant, she."

"For God's sake. Get up and walk with me to Tin Can's place down by the creek."

"Why?"

"I've got to find her. Come on. I'll tell you while we walk."

"The spitfire wench needs a knight to protect her from the wrath of her enemies."

She smiles in spite of her annoyance. "That'll be the day—when I need *you* for protection."

He gets to his feet, slowly, wincing as he straightens his bad knee, which Sarah Jane knows looks nothing like a knee, more like a lump of dough, all scarred and swollen under his filthy khakis.

"One moment, please." He walks off a few feet and turns his back. "The knight pisseth," he says over his shoulder as he urinates a long stream against a tree. Then he turns around, zipping his pants, and says, "Lead on."

As they walk south on Red River in the blazing noonday sun, Sarah Jane tells him what happened under the deck Monday night, about Tin Can running off.

Lufkin is quiet, seemingly caught up in the story. When she finishes, he says, "What did those dudes talk about up there on the deck?"

"Like I said, I don't remember much."

"Try," he says.

"Okay. It's so dumb. The Billy Goat Gruff one was supposed to kill everyone in the chamber, you know, the Senate chamber, with some poison so deadly that Hitler wouldn't even use it." She glances over to see his response, expecting him to be laughing, but he's not. "And the other one, Toetapper, paid him some money from some group, a posse, I think, and, hell, that's all. I don't remember the rest."

"When is this supposed to happen?"

"Whenever some bill on guns is voted on. Monday, I think."

"Shee-it!" Lufkin says. "You got yourself a goddamned hornet's nest in your outhouse."

"Huh?"

"A honest-to-God *moral* problem."

"What say?" She glances at his hairy profile bobbing along next to her, his bad leg dragging behind. He is the strangest creature.

"A *moral* problem," he repeats. "You ever hear of morals?"

"Bullshit."

"No. This is serious. You can't just let these honchos go and poison folks up there in the Capitol, can you?"

She is stunned by this take on it; it never occurred to her. "Got fuck-all to do with me."

"Cow Lady! How you gonna feel when you hear they've gone and done it, and folks have died?"

"I won't feel any way in particular. Except surprised. This was just men talking big."

"Maybe. But sometimes people do what they say. They

say they're gonna bomb buildings and shoot Presidents and goddamned if they don't go out and do it sometimes. You gotta pay *some* attention."

Sarah Jane shrugs. What a ridiculous man, with his newspapers and his morals. "Let me get this straight. Here you are, a bum who would steal a bottle from a baby if you got the chance, and you're preaching to me like it's a Baptist Sunday morning."

"I ain't preaching. But you gotta remember—"

"I hope you aren't gonna say 'What goes around comes around.'"

"But it does. Didn't you never go to Sunday school or nothing?"

She remembered her gramma dragging her, unwilling and resisting, to Sunday school every week while her mama slept off her Saturday night benders. "No."

"Anyway," he says, "you can't just ignore this."

"Watch me."

"You should tell the police."

She shakes her head firmly. That she can never do.

"Why not?" he asks.

She's never told anyone about the howler and all the blood and what a fast getaway she had to make from Houston. "Cops," she mutters, "think they own the world."

"Well, just remember I told you: what goes around comes around. You do the wrong thing here, it'll come back and bite you in the ass."

"Wouldn't it be just awful if I lost everything and had to live out on the street?"

"There's worse things," Lufkin mutters.

They are getting close now to the Creekside Grill. Sarah Jane leads the way to an old railroad bridge and a hidden path down to the creek. This is terrain she knows so well she can do it in the dark, and often has. It has magic for her because it is a wild place right in the middle of the city and it is hidden, so most people don't know it is there. She pushes aside a branch and holds it for Lufkin. The path of trodden-down earth winds its way down the bank to a flat grassy area that is pocked with debris. Brown bags, flattened cardboard boxes, beer cans, and Styrofoam cups mark it as an occasional encampment for the homeless. But no one is around today.

As they descend, the temperature drops several degrees, and it is darker with the high banks and the foliage overhead blocking all but a dappling of sun. The air is so muggy Sarah Jane can barely breathe. Lufkin starts to call out for Tin Can, but Sarah Jane hushes him.

They walk silently along the stony creek bed. It reminds Sarah Jane of playing Indian as a child; she has always been able to move quickly and quietly in spite of her size. They stop when they get to the familiar clearing where Tin Can's oil drum cooker stands close to the creek. They look around in the dappled light for the woman and her calico cat. Sarah Jane glances apprehensively up toward the Creekside Grill, but it is not visible from down here. She takes a chance and calls out very softly, "Tin Can! You here?" They listen to the silence.

Lufkin sits down on a boulder and pulls a pack of cigarettes and a lighter from his breast pocket. "Lord, I'm still wasted. What day is it?"

Sarah Jane doesn't answer. She is walking around the clearing, peering up and down the creek as far as she can see into the dark bends. She looks into the oil drum, hoping there might be signs of recent cooking, but the remains of burned charcoal and wood look ancient. She sniffs, but there is only the acrid odor of old fires and damp, decaying vegetation and her own sharp sweat.

Sarah Jane wonders if Tin Can could possibly be under the deck, but she doesn't want to go up there. She crosses her arms over her chest and looks down into the few inches of water trickling over the rocks. She is stymied, not used to making decisions. She's gotten rusty.

She turns to Lufkin. "Well, damn. The little shit is avoiding me. She's hiding. She's scared I'm gonna be mad. And I am mad."

Lufkin is sitting on the rock with his eyes closed, smoking, looking very much at peace. It makes her want to poke at him, stir him up, make him feel as anxious as she does.

This is all his fault, anyway. She says, "Help me look some more. You go upstream a bit toward the Grill, and I'll walk the other way."

He blows out a trail of smoke. "Knee's resting."

"Well, give me a smoke then." She rarely buys cigarettes since he always has some and never refuses to share.

He pulls the crumpled pack out of his pocket and holds it up to her. "Fair lady, I endow thee with all my worldly goods."

"Crap." She takes a cigarette and leans down for him to light it. He flicks his lighter, and she drags deep, taking that first heavenly hit down to the center of her body. "I might stop drinking someday," she says, "but I'll never give up smoking."

That's when they hear the faint meow.

"Silky," Lufkin says.

Sarah Jane looks across the creek in the direction she thinks the meow came from. If that is Silky, then Tin Can's around; the two are never separated. They must be hiding. She surveys the opposite bank and then she has a sudden jerk of memory. "Oh, Lufkin. The pipe. That drainage pipe where Tin Can keeps her junk. You remember where that is?"

He points with his cigarette to a place about twenty yards down. "Around where that big tree is yonder, if I recollect right."

She studies the bank. She's been there once with Tin Can, to help her with the huge bags of cans Tin Can always collects. It was when Tin Can was sick with pneumonia. But that was during the winter and the growth was not so thick then. Now the bank is a wild tangle of cedar and weeds and vines, covering everything. But she remembers the pipe as a huge thing, probably three feet across and made of galvanized metal. It shouldn't be hard to find. "Come on," she says, starting in that direction.

"Nah. Knee's still resting." Lufkin closes his eyes again. She knows how stubborn he is, and how lazy, so she leaves him and walks along the creek, smoking and studying the bank for signs of the pipe or just a break in the greenery. She gets to the large tree Lufkin has pointed out and stops. It's got to be right near here.

She crosses the creek, stretching her long legs from rock to rock. It is only a few inches deep and she makes it without even getting her feet wet. "Silky," she calls, feeling silly talking to a cat who isn't there. "You here, Silky?"

Another tiny meow comes from the bank, so close it makes Sarah Jane jump. She calls again, "Silky?"

She listens, but the only sound is the trickle of water and the faint whir of traffic in the world above. She looks back to where Lufkin is sitting. She wants to call him, but she'd have to raise her voice and she's afraid to. She tosses her cigarette down into the water.

She steps to the place on the bank she thinks the sound came from and pulls at some vines in an effort to see underneath them. Then she remembers: when she came here with Tin Can, the pipe was hard to get to. They had to climb to get there, but just a little.

She looks up at the steep bank and sets her bag down on a rock. She hates to be separated from it, but she can't make it up the bank if she has that extra weight. Grabbing hold of a bush, she hoists herself up the bank, one step, and then another. She starts to pull at the dense shrubs and vines. With the heavy rains everything has gone wild. It is slow work: she is sweating and her feet keep slipping. She can use only one hand to pull things aside because she has to hold on with the other.

"Silky," she calls in a voice she tries to make sweet, but it comes out like a threat. "Silky!"

She hears the meow just as she catches a glimpse of galvanized metal. She scrambles closer and pulls the underbrush away to uncover it.

There it is—the metal pipe, about three feet across just like she remembered it, the whole opening crammed full of bulging green garbage bags. Yes! She can see the shapes of the cans underneath the stretched plastic. This means Tin Can has not left town; she would never go without selling these; it's how she earns her money.

She reaches up and tugs at one of the bags. It doesn't budge; it's wedged in tight.

A series of shrill meows comes at her now, louder, desperate-sounding. "Come on, Silky," Sarah Jane says. "Come on."

She is answered by a yowling.

Silky is trapped inside the pipe, she realizes. Behind the barricade of bags.

"Jesus," she says under her breath. "Poor thing. I'll get you out of there."

She scrambles a little higher up the hill and braces a foot against a cedar trunk so she can use both hands to pull at the bags. It is hard to get a good grip because the bags are so full. She grabs what she can and jerks. The bag is wedged in so tight the plastic starts to tear in her hand. She finds another gripping place and pulls with her whole weight. The bag rips open and unleashes a cascade of cans. They tumble down the bank with a clatter. Now the bag is half empty and she can grasp the torn plastic and jerk it out. She drops it down the bank. Another bag remains in the opening, but half the pipe is cleared now.

From the dark void something shoots out at her. She shrieks and ducks. She knows it's Silky, but it shakes her up anyway. The cat lands near her feet. Immediately, he butts his head hard against her ankle. But Sarah Jane doesn't even look down. She is rooted in place. The stench has hit her. It assaults her, sends her into a fit of sneezing, as though black pepper has been pumped up her nose. It is the worst thing she has ever smelled.

But she does not look away. She cannot. She has come this far, and she will look.

She holds her breath and drags the remaining bag out of the opening, letting it bump down the bank. She looks into the pipe. It is dark as midnight inside, but in the faint band of light at the edge of the darkness lies another green garbage bag. And reaching out to her from a ragged hole torn in the plastic is a hand. A small, short-fingered hand, with shreds of bloody flesh remaining on two of the fingers.

The palm and the other fingers have been stripped bare, right down to the bone. *Hey, diddle, diddle, The cat and the fiddle.*

Just visible at the wrist is some black and white fabric that Sarah Jane knows as well as she knows her own body. *The cow jumped over the moon.* Slowly she sinks down to a squat and leans forward into the bank so she doesn't fall backward. *The little dog laughed to see such a sight.* She rests her forehead against the earth.

Now she will never get her coat back.

11

RING AROUND THE ROSEY
A POCKET FULL OF POSIES.
ASHES, ASHES.
WE ALL FALL DOWN.
                    —MOTHER GOOSE

"Franny says Aunt Harriet called you that week. Did she tell you she was trying to get Daddy to see a shrink? I never knew that." Molly was trying to keep the whine out of her voice.

Parnell looked up from the notebook computer that sat on his huge mahogany desk—the sole sign of modern technology in an office that otherwise looked the same as Molly remembered it when she had visited it as a child—dark-paneled and dignified, with rich green carpet and heavy old furniture. "Harriet called me a couple of times that week," he said. "I think she did mention wanting to get Vern to talk to a psychiatrist."

"You never told me that."

"Sure I did, honey," Parnell said. "After the funeral. You and I talked a lot, as I recall. When they ruled the death a suicide, I said it was possible since he was feeling so blue toward the end. I told you then. But back in those days"——he looked her hard in the eye—"you had some difficulty listening to what you didn't want to hear. Especially if it didn't fit in with your theories."

It had happened so long ago, and she had been so upset. They probably had discussed it. And he was right: listening to things she didn't want to hear was not her strong suit and never had been.

She turned back to the wall of old photographs she'd been studying. The one that kept drawing her back was of a young Parnell, his hair still full and wavy, standing with Vernon Cates and Lyndon Johnson and Lady Bird. The photo was signed on the corner, "To my good friend Parnell Morrisey, Lyndon B. Johnson." Parnell, his face homely, but animated and unlined, was cradling a beagle puppy in his arms. Her daddy, wearing a Stetson and a red shirt, was looking down at Lady Bird, laughing. She was looking up at him with that light in her eyes women tended to have when Vernon Cates was around.

"When was this taken, Parnell?" Molly asked.

He glanced up from his chair to see which photo she was looking at. "Oh, that one out at the LBJ Ranch? Let's see. It was a barbecue out there in Johnson City, must've been around 1963, spring, I think, when he was still Vice-President. That was right before your mother died, Molly." He turned to Rose, who was sitting in the green leather chair with her needlepoint in her lap. "You weren't there either, Rosie, were you?" He walked over to take a closer look at the photograph. "Oh, yes, I think both you and Josephine were in the hospital at the time and couldn't come. You ladies missed a good party."

Molly remembered spring of 1963 very well; she'd been nine and it had been clear to her for many months, even though no one had told her, that her mother was dying. Her daddy had been away often and Molly and Aunt Harriet had spent lots of time waiting at the hospital for the next installment of bad news.

"What were you in the hospital for, Rose?" Molly asked.

Rose looked up at the photo. "In 1963? Pneumonia, I believe. I was only there for a few days."

Molly didn't remember that, but she probably hadn't been paying attention. Her own world had been collapsing, and the private lives of the adults around her had seemed an impenetrable mystery. It was amazing how you could live through national disasters—assassinations and wars—and the private disasters of people close to you and yet remember from that time nothing but your own fear and loneliness.

Parnell was still staring at the photograph. "It's hard to believe we were ever that young," he said. Looking at him in profile, Molly noticed that he'd cut himself shaving and there was still a tiny shred of tissue stuck to the dried blood on his jawbone.

But she had only two hours before her flight to Lubbock and she wanted to get Rose and Parnell's reaction to what Franny had said. "So," she said, "when Aunt Harriet told you Daddy was going off the deep end that week, what did you think?" She directed the question to Rose, who was looking down at her needlepoint but not working on it. Ever since Molly could remember, Rose always had some handwork with her; in recent years it was needlepoint that she made into pillows and Christmas stockings to give her friends. Molly and Jo Beth both had numerous flowered pillows Rose had given them over the years.

"I was out in Lubbock with my mother, Molly, so I was out of the loop," Rose said. "You probably don't remember, but she was doing poorly then. She passed away about seven months after your father." She glanced up at the photograph. "It was a year of losses."

Molly looked back at Parnell, who was still studying the photograph. "What did you think, Parnell?"

"I was worried about him, Molly, but when I called, Vern told me in no uncertain terms to leave him be in his misery. I got the idea he and Franny were having a lovers' quarrel, so I butted out."

"Did he say it was a lovers' quarrel?"

Parnell looked thoughtful. "Not in so many words. It's hard to remember back that far exactly what he said, even though I went over it in my mind a lot after it all happened. I think he said there was nothing I could do, nothing anyone could do, just to let him be."

"Did he talk about any old business in Lubbock?"

"Not that I recall, sweetheart. Why?"

"Well, Franny says he got this phone call a week before he died, and it changed everything. He told her it was an old business acquaintance from Lubbock, and he had to take care of it. The next day he broke off their engagement. Did you know that?"

"I reckon I did, Molly. I know I should of done more." The old man's gray eyes were misting up, and the bags under them were dark and puffy, dragging the lower lids down in a mournful, hound-dog way. Molly knew it was unkind to make him rehash this painful memory, and she knew she'd gotten him at a bad time when he had lots of pressures. But there was no good time to discuss this, and, anyway, she couldn't stop herself.

Parnell said, "I offered to go out there to the lake, or have him come and stay in town with us awhile, but he said no, absolutely not. I should have gone anyway. We were in session and I was real busy at the time, sponsoring a bill, but I should have gone. If I had, I might have stopped it." He looked at Rose. "*We* might have stopped it. Hindsight—" He shook his head. "Well, it's got perfect twenty-twenty vision, doesn't it?"

"I guess," Molly said. "But, until I talked with Franny, I didn't realize how *really* bad off Daddy was that last week. She says the last time she saw him, the night before he disappeared, he was drunk on the deck of the houseboat office, and he told her to get off his property. Can you believe that? To get off his property!"

"He was in a bad way," Parnell said softly, "not himself."

"Yeah. I wish I knew why."

"This wasn't Vern's first bout with depression, Molly. You know that. And there doesn't really need to be a reason."

"But this was so extreme."

"It was that. Maybe the Quinlans' detective came up with something. What's his name again?"

"Palmer. Julian K. Palmer. Palmer Investigations."

He looked down at his wife. "Rosie, maybe that was the fella came to see us a few years after Vern died. Said he was working for some oilmen's association. Asked questions about Vern. Remember that?"

Rose thought about it for a few seconds. "I believe he was from Lubbock, but I can't remember if that was the name. I can't seem to remember anything lately." She gave a little laugh of apology, as if to acknowledge that she was complaining and that was something she didn't believe in doing. Like Aunt Harriet, Rose had always subscribed to the Southern-woman credo of putting the best face on everything. She rarely mentioned any of her numerous health problems, especially her arthritis, even though it was clear she had a great deal of pain from it.

Molly noticed that Rose had a yellowish spot on the front of her white silk blouse. It was the first time she had ever seen her other than meticulously dressed and groomed. Here were these two old people, neither of them in good health, and she was harassing them with painful history, visiting her problems on them just as she had always done. It was probably way past time for a changing of the guard here, for her to start doing the caretaking. But she was so accustomed to the old pattern: she was the willful, obsessed orphan child and they were the responsible adults who always counseled moderation, but forgave her inevitable excesses.

"I can't remember either, Rosie." Parnell looked at Molly and shrugged. "So Frank Quinlan is trying to atone for his father's sins, I reckon. Frank is one of the better Quinlans. Is he making Franny happy?"

The question surprised her. "Yes. Yes, I think so. Do you know him pretty well?"

"No. Back when Vern was ferreting out the white oil affair, old Jasper sent Frank to see me. Tried to get me to call Vern off. Then a couple of times over the years he's asked for help on oil issues—all reasonable constituent requests. I've tried to accommodate him. But I've never gotten to know him well."

"Of course," Molly said, raising an eyebrow at him, "Quinlan Oil contributes to your campaigns."

"Handsomely," Parnell said. "If I refused contributions from every company that had ever done something shady, I'd have an empty coffer, Miss Molly."

"I know."

"What do you think about him, Molly? Why's he doing this now?"

"I don't know. I can't come up with any motive for what

he did yesterday except what he says—that he wants to help me put this to rest because of his son's suicide."

Parnell rubbed his jaw, pulling off the shred of tissue in the process. The cut began to ooze blood again. Parnell used the back of his hand to blot at it. "Molly, may an old man give some advice?"

"Since when have you asked permission?"

"Well, this is your touchy area. I don't want you going all ballistic on me."

"You're going to tell me not to waste time on this."

"Ah." He managed a smile. "I hate being so predictable. But I can't stand by and not say this. If I know anything in this world, it's that Vern would want you to live your life, honey, not dig into this old can of worms again. I sure hope you aren't getting all het up again."

"Het up?" She turned her face away so he wouldn't see how annoyed she was getting. "No."

"Well, that's good. I thought I discerned the signs of heavy breathing in you. I must have been wrong."

"Frank Quinlan offered to let me see the file," she snapped. "I can't imagine anyone turning that down."

"Now don't get your feathers all ruffled. Just hear me out. You're in the middle of a story—two stories. That's your work and you're good at it. You have a life here. You're just going to drop everything and go to Lubbock to bury yourself in ancient history? Let it go. We all have some uncertainties to live with."

"Everyone tells me that. Grady and Jo Beth and you. And the other day a naked bag lady in the bathroom told me the same thing." She looked at Rose, who was running her fingers over the half-finished pansies and stars of her needle-point design. "You're being awfully quiet, Rose. Don't you want to join the chorus?"

"I know better." Rose's large dark eyes took on the misty, faraway look she got when talking about the past. "I remember when you were just a little thing, everybody telling you not to do something ensured that you would go right out and do it. Remember the bull in the east pasture? Old Jocko?"

Instinctively Molly's hand found the place on her left

thigh and fingered it through the light gabardine of her slacks—a five-inch raised scar where old Jocko had hooked her. It had been a Cates family law that no one ever went into that pasture when Jocko was there. But, as a daredevil eleven-year-old, armored with the invulnerability of youth, Molly had galloped her horse into the pasture with the intention of tapping Jocko with a stick and racing out. She'd just read a story about how the Comanches proved their courage by counting coup on their enemies, and the idea had electrified her. She craved the excitement and was certain her skill and luck would keep them out of trouble. But Jocko had turned and charged like a lightning bolt, nearly disemboweling the horse and goring Molly's leg to the bone, tossing her over his head like a rag doll.

"Oh, yeah," Molly said, tracing the scar. "I remember old Jocko *very* well."

"But did you learn anything from him?" Parnell asked.

"Well, I didn't learn to stay out of the pasture, but I think I learned not to underestimate the adversary."

Parnell's ugly, drooping face came to animated life with his smile. "That cantankerous old bally bastard Jocko." Admiration lit up his eyes. "That bull was faster than a six-legged jack rabbit."

"And meaner than eight acres of snakes," Molly said, knowing the Morriseys would recognize it as one of her father's favorite expressions.

They all laughed. Rose fished a tissue from her purse and blotted a tear from under her eye.

"Don't worry about me," Molly told them. "I'm a sane and sensible middle-aged woman, forty-five next month. I give the Jockos of the world wide berth now, and I don't take things to extremes."

Parnell rolled his eyes.

Rose smiled and shook her head.

The door opened and Parnell's secretary stuck her head in. "Senator Haney called, Senator. He says you're late and they're waiting on you."

Parnell clapped his hands. "Ladies, I'm off. Rosie, are you going to stay here, or you want to come along?"

"I think I'll stay here, dear, and work on my needlepoint."

Parnell turned and put his hands on Molly's shoulders. "Safe trip, sweetheart." He kissed her on the cheek. "Give your Aunt Harriet my love." He started to turn away, then paused and turned back. "Molly, she's always been a fine woman, your Aunt Harriet—loyal and strong. I'm not sure you ever appreciated that fully."

"Probably not," Molly said.

Parnell leaned down and kissed Rose, gathered some papers from his desk, and left quickly.

When the door had closed, Rose said, "Molly, my dear, do you have time to sit with me a minute?"

Molly settled on the green leather footstool so she could be close to Rose. "I'm behaving badly, aren't I, Rose?"

Rose laughed her old tinkling laugh that always reminded Molly of picnics and evenings on the front porch long ago. "You're behaving like Molly Cates."

"It's time for me to grow up, isn't it? That's what Aunt Harriet would say—if she could still say anything. Here I am, the mother of a grown daughter, about to have my forty-fifth birthday, and I still don't feel much like an adult."

"I never could understand Harriet putting such stock in the virtue of being an adult. I think it's greatly overrated, Molly. I know this is shallow of me, but I hate being old. If I could go back to being twenty, I would do it in a snap."

Molly considered it. Certainly physical decay was the pits, and especially painful for one who had once been as beautiful as Rose. One of the few advantages of not being beautiful, Molly consoled herself, was that you didn't have so much to lose with age. "I don't think I would," Molly said. "It was too painful."

"But you haven't experienced real decay yet." Rose put the needlepoint down on the table next to her. "I started this damn thing last year, Molly. Haven't done a stitch on it in two months." She held her clawlike hands out in front of her and studied them. "My hands are too stiff." She let them drop into her lap, rested her head back on the chair, and closed her eyes. "It's like having some big dead lobsters grafted onto my wrists." She gave a mournful chuckle. "Don't get old, Molly."

It was rare for Rose to be so candid. Molly studied the beautiful old face in repose—the delicate chin and finely sculpted nose, the wide, generous cheekbones, the large eyes, set far apart. It was all still there under that thin layer of old, wrinkled skin—the same face, the same woman. Even white-haired and nearly crippled, she managed to retain the glamor she'd always had for Molly. "Rose," she said, "you're still the most beautiful woman I know."

Rose laughed. "Molly, Molly."

"You have any messages for Aunt Harriet?"

Rose thought for a minute, her eyes still closed. "Tell her I think about her. I feel badly I haven't seen her since Christmas."

"Neither have I." The familiar lump of guilt and regret nearly gagged Molly. "I'll see her tonight."

"Tell her we'll come after the session's over, when we're back at the ranch."

"I'll tell her," Molly promised, thinking that Harriet was long past caring whether any of them came or not.

CHAPTER 12

CAPTAIN LEANDER H. MCNELLY OF THE TEXAS
RANGERS . . . WAS NOT A LAW-MAN, BUT A GUER-
RILLA SOLDIER, IN A LAND WHERE THE ESTABLISHED
FORMAL LAW WAS A FICTION.

—T. R. FEHRENBACH, *LONE STAR*

Since she had about an hour before she absolutely had to leave for the airport, Molly stopped in at the Senate hearing, the last one before Monday's vote on the concealed handgun bill. The room was packed, every seat taken and people standing in the back. The seven members of the Criminal Justice Committee sat at the front, high on the dais, behind a curved table, while a representative of the Texas Police Chiefs Association read into the microphone a prepared statement about how allowing more guns out on the street increased the danger for police officers—a message Molly couldn't believe was news to anyone.

She surveyed the crowded hearing room, surprised to see DPS officers in their olive uniforms and Stetsons stationed every few yards around its perimeter. She counted seven of them, five more than usual. It made her wonder if something was brewing. When one of the officers she knew slightly passed by, she followed him. He stationed himself in a corner, standing with legs braced wide, hands clasped in front of him, eyes panning the room.

"What's going on, Officer?" she asked quietly. "You guys having a convention here?"

He hooked his thumbs into his belt and frowned down at her. "Ma'am?"

"Why do they need seven of you for this little bitty room? You expecting a nuclear attack?"

"They tripled us up for this hearing, ma'am."

"How come?"

"This bill's the hot one of the session. Tends to get emotions stirred up."

"True."

"Also, you get lots more folks carrying."

"Carrying guns? Right now? Here?"

"Yes, ma'am."

Molly looked around at the crowd. "How do you know?"

He leaned down and said under his breath, "Well, you got to know where to look. See that fella there, standing off to the side next to the woman in red?"

Molly located him, a fat man with horn-rimmed glasses. "The fat guy?"

"Uh-huh. Watch when he moves. His jacket's so tight you can see the outline of his weapon under his left arm."

Molly watched until the man turned to talk to the woman next to him and sure enough, there it was. "He needs a better tailor," she said.

"Or a smaller firearm," the officer said, cracking a tiny smile. "I reckon a third of the folks in this room are carrying."

Molly looked around the room. "A *third*? No way."

"Look. See the guy leaning against the wall in back? Blue shirt, no jacket. See that pager on his belt?"

"Yeah."

"See how lumpy his hip looks below the pager? He's got one of those pager-pal holsters. Fits inside his pants."

"Looks damned uncomfortable," Molly said.

"And him." The trooper looked to where the tall man in fatigues and yellow beret Molly had seen often before stood next to the door. "He's certainly carrying, even if you can't see it."

"How do you know?" Molly asked.

"The type. He's militia. I'd bet the farm on it. And, of course, with the ladies there's no telling 'cause they usually carry in their handbags. But there's Wanda Lavoy in the first row, and everyone knows she carries."

"How does everyone know that?"

"The talk, rumors. And that guy waiting to testify." He pointed to a man in a brown polyester suit and string tie. "Right ankle. See how thick compared with the other one?"

"Yeah, but he looks like law enforcement."

"Sure. He is, but most of them are carrying illegally."

"So why don't you arrest them?"

The trooper smiled. "We have orders just to watch them. So I'm watching. That's why we're tripled up."

"Have you had any trouble?"

"This session, you mean?"

Molly nodded.

"Not with weapons. There was the fistfight between those two representatives—that actually spilled blood—and the guy who tried to bring a jackass in, actually got it into the elevator and up to the second level. That and a coupla vagrants who like to sleep up in the gallery is about all."

Molly thought about the naked woman in the ladies' room. "What's the policy on them?"

"Vagrants? Oh, we don't bother them if they don't bother no one, if they don't smell too bad. You know."

"So, other than the nature of this bill, you don't have any special reason to worry about security?"

He straightened up, suddenly remembering he wasn't supposed to be talking. "No, ma'am."

Molly was thinking it was time to leave when the next witness was called: Cullen Shoemaker. Surprised, Molly watched as he strode to the microphone. Dressed, as usual, in a dark suit, white shirt, conservative striped tie, and shined shoes, his bearing was even more self-important than usual—a young man with a mission. As he stood at the microphone and faced the committee, his back to the audience, Molly could see enough of his profile to notice that his face and even his scalp under the military-cut blond hair were flushed a tomato red. But he began in a strong voice that revealed no trace of nerves or doubts. "Mr. Chairman, committee members, and fellow Texans, my name is Cullen Shoemaker and I am speaking against this bill."

Molly stood where she was, amazed. *Against* the bill. He couldn't be.

Senator Garland Rauther, sitting up on the dais, stared down at the witness with his mouth gaping. It was clear he hadn't known his young protégé was planning to speak against the bill he was sponsoring, the bill they had both been working to get passed.

Molly looked around the room to see if Elizabeth Shoemaker was here. She spotted her down in front. She was leaning forward, her eyes fixed intently on her son.

Cullen said, "I am speaking now as a representative of the McNelly Posse. We are a service fraternity of two hundred native-born American sons, all students at the University of Texas.

"In the interest of full disclosure"—he cleared his throat—"I was also an aide to Senator Garland Rauther, one of the sponsors of Bill 98. I was, that is, until right now." He paused and looked up at Garland Rauther, still sitting stock-still with a stunned expression. "Senator, I am tendering my resignation, effective right now."

The speaker paused for dramatic effect and it worked. There was a rustling and murmuring around the room. Cullen Shoemaker was well known among those who took an interest in this bill. The senator wasn't the only one he'd just sandbagged.

"I want to explain my reason for resigning. It is because I have changed my mind about this bill. Let me explain why.

"Most of you probably know that my sister and her three children were slaughtered two years ago at the Pizza Parlor in Liberty. My mother was shot, too, and nearly died. If my mother had been armed she could have halted the massacre there.

"I believe our right to bear arms is the rock our democracy rests on, and when I started working for Senator Rauther, I believed this bill would help us enlarge that right." Cullen's left foot, Molly noticed, was drumming up and down on the base of the lectern. He was a man loaded with nervous energy. "But this bill is not what I thought it was. And it is not what you good people out there believe it is. I have new information it is critical that I share with you." He leaned forward toward the committee. "I now know, beyond a doubt, this bill is part of a secret plot of the federal government up in Washington, D.C., to disarm all of us."

Cullen paused to let it sink in.

"Now I know many honest people are supporting this bill, like the senator I worked for, the honorable Garland Rauther." He nodded at his former boss, who was still staring at him open-mouthed. "Senator, I admire you. I know how much work you have put into this bill."

He gestured to the left side of the room. "And the other folks working for this bill, the Texas Rifle Association and the National Rifle Association. These are honorable men. They believe in the Bill of Rights and the Second Amendment. They believe this bill will advance the cause of our freedom to bear arms, as I once believed. But they are wrong. Deluded."

He paused, letting the silence work for him. Molly looked around to see what the audience reaction was. Everyone was rapt. Cullen Shoemaker was a certifiable nut, but an effective speaker.

"Here's what this bill will result in, pardners: licenses that lead to lists, lists of honest citizens who apply for licenses to carry handguns. The lists will go right to the federal government up in Washington, D.C., to the computers at the Bureau of Alcohol, Tobacco, and Firearms and, before you know it, they will come knocking on our doors." He rapped his fist hard on the lectern, three times, and shouted into the microphone, " 'Open up! It's the ATF, come to confiscate your guns. We *know* you got 'em because you're on our list.' "

He paused again, looking hard at each member of the committee.

"So licenses lead to lists, which lead to loss, which leads to lament, and lament is where we are headed with this bill. Believe me, pardners, there will be plenty of lamenting and wailing and gnashing of teeth across the land when they come to take our guns away.

"Let's not play into the hands of these jackbooted Nazi thugs. Anyhow, this bill is not necessary, is it? Why should my mother be required to get a *license* to exercise a right she already has? Do we need a *license* to practice our religion or express political opinions under the First Amendment?" He looked at each member of the committee in turn, as if demanding a response. "No, we do not," he continued. "And we don't need a *license* to bear arms, which is already guaranteed under the Second Amendment of the U.S. Constitution and Article 1, Section 23 of the Texas Constitution."

He ran his hand over his crew cut, then said, "Before I stop, let me tell y'all about the McNelly Posse, the group I represent. We are a committee of vigilance modeled on the committees forced into existence on the Texas frontier of the nineteenth century. Our group is named in honor of Captain Leander H. McNelly of the Texas Rangers, a man of vigilance and action, a man who could teach us all a thing or two about enforcing the law. Back in 1875, when the Mescans and the Indians were in the unfortunate habit of raiding across the border and stealing Texas cattle, Captain McNelly did something no one else had the gumption to do: he got back the only stolen cattle ever returned to the Texas side."

Cullen paused and glanced back at the audience behind him, at his mother who was nodding solemnly. "The only time, pardners, that hard-working Texas ranchers ever—in all Texas history—got back property stolen from them by foreigners making raids across our borders. Now how did McNelly do this? Not by getting a permit from the local police to carry a gun, I'll tell you that, pardners. And not by opening his arms to welcome every foreigner who sneaks across our borders to steal, rape, and murder. No. Captain McNelly led his men down to the border and crossed that river and attacked those thieves and took the cattle back and brought them home to their rightful owners here in Texas. He got those cattle back by being tough and, pardners, he got them back by being *armed*.

"Now I know better than most of you that this bill has enough votes to pass the Senate vote on Monday. But I believe it will lead to lists, loss, and lamenting. Senators, I beg you to rethink this. On behalf of the McNelly Posse and all law-abiding, freedom-loving native Texans, I ask you to defeat bill ninety-eight. Stop it right now by refusing to report this bill out of your committee. Stop it before they disarm us, pardners, and do to us the same thing they did to those folks in Waco—cold-blooded massacre. If we let those jackbooted thugs from the ATF get us on their list, then we are up shit creek with no paddle. That will be the end of our freedoms, pardners, *the* end."

As he walked away from the microphone, there was just enough applause to send a little ripple of fear through Molly; surely no sane person could see that speech as anything but rabid paranoia. Senator Rauther was sitting back in his chair, staring down at the papers on the desk, looking shell-shocked. Molly yearned to be a fly on his office wall later to hear the discussion when he got hold of Cullen Shoemaker.

Molly checked her watch. She'd already stayed far longer than she intended, but she was eager for a few words with Cullen Shoemaker, so she rushed to the door to intercept him before the rest of the crowd got to him.

"Cullen, I am astonished," she said.

He stopped and regarded her gravely. "Why's that?"

"I didn't know you were such an accomplished public speaker."

"I've been going to Toastmasters."

Molly had to restrain herself from smiling at this. "Well, it sure is a recommendation for Toastmasters. But I had no idea you felt that way about the bill."

"Then you haven't read my manifesto yet?" His blue eyes were icy.

The paper he'd given her—she'd totally forgotten about it; it was probably still in her purse, stuffed down at the bottom. "Not yet, Cullen."

"I'd really like to get your ideas on publication." He glared at her.

To change the subject she said, "The McNelly Posse? I'm

a little weak on my Texas history, but wasn't McNelly the one who wiped out the wrong village on the way to get those cattle back?"

He glanced at his watch, then snapped his fingers. "Oh! About your interview—Rauther says he's real busy this week, but he'd be glad to talk to you right after the Senate vote on Monday. You're planning to be here for the vote, aren't you?"

"Yes."

Cullen's face softened into something like a grin. "That would work out then. The senator's going to host some of the press in his office after the vote—sort of a celebration—and he'd be honored to have you come."

"So you think—" Molly stopped mid-question. Olin Crocker was approaching. Her breath felt sucked right out of her body. It had been inevitable for them to meet, but she was unprepared for the intensity of her revulsion. He wore his star belt buckle again and carried a briefcase. He said, "My God, Cully, the McNelly Posse? Sounds like a rich-kid militia. How come you never told me about this, boy?"

Cullen replied, "You never asked, pardner."

"I've got to hand it to you—coming out at the last minute on the losing side. It's like being airlifted to the *Titanic* as it's sinking. You sure know how to pick a losing cause, boy."

"Miracles happen, pardner." Cullen took a step back, clearly eager to make an escape from the group that was gathering to talk to him. "Sorry, Mr. Crocker, Miz Cates—I believe Senator Rauther will want a word with me." He took off, leaving Molly face to face with Olin Crocker.

He looked her over. "Miz Cates."

Molly's jaw was so tense, it was difficult to speak. "Mr. Crocker," she said through tight lips. "Long time."

"Yes, ma'am. I thought maybe I saw you day before yesterday in the gallery." He shifted his weight forward slightly so his belt buckle angled toward her. "And I thought to myself, That sure looks like that little Cates gal from that unfortunate situation out at Volente, but—"

"You mean my daddy's murder, Mr. Crocker? *That* unfortunate situation?"

"His death, yes, ma'am."

"Well, I recognized you right off, Mr. Crocker. You're doing your hair a little differently, but other than that you haven't changed much."

Crocker put a hand to the top of his head to see if the strands were in place over the bald spot. Molly smiled sweetly at him. "I hear you've come out of retirement to do some lobbying, Mr. Crocker."

"Well, I'm just helping to educate folks on the need for this carry bill," he drawled.

"So you're in the education business now instead of law enforcement."

"Yes, ma'am, I am. And I heard you're a writer now, writing an article about the bill for *Lone Star Monthly.* Isn't that a coincidence?"

"How so?"

"Well, we're both interested in the same bill," he said. "If there's any little thing I can do to help educate you, ma'am, I'd sure be pleased." He reached into his shirt pocket and pulled out a card. "Here's my card. Give me a holler any time I can be of help."

"Miz Cates!" Parnell's secretary hurried toward them and handed Molly a folded slip of paper. "Senator Morrisey asked me to try and catch you before you left. Phone message just came for you. The caller said it was urgent."

Molly unfolded the note. It said, *Call me right away please. Urgent. Grady.*

"You can use a phone in the office," the secretary said.

Molly looked at her watch. She had only an hour left. "Thanks, but I've got a plane to catch. It'll be quicker if I use a pay phone on my way out."

Alarmed by how little time she had now to get to the airport, Molly nodded to Olin Crocker and nearly ran to the bank of pay phones in the hall.

"Molly," Grady said, "I'm glad I caught you. Listen, sweetheart, I'm afraid this is going to be bad news for you. Shawcross caught an angel here. Couple of kids found her in a drainage pipe along Waller Creek. Dead a few days. Transient female, throat cut. I think she might be one of your bag ladies."

"Oh." Molly turned toward the wall and leaned her head against it.

"Didn't you tell me you'd interviewed one called Tin Can? Small, mildly retarded. Missing several front teeth."

Under her closed lids, Molly saw the image of the woman with the sun behind her, the cat stretched out on her lap. "Her real name is Emily Bickerstaff."

"That's the one. We just got an ID from one of the counselors at HOBO. We'll double-check with the prints and dental casts at the State Hospital. But I think it's pretty definite. Will you come in and confirm, tell us about your interview with her? We're real interested in who her associates were."

"Grady, I would, but I've got to catch my plane in less than an hour. The photographer who took pictures of her—Henry Iglesias—could identify her. And he's got photos, recent ones, taken about two weeks ago. I've got his number in my bag." She held the phone to her ear by scrunching up her shoulder while she pulled her address book from her bag. "Is this a homicide for sure?"

"Unless she cut her own throat, bled all over the ground outside the pipe, crawled inside a garbage bag, and tied it shut with three knots. We are keenly interested in her associates, as I said."

"Grady, all I know is that she was friends with another homeless woman they call Cow Lady. A large woman, around fifty, I think. Wears a black and white coat with spots like on a cow."

"Know where to find her?"

"No. Well, maybe the Salvation Army. Or here at the Capitol, Grady. I saw her in the third-floor ladies' room on Monday."

"Shawcross will want to hear more about this. Molly—can't you put this trip off? Given the circumstances."

"I have an appointment in Lubbock this afternoon."

"Change it."

"Sorry, I can't."

"Please."

"No."

"We're interested in your notes," he said.

She glanced at her watch again, feeling harried and much too warm. "Oh, Grady, you know better than that. Anyway, I haven't transcribed my tapes yet. But when I get back I'd be glad to tell Shawcross what little I know about her. I'm in a time crunch here and—"

"Listen, I don't want to be crass, but think about this: you are interviewing several homeless women over a period of time to see what happens with them, and now one of them has been killed. Murdered. Something major has happened. Isn't this of some interest to your story?"

"Yes. Of course. But I won't be gone long. She'll still be dead when I get back."

"Molly, this is making me uneasy."

"I don't know why. I'll be gone twenty-four hours on family business. Aunt Harriet is expecting me for dinner tonight."

"Aunt Harriet? Expecting you! She doesn't even *recognize* you."

"Grady, I'm going to be late. I've got to go. I'll call you tonight."

She put the phone down before he could reply. There was no time to argue; as it was, she'd have to skip going home to pack.

13

THEN UP SHE TOOK HER LITTLE CROOK,
DETERMINED FOR TO FIND THEM;
SHE FOUND THEM INDEED, BUT IT MADE HER HEART
    BLEED,
FOR THEY'D LEFT ALL THEIR TAILS BEHIND 'EM!
—"LITTLE BOPEEP," VERSE 3, *MOTHER GOOSE*

Molly stood panting at the top of the stairs, blood thrumming, heart pounding. It was only one flight up, but she felt as winded as if she'd been running all day. She'd parked her car illegally at the Austin airport, made a mad dash for the gate, and caught her flight to Lubbock by the skin of her teeth, just as the last passengers were boarding. But she'd made it, ten minutes early for her appointment with Shelby Palmer at the Cap Rock Office Park.

She ran her tongue over her dry lips. Forty minutes in Lubbock and already her lips were peeling and she felt grit on her teeth from the blowing dirt. Welcome home.

She studied the closed door bearing the tiny discreet brass sign—PALMER INVESTIGATIONS— and forced her breathing to slow. She needed to approach this in a deliberate, grown-up way instead of the passionate, seat-of-the-pants way that had not served her well in the past. She was, after all, a forty-four-year-old investigative journalist now, a methodical researcher. If she kept her cool, she could bring the skills she'd acquired over the past two and a half decades to solving this old and agonizing puzzle.

She turned the shiny brass knob and stepped inside.

The white-haired woman at the reception desk glanced up. "Miss Cates, I bet."

Still huffing, Molly nodded.

"Sit yourself down, honey. You look like the heat's got to you. I'll let Shelby know you're here."

While Molly was still circling the furniture, trying to calm down enough to sit, Shelby Palmer appeared. He was a short, solid man in his fifties with curly gray hair and a gray seersucker suit. He pumped her hand vigorously. "I see you found us. Come on back." He turned to the receptionist and said, "Thanks, Mama. You go on home now. I've got to stay for my six o'clock, and I think I just might manage to take care of Miz Cates all by myself."

As he led Molly down a hallway he said, "This is very unusual, Miz Cates. When Mr. Quinlan called, I was real surprised. Occasionally we need to locate old files for one reason or another, but I don't believe we've ever had anyone come to look at a file in quite these circumstances."

"What circumstances?" Molly asked.

Palmer turned his head to look at her. "Well, you are one of the subjects of the inquiry. I've never had a client ask me to open a file to a subject before. And then there's the timing. This is a twenty-five-year-old case. If Mama wasn't such a stickler for keeping everything, the file would have been destroyed a long time ago."

He opened the door to a small windowless room dominated by an oval table and six chairs. "Our humble conference room." At one end of the table sat a brown accordion file with several tabbed manila folders inside. Molly's eyes locked on it hungrily.

"I've looked the file over," Palmer told her, "and you're in luck. Most of my dad's notes got typed. You'll see why that's important when you try to read the handwritten ones. When you get to those, I'll try to help. If I can't decode them, we'll bring in the real expert." He nodded toward the front office. "Mama will probably stay around even though I told her to go on home. She's only supposed to work a half day. At seventy-nine she—" He went on talking about his mother's prodigious working habits, but Molly was no longer listening. She was staring down at the file and willing him to shut up and leave.

As if he'd gotten the message, he stopped talking and nodded. "Well, then, I'll leave you to it. If you need anything—coffee or a soda water—just holler." He closed the door quietly as he left.

Molly sat down at the head of the table and looked around at the room. She was pleased there was no window because she was in no mood to look at Lubbock. She pulled the file toward her, then looked at the neatly typed labels on the three inner folders: CATES, VERNON; CATES, MOLLY; and CROCKER, OLIN T. Just seeing Crocker's name made her teeth grit; a quarter century had not dulled her hatred one iota.

She pulled out the folder with her name on it. Best to get this little piece of hell over with first.

Stapled to the inside cover was a color photograph of a sullen-looking, dark-haired girl standing in front of a white frame bungalow, a laundry bag slung over one slumped shoulder. She wore a very short green dress that revealed her thin, pale legs to mid-thigh. The girl's long hair, parted in the middle, looked wet, as though she'd just stepped from the shower, and she was gazing down at the sidewalk with the intensity of someone trying to remember something important. Molly Cates at twenty-one.

Molly Cates at forty-four couldn't remember what she had been doing or thinking, standing on that sidewalk holding that laundry bag, but she recognized the bungalow on Avenue D, and the green cotton dress, and the state of profound unhappiness she had been in then. She was certain she hadn't known the photo was being taken; if she had, she would have stood up straight and smiled for the camera—a lifelong habit of putting on a happy face in front of the lens.

The folder contained twelve stapled sheaves of onionskin paper. On top lay five loose sheets typed back in the days before word processors. Single-spaced. The date at the top was 11/2/75. The heading was: "Subject: Cates, Molly. DOB 6–3–54, SS#460–88–5099."

Molly closed her eyes, giving herself a few seconds' reprieve before facing November of 1975—surely one of the worst times of her life. She opened her eyes and began to read.

SUBJECT: MOLLY CATES, TWENTY-ONE-YEAR-OLD MARRIED WHITE FEMALE—RETAINED MAIDEN NAME—RENTS DUPLEX, 2324 AVENUE D, AUSTIN— HUSBAND: SENIOR PATROLMAN GRADY TRAYNOR, AUSTIN POLICE DEPARTMENT—MOVED OUT FIVE MONTHS AGO—STILL PAYS RENT—DAUGHTER: JOSEPHINE ELIZABETH TRAYNOR, AGE 2—RESIDES WITH SUBJECT'S AUNT, HARRIET CAVANAUGH, 4700 MESQUITE TRAIL, LUBBOCK. SUBJECT EMPLOYED AT AUSTIN, *AMERICAN-PATRIOT*, 1974–1975—ON LEAVE NOW—NO VISIBLE MEANS OF SUPPORT.

Molly stopped reading. Christ. This twenty-one-year-old white female being summarized here, the subject, the intense and unhappy girl in the picture—what did that person have to do with her? Same name, same birth date, same Social Security number, but was there a single cell in her body now that was present in the body of that young woman who lived in such misery on Avenue D? She doubted it.

She forced her eyes to the next paragraph.

SUBJECT DROPPED OUT OF HIGH SCHOOL AT 16, 1970, AFTER FATHER'S DEATH—JUNIOR YEAR AT LAKE TRAVIS HIGH—EXCELLENT ACADEMIC REC- ORD, GIRLS' TENNIS TEAM, HONOR SOCIETY.

PERSONALITY CHANGED AFTER FATHER'S DEATH, SAY PEERS AND NEIGHBORS (SEE ATTACHED IN- TERVIEWS)—UNBALANCED, IRRATIONAL, OBSESSED WITH FATHER'S DEATH—REJECTED ALL EVIDENCE OF SUICIDE, INSISTED HE WAS MURDERED THOUGH MEDICAL EXAMINER RULED DEATH SUICIDE, JUNE 1970 (SEE ATTACHED REPORT).

SUBJECT CALLED SHERIFF'S OFFICE 40 TIMES IN JULY 1970—DEMANDED COPIES OF ME'S REPORT—

TRIED TO OBTAIN SHERIFF'S NOTES, THREATENED
TO TAKE HIM TO COURT—BROKE INTO HIS OFFICE
TO STEAL NOTES, SHERIFF ALLEGES.

RUMORS OF HEAVY DRINKING AND SEXUAL
PROMISCUITY AFTER FATHER'S DEATH (SEE AT-
TACHED INTERVIEWS).

Heavy drinking? Sexual promiscuity? Molly considered
it. She had gotten drunk from time to time, yes, but she had
never thought of it as heavy drinking. And sexual promiscuity? Well, you might call it that, that desperate prowling and
grappling, that nervous groping for something she could
never quite pinpoint. But calling it sexual promiscuity made
it sound like a lot more fun than the sweaty, lonely disap-
pointment those pathetic couplings had been.

She read on.

SUBJECT FREQUENTED BARS IN LAKE TRAVIS
AREA—DRANK BEER—PICKED UP MEN—PROMISCU-
ITY DIFFICULT TO DOCUMENT BECAUSE SUBJECT
WAS UNDER AGE AND MEN WILL NOT TALK ON
RECORD.

Molly wondered which ones Julian Palmer had found. Not
that she could even remember their names now, those long-
legged, slow-talking cowboys and carpenters and truckers
she had preferred back then.

1970–1971—SUBJECT LIVED ALONE IN RENTED
HOUSE IN VOLENTE—RAN OUT OF MONEY—MOVED
TO BOARDINGHOUSE IN AUSTIN—RECEIVED FA-
THER'S $100,000 LIFE INSURANCE BENEFIT—DE-
POSITED IT AT MERRILL LYNCH, DID NOT SPEND
ANY OF IT. SUBJECT'S FATHER'S SISTER, HARRIET
CATES CAVANAUGH, A RESPECTABLE MARRIED
WOMAN IN LUBBOCK, TRIED TO GET SUBJECT TO
COME BACK TO LUBBOCK, BUT SUBJECT STAYED IN
AUSTIN.

Now there was an understatement, Molly thought. Subject and her respectable married aunt had indulged in frequent screaming fights over that very issue. Aunt Harriet had begged Molly to come back to Lubbock to live with her and finish school. Molly had refused, even when Aunt Harriet had threatened to bring the law into it. Molly had been too far gone at that point to care, too sunk in her grief and the need to know what had really happened to her daddy out there on the lake.

She was tempted to quit reading here. It was like overhearing people gossiping about you and having the choice to go on listening to them or leave. It was just inviting pain to go on listening.

She went back to reading.

SUBJECT MARRIED GRADY TRAYNOR, AUSTIN POLICE DEPARTMENT PATROLMAN 1972—DAUGHTER BORN 6 MONTHS LATER—ADEQUATE IF UNCONVENTIONAL MOTHER FIRST 2 YEARS. FEBRUARY 1975, QUIT JOB—LEFT BABY IN LUBBOCK WITH HARRIET CAVANAUGH—STARTED NEW ROUND OF QUESTIONING RE VERNON CATES'S DEATH.

The disapproval permeating the tone of this dead investigator stung her where she was most vulnerable. She wanted to talk back to him, explain the extenuating circumstances. Maybe she had neglected her daughter, but she'd discovered something that had set her off again: four years after his death, some of her father's rare Mexican gold coins had turned up in an Austin pawnshop that specialized in old coins. The burglary suspect who had pawned them was in the Travis County Jail and Olin Crocker had talked with him. She'd been desperate for information about this because she was certain the coins had been stolen from her father's houseboat the night he was killed. It could lead to the killer. How could she *not* follow up on that? Julian K. Palmer had been an investigator; surely he knew how compelling such things were.

CROCKER SAYS SUBJECT STARTED TO HARASS HIM AGAIN, WORSE THAN BEFORE—CALLS CATES A "DANGEROUSLY DERANGED YOUNG WOMAN."

MAY 1975—SUBJECT'S HUSBAND MOVED OUT. INITIATED DIVORCE ON GROUNDS OF INCOMPATI-BILITY. FRIENDS WERE SURPRISED, THOUGHT COU-PLE HAD BEEN VERY MUCH IN LOVE.

Molly felt so tired. What a mess these people had made of their lives, this subject and her policeman husband. How could people be so stupid?

SUBJECT BLAMES QUINLAN OIL COMPANY IN LUBBOCK FOR FATHER'S DEATH (SEE ATTACHED AR-TICLE)—CLAIMS QUINLAN OFFERED FATHER A BRIBE NOT TO PUBLISH ARTICLE HE HAD WRITTEN ON AN ALLEGED SCAM QUINLAN WAS CONDUCTING IN ITS DALHART OIL FIELDS—CLAIMS QUINLAN HAD HIM KILLED, HIS NOTES DESTROYED, TO STOP PUBLICATION.

QUINLAN PRESIDENT JASPER QUINLAN AND VICE-PRESIDENT ROGER QUINLAN DENY CHARGES. SUBJECT NEVER PRODUCED ANY EVIDENCE TO SUP-PORT ACCUSATIONS AGAINST QUINLAN OIL.

IN CONCLUSION: MOLLY CATES APPEARS TO BE DISTURBED YOUNG WOMAN UNABLE TO ACCEPT FA-THER'S SUICIDE. BECAUSE OF UNCONVENTIONAL LIFE STYLE AND IRRATIONAL BEHAVIOR SHE WOULD MAKE EXCEEDINGLY POOR WITNESS IN ANY SORT OF PROCEEDINGS.

The article from the *Lubbock Morning Clarion* was at-tached. The rest of the file was transcripts of taped interviews with people she could barely remember: high school acquain-tances, teachers, neighbors in Volente and on Avenue D, fel-low workers at the paper.

There was no denying that this Julian Palmer was a thorough researcher, and an accurate one; there was nothing in the entire file that was out-and-out wrong. His prose was abominable, but his investigating was sound.

When she finished skimming the typed interviews and reports in the Molly Cates file, she looked back at the photograph. That girl, the subject of this sorry story, must have walked right past Julian Palmer without noticing that a strange man had a camera pointed at her. All this information had been gathered right under her nose, without her being aware of it. To think that a business she'd never heard of, in an office park she hadn't known existed, in a part of Lubbock she'd never been in, contained this file of intimate information about her that she hadn't known was being compiled at the time. It was a chilling glimpse into a parallel universe that had been operating right next to her, unseen.

It made her wonder about other universes out there right now, universes she couldn't see that were destined to collide with hers at some point, and when they did, she'd ask herself, once again, how she could ever have been so oblivious to what was going on around her.

With relief she slipped the folder back in the accordion file. Her hand hesitated over the other two. She drew out the one marked Cates, Vernon. Let Sheriff Olin Fucking Crocker wait. For years that sorry weasel had been a pustule festering on whatever organ in her body was the opposite of the heart—the spleen maybe—and he could damn well wait a little longer.

She opened the Vernon Cates folder slowly, fearful she might be confronted with the bloated, rotting monster face that had appeared in the autopsy photo. But stapled to the inside cover was the lean, suntanned face of her daddy, smiling and very much alive. It was the photo that had run with a magazine story he'd written for *Texas Backroads*, taken six months before his death. The crinkled skin around his eyes revealed his forty-five years in the sun, and his slicked-back hair, though still dark, had receded just slightly from the forehead.

This folder was twice as thick as hers. The date at the top of the first sheet was November 21, 1975, the subject, Vernon Matthew Cates, birth date 1/4/25.

It began with a factual account of his death taken from news stories and the medical examiner's report. The autopsy was attached, as were news articles that had appeared in the *Austin American-Patriot* and the *Lubbock Morning Clarion*. Molly had to admire Julian Palmer's thoroughness: nearly five years after the death and he'd found all the sources and gotten it right.

A six-page typed biography followed and the tone of it puzzled her right from the start. It stuck to the facts of Vernon Cates's life, but it presented him as a man who had failed at almost everything. This Julian Palmer had clearly not understood what her daddy had been about. Palmer described him as the ne'er-do-well son of a West Texas rancher, who'd let the ranch he'd inherited languish and managed money badly. Though he'd gotten a history degree with honors from Texas Tech and been on the debate and track teams, he'd never lived up to the promise of that early academic success.

Right out of college he'd gotten a routine job as a well inspector for the Texas Railroad Commission, the state agency that regulated the oil business. After eight years of that state job, with no promotions and an undistinguished record, he'd quit. After that he'd done whatever free-lance writing jobs he could scrounge up for various small local publications.

In 1968, plagued with debt, he sold the family ranch, which had never made a profit under his management, and moved with his teenaged daughter to Volente near Austin. Julian Palmer made their move from Lubbock sound like a defeat rather than the courageous escape from the past that it had in fact been. The information was all correct, but the spin he gave it was all wrong. It was upsetting, more upsetting than anything else she'd encountered in this report, and it made her damn angry. If this Palmer person had encountered her daddy when he was alive, he'd have understood that Vernon Cates was not your run-of-the-mill West Texas rancher; he was cut out for other things, better things. It was true Vernon Cates had not been a financial success, but money hadn't been something he'd valued that much. And while it was true his writing had been low-paying assignments for small local publications, he was on the verge of success when he'd died. He just hadn't gotten his big break.

She forced herself back to Julian Palmer's staccato prose:

SUBJECT HAD HISTORY OF DEPRESSION—AFTER WIFE'S DEATH AND AT TIMES OF FINANCIAL STRESS—DRANK TO EXCESS AT TIMES (SEE INTERVIEWS B, D, AND F). SUBJECT HAD REPUTATION OF BEING LADIES' MAN, EVEN BEFORE WIFE DIED IN 1963—LOTS OF RUMORS—NO ONE WILL TALK ON THE RECORD.

Molly jiggled her shoulders to try to get them to unclench. She'd seen her father drink too much, but only occasionally. All the men of her childhood had been two-fisted drinkers; it was expected. Of course she had to acknowledge the strain of melancholy in him, the same strain with which she was afflicted, but she would never go so far as to call it *depression*. The rumors of other women she didn't like much, but it was possible. Her mother had been sick for several years. He had been undeniably attractive and he had always loved the company of women. It was possible. Harriet would know about this, but of course she'd never tell, even if she were still in possession of her wits. Of her many staunch loyalties, Harriet's devotion to her little brother had been sacrosanct, her fiercest allegiance.

AT TIME OF DEATH, SUBJECT WAS WRITING ARTICLE EXPOSING ALLEGED ILLEGAL DRILLING ACTIVITIES OF QUINLAN OIL—TEXT AND NOTES LOST WHEN THE HOUSEBOAT-OFFICE WAS SUNK. FRIENDS SAY IT INVOLVED ALLEGED WHITE OIL SCAM IN QUINLAN'S PANHANDLE FIELDS. QUINLAN GOT AROUND REGULATIONS LIMITING NUMBER OF WELLS THEY COULD DRILL BY REPRESENTING THEM AS OIL PRODUCERS RATHER THAN GAS PRODUCERS. MISS CATES SAYS QUINLAN OIL PRESIDENT JASPER QUINLAN OFFERED CATES MONEY TO

KILL ARTICLE. MR. QUINLAN DENIES IT, BUT SEV-
ERAL SOURCES (SEE ATTACHED INTERVIEWS B, D,
AND E) CONFIRM BRIBE—SAY CATES REFUSED OF-
FER. THE ALLEGED OIL SCAM IS BEYOND SCOPE OF
THIS INVESTIGATION.

Julian Palmer's acknowledging the attempted bribe
boosted him in Molly's estimation. Here was a man not
afraid to nip the hand that was feeding him. After all, Jasper
Quinlan was paying the bill for this investigation and he was
a powerful force in Lubbock who could throw lots of business Palmer's way, or ruin him.

There followed interviews with neighbors in Lubbock and
Volente, a former boss at the Railroad Commission, and an
editor at the *Morning Clarion*. All mentioned Vernon Cates's
poor financial management, depression, and sporadic heavy
drinking. It surprised Molly to see these things come up
again and again.

One of the interviews was a short one with Rose and
Parnell Morrisey. They described him as a lifelong friend of
theirs who was brilliant but moody. They said he had been
very depressed the last week of his life, though they didn't
know why.

A note at the bottom said that Harriet Cates Cavanaugh
refused to see the investigator or talk to him on the phone.
Well, of course. Aunt Harriet would keep faith with her baby
brother past the bitter end.

There were also Xeroxes of four articles written by Vernon
Cates for some local magazines. Molly picked one up. It was
from the *Lubbock Rancher*, dated May 1966. It was about
the big drought of the 1950s. As she read, her throat tightened; it wasn't what she'd expected. The article was simplis-
tic and amateurishly written. It was the work of a beginner
who was none too careful about his craft. Molly was stunned.
She hadn't read any of her daddy's writing since she was sixteen because all his papers and files had been destroyed when
his houseboat was sunk and she had never, for some reason,
tried to ferret out any of these old pieces.

She picked up another one, this one from the *West Texas Oilman,* about Texans in the Civil War. After reading one paragraph, she stopped and slid it back into the folder, feeling as though she'd suddenly walked into a room and surprised a parent in some secret and shameful activity.

A weariness was settling on her, making it hard to keep her head up. She tapped the file on the table several times, to wake herself up as much as to align the pages, and stuck it back in the accordion file.

Now it was time for Olin Crocker.

She drew the folder out and opened it. The photograph was one she'd seen before, the glamor shot that his office gave out to the media. He was smiling, if you could call that upward twist of barbed wire a smile. His fleshy-lobed ears, lumpy cheeks, and off-center nose gave him the look of a crudely modeled clay pot. It was rare for people to look like what they were, but Olin Crocker looked every bit the coarse and corrupted cracker sheriff she knew him to be.

The photograph showed just head and shoulders, but Molly could picture the whole body—every detail of it, still—the fringe of thick black hair growing on his sloping shoulders, the soft white belly bisected by the jagged line of black hair, the short bowed legs that looked out of proportion with the bulky torso.

The date at the top of the report was 12/5/75, so this part of the investigation had been done after the other two. Without planning it, she had read them in chronological order.

The heading at the top of the page was Crocker, Olin T., birth date, 7–1–37. Molly did a quick calculation. God, he'd only been thirty-eight when this report was written, which was the same year she'd had her final encounter with him. She had thought of him as a dirty old man, but he hadn't been old at all. He'd just been weathered by excess flesh and alcohol, and, of course, she'd been looking at him through the eyes of extreme youth.

SUBJECT: OLIN CROCKER, 38, TRAVIS COUNTY
SHERIFF SINCE 1964—STARTED AS CORRECTIONS

OFFICER AT TRAVIS COUNTY JAIL, THEN COUNTY
DEPUTY.

SUBJECT IS MARRIED—FIVE CHILDREN, AGES 2
THROUGH 15—GRADUATED CROCKETT HIGH
SCHOOL—STUDIED CRIMINAL JUSTICE AT SAM
HOUSTON STATE IN HUNTSVILLE TWO YEARS—
MARRIED RUTH HANSON 1959—WENT TO WORK
FOR COUNTY—CAMPAIGNED FOR SHERIFF ON
PROMISE TO BEEF UP SECURITY AT JAILS, CUT
DOWN ON FRILLS FOR CRIMINALS—WON BY SLIM
MARGIN.

She read quickly over the innocuous account of Crocker's
eleven years as sheriff and his very close reelection campaign
in 1972, during which his opponent, Jim Ray Toser, charged
him with having taken indecent liberties with some female inmates he was in charge of. All this Molly knew already from
following it in the news and from her own research, when she
had read all the back newspaper accounts looking for ammunition to use against him. Her experience with Crocker made
her certain he was guilty of the sexual harassment; it was his
style to use his power to bully women sexually. Oh, was it ever.
But a piece of information that followed caught Molly's
attention:

DURING 1972 CAMPAIGN, TWO WOMEN, FORMER
INMATES TRAVIS COUNTY JAIL, SUED CROCKER.
CHRISTINE FANON, 17, AND SYLVIA RAMOS, 18,
DROPPED SUIT TWO DAYS AFTER FILING. CON-
TENTS OF SUIT UNAVAILABLE.

Molly found herself waking up. This was something she
hadn't known. These women would be forty-two and forty-
three now, maybe still in the Austin area. She'd ask Shelby
Palmer about trying to locate them. She'd love to hear what
they had to say.

INVESTIGATION OF CATES'S DEATH WAS
SLIPSHOD—LEFT SEVERAL IMPORTANT LEADS

UNEXPLORED—VEHICLES STRANGE TO AREA WERE
SEEN BY NEIGHBOR—NO ATTEMPT TO LOCATE
THEM—NO DRAGGING LAKE FOR SUICIDE GUN—
PULLED SUNKEN HOUSEBOAT UP THREE WEEKS AF-
TER BODY WAS FOUND—VALUABLE COLLECTION OF
MEXICAN GOLD COINS UNACCOUNTED FOR.

Under the heading "Conclusion," Palmer wrote:

SHERIFF'S INVESTIGATION WAS POOR, BUT
FINDING OF SUICIDE SEEMS WARRANTED BY EVI-
DENCE. NO EVIDENCE THAT QUINLAN OIL COM-
PANY OR ANYONE ASSOCIATED WITH IT WAS IN
ANY WAY INVOLVED IN THE DEATH OF VERNON
CATES.

The typed report ended here, but paper-clipped to it were
two handwritten pages on yellow legal paper. The heading
was easy to read because it was printed: "12/18/75. Adden-
dum. Delivered orally, no written copy provided."

The rest was written in cursive, tiny and crabbed, so difficult to read it might have been written in code. But after she
deciphered the first sentence, she would have walked across
burning coals to figure out the rest:

12/18/75, AFTER REPORT WAS TYPED, NEW INFO:
JIM RAY TOSER, CROCKER'S UNSUCCESSFUL OPPO-
NENT IN 1972 SHERIFF'S RACE, CALLED—SAID HE
HAD EVIDENCE CROCKER IS CROOKED AS THE
DEVIL'S BACKBONE—

Here the handwriting became increasingly impenetrable.
Molly jumped up and hurried down the hall, letting out a
gasp of relief when she saw Mrs. Palmer still at her post.

"Mrs. Palmer, would you please help me figure out some
of the handwritten parts? I think I've gone as far as I can
without your help."

The white-haired woman looked up from her keyboard. "Honey, you look frazzled. Get yourself a Coke out of

the fridge. You don't want to let yourself get dehydrated. I'll finish this paragraph and then take a look." She gave Molly a smile and went back to typing.

Molly walked in the direction indicated and found a tiny kitchen. She opened the little refrigerator and took out a Diet Coke. She drank a long swig and carried it back to the conference room.

In a few minutes Mrs. Palmer came in and sat down. "Now let's see that chicken scratching he called handwriting. I was probably supposed to type these up and never did get around to it."

Molly handed her the yellow pages. The woman squinted at them for a few seconds. "That man must have been dropped on his hands as a baby." She set the pages down and began to read slowly:

"12/18/75, AFTER REPORT WAS TYPED, NEW INFO: JIM RAY TOSER, CROCKER'S UNSUCCESSFUL OPPO-NENT IN 1972 SHERIFF'S RACE, CALLED—SAYS CROCKER IS CROOKED AS THE DEVIL'S BACK-BONE—CROCKER THREATENED TWO FORMER INMATES, CHRISTINE FANON AND SYLVIA RAMOS, INTO DROPPING COMPLAINTS AGAINST HIM."

She looked up. "The writing gets even worse here. I believe I'm the only one in the world who could decipher this."

"Bless you," said Molly Cates. "Read on."

"CROCKER INVESTED $51,000 CASH IN A HOUSE IN SOUTH AUSTIN. DATE OF PURCHASE, AUGUST OF 1970."

Molly's breath was coming faster. He *was* paid off, the weasel.

Mrs. Palmer kept on reading, stopping occasionally to work out a hard word.

"TOSER SAID CROCKER'S RECORDS AT BERTRAM BANK OF THE HILLS SHOW MAXIMUM $750 IN

ACCOUNT, AT ANY TIME THE LAST TWENTY YEARS. I
CHECKED AND CONFIRMED. TIMING OF INVEST-
MENT CONSISTENT WITH POSSIBILITY OF PAYOFF
IN VERNON CATES MATTER. NO EVIDENCE FOR
THAT, BUT I INCLUDE THIS ADDITIONAL INFORMA-
TION FOR COMPLETENESS.

"N.B. TOSER IS *NOT* A NEUTRAL SOURCE, HATES
CROCKER, PLANS TO RUN AGAINST HIM AGAIN IN
'78. HOPES TO FORCE CROCKER OUT OF THE
RACE."

"Crocker *did* drop out of the race!" Molly exclaimed. "I've
often wondered why."

"Shall I finish?" Mrs. Palmer asked. "Just one more paragraph."

"Please do."

"TOSER OFFERED TO HIRE ME TO INVESTIGATE
WHERE CROCKER'S FIFTY THOUSAND CAME FROM
AND TO LOOK FOR OTHER INMATES WILLING TO
TESTIFY TO CROCKER'S SEXUAL HARASSMENT.
SINCE IT WOULD BE UNETHICAL TO ACCEPT JOB
WITHOUT FIRST CHECKING WITH JASPER AND
ROGER QUINLAN, I TOLD THEM ABOUT OFFER,
ASKED IF THEY HAD ANY OBJECTION TO MY CON-
TINUING TO INVESTIGATE OLIN CROCKER FOR NEW
CLIENT. THEY HAD NO OBJECTION."

"So he did accept it?" Molly asked.

"Yes."

"Oh, Mrs. Palmer, might I take a peek at that
report?" Molly held her breath.

"Tsk, tsk. Miz Cates, you know better than that."

"Yes, but I hoped—"

"You'll have to talk to Shelby."

In a faint voice Molly said, "He was a good investigator,
your late husband."

Mrs. Palmer stood up. She handed the two yellow sheets

back to Molly. "The best. And the most honest. If he wrote it, you can believe it."

"And how about your son?"

Mrs. Palmer beamed. "He's his daddy's boy."

"I want to hire him," Molly said. "Right now, before his six o'clock gets here."

14

ROUND, AROUND, AROUND, ABOUT, ABOUT,
ALL ILL COME RUNNING IN, ALL GOOD KEEP OUT.
—*MACBETH*

Sarah Jane Hurley is standing outside the library shaking so hard her teeth are rattling. There's so much to make a person shake she's not sure whether it's the fever, or the shock of seeing Tin Can like that, or the drinking finally getting her.

She peers in the window, trying to see who's working today. If she's real quiet and careful she might slip past them and go upstairs to do her research. Since she's not wearing her coat they probably won't recognize her anyway.

She takes another peek. It's damned unfair. All those other people, some of them streets just like her, are sitting on the soft green chairs where she used to sit, and all they're doing is just wasting time, pretending to look at the newspapers. Well, she has as much right to be there as they do, and she's got some real research to do, important research that might be a matter of life and death. But those we-own-the-world snots who threw her out think that just because she's living on the street she doesn't *have* any rights.

Well, she's not going to let that stop her. She's going to walk in there right now, and do what she needs to do. After all, it's the *Public* Library and she's a member of the public, isn't she? She wraps her arms around herself and breathes deeply to slow the shaking. She walks to the door and enters, looking around for the bozos who hassled her last week. She's in luck, for once. The security guy checking people's books at the exit is new, and the people working the check-out desk don't seem to recognize her, or even notice her. She hobbles up to the information desk, where a small young woman with frizzy reddish hair sits next to a computer and a shelf of fat reference books.

The young woman actually smiles up at Sarah Jane. She must be new. "Can I help you, ma'am?"

The air conditioning has hit Sarah Jane's wet skin with a vengeance. "Cold in here," she says to explain the new on-slaught of shaking.

"Sure is," the girl says. "Can I help you?"

"Yes." Sarah Jane tries to keep her voice low so she won't attract attention. "I want to find out about a poison. It's called soman, I think, something like that. Can you look it up and see if you got anything about that?"

"S-o-m-i-n?" the girl asks.

"I'm not sure how it's spelled. Maybe that's it."

The young woman types on her keyboard and watches the computer screen. "Nothing under that spelling." She hits a few keys. "Or e-n or a-n. What kind of poison is it?"

"What kind?"

"Yes. Like is it an insecticide or what?"

"Well..." Sarah Jane tries to remember back to the dis-cussion on the deck. "It's this poison Hitler had but didn't use in the war, even though he could have. It kills people. They breathe it. Real deadly."

"A poison gas?" the girl says, brightening up. "Like mus-tard gas maybe. Let's try gases." She types and watches the screen again. Sarah Jane thinks it must be wonderful to have that power in your fingertips, to find out things just by typ-ing. She loves to type and was always good at it. She was one of the fastest typists in her class at Comstock Business Col-lege—seventy words per minute—before she met old slack-jawed Harold, and got married and had the children and was trapped in the house with them all the time and got to drink-ing and all and things went to hell in a handcart.

"Ah, this looks promising—" the girl says, "Gases,

asphyxiating and poisonous, war use. Here's a book on the subject. We've got it at this location if you want to take a look. It might discuss the poison you're interested in. Here, I'll write down the call number for you." She copies from the screen and hands the little square of paper to Sarah Jane.

Sarah Jane stands there looking at the paper—a title and a number. She has no idea how to use it. She hasn't hunted for a library book since she was in high school and she's forgotten how.

The girl cocks her head to one side. "Ma'am, that number should be up on the third level. Toward the back."

"Uh, thanks."

"And when you find the book, you can look in the index in the back to see if the poison you're interested in is included. That's a quick way to see if the book's going to be useful."

"Oh, okay." Sarah Jane looks toward the big central staircase and then she notices for the first time that a thin man wearing a bow tie is staring at her from behind the circulation desk. She looks away quickly and heads for the elevators to get out of his line of vision. She takes the elevator to the third level and hurries through the stacks, figuring out the way the numbers work. It reminds her of the Galveston library, where Gramma used to take her when she had a school paper to do. She's always loved being in a library—so quiet and cozy and orderly, the wooden drawers with the cards inside, the tables with green-shaded lamps, the people sitting quiet, but busy.

Studying the numbers on the tall shelves, she finally locates the shelf where her book should be. When she actually finds the right book, she feels a rush of pleasure. She pulls it out and looks at the cover, which has a picture of a man in a gas mask on the front. It is called *A Higher Form of Killing* and now she remembers Billy Goat Gruff saying those exact words. When he was explaining how it took just the tiniest bit to kill a person, he'd said, "It's a higher form of killing." This is what she's looking for. She tingles with the certainty that fate is about to show her what's what. She carries the book to a table where she hopes she won't be noticed. It's in a deserted corner at the end of a row of shelves.

She is shocked to see how tiny the print of the index is. Since she last looked at a book, the print has gotten smaller, she thinks. But if she gets way back from the print she can just make it out. She pages through, looking for entries that begin s-o-m. It takes awhile, but she finds an entry for "soman (GD)" with three page numbers after it. She looks at the first page listed and is excited to see it has to do with Hitler and something they call "secret nerve agents." This must be right. At the bottom of the page she reads:

> IN ADDITION TO THE TWO FACTORIES WHERE THE NAZIS WERE PRODUCING TABUN AND SARIN, THE RUSSIANS ALSO DISCOVERED THE SECRETS OF AN EVEN MORE POISONOUS NERVE AGENT WHICH THE GERMAN SCIENTISTS HAD REFINED BUT NOT MANUFACTURED IN QUANTITY. THE CHEMISTS HAD FIRST PRODUCED THE SUBSTANCE THEY CALLED SOMAN, LATER KNOWN AS GD, IN THE SPRING OF 1944. TESTS HAD SHOWN THE NEW NERVE AGENT TO BE EVEN MORE TOXIC THAN THE TWO SUB-STANCES THE GERMANS HAD ALREADY ADOPTED FOR USE AS WEAPONS.

Wow. Sarah Jane feels a little thrill at finding what she was looking for. She also feels a growing dread. She goes back to the index for the next page listed and turns to it. She reads:

> SOMAN IS THOUGHT TO BE THE FAVORED SO-VIET NERVE AGENT, FAR AND AWAY THE MOST POW-ERFUL OF THE G-AGENTS, AND ABLE TO BREAK THROUGH THE BLOOD/BRAIN BARRIER WITH EASE.

Lordy—the blood/brain barrier. She doesn't know what that is, but she's certain it has to do with what Billy Goat Gruff was saying about how it kills people. She flips to the middle where there are some photographs. They are awful: battlefields and corpses and people with grotesquely swollen blackened and blistered limbs from poison gas. This is what Toe-tapper and Billy Goat plan to do to the people up there in the Senate—the senators and the schoolchildren and the tourists and the people who work there and the people like her who just need a cool place to sit. She believes it now.

She closes the book. There really *is* a poison like Billy Goat Gruff was talking about. He wasn't bullshitting about that. And now she is convinced of what she has suspected since this morning—he killed Tin Can. It is crazy, but it must be true.

She lets herself remember now. The manager at the Grill, the one with the suck-up voice, told Billy Goat and Toe-tapper about the bag lady in the spotted coat. So they came looking and they found a bag lady in a spotted coat, down by the creek. They killed Tin Can because they thought she was the one who heard them talking and saw them up on the deck. They killed her because she was wearing the cow coat. If Sarah Jane had been wearing it, they would have killed her instead. Poor Tin Can, the simple little twit, just got herself scooped up by that old claw of fate. She probably thought Billy Goat was real nice right up to the end.

Sarah Jane's shivering has started up again; this place is like a refrigerator. They killed Tin Can. They *killed* her and stuffed her in a garbage bag. And they really are going to kill everyone in the Senate. Even the children. They think they can do anything they want and get away with it, like kings of the world. She feels that familiar old hot blue flame licking up, scorching her cheeks.

Lufkin was right.

She has to do something. But what? She can't just go and tell the police what she heard under the deck. If she does that, they'll make her give her real name and then they'll find out about Houston. And she'll have to tell them about Tin Can and take them to her body and maybe they'll think *she* killed her and that she is some crazy serial killer of homeless women and is making all this up, and she'll be in some real trouble then and she'll be sorry she ever got involved.

Anyway, they probably won't believe the poison gas thing because it sounds, even to her, like something a crazy woman would rave about. Just the DTs, they'll say, an old bum having hallucinations.

She needs some sort of proof. The book might help. She glances around to see if anyone is watching. There's no one in sight, so she drops the book into her bag quickly. She'll bring it back when she doesn't need it anymore.

Then she freezes. Someone *is* watching her. He's standing at the end of the high shelves and he could have seen her drop the book in her bag. Oh, no. She lowers her head, watching him from the corner of her eye. He is walking down the aisle, slowly, studying the books. Maybe he wasn't looking at her.

He is a large, gray-haired man in a blue-jean jacket—not one of the library workers, thank God. She's been worried about the bow-tie man who stared at her downstairs. But this man doesn't seem interested; he is just looking for a book.

She sits quite still, waiting for him to finish and move on. As he reaches the end of the shelf, he slows his pace even more. Then he comes to a standstill uncomfortably close to her table, and suddenly is leaning down, as if he's going to ask her something. Instead, he reaches into her bag and lifts the book out. He *did* see her take it. She turns to explain that she is not stealing it, but then she sees that he's holding something in his other hand—a straight razor. It's open and it's heading toward her neck.

Her brain explodes in panic. She throws herself backward with such force that the chair tips and she crashes to the floor. The man grunts and leans down over her. The razor is right in front of her eyes, coming at her. Jesus Christ, he's gonna kill her, right here in the library.

She scrambles backward, desperate. But he is fast for such a large man. He takes a swipe at her throat.

She screams and jerks away from the blade. But it catches her this time, nicks her collarbone as she backs up.

Terrified, Sarah Jane flings her arms in front of her face to ward it off. She squirms backward. He climbs on top of her to pin her down. She screams again.

He grunts and takes another swipe with the razor. It cuts into her forearm, right through her heavy black sweatshirt.

"Ow," she yells. "Help! Someone help me!" The words sound ripped out of her.

As if on command, a man appears from the shelves. "Stop this!" he shouts in a voice you would use for unruly children. Sarah Jane glances up. It is the skinny man in the bow tie. She's so glad to see him.

A woman in a red dress appears at his shoulder. "Call the police," he says to her.

The big man scrambles off her to his feet. He is wearing black boots, jeans. His gray hair is crewcut. He is huge. She realizes with a flash of heat that this must be Billy Goat Gruff from the deck. How the devil has he found her?

"What's going on?" the man in the bow tie asks.

Billy Goat backs away. "This crazy woman attacked me," he says, "this old bum." It's the low voice, the accent. Now she's sure: it is Billy Goat. He raises his hands and there is no razor to be seen. "She was stealing a book and I told her to put it back." He points at Sarah Jane. "Look in her bag." He turns and heads toward the stairs, walking very fast.

"Hold on!" says the bow-tie man, but Billy Goat is already running down the stairs.

Sarah Jane tries to talk but it comes out as sputtering. It takes a few tries before she can get the words out: "He had a razor. He was trying to kill me."

The bow-tie man points at her. "*You* stay right there."

He takes a few steps toward the table and looks down into her bag. He reaches in for the book. "Were you planning to steal this?" Then, looking more closely at her face, he says, "Say, don't I know you?"

Sarah Jane scrambles to her feet. She grabs her bag and heads for the stairs.

"Stop right there!" the man calls out.

Sarah Jane needs to get out, quick. The cops have already been called, and she can't let herself get trapped in here. Without looking back she limps to the stairs and hurries down them, running toward the exit. When she passes through the arch in front of the door an alarm goes off in her ear.

Outside, she looks up and down the street—no cop car insight, and no Billy Goat, thank God. But she'd better hustle.

She turns the corner onto Eighth Street to get off the main road. Before she gets a block away, she hears sirens. She's a sitting duck; they'll spot her right away. She feels an animal instinct telling her to go to ground. She looks around desperately for a place to hide, a safe place just to sit for a while. Across the street stands a huge stone building with a sign saying AUSTIN WOMEN'S CLUB. Fate again. She's a woman, after all. She runs across the street. Behind the building a sunken parking lot is surrounded by high stone walls with patches of overgrown bushes at the edges. Perfect. She hurries downhill and turns on Nueces to get to the entrance. The whole lot is empty. The sirens are louder now; they must be in front of the library, just two blocks away. She hobbles across the lot to a shady corner where a pile of old stones and high weeds provide a hiding place. She clambers over the stones. She drops her bag and sits with her back braced against the old darkened stone wall.

She is burning hot and panting like a steam engine. Her left leg hurts worse than ever from the running and there's blood all over her hands. She knows she's been cut, but she can't feel any pain yet. Carefully, she pulls the arms of her sweatshirt up to see how bad it is. On her right forearm is a long cut, but it doesn't look very deep and has already stopped bleeding. She pulls the sleeves back down. Nothing to worry about—just a few more drops in that endless flow of lost blood.

She tries to look down at her collarbone, but she can't see it and she has no mirror. It doesn't matter anyway.

She rests her head back against the wall. The stones are cool and damp. She closes her eyes. She's tired. She's so tired.

Now she'll never be able to go back to the library. After all that mess today, they'll *never* let her back in. Just one more place she can't go back to. That's pretty much the story of her life—a steady drying up of places to be. One by one. So there's not a single place on the face of the earth for her to go to. She can't go back to her spot under the deck. She can't go back to Ellie's house in Brenham. She certainly can't go back to the shelter in Houston, or the one-room apartment, or to Donner's boardinghouse. She can't go back to the house in Baytown where she lived with old slack-jawed Harold. She can't go back to Gramma's in Galveston. There is no place for her. She is *truly* homeless now.

She doesn't know what in the world to do.

It's surprising, but the person she'd most like to have here with her now is Tin Can. Even though she was a retard,Tin Can was good for talking things over with. She had horse sense and she'd listen to whatever you wanted to say, for however long it took you to say it. Sarah Jane wants to talk to her right now, needs to. But she's dead, and they'll never talk again.

Then it occurs to her that, besides her and Lufkin, and Billy Goat who killed her, maybe no one else knows Tin Can is dead. Maybe no one has found her body. She feels the loneliness of that body lying there in that empty place. It's just not right.

She thinks about the writer woman, Bopeep, the one in the bathroom—what was her name? She'd want to know about Tin Can because she's writing about her and she said she liked her. And Tin Can liked *her* and thought she was a good listener.

Sarah Jane sure needs a good listener. She remembers the card the woman gave her, but she doesn't know if she still has it. Eyes still closed, she reaches into her bag. The first thing her bloody fingers touch is a smooth surface, a small rectangle. She takes hold, pulls it out, and opens her eyes. "Molly Cates," it says, "Associate Editor, *Lone Star Monthly.*" At the bottom is a phone number.

That's it. Fate.

She'll call her.

She'll tell her about Tin Can, and about what she heard under the deck, and about the book and what it says about soman, and about Billy Goat attacking her in the library. She'll tell Bopeep everything and make her believe it. Then she'll ask *her* to tell it to the police. That's a good idea. She's respectable. They'll believe her.

After she rests awhile, calling Bopeep still seems like a good idea, and there have been no more sirens and no police cars that she can see, so Sarah Jane gets up and hoists her bag to her shoulder. She starts walking west, looking for a pay phone. After many blocks she spots one right inside the door of a convenience store. She enters, ignoring the hostile glares from the two men behind the counter.

She rummages around her bag, first for the card, then for her coin purse. She unzips the little purse. Inside is one quarter. That's all—just one quarter. Fate again. She is meant to make this call.

She dials the number on the card. The phone rings three times, then a voice says, *"Hi, this is Molly Cates. Leave me a message at the beep and I will return your call."* Then there is a long beep, and silence.

Sarah Jane is flustered. She doesn't know what to do, so she says, "Uh, hello. This is..." She pauses, recalling that she never told the woman her real name. "This is the friend of Tin Can, the one in the bathroom the other day. Remember? I'm Cow Lady and you gave me a card and said to call if I wanted to talk sometime. Well, I...want to talk. It's important. But I got no number for you to call me back at. And this is my only quarter, so I'm not sure what to do." She pauses. "I know! They take messages at HOBO. Maybe you could call there. I don't know the—" A quick beep cuts her off, then a dial tone. The fucking machine has hung up on her! She stands there holding the phone to her ear, feeling abandoned.

Slowly she puts the receiver back and watches the coin return, hoping her quarter will slide down. It doesn't, of course, but she sticks her finger in just to make sure.

"You need something, lady?"

One of the men has come out from behind the counter. He is staring at her, his hands on his hips.

One more person who thinks he owns the world—they're everywhere. But Sarah Jane is too tired and shaky to give him a hard time. She shakes her head.

On her way out she glances over at the cooler against the wall where they probably have some Thunder Chicken, but the only money she has is Ellie's hundred-dollar bill pinned in her shirt and, of course, she can't spend that. Anyway, the drinking is killing her. Maybe it's time to stop.

She steps outside, out of the air conditioning into the heavy afternoon heat, and wonders where Lufkin is hanging. She thinks she'll look for him. Then she'll check HOBO for a message. If there is a message, she'll scrounge a quarter to call Bopeep back, and she'll tell her everything.

She'll leave it in the hands of fate, right where it's always been anyhow.

CHAPTER 15

RIDE A COCK-HORSE TO BANBURY CROSS,
TO SEE AN OLD LADY UPON A WHITE HORSE.
RINGS ON HER FINGERS AND BELLS ON HER TOES,
SHE SHALL HAVE MUSIC WHEREVER SHE GOES.
—*MOTHER GOOSE*

It was the land of the living dead.

Eyes as faded and vacant as milk-glass marbles, they sat staring at motes of dust drifting through shafts of rosy evening sunlight. Their skeletal, blue-veined hands plucked at their clothes or at the blankets across their laps or at any warm-blooded creature passing within their range. This common room with its chintz-covered wicker furniture and big-screen TV was the antechamber to eternity, where the half-dead, slumped in wheelchairs, waited for whatever was to come next. Molly Cates hoped that eternity would prove more interesting for them than the assisted living wing of the Regency Oaks Senior Care Center in Lubbock, Texas.

As she walked down the hallway toward Harriet Cates's private room, she steeled herself against the familiar waves of guilt. It was more than three months since her last visit. And the only reason she was here now was that she wanted something. She was a piss-poor excuse for a niece, negligent and squeamish, repelled, in spite of her efforts not to be, by sickness and decay. Her repugnance, she acknowledged, was born of fear: this place was her worst nightmare. These frail, helpless old people filled her with dread for her own future, her own vulnerability, her own inevitable losses. Maybe she would grow up someday and come to terms with death, but she would never come to terms with incontinence and senility. Never. She turned the corner and came to a stop outside room 136.

The door stood open and the last rays of daylight streamed in from the west-facing window. The hospital bed with its crisp white sheets was so expertly made that even the Harriet Cates of old, the perfectionist whose house stood ready day and night just in case *House Beautiful* should arrive to photograph it, would have approved. The cream-colored linoleum floor was sparkling clean and a fresh yellow rose stood in a cut-glass vase on the night table. This place, Molly conceded, was as good as nursing homes got; she'd chosen it herself, mainly because they managed, somehow, to avoid the usual urine and disinfectant reek, and Aunt Harriet had always been particularly fastidious about odors. In the hallway the only discernible smell was of chicken cooking.

In a chrome wheelchair next to the window sat Harriet Cates Cavanaugh. She looked thinner than she had three months before. Her head was tipped back slightly and on her face was an expression of pure bliss. Behind her stood a nurse's aide gently brushing the old woman's sparse yellowish-white hair. Molly had to swallow twice before she could find her voice. "There you are, Aunt Harriet." She walked in slowly, watching her aunt's face closely for some spark of recognition. On her last visit, Molly had stayed for several hours and had dinner in the dining room during which they'd talked about the food and her aunt's pains and the weather, but she'd left uncertain whether Harriet had known who she was.

She bent and kissed her aunt's cheek. Under her lips, the skin felt as dry and ridged as corrugated paper, dead and loose, as if it had separated from the supply of warm blood underneath and was being sloughed off. It seemed to Molly that the old woman's journey toward death had been a piece-by-piece shedding of body parts—teeth, hair, a breast, muscles, brain cells, and now skin. What continued to surprise Molly was how much of your original body you could live without—all those things you once believed essential.

The old woman turned her face toward Molly. The eyes that had once been large and dark and almond-shaped, snapping with irony and opinion, just like her younger brother's, were now cloudy and nearly obscured by hanging folds of cracked skin like some prehistoric lizard's. But Molly thought she glimpsed a response there—a slight narrowing of the eyes and a squeezing together of the eyebrows. She was staring at Molly with the intent, unsettled, dour look of someone trying hard to remember past grudges.

"Aunt Harriet, hi. How are you?" Molly squatted down, took her aunt's fragile hands in hers. "It's so good to see you."

Harriet said nothing, but Molly thought the corners of her aunt's mouth curled up just an iota.

Molly glanced up at the nurse's aide, a young black woman with smooth tight skin over plump cheeks. "Miz Cavanaugh's been waitin' on you all day," the woman drawled. "We been telling her you coming, and she's been real excited."

"Really?" Molly was never sure how much of what the staff here said about the patients was sensitive observation and how much of it was wishful thinking, like anthropomorphizing animals to make them more lovable. She looked at her aunt's knit brow and narrowed eyes: somewhere behind those dulled eyes did the real Harriet Cates Cavanaugh still live? Maybe all her memories were still there intact, bundled up inside that Alzheimer's mess of neurofibroid tangles, waiting for Molly to tap into them. If she just knew how. The phone call, for example, the one Harriet made to her brother a week before he died, the call that changed him, caused him to break his engagement. Surely something that important was still in her memory bank. What had they talked about? Why had she never told Molly about it?

"Really?" Molly repeated. "She was excited I was coming?" Then she looked back at Harriet apologetically. It was inexcusable to talk about someone as if they weren't there, even if they were senile, but she felt desperate to know what she could expect, if she had a prayer of getting what she came for.

"Oh, yes, ma'am," the nurse said. "Real excited. She said you was her niece and she wanted to look good when you came." She patted the old woman on the head. "Wanted to get yourself pretty for your niece, didn't you, sweetheart?" She slipped a pink ribbon under Harriet's thin hair at the back of the neck and, with one smooth movement, tied it in a bow on top of her head. "Now don't she look pretty!" she said, stepping back and surveying the old woman in the wheelchair.

Molly looked at the ridiculous pink bow perched on top of her aunt's head. This was an indignity Harriet, the real Harriet, that striking woman with sleek black hair and flawless taste, would never have allowed. She had always dressed simply and elegantly in dark colors—no ruffles, no frills, and no pink bows, for God's sake.

"Really?" Molly felt like a broken record. "She said her niece was coming?"

"She sure did." The nurse put the brush back in the dresser drawer. "I'll leave you two ladies to it. Have a real nice visit. We hope you'll stay for supper. It's at six. Miz Cavanaugh will tell you what's on the menu."

"Thanks," Molly said, standing up.

After the nurse left, Molly drew the door shut, pulled the room's one chair close to the wheelchair, and sat facing her aunt, who had not once taken her eyes off Molly's face. Molly reached out and picked up the frail dry hands. "Aunt Harriet, it's me, Molly."

The old woman nodded.

"That's right. I came to see you. And I need to ask you something important."

Harriet withdrew her hands from Molly's grasp. She held them out in front of her, palms down. "Where's my ring?" she asked in the rich contralto of her old self, only slightly shaky. "Do you know where it is?"

"Your diamond ring, you mean? Your engagement ring?"

"My diamond ring." She lowered her voice. "I think they stole it."

"No, Aunt Harriet, they didn't steal it. It's in your lock-box—for safekeeping. You remember when you came here it was one of the rules: all valuables have to be kept in the lock-box in the office. Your good watch and some of your other jewelry are there too."

"Where's my ring?"

"In the lockbox. We can get it out after we talk. You could wear it to dinner if you want."

Harriet nodded.

"It sure is good to see you and hear your voice, Aunt Harriet. I hope they're taking good care of you here. Are they?"

Harriet squinted and looked confused. Finally she patted her hair and said, "They fix my hair for me."

"Is there anything you need? Anything I can do for you?"

There was no response.

Molly looked into the hooded eyes. "Well, Aunt Harriet, there's something *you* can do for me." As soon as she said it, she realized how much a part of their lifelong pattern this was. It had always been Molly in need of something—a place to stay, a loan, a car, a shoulder to cry on, someone to take care of her daughter, comfort, support—she had always needed something.

"As usual," Molly said with a rueful smile, "I've come because I need something from you. Hasn't that always been the way? I come back to you when I need something."

Harriet nodded in a matter-of-fact way, as if acknowledging that it was the proper course of things.

"You remember Franny Lawrence, don't you?"

Harriet looked vacant.

"The woman Daddy was going to marry, at Lake Travis. Franny. Well, I was talking to her and she told me something I hadn't known. She said that, a week before Daddy disappeared, she was at the houseboat with him. He got a phone call and it was from you. You called Daddy and told him something, maybe that someone from Lubbock was coming to see him. It might have had to do with some old business. You remember that?"

Harriet's eyebrows moved closer together, as if she were thinking hard, trying to remember. It gave Molly a faint ray of hope.

"You remember that phone call?" Molly prodded.

Harriet pursed her lips.

"Franny says Daddy changed after that. So I wondered who it was who came to see him. I'd really like to know that, Aunt Harriet."

Harriet didn't speak.

"You're the only one I can ask, the only one who knows. Please tell me. Please try to remember."

The line of concentration between Harriet's eyebrows deepened, as if she were making a supreme effort. "They *told* me what it was."

Molly was electrified. "Who told you? What?"

Harriet looked up to the ceiling, as if searching for the answer there.

"Let me help you remember," Molly said, excited, eager to jar loose some more words. "It was May of 1970, a year after we'd moved from Lubbock. Remember? You were unhappy we'd left, lonesome. Uncle Donald had died two years before and Daddy tried to get you to move to Austin to be closer to us, but you decided to stay in Lubbock in your old house. I was a junior in high school. Remember? We talked on the phone a lot. I was sixteen and I had a boyfriend, and you used to warn me about being careful. Remember?"

"I think so," she murmured with a faraway look.

Molly's pulse raced. It was working. "It was May and I was being inducted into the National Honor Society, and Daddy asked you to come, but you said no because you were planning to come for his wedding in just a few weeks. Daddy was going to marry Franny Lawrence. Remember? He was so happy and so much in love. And you kept telling me I needed to be nice to Franny because she was a very nice woman who loved Daddy, and she was going to be my stepmother whether I liked it or not, but I wasn't nice. And you know something, Aunt Harriet? You were right. She *was* a very nice woman."

Molly was excited because the old woman's eyes had come alive with interest and response. Talking to her about it was working. "But after that phone call, Daddy broke his engagement to Franny. He said he couldn't marry her or anyone. Why not? What happened? What did you talk about? Would the date help? I figured it out. It would have been May14." Molly stopped to catch her breath.

Harriet's face was suddenly animated, her mouth open, eyes shining.

"The phone call," Molly said. "You're remembering it."

Harriet put her fingers to her temples.

"What did you and Daddy talk about? What?"

Harriet suddenly lifted her hands in the air and opened her eyes wide, as if she were miming a person having an idea. "Oh, yes!" she said.

Molly's heart hammered her ribs. "Yes—?"

"Fried chicken and mashed potatoes. Peach cobbler. They told me and I remembered."

"What?"

"For dinner. Things you like."

Molly exhaled slowly. She could not believe this. "Dinner?"

"Stay." Harriet reached out and gripped Molly's wrist with her clawlike hand. "Please stay."

All this time the old woman had been trying to remember the goddamn dinner menu, not the phone call. Molly felt like taking her by the shoulders and shaking her until the memory Molly needed came unstuck.

"Yes," Molly said slowly, "of course I'll stay." She needed to get control of herself.Trying to hector this poor senile old woman into remembering something she didn't remember was stupid. Worse! It was cruel. But this was the last chance. Each time Molly came to visit, Harriet was more confused and disoriented. Now the fog of senility was poised to engulf her totally. Molly could see it hovering behind her aunt.

It was now or never.

She *had* to try.

Molly looked into the dark, hooded eyes. "You remember I like fried chicken and peach cobbler. And you remember the dinner menu they told you, right?"

Harriet cocked her head, listening.

"So you *can* remember when it's important to you. I think

you can remember that phone call, too. And the other phone calls after that, the week before Daddy died. You can do it if you try. Like you did with the fried chicken just now."

Harriet was watching her intently, the skin on her forehead cracked into a web of anxiety.

"Now, Aunt Harriet," Molly said, "let me walk you through it. You were in Lubbock. You called Vernon at the houseboat, his office number. It was May, and Vernon was planning to get married in two weeks. They'd just told us. Remember what a surprise that was?"

Harriet nodded.

Molly felt her pulse race; of course she remembered. It was just a matter of extracting it. "You talked to him on the phone and—"

"At two," Harriet said wistfully, "he could talk like a grownup. He could sing the whole alphabet song. I taught him. I taught it to you, too, and then...Jo." She had to grope for the name. "Jo Beth, yes. Vern, then Molly, then Jo Beth. But he was quickest." Her face was infused with the pleasure of a warm memory. "We sat on the porch in the big rocking chair. And he sang on tune. The smartest little boy I ever saw."

"Yes, he was smart. He was forty-five, though, when you made that phone call. The week before he died. Remember?"

The smile faded from her face. She *was* remembering. Just a little more pushing and she might get there. "We'd been living there a year and this was the week before he disappeared. It was awful—that five days he was missing. And then they found him in the lake. Remember?"

Harriet began to hum low in her throat. It took awhile, but Molly finally recognized it as the alphabet song. "H-I-J-K-L-M-N-O-P," she hummed.

Molly was desperate not to lose the ground she'd gained; she went on talking right over the humming. "What about the week before he disappeared? Franny says Daddy was depressed and you and Parnell talked about him going to see a psychiatrist. Parnell says so too. You never told me that, Aunt Harriet. How come?"

"He was so smart he skipped first grade. Did you know

that? The first week they saw he could read and all, so they put him ahead a year. And I taught him. I was the one taught him to read. And write. I taught him cursive. I saved all his papers he brought home—A's and gold stars mostly. Mama and Papa didn't bother with that much, but I did. I saved all his drawings and stories, everything he ever wrote, even later on. And he always told me everything that happened at school and I—"

Molly had heard all this hundreds of times; she was sick of it. "I know. You were such a good big sister. You two were very close. But later when he was a grown man and we moved away from Lubbock—that's what I want to know about. The last week of his life. Help me, Aunt Harriet. Help me one last time."

"He was so smart in school. He could have done anything he wanted. But it's hard to settle on just one thing when you're so smart. At six he was reading chapter books and by eight—"

"I know," Molly interrupted, "by eight he was reading Sir Walter Scott." Tears of frustration welled up. "You always tell me how wonderful he was. Tell me something I *don't* know. Tell me about his other women. Did he do that while my mother was still alive? Tell me about his failures, his money problems, his drinking, his depressions. You never talk about those things, Aunt Harriet. Tell me about his writing. Was he good at it?" She was losing control. She felt like screaming, kicking, demanding what she had every right to know. "For God's sake," she hissed, "tell me. Help me while you still can."

Harriet squinted as if in pain from a splitting headache. "Bad things. I don't think about the bad things and you shouldn't either. He was a good man. And the *smartest* little boy." She began to wring her hands, a gesture she'd begun making about a year ago when she was exceptionally frustrated and stressed. "Don't think about the end."

"Everyone gives me that advice. But I need to know. Tell me just one thing—about that phone call. That's the thing I really need to know. Please tell me and then we won't think about it anymore. Okay?"

Harriet's hand-wringing accelerated. It made Molly's nerves jump and twitch. It made her talk faster, push harder. "He answered the phone," she mimed putting a phone to her ear, "and you said, 'Hi, Vern,' and maybe he said that Franny was there with him and you said . . . what?"

Harriet squeezed her eyes closed as if she were expecting a blow to fall.

Molly leaned forward so she was just inches from her aunt. "What did you say? You *must* remember." Her voice was rising, but she couldn't stop it. Maybe it took some volume to break through those dense tangles in that shrunken brain. "What? What did you say to him?"

Harriet's face was scrunched into a mask of misery. From under her closed lids a few fat tears slid out and slowly ran down the deep crevasses in her cheeks.

Molly looked with horror at the tears. She had never seen Harriet cry before, never, not when Harriet had her miscarriages, not when her husband Donald had died, not when Vernon Cates had floated to the surface of Lake Travis, not when Molly had made her move out of her house and into this place. But now Molly had made her cry. What in God's name did she think she was doing? This was her sick, feeble old aunt who had loved and cared for her all her life. Now that it was Molly's turn to do the caretaking, here she was bullying her, making her cry. It was inexcusable. She was acting like a spoiled child, throwing a tantrum to get what she wanted.

Molly sat back in her chair. She'd failed to meet even the minimal standard for love and compassion. "Aunt Harriet, I'm sorry," she said very softly.

Harriet opened her eyes slowly. "Molly, Molly," she said, as if she were speaking to a bad but beloved two-year-old. "You shouted."

"I guess I did. But I've always been a royal pain in the ass, haven't I?"

Harriet let out a puff of air that sounded exactly like a chuckle.

Molly said, "But you did your share of the shouting, Aunt Harriet. In the old days. Oh, the fights we had! Remember the knock-down-drag-out about my staying out past midnight? And where I was going to live after Daddy was killed? You know something? I miss those fights. Now there's no one who cares enough to fight with me."

They had never been demonstrative with one another, rarely expressed mutual affection, so between the two of them this amounted to a gush of emotion. Now that she'd started, Molly went on with the things she'd always meant to say and hadn't. "All my life I've counted on you, Aunt Harriet. To be there for me, no matter what I did. And you always were. Always. I don't think I've ever thanked you, have I?"

They looked at one another in silence for a while. Then Harriet began to sing slowly, "A-B-C-D-E-F-G-" She stopped and her eyes rolled in panic. She'd forgotten what came next.

"H-I-J-K-L-M-N-O-P," Molly carried on for her.

"Where's my ring?" Harriet demanded, holding her hands out."I think they stole it."

There was a knock on the door. It opened and the young nurse stuck her head in. "Ladies, supper," she chirped.

"Fried chicken?" Harriet said, squinting at Molly. "Mashed potatoes?"

"So I hear."

"Stay, Molly."

"I will." Molly leaned forward and untied the pink bow in her aunt's hair. "Of course I'll stay." She pulled the ribbon off and dropped it into the wastebasket. "Let's go get your ring from the lockbox. Okay?"

"I'll wear it to supper," Harriet said with a smile.

"Yeah. We'll go formal."

NO OBSERVER, SEEING THE VIOLENCE THAT FLARED
CONTINUALLY ON TEXAS' LONG FRONTIER, CAN
FAIL TO UNDERSTAND THE ENSUING PROBLEMS OF
LAW AND ORDER THAT BESET THE STATE. BY 1835,
ANGLO TEXAS WAS DRAWING MEN WHO SOUGHT
VIOLENCE LIKE STRONG DRINK; IF THEY COULD NOT
FIND A WAR, THEY WERE DISPOSED TO MAKE ONE.
—T. R. FEHRENBACH, *LONE STAR*

Molly didn't use her free morning in Lubbock to drive out to
the old ranch near Crosbyton. She didn't drive by Aunt
Harriet's house either—the old Victorian house on Mesquite
Trail, where she'd lived during ninth and tenth grades because her father wanted her to go to high school in Lubbock
rather than the little school in Crosbyton. She didn't call the
one high school friend she still kept in touch with. She didn't
call home for her messages as she usually did. She didn't call
Grady as she had promised. She didn't even get out of her
bed at the Ramada Inn until two hours before her noon appointment with Shelby Palmer.

She couldn't face Lubbock—the eternal wind, the red
dust, the flatness. The past. And she couldn't face Julian
Palmer's version of her father as a depressed, womanizing
ne'er-do-well. During her eighteen hours in Lubbock, she
had managed to be inside the entire time except for the
drive from the airport to Palmer's office, then to the nursing
home and the motel. It was possible, if you kept your blind-
ers on, to travel to a city and never actually *be* there.

She kept the motel room cold and dark and tried to sleep,
but ended up lying in bed with her eyes closed. She hoped

that if she stayed very still and pretended to be asleep the flood of mood-darkening chemicals she felt marshaling force in her bloodstream might just peter out without her feeling them.

It seemed to work, because when she finally got up and took a long shower she felt better. She'd forgotten to buy a toothbrush, so she scrubbed her teeth with a washcloth. After putting yesterday's clothes back on, she glanced around the room to see if she'd forgotten anything. No suitcase and nothing to pack. It sure made checking out simpler. It felt so free, Molly decided to try it more often; over the years she'd become increasingly encumbered when she traveled, hauling around accouterments like hair dryers and travel clocks, extra shoes and books, sweaters and raincoats—things she might need, but usually didn't.

While she was waiting for a late breakfast of cornflakes and fruit at the coffee shop, she rummaged through her purse for the paper Cullen Shoemaker had given her on Monday. She found it crumpled at the bottom. Until yesterday she'd had no intention of reading it, but after hearing his rant yesterday she felt a morbid curiosity.

She smoothed it out and read it as she sipped her coffee. His thesis was that Jews and blacks and immigrants and women's libbers and intellectuals and the mass media had taken over the government. They were conspiring with the ATF to disarm white Americans and then force on them their "Jewish-liberal-equalitarian plague." The only hope was for white native-born males to band together in armed vigilance committees like the McNelly Posse to defeat the "mulatto zombies." If violence was necessary to accomplish that, then violence it would be.

His speech at the hearing had been a greatly sanitized version that stuck pretty much to the concealed handgun issue. This "McNelly Manifesto," as he titled it, went way beyond that. It was hair-raising stuff. Just reading it gave her an unclean feeling.

What was particularly unsettling about it was Shoemaker's insistence that all forms of gun control and registration should be resisted to the death.

It was so unsettling that Molly thought she ought to pass it on to someone, but she didn't know who. She'd ask Grady or Parnell if she ought to do something with it.

She drove her rental car back to the Cap Rock Office Park and again arrived ten minutes early at Shelby Palmer's office. This time, when she walked in, she didn't get a smile from Mrs. Palmer. "He was up all night on your matter," the white-haired woman said. "Man his age with an ulcer ought to know better. You can go on back."

Shelby Palmer was wearing the same clothes, too, and he looked rumpled and discouraged, which made Molly's fragile spirits sink. He came around from behind his cluttered desk to shake hands with her. "Miz Cates, sit down. Coffee?"

"Never past noon. Thanks."

He looked at his watch. "You've still got six minutes."

"Oh, I'd love some then."

He hollered out the door. "Two coffees, Mama?"

He went back to his desk and picked up a yellow legal pad. "Computer sure is a boon to this business."

"I bet."

"In the old days it would've taken me weeks to do what I did last night. I read the Toser file and I'm sorry I can't let you see it, but you know how unethical it would be without Jim Ray Toser's okay. I finally got hold of him this morning, and he emphatically did *not* approve my giving you access to the file. He recognized your name and said the last thing he wanted was to see this smeared all over *Lone Star Monthly*. But when I explained your personal interest, and promised him you wouldn't write about this—" He paused and looked hard at her. "You *do* promise that?"

Molly nodded solemnly.

"Good. When I explained all that, Toser said it was okay to share with you the part about the money—the fifty thousand cash, since that's really the item which might pertain to your matter."

He sat down. "Unfortunately, there's nothing of substance to share. Dad never figured out where it came from. Tracking cash is almost impossible." He looked down at his yellow pad. "He did narrow it down some. He talked with

Crocker's wife, who was by then about to be his ex-wife, and whoever said hell hath no fury like a woman scorned must've had Ruth Crocker in mind. She said Crocker was interested in two things: making money by any means and getting into young girls' pants. The reason she finally divorced him, she said, is that he was even bringing the girls home, and some of them were younger than his own daughters. Anyway, she said that the fifty thousand dollars did not come from anything she knew of. No rich uncles, no insurance policies. And he sure as hell didn't save it up. Crocker never had so much as a pot to piss in the whole twenty-two years she knew him. She said she didn't even know about that house investment until Toser came around asking about it. Her bet was the money was ill-gotten, but she wanted her community property half of that house anyway."

Mrs. Palmer entered with two steaming Styrofoam cups. "What do you take, Miz Cates?"

"Just black. Thanks."

"Makes it easy. Mr. Trion called," she told her son. "He'll be here at one-thirty. You should take a nap first."

"Thanks, Mama."

When she'd gone he said, "I checked the property records, and Dad was right on, as usual. Crocker put down $51,432 cash for the house on August 13, 1970. Where the money came from is anybody's guess. I imagine the only people who know are Crocker and whoever paid him."

Molly looked down into the black depths of her steaming coffee cup and marveled at how many dead ends one question could have. Here was another. She should be getting used to it by now, but she felt as frustrated and inadequate as she always had.

"You look lost," Shelby Palmer said.

"Yeah? A bag lady I ran into the other day called me Little Bopeep, because I looked like I just lost my sheep. It's pretty bad when you have bag ladies feeling sorry for you."

"I know you're disappointed, but here's something else I can tell you. That house Crocker bought was leased by a business called Miracle Massage. It was a front for prostitution.

According to Ruth and several other pretty good sources, none of whom would ever testify to it, Crocker was involved in the business and was not just an unwitting landlord. Miracle Massage is now defunct, but it operated right up to '88. I believe the profits from this made it possible for Crocker to retire and be the gentleman farmer he now is."

"Where's Ruth now?"

"Living in Oklahoma with her oldest son and his family. Works for the city, never remarried."

Molly blew on her coffee. "Have there been other wives?"

"Ah, you're getting ahead of me. There have been two more—Jeanette and Kelly. The most recent one, Kelly, divorced him last year. When they got married she was nineteen, he was fifty-nine. She's so angry she makes Ruth sound like a purring kitten. It seems she caught Crocker diddling girls from the local junior high—repeatedly."

"*Junior* high?"

"Yup. She's also mad that Crocker out-lawyered her in the divorce and she ended up having to go back to work at the Dairy Queen."

"I wonder if Kelly would testify if we could get an indecency with a child charge brought against Crocker?"

He did a little drumbeat on the desk with his fingers. "I had a feeling you'd want to know that. She says she might, and if she did, she could nail his balls to the barn door—that's a direct quote."

"That's interesting. Would you call her back and see if you can get the names of some of the girls who got diddled?"

He made a note on his yellow pad. "Sure. Now, we come to your second question—the two young women who initiated the suit against Crocker back in '75. I don't know if this is worth the vast sum you're about to pay me for having stayed up all night, but I did track them down. The first one, Christine Fanon, is dead, I'm sorry to say. Heroin overdose in '84 in Houston. Prostitute, IV drug user, long record of drug and prostitution charges. The other one—Sylvia Ramos—has a prostitution record from Austin and Houston. She's living in El Paso now. But more than that I couldn't get. She doesn't have a driver's license or pay property taxes, but she is on the voter rolls."

Sylvia Ramos in El Paso. Molly found her interest picking up here. "Mr. Palmer, I'd like to hire you to fly down to El Paso and follow up on Sylvia Ramos. Today, if possible."

"Sorry, Miz Cates. I can do the phone follow-up with the third ex-wife because that won't take long, but I can't go anywhere. I'm booked solid for the next three weeks at least, and so is my associate. Last night I fit you in because Mr. Quinlan had asked me to give you all possible assistance."

"I see. Have you got an address in El Paso for her?"

"Yes, ma'am. It's in the report Mama's typing up for you right now." He shook his head. "But you don't want to do this yourself."

"Why not?"

"My hunch is Sylvia Ramos lives in circumstances a lady shouldn't go into by herself."

"A lady?" Molly said, raising her eyebrows at a word she hated. "I don't see any of those around here."

"Sorry. I'm old-fashioned. But even if it weren't dangerous, what is there to learn from her? That Crocker was guilty of official misconduct twenty-some years ago? We already know that and the meter's run out on any crimes he may have committed back then."

Molly nodded. He was probably right, but she had a long tradition of leaving no lead unfollowed. And this was the only one left.

"You ready for question number three?" he asked.

"Definitely." She took a swig of coffee.

He looked down at his yellow pad. "Olin Crocker lives on a farm near Taylor. Alone, since Kelly divorced him last year. He's got fifteen hundred acres. Bought them in '82. Listed on the tax rolls as worth more than two million, but they're in cultivation so he's got an agricultural exemption. He's a prosperous citizen, done right well for himself. He's got four hundred thousand dollars in CDs at the Williamson Bank. In January of this year he registered as a lobbyist for TEXRA, just as you said. But other than that he hasn't worked since 1974 when he left the sheriff's office."

"Got an address and phone?"

"Yes, ma'am. Both unlisted. They'll be in the report."

"I understand you can't let me read the Toser report, but could you tell me how Toser used the information? I'm assuming if there had been something indictable Toser would have gone for it."

"My guess is he used it to scare Crocker out of the race."

"Anything else?" Molly asked.

He looked down at his pad again, then shook his head. "That's it."

She stood up. "Many thanks for taking this on when you're so busy."

He reached out his hand. "I wish we could've gotten more for you."

"Well," Molly said, taking hold of his hand, "it may turn out to be enough."

"You aren't going to El Paso, are you?"

"No. I'm going home."

"Good."

On the way out Molly picked up the report from Mrs. Palmer and wrote a check for four hundred dollars for a night of Shelby Palmer's time. It felt like a bargain.

Molly didn't know for sure what she was going to do until she got to the Lubbock airport and saw the flight to El Paso listed. It was leaving in a half hour, before the next flight to Austin. There was one seat left; it felt like fate beckoning. She bought the ticket and, with no bags to check or carry, headed straight to the gate. She'd planned to call home for her messages, but there wasn't time. She stopped at the newsstand, bought a *New York Times* and a toothbrush, and boarded the plane, with a quivery feeling in her chest.

She sat down in her window seat and looked out at her hometown framed in the tiny window. The brown earth was so relentlessly flat and featureless there was almost a purity to it. As the plane taxied down the runway, the vibration of the engine set the quiver in her chest to humming a familiar tune. If she were forced to give words to the tune, it would be

Willie Nelson's "On the Road Again." She felt light and un-encumbered, like a young girl again, running away from home and destined for danger and illicit excitement. She had felt some version of this every single time she left Lubbock.

By the time they landed in El Paso an hour later, she'd fin-ished the crossword puzzle and read everything in the paper except the business pages, which she always intended to read and never did. One look out the window at the encircling mountains, all mauve and rust and pale green, and she knew she wasn't in Lubbock anymore.

She rented a car and enlisted the agent's help in finding Sylvia Ramos's address on the map. It turned out to be less than two miles from the airport. Fate again.

She'd been to El Paso only once before and that was thirty years ago with her daddy on one of their road trips. But it had made an impression on her. Ever since that visit she'd thought of El Paso as the place she'd run away to if she ever needed to lose herself. The city was an escape fantasy, as far west as you could go and still stay in Texas. It had for her that romantic, last-chance, end-of-the-line, barely civilized feel that border towns had. Here anything could happen. You could change your identity and get away with it; you could live life on the edge.

Chester Avenue was a block from Highway 54 and four blocks from Fort Bliss, in a neighborhood that could easily have been found in Mexico. Not surprising since the border was only three miles to the south. The house was a tiny cinder-block box painted bright blue. The yard was packed dirt that looked like it had been swept with a broom recently. When she got out of the car, three nearly naked children and a skinny mongrel in the yard next door stared wide-eyed, as if she'd dropped from Mars. There was no doorbell, so Molly knocked on the unpainted, warped screen door, carefully, to avoid getting splinters in her knuckles. A man in his twenties, wearing only a pair of blue jeans, opened the door and glared at her.

"Hi. I'm looking for Sylvia Ramos. Is she home?"

"Sylvia?" He looked panicked. "Ma!" He bellowed it like a cry for help as he walked away. "Ma!"

A woman with strands of long white hair stuck to her sweaty face came to the door, drying her hands on a dishtowel. Sylvia Ramos would be forty-three now, Molly figured, and even taking into account the wear and tear of a hard life, this woman was too old. She squinted at Molly through the screen.

"Hi. I'm Molly Cates. Sorry to bother you, but I'm looking for Sylvia Ramos."

Her face stony, the woman stared at Molly and continued to dry her hands. "Sylvia? What for?"

"I have a message for her."

"You give it to me. I see she gets it."

"Are you related to her?"

The woman shrugged and started to close the door.

"Wait!" Molly said, resisting the impulse to stick her foot in the door. "I need to see her. It's really important. I flew here from Austin just to talk to her."

The woman paused with the door half closed.

"I need help," Molly said, looking her in the eye. "Please. I'm not with the police or immigration or anything like that. I promise I won't hurt her in any way."

"What you want with Sylvia?"

"A man who did something very bad to her, a long time ago, also did something bad to me. I just want to talk about it with her."

The woman was silent, looking Molly up and down.

"Where can I find her?" Molly asked.

"You want Sylvia," the woman said, "try downtown tonight. Cebeda Street. After nine."

"But how will I find her? I don't even know what she looks like."

She shrugged. "Ask anyone. Corner Cebeda and Duranzo. There's a bar—Las Brujas. They all know her there. La Risa, they call her." Her mouth tightened, sending out rays of wrinkles from her lips.

"I'm only in town for a few hours," Molly said. "Isn't there somewhere I can find her now? A phone number where I could call her?"

The woman shook her head.

"Well, I can understand that you wouldn't want to give out her number to a stranger. Maybe you could call her and ask her to—"

"She got no phone. You want to see her, you look for her tonight."

Molly unfolded her map. "Cebeda and Duranzo, you said? Could you—"

Before she could ask, the woman closed the door.

Molly got into her rental car. She was still close enough to the airport to get back there for the five o'clock flight to Austin. But only if she left now. If she didn't catch that flight, she'd have to stay here tonight and she wanted to get home, needed to get home. This was going to be a waste of time—it had all the signs. Sylvia Ramos would turn out to be a strung-out whore who wouldn't even remember she had ever been in Austin.

But she was here now and her blood was beginning to simmer with the chase. By the time she drove the few blocks to the highway, she knew she'd stay. She pulled into the first motel that looked clean, an Econo Lodge, and checked in.

Once in her room she turned up the air conditioning and called home for her messages. There were lots since she hadn't checked them for more than twenty-four hours: Jo Beth wondering if Molly would be back for exercise class; her editor reminding her to cover the actual passage of the bill, which his sources told him would happen in two days; her friend Barbara inviting her to go out and get drunk and listen to her latest tale of romantic woe; Cullen Shoemaker checking to see if she'd gotten his fax confirming her Monday interview with Garland Rauther and apologizing that he wouldn't be there because he'd gotten fired and was taking his mother on a vacation; a really strange one, from the bag lady she'd met in the Capitol bathroom, wanting to tell her something, asking her to leave a message at HOBO; Grady, upset she hadn't called last night; Grady again, worried about her, telling her Calvin Shawcross wanted to talk to her about Emily Bickerstaff.

Molly played them again to hear the bag lady message. It had come in yesterday at five-thirty and got cut off in mid-sentence. The woman's voice had a desperate sound, very different from the belligerent tone Molly remembered from their encounter in the bathroom. She sounded sick or upset, or both. She must have gotten the news about her friend Tin Can getting killed. Shawcross would surely want to talk to her if he hadn't located her already. She should call him and tell him to pick the woman up at HOBO if he wanted her. But the woman wanted to talk to Molly; to call the police seemed like such a betrayal of confidence. Still, alerting Sergeant Shawcross was the responsible thing. Damn. She didn't know what to do. She picked up the phone and dialed Grady's office number. She got his pager and punched in the Econo Lodge number.

She called information in Austin and got the number for HOBO. A man answered. She asked if he knew a woman called Cow Lady. "Sure do," he said. "You want me to see if she's around? Wait a sec." Moments later he came back on the line. "They tell me she was here, but she left."

"I'd like to leave a message for her. In case she comes back."

"What's the message?"

"Tell her to call Molly Cates right away, collect at this number." Molly read the number off the phone and had him repeat it. "I'll be waiting for her call," Molly said. "It's important. Please make sure she gets it."

Then she lay down on her bed and wondered what the hell she was doing in a motel in El Paso late on a Friday afternoon when she wanted to be home. She wanted to go out to dinner and to a movie with Grady. She wanted to take him home to bed.

The phone rang.

"You alone?" said the low, mellow voice that had always had just the right amount of hoarse male rasp.

"Uh-huh."

"Lying on your bed?"

"Where else?"

"In a cheap motel?"

"Uh-huh."

"Shades drawn?"

"Uh-huh."

"Naked?"

Molly looked down at her wrinkled slacks and blouse. She hadn't even taken her shoes off. "Yes."

"No, you aren't."

"How would you know?"

"When you're naked your voice is lower, all languorous and liquidy."

"Well," she said, "I could get naked. If you will."

"Mmmmm. Problem is, Captain Lahar and four rookies from Vice are here watching me. Just hearing the word 'naked' makes them get their handcuffs out."

"Too bad."

"Yeah. Vice would be out of business if folks confined themselves to telephone sex. Where the hell is area code 915, Molly? Not Lubbock."

"El Paso."

"Why El Paso?"

"Oh, there's this whore I need to talk to."

"Molly." His voice had gotten suddenly cool.

"Just getting some pointers. Listen, Grady, I got a problem. There was a message on my machine from this homeless woman I told you about—Cow Lady, the one who hung out with Emily Bickerstaff."

"Sarah Jane Hurley."

"Is that her name?"

"Uh-huh. We've been looking for her. What was the message?"

"Well, wait a minute—"

"Molly, don't be coy. Hurley's the primary suspect in a homicide. What was the message?"

"Primary *suspect?*"

"You bet. She was known to be in a dispute with the deceased over a coat, she has an old warrant in Houston for aggravated assault, *and* yesterday she was involved in a fight at the public library. What was the message?"

"Whoa a minute. Was the coat in dispute black- and white-spotted?"

"Yup."

"She was wearing it when I saw her on Monday. Remember, I told you that."

"Well, her dead buddy was wearing it yesterday. What was the message?"

"Oh, Grady, she sounded sick and she wanted to talk to *me*."

"Molly, please."

"If I tell you, will you go pick her up yourself? Shawcross is so intimidating."

"Yes, I'll go myself."

If he said it, you could count on it, and he was the rarest of creatures—a cop with a gentle bedside manner, especially with women. "Okay. She said I should leave her a message at HOBO and she would check there for it."

"When did the message come in?"

"Yesterday at five-thirty. I just called HOBO and left her a message to call me here collect. They said she had been there but wasn't now. Maybe she gave up on me."

"I'll go check."

"Grady, I don't think she did this."

"Molly, you exchanged a few words with the woman in the can and that qualifies you as an expert on her capabilities?"

"She recites nursery rhymes, Grady. What happened in the library?"

"She got in a fight with an unidentified man. There was a razor involved, and she stole a book."

"Was the man injured?"

"We don't know. They both took off fast, but there was some blood on the rug."

"What were they fighting about?"

"We don't know, but she said he was trying to kill her and he said she was stealing a book."

"What book?"

"Oh, Molly, I love you. The title is *A Higher Form of Killing*. It's about chemical and biological warfare, mainly poison gases."

"Poison gases? Really?"

"Molly, I gotta run, sweetheart."

"Call me after you've talked to her?"

"Okay."

Molly put the receiver down, wondering what a bag lady wanted with a book on poison gases and why she would steal it, and whether she really did slit her friend's throat in a dispute over a coat and if the man in the library really was trying to kill her. What was it she wanted to talk to Molly about? Why had she been at the Capitol? She spoke like a woman with some education and more than a little intelligence. What happened to put her out on the street?

The questions were giving her a buzz. There was a story there that she couldn't bring into focus, a jigsaw puzzle with some pieces missing. Molly had a feeling that if the picture ever got reconstructed it would be a fascinating one.

But it wasn't her story. It wasn't what she'd come to El Paso for. For a moment she yearned to be working on the Sarah Jane Hurley puzzle instead of the painful one she was trapped inside of. Puzzles were much more fun and easier to assemble when you weren't personally involved, when it was other people's families and other people's failures and other people's disasters.

She put her head on the pillow.

Maybe this was a wild-goose chase, a waste of her time.

Maybe she was wrong and everyone else was right— Grady and Jo Beth and Parnell, the people she loved. They all said let it drop. Well, maybe El Paso was the end of the trail, anyway. Maybe this nighttime rendezvous with a whore on the Texas border was the last gasp.

17

THERE WAS AN OLD WOMAN TOSSED UP IN A BAS-
   KET,
SEVENTEEN TIMES AS HIGH AS THE MOON;
WHERE SHE WAS GOING I COULDN'T BUT ASK IT,
FOR IN HER HAND SHE CARRIED A BROOM.

"OLD WOMAN, OLD WOMAN, OLD WOMAN," SAID I,
"WHITHER, OH WHITHER, OH WHITHER SO HIGH?"
"TO SWEEP THE COBWEBS FROM THE SKY!"
"SHALL I GO WITH YOU?" "AYE, BY-AND-BY."
                                          —MOTHER GOOSE

Sarah Jane Hurley feels doomed to keep relearning life's les-
sons. Now she remembers this one: if you swear you'll never
do a certain thing, right away fate starts slamming gates so
that eventually all paths are blocked except one, and that one
leads back to the exact thing you swore you'd never do.

After that one night in the Patchwork Pit when she first
arrived in Austin, she left vowing to the heavens that nothing
in the world could ever make her go back there. It has been
more than a year, but now she is heading back, because it is
the only place left to go. Even though she recalls all too
clearly what happened the last time—the cries and pleas of
the old bum Squint and Roylee and some others tortured and
beat nearly to death because he had told the cops that Squint
was running a scam at the day labor cage. Everyone on the
street knew that Squint got the first ten bucks of any day labor job picked up at the cage. If you didn't pay, you ended
up with broken legs.

But this man who squealed got lots more than his legs broken. First they dragged him to the fire and held his fingers in the flames until he confessed he'd done it. Then they beat him to a bloody pulp and dropped him in a vacant lot. Sarah Jane Hurley has sunk pretty low and has even drawn blood herself. But what they did to that old man that night was way beyond what she could stand.

Just south of Town Lake, the Patchwork Pit lies in a draw hidden from sight in a densely wooded area not far from one of the busiest intersections in town. It is well known among the homeless as a vile, bottom-of-the-barrel camping place, dirty and dangerous, where derelicts prey upon one another, where Squint and Roylee bully the down-and-out and manage to squeeze some sort of payment out of them. In exchange, the transients at the camp are not hassled by the law. For some reason having to do with Squint, the cops leave Patchwork pretty much alone, even with the new ban on camping on public land.

So, in spite of it all, she's heading down the dirt path back to Patchwork.

She knows this much: she is sick and exhausted. She needs a place to lie low. Last night after checking for messages at HOBO, and finding none, she was planning to crash on the loading ramp, but she was scared off when she saw a man she was sure must be a cop entering the building. He wasn't in uniform, but he had the look of a cop, so she ended up walking around all night, afraid to settle anywhere, afraid to go back to HOBO. Billy Goat is surely trying to find her again, and if the cops aren't looking for her now, they will be when Tin Can's body is found. Everyone on the street knows she and Tin Can were hanging buddies.

Maybe they already have found Tin Can. It's been more than a day since she and Lufkin found her body. Maybe that's why Lufkin has disappeared. After the library, she looked for him everywhere, hoping he might have scored some bus tickets, but he was in none of the usual places. Maybe she can get a loan from Squint; he did say he'd make it worth her while if she came to Patchwork. She finds she is shivering, even though it is a warm afternoon and not raining yet. Out of cigarettes, she sucks on a piece of grass and hums to keep her courage up.

She smells the Patchwork Pit before she sees it—a stinking mix of rotting garbage, sweat, dog shit, and acrid smoke, which hovers in a filthy haze over the camp like an evil miasma. It is the smell of the bitter end. She tries to straighten up and control her shaking because in a place like Patchwork you can't show weakness.

A dog barks, and several more join in.

Sarah Jane stops and calls out to announce herself. "I'm coming in. It's okay. It's me, Cow Lady." That's so she doesn't alarm them. With the ban on public camping, everyone has gotten real spooky and the folks at Patchwork have better cause than most to be wary.

She pushes through the thick bamboo stand that surrounds the camp and there it is—the rock bottom, the place where you go to wait for the worst life has to offer. The packed dirt clearing is still covered with the squares of old carpet remnants that give the place its name; the fire pit in the center has the same black-encrusted cooking pot sitting on the charred wood. Four dogs and ten people are sitting and lying on the ground, eying her with suspicion. Bedrolls and garbage bags and bottles litter the place. The dogs quiet down but no one greets her.

Out of breath, Sarah Jane lowers her bag to the ground. There is only one other woman; she is sitting with her back against a tree trunk, a filthy child sprawled sleeping in her lap. Sarah Jane surveys the men, looking for Squint and Roylee, but they don't seem to be here, which is a relief.

Across the camp she spots someone she knows— Rhyming Rudy, a small black man who was in the State Hospital with Tin Can and got released about the same time. He used to hang with them down by the creek. Sarah Jane is pleased to see Rudy. He's got this gimmick she really likes: he sells rhymes to people on the drag for a dollar a line. They tell him what the poem should be about and he writes it. It sure beats selling blood. Sarah Jane has always loved rhymes, from when she was a little girl and Gramma read her *Mother*

Goose every night. And she read the same rhymes to Tom and Ellie back in the good days, when she was still trying to be a proper mother.

She hoists up her bag and walks over to talk to Rudy. He is sitting on an upside-down yellow bucket, holding a taco about an inch from his eyes and staring at it. He's one of the smallest men she's ever seen—about eighty pounds. He looks like a little boy sitting there on the bucket.

She surprises herself by saying, *"Little Jack Horner sat in the corner, eating of Christmas pie."* She doesn't usually let the nursery rhymes out, but lately they've been erupting and it worries her. It's this dizzy head of hers, whirling bits of her inner thoughts out into the air against her will.

Rudy looks up at her, his black face scrunched in puzzlement. Then he says, "Cow Lady?"

"Yeah, it's me."

"I didn't hardly know you without your coat, woman."

"Me either."

"What happened to it?"

"I gave it to Tin Can."

Rudy smiles. "Tin Can, she my man."

Suddenly Sarah Jane feels like weeping, something she hasn't done in years. There is a big, sucking, hollow space in her chest. It's Tin Can, that dumpy little twit, that dumb retard. She misses her so much she can barely breathe. "Can I sit down?"

"Take your rest," Rudy says, "be my guest." He studies her face, then says, "Don't look so hot. What bug you got?"

Sarah Jane lowers herself to a carpet square. It is filthy and she can see the fleas bouncing around on it, but she doesn't care. "What bug?" She touches her left leg where the swelling is tender to the touch. "Fire ants."

Rudy finally takes a bite out of the taco. "That big dude ever find you?" he asks with his mouth full.

"What big dude?"

"You know." He lowers his voice and tries to do a German accent. "Talks like Arnold Schwarzenegger."

Sarah Jane shudders. "He was *here?*"

"Yup."

"When was this, Rudy?"

"Yesterday. No, the day before that. I dunno. I lose track."

"What did he want?"

"Don't know." Rudy swallows. His neck is so thin Sarah Jane can see the lump travel down it. "Squint'll know, but he ain't here now. They talked a spell. Then Squint akst me where you was hanging and I tole him down by the creek behind the Grill. Di'n't he find you?"

Sarah Jane can't believe how dense she's been; it must be the fever. "What did the guy look like?" she asks, just to confirm what she already knows.

He shrugs his narrow shoulders. "White dudes. Mike and Ike, all alike."

"But you said he was big and talked like Arnold Schwarzenegger."

Rudy takes another bite and nods. "Big old bear, short gray hair."

She feels her body heat rising but she fights down the fear and turns it to anger. "Rudy, why did you tell him where to find me?"

His eyes shift away from hers. "It was Squint told him, not me. I just give a answer when Squint ast me a question."

"He might of been a cop."

"No. You could see he wasn't no cop. No way, José." Rudy keeps his eyes averted, chewing much longer than necessary.

Sarah Jane has a flash of insight. "He paid you," she says.

He keeps on chewing and doesn't deny it.

"And Squint?" she says. "He got paid too?"

Rudy meets her gaze. "Squint's the chief, he got the beef. If I got twenty, you know he got plenty."

It takes her a few minutes in her woozy and overheated state, but Sarah Jane forces herself to think it out, step by step: Billy Goat came here handing out money and looking for the bag lady in the cow coat. With Rudy's help, Squint sent him to the creek behind the Grill. Billy Goat found Tin Can there wearing the coat and he killed her. After Sarah

Jane ran into Squint and Roylee yesterday, they must've gotten hold of Billy Goat and told him about the coat mix-up and that the real Cow Lady might be found at the library. They sold her out. And they'll do it again if they get the chance.

She tries to stand up, but her legs are so rubbery she can't do it. "I've got to go," she mumbles, deciding to sit for a minute, then try again.

"You just come." Rudy holds out to her a bottle with some deadly looking amber liquid in it.

"What is it?" she asks.

"Rye whiskey." He pushes the bottle against her chest. "Not too risky. Make you frisky."

Sarah Jane's head is already spinning. "Better not. I got to go. I really do."

Suddenly the dogs jump up and start barking. It may be too late now. If this is Squint, she's a goner. She watches the entrance and lets out a breath of relief when she sees Lufkin walk in. But she can tell from all the way across the camp that he has not been successful. It is amazing that a face so covered in hair can be so expressive.

Lufkin spots Sarah Jane and heads her way, dumping his backpack next to hers. She knows what he is going to say before he says it: "Fair lady. No luck." He lowers himself to the ground. "Hey, man," he says to Rudy.

Sarah Jane moves closer to him and tells him what happened at the library and what Rudy has told her and how she's sure now that Billy Goat killed Tin Can and that he will kill her, too, if he finds her here.

"Woo-ee. Like some movie," Lufkin says, shaking his head. "You think nothing more can go wrong and then it does."

"Yeah, but this is *real.*"

"Cow Lady," he says with surprise on his face, "you're scared."

"No." She will never admit to that. Sarah Jane Hurley is no scaredy-cat, not since age eight anyway, when she discovered that the way to tame fear was to get mad and kick butt.

Then she became the toughest kid on the playground. She prides herself now on being free and fearless, on walking the world alone and unafraid, going anywhere and everywhere.

"Yes, you are," Lufkin insists. "You're scared. Anyone would be."

"I'm sick," she says. "But I got to move on."

"Me too." Lufkin leans over to his pack and pulls out a newspaper. "Listen to this," he says. "Today's paper." He begins to read, his voice almost a whisper: " 'Two ninth graders collecting water samples for a school science project yesterday found the body of a woman inside a drainage pipe near Waller Creek. The woman has been identified as Emily Bickerstaff, 43, originally of Phoenix, Arizona. Her local address was the Salvation Army. APD Sgt. Peter Ramirez says police are seeking for questioning several other homeless people who were friends of the dead woman, who was known on the street as Tin Can. Police did not comment on the cause of death, but they suspect foul play.' "

Sarah Jane's head spins faster. "I didn't know she was from Arizona, did you?"

"There's more news." Lufkin folds the paper to a different page. He pauses and studies her face. "You up to it?"

"Shoot."

"It says here the Senate is gonna vote on that bill on Monday." He taps his finger on the article and holds the paper out to Sarah Jane. "See here."

She pushes it away without looking at it. "I *really* got to go. I can't be here when Squint comes back. I got to find someplace I can lie down."

"Maybe the hospital, the ER," he says. "You look real sick."

"No. The cops'd get me right away. And I'd be all closed in." She rests her head on her knee and thinks about just giving up. "There's no place to go," she says softly.

Lufkin rubs his beard, a nervous gesture Sarah Jane knows so well. "I don't know," he says, "maybe that Mother Teresa."

"Oh, shit," Sarah Jane says, "this is serious."

"No, really," he says. "That's what she calls herself—that tall black woman. Looks like the Queen of Sheba or something. Wears a turban and all them clothes."

Sarah Jane knows who he means; she has seen the woman around the Plasma Center. "She's bonkers."

"Yeah, but she's got a shack and she talks about how God sent her to take care of sick folks. Says she used to be a nurse, in a hospital."

"Bullshit."

"Shack's near here. I just about tripped over it one day."

"How far?"

"You walk south a bit, you come to this old cracked road, ain't been used in years. Just past it, there's this wood box-like thing she lives in."

It's crazy, but Sarah Jane has no other ideas. Maybe it's fate. If she doesn't get up now, she never will. She manages to stand up by bracing herself on Lufkin. Then she picks up her bag. "I'll try it," she says.

"I'm gonna talk with Squint about finding me some day job," Lufkin says. "I'll get some money tomorrow and then I'll come find you."

"Sure," she says, knowing she will never see him again. They have come to that hard place where everyone bails out; she knows this because it's always happened like that in the past. "Sure."

Sarah Jane shuffles off, without looking back at the camp, heading south. She understands now why old people shuffle; it's easier to keep yourself from falling if you keep both feet on the earth at all times, and what she wants right now is simply not to fall.

She leaves the Patchwork Pit behind and makes her way through the woods, her ears buzzing, head whirling, eyes blinking against the light. The woods, the sky, the ground appear to her in sharp little flashes, as if a flash bulb just went off in her face. She keeps shuffling on, but after what seems like a very long time she still hasn't come to the crumbling road Lufkin talked about and nothing is familiar.

She is lost.

Mother Teresa—what a laugh. There is no point in walking anymore, she'll just get more lost. She comes to a stop and sways back and forth.

To steady herself, she puts her bag down and reaches her arms out. One hand finds a tree trunk; it is there for her as if by magic. This is where she's been heading, she realizes. This is her stopping place. She shuffles closer to the tree and stretches her arm around it. Oh, what a tree! So strong, so steady. She leans into it and rests her cheek against the rough, fragrant bark. She looks up into the spinning branches. The sun lights the leaves from above, and they glow green, the greenest green she's ever seen—new green, electric green, neon green, green-bean green, spring green, gardener green, Galveston green, Gramma green. These magic leaves whirl and glow, they shimmer, they dazzle, they break the sky into pinpoints of light that flash and flame like tiny sky-stars twinkling in the mess of spinning green. All of it moving, whirling, reeling. Alive. She is dizzy with the wonder of it. Her head hangs back and she gazes up and up, dazed, adoring. Never, never has she seen such a tree.

A thought pops to her lips and forces her to speak out: "I am just beginning." She laughs when she hears the words. Just *beginning?* Someone else must have spoken this with her lips. She is, after all, at the end. She is the dead-end girl, the old drunk, the crazy bag lady people are embarrassed to look at, the throwaway woman who has no place to go. But she is much worse than that. Whirling free like this, she can confess it all to the tree: She is the drunken mother who didn't take care of her children; she nearly burned them up once. Harold was right to take them away. She is the unfaithful and bitter wife, the old woman who lived in a shoe and wanted out. She is also a wanted criminal who stabbed another human being in the chest. The woman was stealing from her, but Sarah Jane was drunk and she stabbed her in anger, meant to kill her. The woman didn't die—it said so in the paper—but Sarah Jane *meant* to kill her. And she has run away, run away from it all. She has shirked responsibility and failed at everything worth doing in life.

Yes, she did all those things, was all those things, but they are all past—water under the bridge, blood under the bridge. They are done, and she is done with them now.

"I am just beginning." She says it again, and smiles; it feels as good as it did the first time.

She wraps her other arm around the tree and embraces it, a friend, a confessor, a lover, a comforter, a fellow beginner putting out new leaves. She continues to embrace it as she slides slowly down, loving the way the bark rasps her cheek and her lips and the palms of her hands. She comes to rest at the roots, still embracing it, finally home. Oh, what a tree!

18

WHAT ARE THESE,
SO WITHERED, AND SO WILD IN THEIR ATTIRE,
THAT LOOK NOT LIKE TH'INHABITANTS O'TH'EARTH
AND YET ARE ON'T?—

—*MACBETH*

Molly Cates left her rental car in the parking lot of the Paso del Norte Hotel for safekeeping and walked through downtown El Paso, heading south toward the border and the bridge of the Americas. The sidewalk still retained the heat of the desert sun, but the air was cooling rapidly as evening came on. She was ravenous because she'd missed lunch. Figuring there was at least an hour until dark, she decided to take time for a serious meal.

She stopped at a Mexican restaurant that seemed to be doing a thriving, noisy Friday night business, with several large tables of revelers and a mariachi band playing on the deck. She asked to sit outside and then threw caution to the wind by ordering the enchilada platter and a Dos Equis. Listening to the music, she ate with abandon. It was the kind of soft, comforting, greasy Tex-Mex food she'd grown up on and she devoured it all, right down to the last grain of rice, the last refried bean, then used a tortilla to soak up what was left on the plate. It infused her with a sense of well-being, but it was not just the food lulling her; it was being close to the border and being surrounded by people who were having an unrestrained good time. It occurred to her that she hadn't had a vacation in years, not because anything was keeping her from it, just because the idea never occurred to her. Maybe she'd try to get Grady to leave his work and his dog and take a long weekend with her here at the Paso del Norte. The rooms were huge, she'd heard, with marble baths, and the bar had a glorious stained-glass dome and a piano player on duty at all hours.

When it started to get dark, she checked her map and headed west. A block away from the intersection of Cebeda and Duranzo she stood in the shadows to watch the street life coming awake as the sun set. Under a flashing green neon sign that said LAS BRUJAS several groups had gathered to talk and smoke. A bunch of men, drinking from beer bottles, kept up a raucous conversation in Spanish with a nearby group of women who were wearing very high heels and very tight skirts. Whenever the bar door opened, guitar music blasted out into the street. Friday night was well under way at the corner of Cebeda and Duranzo—five blocks from the Rio Grande.

Outside the well-lighted area around the bar, women lined Cebeda Street, each one standing alone, separated from the next by about twenty yards, as though they knew the environment could support that density and no more. Molly never saw these women arrive. As the sun set they just seemed to appear, to rise up out of the earth—women dressed in form-hugging, garishly colored clothes that barely covered their breasts and hips. They arranged their bodies in provocative poses and called out to cars cruising by. If they slowed down, the women approached the open windows to negotiate. Occasionally a car door opened and one of the women sashayed over and got in. The women all looked Hispanic and, from where Molly was standing, they all looked far too young to be Sylvia Ramos, who, at forty-three, could be the mother—or grandmother—of any of them. In this ancient and ubiquitous business of women renting their bodies to men, Molly wondered, was there a niche market for mature flesh?

More people joined the groups in front of Las Brujas and

the noise level boomed. Lazy swirls of cigarette smoke rose and formed a cloud overhead, which the neon illuminated into a green miasma, flashing on and off, on and off.

After watching for several minutes, Molly decided to bite the bullet. She walked to the intersection and approached a tiny woman standing alone under a streetlight. She was wearing black short shorts and a shiny red tank top. "Hi," Molly said, chagrined as always that she'd lived forty-four years in Texas and never learned Spanish. "I'm looking for La Risa. Do you know her?"

Even though the woman wore stiletto heels that must have been five inches high, her head barely reached Molly's chin. Molly looked down into the heavily made-up face and saw beneath the clownlike layers of pancake and rouge and mascara the small, undeveloped features of a child. The girl looked Molly over, with a smirk of amusement on her bright red mouth. Then she pointed across the street to one of the groups gathered in front of the bar.

"Which one?" Molly asked.

The girl looked at her as if she were an idiot. *"La monja,"* she said, giggling.

"What?"

"La religiosa."

Molly looked back at the cluster of women the girl was pointing to. Three of them wore short skirts, one wore skin-tight flowered pants, and the fifth wore an ankle-length black skirt and tennis shoes. On her head was the short coif of a modern nun. Molly hadn't even noticed her before.

"The nun?" she asked in disbelief.

"Sí. La monja."

Molly was nonplused. "That's La Risa?"

The girl nodded and looked anxiously toward the cars passing in the street. Molly was interfering with business.

"Gracias," Molly told her.

The girl sauntered away, swinging her tiny hips.

Molly studied the group across the street. One of the women, a plump teenager in fuchsia skirt and turquoise jog bra, talked in loud, angry, animated Spanish, using her hands to emphasize her points. When she finished, the nun spoke to her in a low voice and the other girls leaned forward to listen, nodding in agreement as she talked. Molly wanted to know what she was saying to them. Her journalistic instincts were aroused by the possibilities of a story about a nun befriending prostitutes on the border. And, oh, the magic Henry Iglesias's camera could work with these women!

She crossed the street and approached the group slowly. The minute they saw her, they fell silent. "Sylvia Ramos?" she said.

The woman with the long skirt stepped away from the group. Her dark eyes, looking Molly over, were wary. "Yes?" She had a perfect oval face with smooth unlined tan skin, full lips, and upswept black eyebrows like a raven's wing. She was much younger than the woman Molly was looking for. She'd found the wrong Sylvia Ramos.

"I'm looking for the Sylvia Ramos who was living in Austin twenty-five years ago."

The young woman's enormous brown eyes reflected the flashing green neon. "You mean the Sylvia Ramos with a police record in Austin? The *puta? That* Sylvia Ramos?"

Molly didn't know how to respond. This was so different from what she'd expected that she was thrown. Finally she found some words: "The Sylvia Ramos who was acquainted with Sheriff Olin Crocker."

The woman crossed her arms over her chest and frowned.

The four girls in the group who'd been watching them immediately sensed the change in climate. One of them walked over, rested a protective hand on La Risa's shoulder, and asked her something in rapid Spanish.

La Risa shook her head and answered in Spanish. The girls drifted several yards away. "Are you that Sylvia Ramos?" Molly asked the nun.

"Yes."

"You don't look nearly old enough."

"That's because you can't see my knees."

Molly smiled. "I'm Molly Cates. Can I buy you a cup of coffee?"

La Risa shook her head. "What can I do for you?"

"Talk to me."

"About what?"

"Olin Crocker."

The beautiful mouth made a Hispanic version of a Bronx cheer. "Waste of breath."

"Everybody tells me that. I thought you might be different."

"Miss—what are you called?"

"Cates. Molly. I'm called Molly."

"I'm working now. Maybe you can't see it, but I am."

"What is your work?"

"I counsel 'ladies of the night.' " She rolled her eyes, making fun of the phrase. "I try to save their bodies from disease and their souls from sin. It is what the Church calls my 'special mission.' "

"Well, *I'm* a lady of the night," Molly said. "Counsel me. I wake up at 3 A.M. in terror, and my soul needs saving from sin."

"What is your sin?"

"Hatred. My heart is so full of it, I can feel the frost forming." She had said it lightly, but as soon as she spoke the words, she knew it was true.

"Who do you hate?"

"The same person you hate. Or did once. Olin Crocker."

La Risa looked down at the sidewalk and shook her head, as if in exasperation. When she looked back up, she said, "We can get coffee if you want. But I'll have to make it quick." She nodded to the neon sign behind them. "Las Brujas okay?"

"Sure."

The smoke inside the bar was so dense, Molly was blinded by it at first. La Risa led her to a table near the back. "Leo!" she shouted to the man behind the crowded bar. *"Dos cafés, por favor."*

They sat in silence while Molly tried to decide how to begin. Her eyes were watering from the smoke, but she surveyed the crowded room. Her attention was caught by a huge painting over the bar. It was of three naked, straggly-haired, withered-breasted old crones huddled around a black pot with a fire burning under it. The painting was very dark, but a spotlight shone on it and made the brilliant oranges, reds, and yellows of the fire glow warm in the dim bar, as if it were a real fire. Sylvia Ramos saw her looking at it. *"Las brujas.* The witches."

Molly hadn't known what Las Brujas meant. She studied the witches' wrinkled, emaciated bodies. "Scary," she said.

"Witches?"

"No. Getting old, becoming a crone. There are mornings when I look like that."

La Risa regarded her with an unreadable expression on her placid features.

The bartender, a squat, unshaven man in a filthy apron, set down in front of them two mugs of coffee and a plate with sugar and cream.

"Gracias, Leo." La Risa smiled up at him.

"Are you a Catholic nun?" Molly asked.

"Yes."

"For how long?"

"Seven years."

"Are you called La Risa by your friends?"

"No. That's just on the street. In the Order, I'm Sister Sylvia Ramos."

"What should I call you?"

"Don't call me anything. Tell me what you want."

"Back in 1975, after you got out of jail in Austin, you and Christine Fanon filed a lawsuit against Sheriff Crocker. I wonder if you could tell me about it and why you dropped it."

La Risa lifted her chin and looked at Molly as if from a long distance away. "Who are you to ask me this?" Her tone was icy.

"I'm a writer. I work for *Lone Star Monthly* magazine in Austin, but this is not connected to my work. My interest is ... personal."

La Risa took a sip of coffee. "Tell me about your 'personal interest.' "

"If I show you mine, you'll show me yours?" Molly said.

"Maybe."

"Okay. In 1970, when I was sixteen, my father was murdered in Travis County. Olin Crocker was the sheriff. He was in charge of the case, but he didn't do much investigating. He called my father's murder a suicide, but I knew it wasn't. I tried to investigate it myself, but I got nowhere, and Crocker was no help at all. Four years later, some new evidence came up and I went to see him. I asked him if I could look at it—the new evidence, something I believed was stolen from my daddy's office when he was killed. Crocker said no, but he had some new information in the case and—" Molly paused here. She was rambling. She'd come to get information, not give it. "Well, he never did show me, and I just recently found out about your lawsuit and I—"

Sylvia Ramos held up a hand. "Stop there. You want me to tell you something embarrassing and painful about my life. But you won't do it yourself."

"Do what?"

"Be honest. One thing about those young *putas* out there"—she gestured to the door—"they know how to tell the truth. When they talk about their lives, they tell it like it is."

Molly was confused. "Are you saying I'm not telling the truth?"

"You think if something bad happens to me or to them we should talk about it, right? But if it happens to *you,* it's private."

Molly's face was heating up. "I just told you about my father's death and why I'm interested in Crocker. That's being *private?*"

"You're telling me the cleaned-up version."

"I told you my history with Crocker. And I asked you about yours. What's wrong with that?" Boy, this woman really had a chip on her shoulder.

"What's wrong is you're bullshitting me."

Molly was incensed. "You're a nun! Is this how you counsel people?"

La Risa looked her in the eye. "Yes. This *is* how I counsel people. I have no time to waste with bullshitters."

"What did I say that was bullshit?"

"You're not telling the truth."

"Yes, I am. That's what happened. I—"

"Look." La Risa leaned toward Molly. "I *knew* Crocker. I can guess what happened: he said he'd tell you what you wanted to know if you'd give him a blow job, or maybe, depending on the mood he was in, if you'd fuck him, or maybe he wanted you to bring a friend along so you could have a three-way. You did what he asked, and the son of a bitch double-crossed. And you're still mad about it. That's why you have that closed look when you talk about him, with your mouth all tight."

Molly was speechless. The smoke was strangling her, stinging her eyes. She needed to get out of here. This woman was intolerable.

La Risa moved her face closer. "Am I shocking you? Well, I'm so sorry." She stood up. "You see, I was a whore for nearly ten years. I hang out with whores now. We talk about blow jobs and butt fucks like bartenders talk about margaritas and Manhattans." She turned and walked toward the door.

Molly struggled to regain her equilibrium. Her face felt burning hot and she couldn't decide if she wanted this woman to go or stay. She had never told anyone what had happened with Olin Crocker. It wasn't anyone else's business. She was here to ask the questions, not to be abused like this. "Wait," Molly called. "Wait a minute."

La Risa turned around. "Why?"

"Because I—" She stopped herself, about to repeat what she had already said. Instead she said, "How did you know?"

La Risa walked back to the table. "Easy. You were a young girl. Attractive. Helpless. That's what Crocker liked, that's what he did."

Molly sat looking into her coffee, feeling totally humiliated. She was a victim like all the rest and she hated it. When she looked up, Sylvia Ramos was looking down at her with eyes full of compassion. "It wasn't your fault, *chica*. You know that."

"Not the first time," Molly said, barely able to meet the other woman's eyes, "when I was sixteen. But the second time, I was twenty-one, a grown woman, married. And I knew what he was."

"Crocker was the worst man I've run into and there's some tough competition out there. He's still alive, I guess."

"Yes."

La Risa sat down. "You tell me what happened. It will lose some of its power then."

"I know." It was something Molly told people all the time to get them to talk to her, and she believed it was true: nothing defanged pain and shame like talking about it. But this subject was so difficult she didn't know if she could even find the words. La Risa had already started supplying them for her, though. Maybe she could.

"Go on. Try it."

"When I was sixteen Crocker came to my house. He said he would tell me all the things about my daddy's case that hadn't been made public, the things the police always hold back, but he would tell me if I would—" Her teeth clenched against remembering it.

"Say it to me. Right out loud. Like this." La Risa turned toward the crowd at the bar and announced in a loud voice. *"Yo mame la verga."*

Every head in the room turned their way. Several men laughed. One applauded.

"What did you say?" Molly asked.

" 'I sucked his cock.' Now you say it." She smiled at Molly for the first time, and it was a gorgeous smile. "Go ahead."

"I sucked his cock." Molly said it forcefully, but her face burned.

"Now that wasn't so bad."

"But then he didn't tell me anything."

"I bet. That was his way. He didn't keep bargains."

"So four years later I should have known better."

"But you didn't. Some of us learn slow. Or we want something so bad, we just keep on trying."

"He came to my house again. My husband was at work. And I did it again."

"Say it—you sucked his cock. You gave him a blow job. You gave him head. Shout it out. It'll make it easier."

"It's not that I'm prudish, usually.... It's just so hard to talk about this."

"When it's forced on you, sex hurts you in one way or another. Crocker was really good at this. He'd make sure you were too ashamed to talk about it."

"But I agreed to it. That's the thing. It wasn't like I was being raped."

"No?"

"I mean there was no force involved. I was twenty-one. I didn't have to."

"Oh?"

"And of course the second time he didn't tell me anything either."

"Hey," La Risa said, "you want a real drink? You look like you could use it."

Molly nodded. "A glass of white wine."

"White wine?" She laughed. "A real drink. Leo will like that." She shouted, "Leo! Give us a white wine and another coffee."

Immediately the bartender brought the order. Molly was impressed with the level of the service La Risa got.

The nun sipped her second cup of coffee and said, "I need to get back out there, on the street. They know that's where they can find me on Fridays. My office hours."

"What do you do for them?" Molly asked.

"Not much."

"That girl I talked to—the one in the red shirt—couldn't be more than fourteen."

"Camilla? She's twelve."

"Lord."

"What I do is listen to what they want to talk about and then I tell them about other choices." She lowered her voice. "I also give them rubbers. The Church doesn't know about that, of course. I have to buy them with money people give me. Leo there"—she glanced toward the bar—"is my big donor."

"What choices do you tell them about?"

"That's the problem. But we're working on a shelter where they can stay if they're trying to get out of the life. Money's real hard to find. Whores are not anybody's favorite charity." She shrugged. "If the shelter gets done, I want to call it the Casa Christine, in memory of Christine Fanon, but the Church says you can't name a place after a whore. They want to call it Casa de Caridad." She took a long drink of her coffee.

"How much do you need? For the shelter."

"To finish the building—about seventy thousand." She pushed her empty mug away. "I got to go."

"I know, but tell me first about the lawsuit."

"Mary, Mother of God—the suit." La Risa tipped her head back and closed her eyes for a few seconds. "Okay, it's really the story of Christie."

"Christine Fanon?"

"My first real friend. I had to go to jail to find a friend. I was eighteen, she was seventeen. I was doing ten months for theft, she was in for possession. First time for both of us. I guess I'd had girlfriends before, but not a soul mate, somebody I'd tell everything to. She was this funny, skinny, freckled blonde girl. Looked like she was ten years old. Came from a family even worse than mine. We hung out together and talked and talked. It made the time pass, which is a big deal when you're in jail.

"I'd been in maybe six months when one day Sheriff Crocker asked for me to come to the warden's office. The warden wasn't there, just Crocker. Did I want an early release, he asked me, so I could get this all behind me?

"'Sure,' I said. 'How about today?' Real cocky, you know. In those days it was all I had.

"He said, 'It'll take a week, but I'll fix you up.'

"'How about my girlfriend up in the block?' I asked. I was so stupid." She took a long drink of her coffee. "I was signing her death warrant.

"'Who's your friend?' he wanted to know. 'Christine Fanon,' I said. 'She pretty like you?' he asked. I still didn't see it coming. 'She's pretty, I guess. In this little-girl way.'

"He said, 'Pretty Mescan señorita like you, I bet you know how to take care of a man, make him feel good, don't you?'

"Until then I didn't understand the deal. He stood right in front of me where I was sitting and he real slow unzipped his pants, like he had the Holy Grail in there. All I had to do was suck him off, he said, show him how grateful I was.

"I was no virgin, but I never did sex for money or favors. I didn't want to. I hated to do it, but I was scared. He was the *sheriff.* And I wanted to get out of there. So I figured what the hell, nobody would ever know and I'd just forget it ever happened.

"And he got me an early release, me and Christie both, but there was a catch. Of course. This was Crocker. There was always a catch. The day we got released he called both of us into the office and said he had us some jobs. In his massage business."

"Miracle Massage in South Austin?"

"You got it."

Molly was aghast; this was far beyond the sexual harassment and abuse of office she'd known about. "Crocker recruited *inmates* to work there?"

"Recruited is not the half of it. He made offers they couldn't refuse. All the girls were on parole, early release for 'good behavior.'"

"So you went to work there?"

"Not right away. Christie said no. And she told her lawyer and the lawyer said we'd sue Crocker. I was scared, but Christie was a fighter, not somebody you could bully. And I loved her for it. So we did it, and it was really a dumb thing. Crocker found us the next day, pissed off like you wouldn't believe. He had papers that revoked our paroles. He said when he got us back in jail he was going to fix us up to be suicides. Even Christie was scared. He told us the only way out was for us to drop the suit. Also we'd have to come work for him. He wanted to be sure he had us where he could keep an eye on us."

"So you did?"

"Yeah. We dropped our suit, and we went to work for him."

"At Miracle Massage."

"Yeah. The miracle was you really got a massage with the sex. The johns could get a massage and hand job for twenty-five, a massage and blow job for fifty, or a massage and full sex for a hundred. The girls got to keep half. Best money I ever made. I got to say this for Crocker—he was a good businessman. He ran a tight prison and a whorehouse where everybody made money."

"Crocker ran it himself?"

"Not day to day. This other guy, Eduardo Bandera, did that. But Crocker brought in the girls and he was the brains."

"He owned the building too," Molly said. "Did you know that?"

"No."

"We've got an intimate connection here."

"You mean we both sucked Crocker's dick?"

Molly smiled and was amazed that she could. "You're a hell of a nun."

"I know. That's what my superior says."

"There's another connection: the house. Crocker bought it the month after he called my father's death a suicide. I believe the fifty thousand dollars he used to buy it was a payoff not to investigate my daddy's death. What I need to know is who paid him."

"And you were hoping I could help?"

"I guess. And I was just curious about your suit. You were my last lead. What happened to Christie?"

"Crocker took a liking to her. He was turned on by women who looked like little girls, and he liked spirit in the women he ruined." She looked at Molly over her coffee mug. "That may be why he liked you."

"No. I was a pushover. Christie sounds like the real goods."

"She was a tiger. But she was weak for drugs and Crocker made sure she got plenty of them. She was easier to control stoned. She never beat the addiction she got there. When we finally ran off to Houston, she was hopeless. The shit finally killed her."

"And you?"

"I never got the habit. And I hated the life. When Christie died, I quit and went back home. My mother took me in." She looked at Molly. "I guess you saw her. That's how you found me?"

Molly nodded.

"I went back to school. Mama wanted me to be a teacher. I wanted to help *putas* and I needed the Church." She leaned over and looked at Molly's watch. "I got to go for real."

"Wait," Molly said. "Let me ask you one more thing."

"Do I miss sex?" La Risa grinned. "Everyone asks that."

"No. If Crocker were on trial for some of his more recent crimes against young girls, would you come testify?"

La Risa shook her head. "Sorry."

"How about giving me the names of some of the other girls who worked there?"

She shook her head again.

"Why?"

"My Church says we're supposed to forgive the bastards who trespass against us."

"Have you done that?"

She laughed. "No, but I pray for the strength. What about you?"

"I think I'd rather get revenge."

" 'Vengeance is mine; I will repay, saith the Lord.' "

"In this case I'm going to help Him out a little." Molly paused. "Well, *do* you miss sex?"

"No. I never liked sex. Not with men, anyway." La Risa stood; she gave Molly a beatific smile. "The peace of the Lord be with you, Molly Cates."

"Fat chance." Molly squinted up at her through the smoke. "Are you *really* a nun?"

La Risa laughed. "You're supposed to say back to me, 'And also with you.' " As she walked out she called to the bartender. "*Qué chulo,* Leo."

When Molly handed Leo a twenty-dollar bill to pay for the drinks, he said, "It's on the house, *señora.*" But he took the money and stuck it in his apron pocket. "I'll put it in La Risa's health fund. Protection for the little *muchachas* out there," he said, gesturing toward the street.

19

FOR EVERY EVIL UNDER THE SUN
THERE IS A REMEDY OR THERE IS NONE.
IF THERE BE ONE, SEEK TILL YOU FIND IT;
IF THERE BE NONE, NEVER MIND IT.
　　　　　　　　　　—MOTHER GOOSE

There was something about being strapped into a vibrating seat inside a capsule hurtling through space at five hundred miles an hour that always stimulated her thinking. The little bottles of white wine helped, too, and Molly Cates made it a rule never to break her reverie by talking to the stranger sitting next to her. She'd formulated the rule some years back, when she'd gotten trapped on a flight from Dallas to Seattle listening to a garrulous stockbroker's nonstop monologue on the municipal bond market.

This morning she'd left El Paso reluctantly, yesterday's eagerness to get home dissipated, possibly because she knew now that with each mile she traveled she was getting that much closer to doing something extreme, very extreme. Something that made her long-ago misadventure with Jocko the bull look like a rational, adult decision. But if she was going to restore herself to balance and shake off the past, she needed to take some action. If it was possible to learn who murdered her daddy, she was going to learn it now. If it was not possible, she was going to forget it. The chain of events that had begun six days ago when she saw Olin Crocker in the Senate gallery demanded that she follow this through to the final link. She was going to do it. But this time she was going to control the situation.

On the way home from the airport Molly made two stops, both of them unprecedented. The first was McDavitt's gun shop, which, on a Saturday afternoon, bustled with men in plaid shirts and boots. She went to the ammunition area and asked for cartridges for a .38 special. The man behind the counter startled her by asking what they were for. He must have noted her confusion, because he added, "Are you fixin' to do target practice, or are they for home defense?"

"Oh. Home defense."

"Alrighty," he said with enthusiasm, "then it's stopping power you need." He pulled a box off the shelf and set it on the counter. "My favorites." The box said *Winchester sxt 38.* "These are the Black Talons, but they changed the name back when there was all the nonsense in the press."

"What nonsense was that?" Molly asked, remembering only vaguely.

"Oh, these hollow points were made out to be evil its own self, but they're just good expansion bullets."

"Expansion." Molly took one of the sleek cartridges out of the box and examined the open serrated point. "They probably hurt a lot."

"Ma'am?"

"I mean they do a lot of damage?"

"On impact they open up just like a flower blooming." He spread his fingers outward to illustrate. "Nearly triple their size. Massive tissue damage. Real dandies."

"Sounds like just what I want."

Molly took the box to the cashier and paid for the bullets as if she were buying a dozen eggs. Only in America.

Her second stop required a bit more fortitude. The porno store called the Pleasure Palace was down near the university. Red neon signs in the window proclaimed ADULT VIDEOS and X-RATED NOVELTIES. NO MINORS. When she walked in, several male heads turned in her direction, then quickly away. The front of the store was lined with boxes of videos turned so the pictures on the front faced out. The images were mostly naked women with balloonlike breasts and legs spread—caricatures of women, as unbeautiful and unerotic as an anatomy textbook. She found herself not repelled but puzzled, wanting to know what it was like to be moved by all these images. Maybe sometime she would do a piece on the porno business, but from the point of view of the consumers. Trying to sell that idea to her editor would be interesting.

She walked to the counter in the back where there were several racks of novelty condoms. She took her time looking and ended up buying a package of four ribbed, lubricated, margarita-flavored, glow-in-the-dark condoms.

When she got home to her townhouse she pulled her truck into the garage and closed the door behind her, something she rarely did. It was best if no one knew she was home. She left the newspapers where they lay on the front walk. They were all soggy-looking, anyway; it must have rained while she was gone. The first thing she did was check her phone messages. Since yesterday, there were five messages and eleven hangups, but none from Cow Lady and none from Grady. The others could wait until tomorrow. She wanted badly to call Grady, to hear his voice, and to find out what was happening on the Emily Bickerstaff murder and whether he'd managed to pick up Cow Lady, but she didn't want him to know she was home yet. What she was going to do she would never share with anyone, especially Grady.

She took a bath, shaved her legs, and washed her hair. She spent more time than usual blowing her hair dry, then rummaged through her drawers to find some lingerie that might pass as provocative rather than comfortable. She came up with a white lace bra and matching bikini pants she'd worn only once because they were scratchy.

She pulled on a pair of tight jeans and a short-sleeved white Henley, leaving the buttons open to reveal a bit of cleavage and the lace on her bra. She did full eye makeup and perfume, which she rarely bothered with. She put on a pair of dangly earrings and then surveyed the finished product in the mirror. Not that bad, really. Of course, she was decades too old to sing a siren song to a man who got off on teenagers, but she was going to give it a shot. She was going to try a brew of sex and bluff and genuine Wanda Lavoy–inspired mayhem on him.

Assessing her reflection, she thought she looked like a handsome, well-tended, middle-aged woman getting ready to try her luck at a honky-tonk on a Saturday night. It reminded her of the time after her daddy died when she used to troll the bars out at the lake. In those days, at sixteen and seventeen, there was no question about being able to attract men; it was automatic, as if a pheromone secreted from youthful sweat gave men no choice but to chase the scent. That sure had been a long time ago.

Really, she thought, continuing to study her image, in spite of all the whining she and her friends did about aging, the physical differences between her body at sixteen and forty-four, nearly forty-five, were quite minor. She put her face right up to the mirror and examined herself coolly. She had a few wrinkles in progress, yes, and some gray hairs, sure, and—she turned and craned her neck to examine herself from the back—her body parts were all lower, yes, but only a fraction of an inch lower—changes that would be barely visible in a smoky bar. It wasn't those small signs of decay that made women feel less alluring in middle age, she thought; it was that men no longer responded to them with the instinctive attention of bird dogs coming to point.

Molly sat down at the kitchen table and scanned Shelby Palmer's report for Olin Crocker's unlisted home number. As she picked up the phone, she paused. This—right here—was the point of no return. Once she dialed the number, she was committed. If she wanted to write this off now, she could still do it. She could call Grady or Jo Beth or Barbara instead and see if they wanted dinner or a movie—the things sane people did on a Saturday night.

She dialed the number. If he answered, she told herself, it was fate telling her to go ahead and do it. If he didn't, well... maybe she should reconsider. The phone rang and rang. All dressed up, she thought, and no place to go. On the ninth ring he answered. "Yes?" He sounded out of breath.

"Olin Crocker?"

"Yes."

"Molly Cates."

There was a pause. "How did you get my home number?"

"Oh, I have my ways," she said lightly, trying to sound like a coy and flirtatious teenager.

"Well, I just bet you do," he said.

"You said I should call you with any questions, remember?"

"I surely do."

"I'd like to ask you a few things—for my magazine piece."

"I'd be real glad to talk to you. Why don't you come by my office Monday?"

"I'm working on this right now, Sheriff. Tight deadline."

"So you wanna do this over the phone?"

"Well, I have an errand out your way tonight.... I thought I might drop in and see you after I finish."

"An errand out *here?*"

"In Taylor, actually, a quick one, but I hear you're close by."

"You know where I live?"

"You're a few miles east of Taylor on Carlson Road, aren't you?"

"Who told you that?" His voice carried a wariness that worried her. She'd have to say something to put his mind at ease. This would never work unless she could disarm his suspicions and appeal to his vanity and his lust.

"When I saw you in the gallery it set me to wondering about you. So I asked around."

"You asked Cullen Shoemaker about me." He said it in a flat voice.

Oh-oh. She should have figured Cullen would tell him about her inquiries.

"Yes. I find myself real ... curious about you, Sheriff."

"We do have some unfinished business, don't we?" he

said in a voice so cold and quiet Molly found her skin prickling.

"Well, how about it?" she asked with an attempt at lightness. "I'd probably get to you around nine o'clock."

There was a long delay. Molly found herself holding her breath. Finally Crocker said, "We better wait till Monday on this."

"Tonight is better. I'll bring the beer. Olin."

"I was planning on getting to bed early. Molly."

"You could stay up for me, couldn't you?" Lord, this was demeaning.

He chuckled. "Oh, hell, why not? You coming alone?"

"Uh-huh."

"Look for the third driveway on the left after FM 4563, the one with the stone mailbox. Don't pay no mind to the dog—bitch is all bark and no bite."

Molly put the phone down. The die was cast.

She dumped out the contents of her big bag onto the kitchen counter. Next, she opened the box of cartridges and loaded six of them into the Ruger, with the gun pointed down, just as Wanda had taught her. She set the gun carefully on the counter. Then she transferred into Wanda Lavoy's pistol-packing handbag the few things she might need—her wallet, a lipstick, keys, and the garish yellow and black condom package; finally she slipped the .38 into its separate compartment on the side of the bag.

She slung the bag over her shoulder, grabbed a six-pack of beer, and headed out the kitchen door to the garage. She pushed the garage door opener. The light came on and the door began its slow, creaky ascent. As she reached for the truck door, she saw something in the corner of her eye and whirled around to look. A pair of long legs was being slowly uncovered by the lifting door. Inch by inch, the door revealed a lanky man dressed in fatigues, standing just outside her garage. She had time to get in the truck or run back into the house, but she didn't. She just stood rooted. She recognized him—the yellow beret, the long face. It was the militia crazy from the Senate gallery. She should have run when she had the chance. She started to retreat toward the kitchen door.

He stepped forward. "Miss Cates, don't worry. Federal Bureau of Investigation. I'm Special Agent Heller."

She hesitated.

"It's okay," he said. "I was just going to ring the bell when I heard you in here. I need to ask you some questions, please."

Molly walked toward the open garage door. She needed to get out in the open, to the street. He stood aside to give her plenty of room to pass. She strode down the drive to the street and waited there for him. It was just starting to get dark and she was relieved to see a car coming their way and a neighbor several doors down weeding his flower beds.

He followed her slowly, careful to give her space. "Sorry to alarm you like that, but I've been trying to call you for two days. You been away?"

"Let me see some ID," she said.

"We don't carry a badge when we're undercover, ma'am."

"Then how do I know you're what you say?"

In a very quiet voice he said, "Rain Malloy sends her greetings."

Molly felt her mouth fall open in surprise.

"She says you're one real standup guy and I should remind you to keep a low profile if things get hot."

Molly found herself smiling at the memory. Low profile, indeed. Rain Malloy was an FBI agent Molly had met eighteen months ago during the Jezreel hostage incident. Before the two of them had entered the cult compound, the agent had instructed Molly to lie flat on the floor and cover her head when the shooting started. It would have been impossible, Molly thought now, for anyone to get her profile lower than Molly had done that night. Besides Molly and Grady, only a few select federal agents knew Rain Malloy had ever been in Austin. The only way this man could know about Molly's involvement with her was from the FBI.

Molly took a closer look at special agent Heller. He was very tall and lean with a long dour face. Dark stubble covered his sunken cheeks. He looked even more menacing than he had when she'd first spotted him in the Senate gallery six days ago. "You aren't a militia crazy from the panhandle?"

"So everyone buys my cover?"

"I did."

"I'd rather no one saw us standing out here, Miss Cates. Could we go inside? I don't think this will take long."

"They'd just think I was interviewing you. I'd had that in mind, anyway."

"Yes, ma'am, but it's much better if we don't stand out here on the street."

It wasn't until this moment that Molly remembered she was carrying a loaded handgun in her bag. It wasn't illegal here on her own property, of course, but once she left home it was, and she'd clearly been on her way out. What rotten luck. The one time in her life she packs a gun—the one time!—a federal agent appears at her door. It was like having sex one reckless time and ending up pregnant. She resisted the impulse to hug the purse closer to her body. Instead she asked, "What's this about?"

"I want to ask you about Wanda Lavoy and her group that meets out at Clem's range."

The light dawned. The white Camry. "Was that *you* parked there on Tuesday?"

"Yes, ma'am."

A car drove by them, catching them in its headlights.

He gestured toward the open garage. *"Please,* Miss Cates."

"Come in, then," Molly said, glancing at her watch. "I've got an appointment, so—"

"Ten minutes," he promised.

"Okay." Molly walked back into the garage and unlocked the door. The box of cartridges on the counter among the other clutter startled her. Without turning on the light, she led him quickly through the kitchen into the living room.

She switched on a lamp, stuck her bag out of sight under the wing chair, and sat down. "Sit down. How did you know about Rain Malloy? I thought that was top secret."

He chose the other wing chair, in front of the big window.

"After I saw you with Wanda Lavoy in the gallery and then when you showed up at the range, I put your name in the computer. It came up with a connection to a past agency action. It was sealed but Agent Malloy's name was attached to it. She was one of my instructors at Quantico, so I called her. I still don't know what the action was, but from the date of the file and the location I'd guess the Hearth Jezreelite matter."

"Are you testing me, Agent Heller? You know I can't talk about that."

"Yes, ma'am. What I'd like to know from you is your impression of Wanda Lavoy and her Women in Control."

"My impression? Why?"

"Well, there's persistent buzz about some pending violence."

"At the Capitol?"

He nodded.

"I've noticed the increased security."

"Oh, I wouldn't call that security. They've put a few more troopers on, is all."

"Is this in connection with the handgun bill?"

"Yes, ma'am. According to the buzz."

"Why Wanda?"

"Her name just keeps on coming up. She talks wild."

"I know, but I think it's mostly talk."

"What makes you think that?"

Molly was silent, unsure how to answer.

"Think out loud," Heller said.

"Okay. When Wanda talks, it feels to me like bravado. I think she's got a world view that makes her scared all the time, so she's got to do a lot of whistling in the dark. Also, she's got no political grievance right now. She supports the bill and it's going to pass and it will enrich her because she'll become one of the instructors for getting a license. Also, there's the gender thing."

Molly thought she saw a twitch at the corners of Heller's long sour mouth. "Which gender thing are you referring to, ma'am?"

"Well, women are just too sensible, and too busy, to shoot

up cafeterias or bomb federal buildings. That's male territory, Agent Heller. Surely all your profiles and computer
printouts tell you this."

"There are exceptions."

"I know, but I don't think Wanda's one."

"Does she carry a weapon?"

Molly shifted her gaze away from him to the darkening
window. She hated this. She wanted to cooperate, but her
personal loyalties had always taken precedence over group
ones. If there really was violence brewing here, she wanted to
help them avert it. But she could not bring herself to answer
this question.

She shrugged. "I can't believe the FBI is worrying about a
bunch of women who get together to do target practice."

"We wouldn't if it weren't for these damn rumors, Miss
Cates."

"Where do the rumors come from?"

"I can't talk about that, but they are persistent."

"If there's violence being planned, I think you're looking
in the wrong place."

"Where would you look?"

Immediately, Cullen Shoemaker and his manifesto
came to mind. "You were there on Thursday when Cullen
Shoemaker spoke. That was bad enough, but I just read this
thing, this tract he wrote—the McNelly Manifesto, he calls
it, and it's scary. Very scary."

"Have you still got it?"

"Yes."

"Could I see it?"

"I think I've got it in the next room. I'll be right back."
Molly went into the kitchen and without turning on the light
picked up the box of cartridges and stuck it in a drawer, trying to close the drawer without making any noise. Then she
rummaged through the pile of things she'd dumped from her
bag until she found the paper. She took it back to the living
room and handed it to him. "It's *Turner Diary*–type stuff—
just unspeakable."

Heller folded it and tucked it into his shirt pocket. "We've already looked at Shoemaker. The McNelly Posse's a militia in the making with one big difference—they're not your usual bitter rednecks. They're college kids with some rich daddies who back them, but they're mostly about posturing, I think. Kids."

"Maybe, but that manifesto is the most vicious kind of hate-mongering. He talks about violence being necessary to resist any sort of gun registration. Don't let Cullen's little-boy looks fool you. I think he's dangerous."

"Well"—he patted his pocket—"I'll read it. Tell me what went on at the range on Tuesday."

"My daughter and I shot at targets of bad guys and when the WIC members showed up they did some quick-draw-and-shoot practice. Some of them are pretty good."

"Hmmm. That's it?"

"Well, before we shot we had some classroom time—the world according to Wanda Lavoy."

"And what is that world?" he asked.

"Oh, it's full of bad guys and danger. Women need to be able to take care of themselves since the police can't do it."

His long face took on an even more dour look. "Well, I can't argue with that. No talk about taking up arms against the government?"

"No. Just against individuals, bad guys."

"And that was it?"

"Yes." Molly looked at her watch.

He stood up. "Thanks for taking the time, Miss Cates. You coming for the vote on Monday?"

"Yeah. I've come this far with it. You?"

"Yeah. I'll be relieved to have it over with. Let me give you a number you can call if you want to get in touch with me."

Molly got a pencil and paper from the table and wrote down the number he gave her.

"Someone answers there, twenty-four hours. Just say it's urgent for Agent Heller and I'll call you back." He stood up.

"What do you think about the bill, Agent?" she asked as they walked toward the front door. "You've been there every day."

"Oh, I guess pretty much the same as other law enforcement folks. Officially I'm against it. Privately, I encourage my wife to carry protection in D.C. at night. That's off the record, of course."

"The issue is a lot more difficult than I thought," Molly conceded.

He stood at the door and patted the pocket where he'd tucked the manifesto. "The worst part of it is that Shoemaker is right."

"What?"

"That the lists of gun registrations and licenses *will* eventually be used to disarm people. He's rabid, of course. There's no conspiracy that I know of, but when tighter restrictions come, and they will, they'll start with the lists."

Molly opened the front door for him. "Tell Rain Malloy hello for me."

"I will." He paused in the open door. "Be careful with that .38 in your bag, Miss Cates. You're a beginner and you wouldn't believe how wrong things can go when a loaded gun gets in inexperienced hands."

The nerve of these cops! Damn him. "I suppose at dinner parties you snoop through the host's medicine cabinets."

"Yes, if I'm worried he might be up to something."

"You think *I'm* up to something, agent?" Molly demanded.

"No, ma'am, but it looks like you've got quite an evening planned."

"I don't believe carrying condoms breaks any law," she said, trying to sound unperturbed, "but illegal searches do."

He glanced up at the darkening sky. "Looks like we're in for more rain. Have a good evening, ma'am."

As soon as he'd left, she closed the door, then locked it. Well, shit. She walked back into the living room and pulled her bag out from under the chair. She took the gun out and opened the chamber. All six cartridges were still there. He was quick, but not that quick. She put the gun back and glanced at her watch.

Time to get going. Saturday night, hot date. Didn't want

to be late. After all, she'd been waiting twenty-five years for this one. Twice before this man had cheated her, but this time she would make it come out differently.

Agent Heller was right about one thing: she had quite an evening planned.

20

AND OFTENTIMES, TO WIN US TO OUR HARM,
THE INSTRUMENTS OF DARKNESS TELL US TRUTHS.
—MACBETH

There were people in the world, or so she'd heard, who could forgive and forget. Molly Cates was not one of them. She rarely took offense, but when she did, she embraced the injury forever. She knew this grudge-holding to be an unappealing trait but, to her credit, she had never taken active revenge in her life. And she certainly did not believe in violent retribution. She'd seen the futility of that during her years on the police beat.

Olin Crocker headed her list of those who had done her harm, but she had let two and a half decades pass without lifting a finger against him. Until now.

Molly was usually pretty good at rationalizing what she wanted to do, but this one was a real challenge. After all, what made her any different from Cullen Shoemaker and his vigilance committee, whose philosophy she loathed? According to the McNelly Manifesto, white male citizens had the right and the responsibility to administer summary justice when the regular legal system failed to punish the guilty. Wasn't that what she was setting out to do tonight? Since the law had not gotten Olin Crocker, she was going to try to nail the bastard herself.

She had the right, she told herself. When for decades

you'd lived life as a responsible adult, doing all the law-abiding things—going to work, paying your taxes, renewing your car registration and dog licenses, stopping at traffic lights, recycling your trash—surely you'd earned the right to step outside the bounds of civilized behavior just once, if the cause was honorable. Every dog was allowed one bite, after all, and sometimes those dogs were sorely provoked into biting. Why shouldn't each person be allowed *one* vigilante act? For hers, her once-in-a-lifetime bite, she was choosing to call in Olin Crocker's debt by force.

Before heading out toward Taylor, she drove around Northwest Hills a little to see if Agent Heller might possibly be following her. After ten minutes of zigging and zagging, making U-turns and watching in the rearview mirror for white Camrys, she felt totally ridiculous. Planning illegal activities had a tendency to make you paranoid.

By the time she got headed east on Highway 290, it was nine o'clock and dark. She thought about calling Crocker to say she was running late, but decided not to. He might tell her it was too late to come. And, now that she was moving in that direction, she was hell-bent on going through with this. No chickening out now.

It was a fifteen-minute drive to County Road 973 and another fifteen minutes through flat farmland to FM 4563. After turning right on Carlson Road, she started counting driveways. Without his instructions she would have had a hard time finding it because the numbers were impossible to see in the dark. She turned in at the stone mailbox, her heart pounding so hard against her ribs it made her arms shake. She gripped the wheel tighter to steady them.

The long gravel driveway ended at a low, sprawling stone house, very substantial and totally charmless. Behind the house, she could make out in the darkness the shape of a barn and some other outbuildings. The porch light wasn't on, but several windows showed light around the edges. The one closest to the door showed the flickering light of a television.

A large yellow dog came bounding around the side of the house, making enough noise for a whole pack of hounds. Molly parked the truck near the house and rolled down her window.

A light came on over the front door and the door opened. A dark shape filled the doorway. "Lady, you yappy old bitch, get up here." The dog stopped barking, trotted meekly up on the porch, and sat at the man's feet, whining.

Olin Crocker took one step out onto the porch and stopped there, staring at the truck. He was barefoot, wearing saggy blue jeans and an unbuttoned white shirt with the sleeves rolled up. Molly's entire body clenched up with disgust at the sight of him. She was wrong: she would never be able to carry this off. She hadn't reckoned on having such a powerful visceral reaction. He'd take one look at her and see her loathing. Her acting skills weren't even close to good enough to carry on a sexual flirtation with this weasel. The idea of touching him made her flesh crawl.

She sat watching him up on his porch, trying to psych herself back into the frame of mind in which she had convinced herself this fool plan might work. Think of it, she told herself, as a trip to the dentist when you've had a toothache that's tormented you for years. The cure might be painful, but it is short-term pain. Think how much better you'll feel when you've done something about it.

She sat up straighter. This was the best shot—perhaps the only shot—she was ever going to have at curing this old and persistent toothache of hers. The worst that could happen was she'd get humiliated . . . or beaten up . . . or raped . . . or killed . . . or sent to prison.

"You gonna sit there all night or you gonna get out?" he called to her. "Don't wet your pants over this little ol' dog. She's not gonna hurt you, are you, Lady, girl?" He leaned down to scratch the dog on the chest. "No, ma'am, she won't bite and I won't neither." His voice contained both a sexual suggestiveness and the kind of condescending reassurance you'd offer to a neurotic child.

Molly had to unclench her teeth to speak. "Good watchdog," she said, opening the door.

"When she's awake, which is about one hour a day," he said. "On a good day."

Molly pulled the six-pack out of the cooler in back, slung her bag over her shoulder, and slammed the door. No turning back now; she was in for the duration.

"Well, howdy." He managed to twist his lips into the replica of a smile.

"Evening, Olin. Nice spread you've got here."

"Well, it's too dark for you to see now, but it's right pretty—fifteen hundred acres," he said with pride in his voice, "one of the biggest spreads in the county."

Good. He loves this place, she thought. I'll use that to put the fear of the Lord into him.

He watched her approach, his eyes wary.

"You've done right well for yourself," Molly said, affecting a hearty twang. If this had a prayer of working, she needed to put him at ease.

"Well." He grinned and shrugged. "They tell me you've become a famous writer. There's just no predictin' these things, is there?" He put his hands on his hips and laughed. "Hell, I remember you as one mixed-up lil old gal. Wild, whoo-eee! And you dropped out of high school, didn't you?"

Molly reached the porch steps and looked up at him. "You're right, Sheriff. There's no predicting anything." You had to be careful who you screwed, Molly thought, because not all of them end up dying of a drug overdose. One of them might turn out to be a vigilante.

He stuck his hands in his pockets. "So what was this errand you had to do in Taylor?"

"A real sad thing. I took a casserole to Mattie Jenks. Her husband died Wednesday, old friend of my daddy—Stuart Jenks. Farmed up by Thrall before they retired and bought that big old house in Taylor. You know him?"

"Jenks?" He gave her a long look. "Don't believe so."

"Well, I guess Taylor's getting to be a big place."

"Too damn big. Yuppies all over the damn place."

He squinted down at her with an intensity that fueled her growing anxiety. The light above his head illuminated his face, accentuating the deep furrows in his forehead and the suspicious narrowing of his eyes. She could see his doubts etched into his skin. Was she prey or predator? he was wondering. Was she crazy like she used to be? What did she really want? And was she really worth taking a chance on?

Now was the moment. He was making up his mind.

She held up the six-pack and announced, "I brought the liquid refreshment, as promised. How do you like that for a cheap date?"

There was a faint rumble of thunder in the distance. He looked up into the dark sky. Then he said, "It's fixing to rain. You might as well come in." She could see in the relaxing of his face that he'd decided—famous writer or not, she was the same gullible pushover she'd been as a girl. Molly heaved a sigh of relief; this might be possible after all. His contempt for women was working in her favor.

"Such hospitality," she said, starting up the steps.

He held the screen door open and let the dog precede her inside.

They entered a large, dreary living room lighted only by the glow from a huge Sony TV, which was on with no sound. A dingy couch against the wall was covered with newspapers and the brown shag carpet looked and smelled badly in need of vacuuming.

"Colored gal who does for me didn't show up this week," he said. "House usually looks better."

The dog settled down with a clunk in the middle of the floor.

"Let's put your beer on ice." Crocker headed toward the lighted kitchen.

She followed him. He took the six-pack of Coors Light from her and made a face. "You *drink* this cat piss?" He opened the refrigerator and leaned over to take two bottles of Shiner Bock from the bottom of the door. "No offense, but we'll drink mine." Molly took a good look as he bent down, to see if he had a gun tucked into his waistband in back. Dressed as he was, it was the only place on his body he could be concealing one. She didn't think he was.

He straightened, twisted the top off a bottle, and handed

it to her. "You 'famous writers' need a glass? Or you drink out of the bottle?"

"We drink it any way we can get it." She took a sip from the bottle.

"Well," he said, opening his and lifting it toward her, "here's to reunions, Molly. No hard feelings, I hope."

She touched her bottle to his. "Hard feelings? After all these years? Shit, Sheriff, who'd stay mad that long?" She put the bottle to her lips and watched him as she drank. He was moving his eyes along her body openly now, assessing her. Grunting his grudging approval, he took a long swig of his beer.

"We did have our differences at one time," he said. "Sure was a bad break your husband showing up like that." A small knowing smile played on his thin lips.

"Sure was," Molly said, barely able, even after all the intervening time, to think about the scene—Grady arriving home to find them in the bedroom, his shocked and icy departure, Crocker running off and weaseling on the bargain.

"I suppose he was real mad, your hubby?"

"Ancient history," she said with a shrug.

"So." He wiped his lips with the back of his hand. "You got some questions for me, huh?"

"Well, I got to admit something to you, Olin."

He raised his eyebrows.

"I came here under false pretenses."

"Did you now?" He leaned back against the refrigerator and his unbuttoned shirt fell open. The skin on his chest wrinkled and sagged like it was two sizes too big for him now, but he displayed it with all the arrogance of a young stud. He pressed the beer bottle against his chest and rolled it slowly between his nipples. "So you don't have any questions for me, Molly? Here I thought I'd be in your article, you'd make me famous."

"Oh, yes, I've got questions, but not about the bill. I'm not much interested in the bill. Never was."

"That right? I thought you were writing about it."

"I am."

"But you're not interested?"

"You know what we women are like." She reached out and rested a finger on his cheek. The skin felt dampish and thick, as though you'd have to go through many layers to hit bone or blood. Slowly she ran her finger along his weak jawline to his chin, his neck, and then very slowly down his chest, alongside the beer bottle which he still held pressed to the center. He stood stock-still.

She smiled up at him. "We're always more interested in the personal than the public." She circled her finger through the hair on his chest. It was gray now, but in 1970 it had been jet black and dense. He'd rubbed it against her face and then pushed her head down. Weak with fear and repugnance, she'd done everything he'd told her to do. He hadn't forced her. He'd just held out the promise of the information she craved, and she had gone along with it.

She moved her finger downward to where his big belly swelled. Then she undulated the finger over it down to his belt buckle, which was not the star tonight, but a plain brass buckle. She stopped there and ran her fingernail horizontally above the belt.

"My questions are of a more personal nature," she cooed.

His breathing had quickened. "Like what?"

"Oh, like where's that handsome silver star buckle? It's what drew my attention in the gallery. I wouldn't have noticed you otherwise." She fingered the brass buckle. "I like it much better than this one." Then she pressed her hand slowly down his crotch. With a crude man like this, any subtlety would be wasted. She knew him to be a lecher eager to get to his main event without wasting time on preliminaries.

And she was even more eager. Her anxiety was mounting and she was desperate to finish this painful charade and get to *her* main event.

"It's in my bedroom." He took hold of her upper arm. "Come on. I'll give you a tour"—he leered at her—"of my closet."

Molly pressed her left arm against the purse hanging on her shoulder for courage and let herself be led from the kitchen, her heart thumping, her hands slick with sweat. He led her through the living room and down a dark hallway. Halfway down the hall, with his hand clamped tight around her arm, the walls closed in on her, sealing off any possibility of retreat. He'd led her like this into her father's bedroom when she was sixteen, when he'd had all the power of male authority and she'd had none. She went along with him, then and now.

The bedroom, lighted by one small lamp on a table next to the unmade king-size bed, had the same brown shag carpet as the living room, and the same stale, unclean odor. He stood next to the bed and turned to face her. Immediately he unbuckled his belt and dropped his pants. There sure wasn't much trick to getting this lamb ready for the slaughter.

Molly set her bottle down on the dresser and carefully arranged her purse next to it.

"What's this going to cost me?" he asked. "You haven't told me your questions."

"Well," she said, slowly unzipping her jeans, "what are we talking about here? What do you like these days, Olin?"

"Same old, same old," he said, pulling his boxers down to reveal his erection.

"How about this?" she said, pulling her shirt up. "We'll finish what got interrupted last time. Then you'll answer one question for me." She pulled the shirt over her head and dropped it on the floor.

He was looking her over. "Well, I don't know. That was the deal before. No offense, but you're a lot older now." He smiled.

She stared back at him, making a show of studying his body the same way he was studying hers. "Forty-five next month," she said, holding her stomach in tight and trying to inject pride into her voice.

His smile faded. "As a rule, women over twenty-five just don't do it for me, but I'm making an exception with you. Unfinished business."

She peeled her jeans down and stepped out of them. "I'm flattered. Oh." She turned to the dresser behind her. "I brought you something." She opened the flap of her purse and put her hand in, hesitating, unsure of whether to go for the gun or the condoms. It might be premature for the gun. . . .

"Turn around real slow," he said behind her.

She did what he said—turned real slow.

He was sitting on the bed with a shotgun aimed at her. Lord, that was quick; he must've had it under the bed.

She raised the hand with the condoms. "Such an overreaction, Sheriff. I know you men don't like wearing these, but *really.*" She waved the packet at him. "Nothing personal. It's a rule of mine." She tossed the packet onto the bed next to him. "The first of my three sexual rules," she purred, leaning back against the dresser, bracing her arms behind her, one hand touching the purse.

He kept the shotgun on her with one hand and picked up the packet with the other. As he glanced down to examine it, Molly slipped the gun out of the purse's side compartment and slid it down the back of her white lace bikini pants, hoping they would hold the weight.

Crocker looked up, his grin wide. "Glow-in-the-dark, huh? Well, we'll see. What are your other two rules, Molly?"

"No guns. You need to put that away."

"And?"

"Nothing that draws blood. Other than that, anything goes."

"Tell you what," he said with the shotgun still pointing at her. "Let me take a look at that handbag of yours. Just to make sure you're abidin' by your own rules."

Molly reached behind her, grabbed the purse, and tossed it onto the bed. He lifted the flap and felt around inside, then tossed it back to her.

He leaned down and put the shotgun on the floor.

"Under the bed," Molly said. "Out of sight."

He pushed it under the bed.

"Okay. Now put one of those rubbers on, Sheriff, and I'll see if it *really* tastes like margaritas. I'm *very* fond of margaritas."

He ripped the package hurriedly and took out the little circle. As he unrolled it on himself, she crossed the room to him quickly. He was sitting on the edge of the bed. She knelt between his open legs, trying not to breathe in his sour smell, which she remembered all too well. "Next time I'll show you how I can put it on with my mouth—a skill for the nineties." She put her hands on his knees. "Here. Lie back. Go on," she crooned.

He lowered his head to the bed, letting his legs hang over the edge. Perfect. She felt like gagging. She slid her left hand slowly up the inside of his thigh while her right hand reached behind her for the gun. She brought the .38 up underneath his legs and pressed it against his scrotum. When she cocked it, the noise was unmistakable.

Crocker let out a little "oof" noise.

"Stay still," she said. "You move and I'll blow your balls to raw hamburger."

She glanced up toward his face to see if he was buying it. His lips looked frozen in a little O. He was terror-struck. There was no denying the powerful thrill of satisfaction that rippled through her. This sudden shift of power felt mighty good. She had the makings of a vigilante after all.

She pushed the gun harder against him. His erection had collapsed, the condom wrinkled like a deflated balloon.

"You wanted to know my question, Sheriff. Here it is, real simple. Who paid you off in 1970?"

The only sound in the room was his labored breathing.

"You owe me an answer. If you don't tell me, I'll shoot one of these fine Black Talons into your soft tissue right here,"—she gave him a jab—"and I'll do it with pleasure." She looked up at his face, which had turned a dark red. "You understand?"

He grunted.

"Okay. Someone gave you fifty thousand. I know that. Who was it?"

"No one." His voice was a croak.

She applied more pressure. He whined and squirmed on the bed.

"Go ahead and move again. Give me an excuse. Gelding you would be a public service. Who was it?"

"You don't want to know." His voice quavered.

"Who was it?"

He was silent.

She'd been afraid of this. She needed to convince him she was serious. She pressed her left thumb against his scrotum right next to the gun muzzle. Then she lowered the gun two inches so it was aiming into the side of the mattress. She closed her eyes and fired.

The explosion shook the small room. He sat up with a shriek, tears running down his face. Molly was dazed and deafened. Crocker made a grab for her arm, still screaming.

She jabbed the gun into his scrotum, hard.

He shrieked again.

"Lie down!" she shouted, cocking the gun.

Whimpering, he lowered himself back on the dirty sheets. "Oww. Stop," he begged. "Please stop."

"That was just a warning. The next one will end your sorry sex life. Who was it?"

"You won't like it." His voice was high with fear and pain.

She pressed harder with the gun. "Who?"

He said in a whisper, "Parnell Morrisey."

"What?"

He spoke it louder. "Parnell Morrisey."

"You liar," she hissed.

"It's true," he croaked.

"No."

"Yes. Molly, really."

"No fucking way."

"Really. The day we got the body he came to ID it and he gave me the money then, in cash." He was talking fast. "Parnell Morrisey. The senator. Right there in my office. All I had to do was call it a suicide and not follow up on the leads, not pull the houseboat up for a while. That's the truth, so help me God. Put that gun away, please. Let me sit up."

Molly's blood thrummed at her temples. "No."

"I swear it. Let me up. I feel sick."

She pressed the gun harder into his groin. He groaned. "You're hurting me bad."

"Good."

"I told you what you wanted."

"Why should I believe a weasel like you?"

"If I was gonna lie, I would've given you some other name." His voice shook. "He told me back then you might be a problem. That you were just a kid, but you were real smart and you never gave up on things. He said not to tell you anything. That's why I never gave you any information."

Molly felt herself deflating as if she'd pumped herself up with phony, hot-air courage and it was all leaking out, leaving her limp and pathetic like that miserable condom. If this was true, what did it mean?

"Who killed my daddy?" The question came out like a plea.

"I don't know what happened. God as my witness, I don't know."

"Parnell?" she asked, amazed she could even entertain the idea.

"Maybe. I don't know. Far as I know, it *was* a suicide, just like I called it."

"But why would he pay you off?"

"I don't know. Let me sit up. I can't breathe. I feel sick—"

Molly backed up on her knees. She kept the gun pointed at his groin. "Okay, sit up."

He swung his legs up on the bed and scootched back to lean against the headboard. His face was blotched, wet with tears, and some long strands of mucous hung from his nostrils.

"Put your hands on your belly so I can see them," she said.

He did it. "Leave now," he whined, "and I won't tell anyone about this."

"Oh, you won't tell anyone." Her entire body was going numb, as though a shot of Novocaine was taking effect. The fear and anxiety were retreating.

"Where's your checkbook, Sheriff?"

He pointed to a small roll-top desk against the far wall.

"I'm going to fetch it for you. Don't you even twitch."

She stood carefully, keeping the gun on him, and backed up to the desk. "Where?"

"Inside. One of the cubbyholes."

"Which one?"

"Top right."

Without looking, she reached in and groped around until she found a plastic-covered checkbook and a ballpoint pen.

She walked back and stood over the bed. "Here's the deal. You're going to make out a check, payable to Sylvia Ramos. Remember her?"

His ravaged face was blank.

"You remember. Pretty Mescan girl. Travis County Jail, 1975, one of your Miracle Massage recruits. The amount of the check will be a hundred thousand dollars. It's a charitable contribution, so you'll be able to deduct it. On that little line where you write what it's for you'll write 'Casa Christine.' That's Christine as in Christine Fanon. Remember her?"

His mouth hung open in disbelief, as though a ghost had just passed in front of him.

"She's dead, of course—drug overdose—but because you want to make some small gesture to atone for all the harm you've done, you're going to contribute to her memorial—a shelter for young prostitutes. It's appropriate since young women in need have been a longtime interest of yours."

She dropped the checkbook on his stomach and the pen on the mattress. "Go ahead. Write the check."

He opened the checkbook. He began to write, painfully slowly, having difficulty controlling his shaking.

"Make it nice and legible, Sheriff. I will Fed Ex it to Sylvia," Molly told him. "The amazing thing is, when I leave here you're not going to stop payment on it. And you will not do anything to retaliate against me or Sylvia Ramos or anyone associated with this matter." She managed a smile. "I bet you want to know *why* you're not going to do those things."

He finished writing the check. She picked it up and examined it. He'd done it just the way she'd instructed. She made a move to put it in her pocket and discovered she was still in her underwear. Suddenly she wanted desperately to get dressed, but didn't know how to do it and still hold the gun on him, so she folded the check and stuck it in her bra.

"Now, Sheriff, do you want to keep this place and the four hundred thou you've got in CDs at the bank? Actually three hundred now, isn't it?" She looked at him, waiting for an answer, but he was staring down at his hands.

"Well, I think you do. You want to continue being a gentleman farmer. At age sixty-one you don't want to go back to being a dumb hick with nothing in the world.

"Listen good. If you stop payment on this check or if you tell anyone about tonight—not that you'll feel much like talking about it—here's what's going to happen to you." She slowed her speech, pronouncing each threat for maximum impact. "I will do everything in my power to see you convicted of sexual assault, indecency with a child, and any other charges we can dream up. I have a war chest of almost a half million to spend on this—investigators, lawyers, the works. You know where I got the money? My father's life insurance. One hundred thousand invested since 1970 in tax-free bonds, compounding and growing, never touched. I've been saving that money for *you,* Sheriff, and I am willing to spend every cent of it pursuing you. If I don't put you in prison, then I *will* bankrupt you. You might beat the rap, but the ride will cost you everything you've got.

"Your ex-wives—Ruth, Jeanette, and especially Kelly— are going to cooperate. They don't like you much. And the private investigator I've had on your case has come up with the names of several minor girls. When I use my contacts in the media to send out the call for other young women who have been abused by you, we will be flooded with responses. You have spread your seed widely, Olin."

Molly was studying his face. It was gray and sullen. "You understand me? I want an answer."

"I understand you," he said in a barely audible voice.

"Good. I'm going to give you another chance now to tell the truth. You'll want to take this chance because I'll check it out and if I find you've lied I will feed you, piece by piece, into the meat grinder of our legal system. Have you told me the truth tonight? Was it Parnell Morrisey who paid you fifty thousand in 1970?"

"Yes, but it was sixty thousand," he said.

Molly felt certainty like a lead lump in her stomach. She believed him.

"Now, Sheriff," she said, "how am I going to get out of here? Do I have to tie you up like you've been doing some kinky bondage and call 911 on my way home to come rescue you? Or shall I just leave?"

"Just leave. For God's sake, just fucking *leave*."

The sound of rain beating down on the roof stopped her for a moment. She wondered how long it had been raining without her hearing it. "You were right about the rain," she told Crocker. "Oh, one other thing. I'm a writer, so of course I've written all this down. My lawyer and my editor both have copies, so trying to do me harm would cause you no end of trouble. And I'll be watching over your ex-wives and those little girls you statutory-raped to make sure you don't contact or threaten them." She poked the gun into his abdomen. "You hear me, Sheriff?"

He nodded.

Without taking her eyes off him, Molly bent and scooped up her jeans and shirt. She got her purse from the dresser and approached the bed. She reached her foot underneath and nudged the shotgun out. It was tricky, but she stuffed her clothes under her arm and picked up the gun with her left hand. "I'll leave this at the end of the driveway."

She backed to the door. "Count to a hundred, please, before you get up."

"Get the fuck out of my house."

"Thanks for your generous contribution. And, Sheriff— you're one lucky son of a bitch. You're getting off easy tonight. But you're going to be under surveillance from now on and, if you mess with any more underage girls, you will end up in jail. That's a promise, and you have cause to know that I never forget a promise."

She took one last look at him. He was just a naked old

man shivering on his bed, tears oozing from under his closed eyelids.

By the time Molly got halfway back to Austin, the rain had cooled the air so much she had to roll up the window. She was shivering, still in her underwear.

21

OLD MOTHER GOOSE,
WHEN SHE WANTED TO WANDER,
WOULD RIDE THROUGH THE AIR
ON A VERY FINE GANDER.

—*MOTHER GOOSE*

Sarah Jane Hurley wakes in the rain. It's dark and she is lying on the ground, one arm still embracing her tree. She loves the feel of the rain, each drop a laughing baby's kiss, cooling her burning skin. Steam is rising from her body, all her anger burned away, vaporized into the darkness.

It is the first time in years she hasn't awakened in fear.

She opens her mouth and lets the rain feed her. She's very, very dry and it is giving her exactly what she needs.

It's raining, it's pouring, the old man is snoring, fell out of bed and broke his head, and couldn't get up in the morning. She used to sing it to Tom and Ellie on rainy mornings when she'd get them up for school, and before that, Gramma used to sing it to her.

If it hadn't rained so hard the morning of the fire, they all said, her children would have died. Tom and Ellie would have been burned alive in the back bedroom. A godsend, a blessing, everyone agreed. It's the thing she's most thankful for in this life. To think about it makes her tremble—such a close call. She was saved by the grace of the rain.

For years she hasn't let herself think about it. Now it seems important to remember. She lets the memory wash over her and flow out, her gift to the tree. Tom was five and

Ellie was seven. Sarah Jane had been out most of the night drinking. *Lady Bird, Lady Bird, fly away home.* She got home at four in the morning and was smoking on the sofa in the living room so she wouldn't have to go into the bedroom and face Harold's angry preaching. She fell into a deep drunken sleep, and the cigarette dropped from her fingers to the floor. It set the newspapers on fire and that set the curtains on fire and then the chair. And instead of coming her way as it should have, the fire crawled along the carpet to the hall and back to the children's room and there it set some wood toys on fire, and then the covers hanging off Tom's bed, and then his Kermit the Frog pajamas, and then the perfect soft baby skin of his arm. *Your house is on fire, your children will burn.*

By the time she'd awakened from her stupor, it was nearly over. She staggered out of the smoky house, still drunk, not even aware her home was on fire, forgetting she had children to take care of.

The firemen said Ellie and Tom would have burned to death if Harold had not crawled in through the flames and got them out. And they said Harold could never have done it without the rain. Instead of Tom just getting some very bad burns on his arm, both children would have burned to death, but the heavens had opened at the last minute and spilled down rain, torrents of blessed rain on their house in Baytown, just in time to dampen the flames so Harold could get to them.

It was the last straw for Harold, of course. He'd divorced her and he'd gotten custody of the children. It was the best thing: he was not a bad father.

She moves her lips to catch the fat drops. She understands now what she is meant to do with this new beginning: she is meant to save those people in the Senate from the poison gas. That's why Fate put her under the deck to hear them talking—so she could pay back what she owes. Why didn't she see it before?

"Thank you," she whispers to the rain, "thank you for helping then, and thank you for helping now."

Sarah Jane goes back to sleep, thinking if she were to worship anything in this world it would be the rain.

22

IT WAS NOT DEATH, FOR I STOOD UP,
AND ALL THE DEAD, LIE DOWN—
—EMILY DICKINSON

Long past midnight Molly Cates sat watching the rain wriggle down the dark window in quivering, wormlike runnels.

It had taken hours for her to calm down enough to start thinking in any coherent way. The adrenaline surge of excitement she'd felt on the way home, the undeniable outlaw thrill of having gotten away with something very dangerous, was finally subsiding. But it was like robbing a bank and discovering what you had stolen was not the gold coins you'd been after but a sack of rotting garbage. She didn't know what on earth to do with Crocker's revelation.

Parnell.

Parnell Morrisey had paid Crocker sixty thousand dollars to call her daddy's death a suicide and close the case.

Why? Why would he have done that? The only theory Molly could dredge up was so completely far-fetched she could barely get her mind around it: Parnell had killed Vernon Cates. Could that possibly be true?

Given the right circumstances, she knew, anyone could kill anyone. After all, mothers killed their children, men killed their best friends, lovers killed one another, people committed vile, incomprehensible acts all the time. But Parnell? That gentle, loving, rational man, her godfather and lifelong protector, killing his boyhood friend—the idea was too out-landish.

But maybe something had happened, they'd had a fight.

Maybe her daddy was going to write something that threatened Parnell's political career.

Maybe the friendship deteriorated after they moved to Lake Travis. It did seem to Molly, as she thought back, that they had seen less of the Morriseys after the move. Even though the Morriseys had an apartment in Austin, just a thirty-five-minute drive from Volente, they had rarely seen them. Her daddy was preoccupied with Franny and his writing. Parnell was busy with the legislature when he was in Austin and running his ranch back in Lubbock the rest of the time. Rose was often ill.

But maybe they'd had a disagreement Molly hadn't been aware of—a feud of some sort.

She would, of course, ask Parnell about it.

She could call him now, get him out of bed, and ask him point-blank: Why did you pay Olin Crocker off? Did you murder my daddy?

But if he had done this, he had concealed it for twenty-eight years and would be unlikely to confess it now.

If only Harriet still had her wits. Her brother's confidante and a lifelong close friend of Parnell and Rose, Harriet would certainly have known if the friendship had gone sour. Her brother would have talked about it, and even after they'd moved away he would have written about it. Her daddy had kept up a regular, weekly correspondence with his lonesome sister left back in Lubbock. They were both prodigious letter writers of the old school, who always preferred writing to talking on the phone.

And Harriet had said she'd saved every word Vernon Cates had written. Maybe somewhere in that vast morass of Harriet's archives there were letters about it, letters from the year following the move.

Molly's spirits sagged at the thought of confronting the archives. Unable to face them before, she'd banished them into storage and neglected them, but she knew it was the inevitable next step. Tomorrow she'd have to have a go at the archives. A needle in a haystack would be easier, and a lot more fun to look for.

When Grady Traynor arrived with his dog at 3 A.M. and saw Molly sitting in the dark living room, he knew enough not to turn on the lights. Without a word, he came in and sat at her feet, leaning back against her knees. The dog thumped down next to him.

Grady joined her in staring straight ahead into the black, rainy window. After a few minutes of silence he asked, "What do you get out of it, Molly?"

She took awhile before answering. In the long years she'd been keeping these monthly vigils she had never tried to explain them to anyone. She had never really understood the need to sit in the dark from time to time and watch the night away. It had started after her father died; certainly it was connected to his death.

Now she found she wanted to understand it. And to talk about it. She said, "I think it's because I don't have any ritual in my life, no religion, no traditions. Maybe it's like lighting a candle or saying Kaddish or ululating or wearing sackcloth and ashes."

"Mourning."

"I suppose."

"But most mourning comes to an end," Grady said very quietly. "Don't you think that's what rituals are for—to bring it to an end after a given time?"

"Probably. But I don't seem to be able to do that. Maybe you have to keep on mourning until you get it right."

"Or until the dead lie down," he said. He was looking up at her now, his pale eyes silvery in the dark.

"Grady, I never even went to the cemetery when they buried him. After the funeral, I just walked away. I didn't say good-bye, and I've never been to his grave."

"Do you want to tell me what's been happening, Molly?"

Yes, she did want to tell him—desperately. He was the best listener she knew, that rare man who didn't thrust himself into a problem and try to solve everything. He was willing just to hear it, to acknowledge it as a problem, to listen to you massage it until you were satisfied. She wanted to tell him about Parnell and the payoff. She wanted desperately to tell him, but she couldn't without telling the Olin Crocker part and that was a subject she could never discuss with him. Secrets had a tendency to cast a shadow much larger than themselves.

"No," she said. "I don't have anything to tell yet."

"Well, I'm around. Any time you're in the mood to talk."

She rested her hand on the back of his neck. "I know."

He turned and knelt in front of her, sliding his hands slowly up her legs. "Listen, Copper and I are badly in need of some sack time. We'd love to have you join us." His hands moved up her belly and brushed her breasts. "We really desire that. Come to bed, Molly."

She leaned over to meet his lips for a long kiss.

"Okay," she said, a little breathlessly.

He stood up, took hold of her hands, and lifted her out of the chair. "Hot dog, Copper," he said. "We just got lucky."

Every time Grady Traynor got up from her bed to go to work, she had to resist the impulse to pull him back, wrap her arms around him, press her body tight against his back, and beg him not to go. She'd never done it, of course, or even told him she felt like doing it, but the impulse seemed to be getting stronger.

They'd beeped him, and he would go, as he always did, immediately alert, without a grumble. Even though he'd had less than two hours of sleep.

She checked the glowing green numerals on the clock radio. "Four-fifteen, Grady. What is it?"

"The Gristead case. Karen Gristead says she wants to make a confession—to me."

"Of course she does. It's your bedside manner." She ran her hand up his bare back. "And she doesn't know the half of it."

He leaned down and kissed her, but it was perfunctory. His attention was already on Karen Gristead and her estranged husband who'd been found dead in his bathtub with a bullet hole where his left eye had been.

Grady picked up his pants, which were in a heap on the floor. "When I leave, are you going back to the window?"

"No. I'm going back to sleep," she said.

But when she heard him shut the front door she pulled on a big T-shirt and went downstairs. The dog followed her, the jingle of his tags the only sound in the silent house.

The window was still inky black, just as she'd left it, and the rain continued to run down the glass. She settled into the wing chair with her legs curled up underneath her.

The dog circled a few times, then thumped down in front of the chair. Copper had been retired two years earlier from the Austin Police Department's K-9 Unit after his handler had been beaten to death. In Molly's opinion, the dog's behavior problems resulted from the trauma. He was still waiting for his handler to come back.

"Oh, Copper," she murmured, "the past isn't really past, is it? You're the only one in my life who seems to understand that."

23

> THERE WAS AN OLD WOMAN, AND WHAT DO YOU
> THINK?
> SHE LIVED UPON NOTHING BUT VICTUALS AND
> DRINK;
> VICTUALS AND DRINK WERE THE CHIEF OF HER DIET,
> AND YET THIS OLD WOMAN COULD NEVER BE QUIET.
> —MOTHER GOOSE

Even a pint of the best Scotch whiskey never gave her a float like this. Sarah Jane is soaring. She is a child rolling down a green grassy slope, a buzzard riding the air currents, a sleepwalker drifting through time, seeing little relics of the past. There's a tiny skull that was once Theobald, the squirrel she tamed to eat nuts out of her hand in Gramma's backyard. There are some rocks Tom found at the creek the year he learned to walk and feathers Ellie collected at the zoo. And there is a lock of long silky brown hair that was Harold's when she first knew him and they made love on the beach. Sarah Jane sleeps, she sweats, she shivers, she wakes, she dreams, she talks, she raves, she laughs, she remembers.

But mostly she dreams. She is sick with a fever and has to stay home from school today. It is raining and the rain pings and dings on the tin-can roof, and some of the rain falls through holes in the tin and hits her face, like when she slept under the deck. "Rain, rain, go away," she sings when a raindrop pings on her cheek. "Come again some other day," Gramma sings.

Gramma brings her something sweet and cool to drink.

She kneels down and her hand shakes as she puts the cup to Sarah Jane's lips. She dribbles some on Sarah Jane's neck. Gramma is wearing antlers trimmed with foil and other shiny things. Sarah Jane laughs to see it. "Gramma," she says, "what big horns you have." "The better to heal you with, my babee," Gramma says, and she laughs too. This is a dream Sarah Jane loves.

Then she dreams of candlelight and being surrounded by tiny clean white skulls and hundreds of bones arranged just so, feathers, pine cones, smooth stones of many colors. But this dream she doesn't like at all. It is too much like being a body laid out for viewing in a funeral home, like Mama was. She sees the chicken feet, and the whole bird's wing which still has some blood on it. The candle flickers as the rain and wind pick up. Dreams can go bad so fast.

"I've got to go," she says.

"Nooooo," Gramma says.

"There's something I've got to do."

"Oh, noooo."

"Really. It's important."

"What be so important, babee?" Gramma asks.

"I don't remember."

"You be sick. Got a fever, an infection."

"I know. But there's something..."

"Don't you know me?" asks Gramma. "I am Mother Teresa."

"No, you're my Gramma."

"Oh, no, God told me take care of the homeless and the sick and the hungry. And there you were, babee, waiting at my tree."

"That's *your* tree?" Sarah Jane asks in awe.

"Oh, yes. It was a sign."

"A sign?"

"The sign say I will make a miracle. God is testing me now I have brought you back to life to see if I make you well."

Sarah Jane thinks about being afraid. There are things here a person might be afraid of, but she needs to remember what she has to do. She can smell the rain as if it were real rain instead of dream rain. It is the kind of drenching rain that makes the earth swell and soften to mud and makes the trees smell overripe, all that wood and greenness turning to sodden decay. Never has she had a dream like this before, so real and so unreal.

She remembers something she was trying to remember— that second verse. *Little Bopeep fell fast asleep and dreamt she heard them bleating. When she awoke, it was a joke, for still they all were fleeting.*

She sits up and remembers what she needs to do: she needs to call Little Bopeep and tell her about the terrible danger the Senate is in. She saw it all so clearly under the tree: her children were saved, now she needs to save people to pay the universe back. "What day is it?" she asks. She can see daylight through the chinks in the wall. Even so, the candle still burns. And it is still raining.

"You are sitting up, babee!" The woman puts her face close to Sarah Jane's. She has taken off the turban with the antlers on it. She has a fuzz of gray hair on her small dark head, which is perched on a long slender neck. "The miracle is complete now. It is accomplished."

"But there's an emergency, something so important."

"What can be more important than a miracle? Tell me that, babee."

Sarah Jane looks into the woman's glowing black eyes which seem to float in a sea of cream decorated with red swirls. She looks around at the circle of bones and rocks surrounding her, at the candles and the bird's wing. She has fallen into the hands of a madwoman. "Tell me about the miracle," she says.

"I found you laying dead and gone. You be cold as the grave. No pulse what-so-ever."

"There was a tree," Sarah Jane says.

"Oh, yes, babee! You are remembering. At the roots of my sacred tree I find you. That is where I perform the miracle. Then I bring you back here."

"How did you do that?" asks Sarah Jane.

"I carry you."

Sarah Jane studies the woman. She is very, very thin. Probably weighs sixty pounds less than Sarah Jane. "That really is a miracle," she says carefully.

"Yes, yes, a miracle. And then I heal you. It is not enough to bring a dead person to life. Also I must heal you."

"I *was* sick."

"Bad infection in your leg. Cellulitis. Dehydration. High fever. Now look."

Sarah Jane lifts her head to look down at her leg. The redness and swelling are nearly gone. Only a few scabs remain.

"It *is* much better. How did you do that?"

"I give you liquids with electrolytes and sugar and salt. This I know from being a nurse's aide at Bellevue Hospital in New York, many years. The infection—" The madwoman raises her hands and wiggles the long, delicate fingers. "It burned itself up."

"Well, thank you," says Sarah Jane, feeling a moment of real gratitude. Her mind is whirring. She needs to get this crazy woman to help her do what she is still too weak to do herself. She needs to get her to call that writer, Bopeep, Molly whatever-her-name-is. Before it's too late to stop Billy Goat from killing all those people.

"What's your name?" Sarah Jane asks.

"Why, babee, don't you know me?" She smiles radiantly. "I am Mother Teresa."

"Of course," Sarah Jane says. "I am Cow Lady. And for this miracle to be really complete we need to let the world know about it."

Mother Teresa claps her hands. "They will build a shrine here."

"I know just the person to tell the world," says Sarah Jane. "She will write about it in her magazine and all the world will know."

Mother Teresa claps again and her face is radiant. "Yes, babee!"

Sarah Jane has lucked into just the right approach. "You will call her and bring her here so she can see what you have done," she says. Then, suddenly, she panics. "My bag! Do you have my bag? The phone number's in it."

Mother Teresa's laugh is a musical scale. "Oh, babee, sure we got your bag." She lifts it up to show Sarah Jane. "We got it right here. Nothing to worry about."

24

MY FATHER DIED A MONTH AGO
AND LEFT ME ALL HIS RICHES;
A FEATHER BED, A WOODEN LEG,
AND A PAIR OF LEATHER BREECHES;
A COFFEE POT WITHOUT A SPOUT,
A CUP WITHOUT A HANDLE,
A TOBACCO PIPE WITHOUT A LID,
AND HALF A FARTHING CANDLE.

—MOTHER GOOSE

Sunday morning arrived dull and drizzly at the window; the rain persisted but seemed wrung out, exhausted with its night's work.

Molly Cates did what she did first every morning: she made coffee, the one ritual that never failed to give her comfort. When she had a cup in hand, she called the Lamar Boulevard Self Storage to find out when the gates opened. A recorded message told her Sunday hours were from ten to six.

She had two hours to kill, so she brought in the papers that had accumulated outside during the past three days. She scanned the *American-Patriot* for news of the Emily Bickerstaff murder. The only mention was in Friday's paper—a small article on the first page of the Metro section that identified the homeless woman and described the discovery of the body near Waller Creek by two ninth graders working on a school science project.

There was also an article about the concealed handgun bill, saying the vote was set for the next day and the bill was expected to pass by a huge margin.

Just before ten she pulled on shorts and an old T-shirt and located the padlock key in a kitchen drawer. Driving through the rain, she thought about Aunt Harriet and her powerful attachment to her worldly possessions.

Three years earlier, when it had become clear to Molly that her aunt was too addled to live alone anymore, there had been a real battle. Harriet didn't want to leave the house she'd lived in for fifty years but, after she nearly burned the house down by leaving a pot on the stove all night, Molly had convinced her it was time to move into the nursing home. That left the problem of what to do with a lifetime's accumulation of furniture and china and clothes and knickknacks and books and pots and pans and, most difficult for Harriet, the voluminous Cates family archives. The old woman agreed to sell her furniture, but not the family antiques she had been particularly attached to. And she was nearly frantic over the archives, which occupied an entire room of her house—an accumulation of photos and letters and memorabilia of three generations of the Cates family, none of whom had ever thrown away so much as a single scrap of paper.

Molly and Harriet finally reached a compromise: Molly would ship these precious things back to Austin and take good care of them. The antiques and the china she'd save for such time as Jo Beth might want them, and the archives Molly would personally maintain during her lifetime. She vowed she would preserve everything exactly as Harriet had done before her.

With this reassurance, Harriet had relented and gone meekly into the Regency Oaks Senior Care Center.

Of course, Molly didn't have room in her townhouse for any of it, especially the five large file cabinets and all the cartons. Every nook and crevice of her small house was already filled with her own accumulation, which had burgeoned out into half the two-car garage and threatened the other half.

So when the shipment arrived in Austin, Molly had it delivered to a storage unit she'd rented for the purpose. As a temporary measure until she had time to sort through it and find a place to keep it at home. But in the three years since then she had not once gone to check on the stuff. She paid the storage rent by the year and, each time it came due, she promised herself that *this* year she would take care of it.

She pulled through the gates, resigned to a day of discomfort and misery. The place was deserted. Even in sunshine, Molly thought it the saddest and loneliest place in the world. In the rain on a Sunday morning, it was unspeakably bleak: long rows of identical flat-roofed barracks with locked doors stretched to infinity. It was a mausoleum for the old possessions people didn't really want but couldn't throw away—a pitiful limbo for material goods.

Three years of rain and heat and nonusage had made the padlock stiff, but she managed to unlock it and open the door. Her energy melted away when she saw how much *stuff* was crammed in the small unit, much more than she remembered, as if some reverse-thief had sneaked in and added all his family rejects to hers. The hot, stale, dusty air filled her lungs with regret. Before we die, she decided, we should burn our accumulated possessions in a Viking funeral, so our families don't have to contend with them.

Piled to the top of the unit on one side was the old furniture Harriet couldn't bear to sell off: a mahogany end table that had belonged to her grandmother, a carved chair that had been Donald's mother's favorite, a small oak dresser, a painted hope chest, and at the top, wrapped in green garbage bags, some shapes Molly couldn't identify. There were also cartons of books, china, and glassware. Harriet had been certain Jo Beth would "marry well" and want all this someday when she had a big house to fill.

On the other side, the archives were packed in tight: five three-drawer file cabinets with four bulging cartons stacked on top. It was enough to make you wish your ancestors had been illiterate.

Molly thought the letters were most likely to be in the file cabinets. She pulled the drawer on one and found it stuck. She tried every one of the fifteen drawers before accepting that they were locked. Was she supposed to have a key? Had Harriet given her one? She had a sudden memory of her last visit to the nursing home. In the lockbox where Harriet's jewelry was kept, there had been some keys. Molly hadn't even wondered about them at the time. Well, damn. She wasn't about to go back to Lubbock.

She got in her truck and called Information for the numbers of some locksmiths with Sunday hours. After four rejections, she finally found one who could come immediately.

The white truck arrived in nineteen minutes. It took him ten seconds to open all five filing cabinets, for which he charged her forty dollars. She paid him in cash, then started the tedious job of going through the files.

Aunt Harriet had kept *every*thing, including the grade school report cards for every member of the family, every tax return of her life, all her canceled checks, her papers from college, her mother's sixty years of daily diaries, her husband Donald's engineering notebooks, maps of every city she'd ever been to, menus, birthday cards. When Molly got to the fourth cabinet, she found Harriet's personal correspondence—an entire lifetime of it. One whole drawer was filled with letters from her childhood friend who'd moved to Chicago and from a pen pal in Tokyo.

In the bottom drawer Molly finally found what she was looking for—letters from her daddy, organized, thank God, in a roughly chronological fashion, beginning from when he'd gone to camp in San Marcos the summer he was nine and moving through college and vacations away from Lubbock. Even back then his handwriting had been exquisite, a legacy from the days when they taught the Palmer method in schools. Seeing the familiar flourish on his *w*'s brought back the scritch of his pen on paper, the silences when he'd look off into space between sentences.

Toward the back of the bottom drawer she found the letters that began in June 1969 when Molly and her father had moved to Lake Travis. All were written with a real ink pen on sturdy gray stationery. Even though he had been an excellent typist and did his magazine work on an old Underwood, Vernon Cates believed personal letters should be handwritten, a prejudice his daughter shared.

The storage unit was hot and stuffy, so Molly took two

handfuls of letters and, hunching over to protect them from the rain, ran back to the truck. She turned on the air conditioning and put her feet up on the dashboard, settling in.

The letters from their first summer at the lake talked about the move, about meeting Franny Lawrence—"this sweet and gorgeous redhead"—and how much both he and Molly loved living on the lake. He wrote a lot about his financial difficulties and thanked Harriet for the loan to help them with the move, something Molly had not been aware of. He wrote about Molly and her adjustment to the move, her initial loneliness, his concern that he was doing the right thing, issues she hadn't realized worried him. By January 1970 the letters talked increasingly about Franny and his growing love for her.

Every letter repeated his wish that Harriet would move to Lake Travis or Austin to be closer to them. Molly was amazed at how dependent he seemed to be on his sister. He asked for her advice constantly; he seemed to need her approval on everything, no matter how small.

Molly had always believed he tried to get Harriet to move with them because he was worried about her being lonely in Lubbock, but really, she discovered, it was because he depended on her for everything and felt lost without her.

There was one brief mention of having seen Parnell and Rose in Austin.

She finished reading the stack she had and ran through the rain to get the rest of them.

Finally, after nearly two hours, she arrived at May 1970. The last letter, dated May ninth, was the one she was looking for. She could have gone to it right away, but she didn't. She'd felt the need to take the letters in order and work her way gradually to the end, to her father's inevitable last letter.

It was two pages long.

May 9, 1970

Dearest H,
After our conversation last night, I was able to sleep, finally.

Thank you. Thank you, dear sister, for taking this on. You have always been so good to me, but this is above and beyond everything. You are an angel. I will never ask you for anything else ever again.

I really think it will be easier coming from you. And she'll have a chance to calm down before I am likely to see her. And then there will be other people around, so she will have to behave and not be so melodramatic.

The fourteenth will be perfect. She's planning to be in Lubbock without Parnell because he is involved in the finance bill and she needs to see her mother. It will be the perfect time for you to tell her. If there is a perfect time for such a thing.

About the wedding—Parnell will want to come, of course, but I wish they wouldn't. Can you think of any way around that problem? I don't trust her to hold up emotionally, she's so fragile, and it's just too awkward. If I said it was just family, maybe that would do it. But I'm afraid he'll still insist on coming and that would be disaster. I don't think she could make it through the ceremony. Do you have any ideas for me, big sister?

Oh, Harriet, I'm so sorry for all this mess. I wish I'd listened to you back in high school when it all started, but I couldn't help myself. She was so beautiful and I'm such a weak man. I know it's been hard for you to understand how we could have kept the relationship going all these years. But you know how hard I tried to end it before and what happened then. But we're older now, and wiser, I hope, so maybe she will take it in stride this time.

The move has certainly helped, as I hoped it might; I've only seen her alone once since we came here, so the old pattern is already broken, which should make this a little easier to take.

Tell her I will always love her as a dear friend, but she can see this new development makes it impossible for me to ever be alone with her again. We have been lucky all these years that Josephine and Parnell and Molly never found out about us, and so we never really hurt anyone with it.

Thank you, sister mine, dearest Harriet, thank you. I owe you the world for taking this on.

Call me when you have talked with her, will you? So I know it is done and can breathe easy. I've been so dreading it. It is the only thing that stands in the way of my great happiness with the soul mate I have finally found.

I remain your little brother, repentant, and happier than ever.

V

Molly sat motionless with the letter in her hand.

Her father and Rose Morrisey.

For more than twenty years her father had carried on an affair with his best friend's wife. It had started during high school before they were married; it had continued while they were married to other people, while her mother was still alive, while she was dying. And Aunt Harriet knew about it all along.

He was asking Harriet to tell his lover he was finished with her, and she was going to do it for him. Her father was not just an adulterer; he was also a buck-passer who got his sister to do his dirty work.

But as she thought about it, Molly saw that passing the buck had always been his style. Whenever she had been in need of disciplining or scolding, he had gotten Harriet to take it on, hadn't he? It was always Aunt Harriet who undertook the unpleasant jobs, played the heavy. How could she have missed seeing that?

And, my God, here was Parnell's motive. He had always adored and treasured Rose. To find out about this could send anyone over the edge.

Molly looked down at the letter in her hand. It was shaking as if in a strong wind.

Parnell had paid Crocker to call the death a suicide.

Parnell had had a powerful motive to want Vernon Cates dead.

Her hand still shaking, Molly folded the letter and stuck it on the dashboard. She bundled up the rest of the letters and put them back in the file cabinet, carefully, exactly as Harriet had left them, keeping the archives intact as she had promised. She closed the door and replaced the lock. It would be a good while, she knew, before she ever came back here.

She sat in the truck for a while, watching the rain fall on this godforsaken place, wondering what to do next. Now that she'd learned this, she was going to have to do something with it. She was going to have to confront Parnell and Rose. She'd come this far; there was no going back.

She rested her forehead against the steering wheel. The whole world was tilting. Her daddy was not the man she had thought he was. Aunt Harriet was not the woman she had thought she was. Rose was nothing like what she appeared. And Parnell—what was he? A murderer? Suddenly there were no constants, nothing to depend on.

The problem with learning a secret like this was that you could never unlearn it.

THERE WERE ONCE TWO CATS OF KILKENNY.
EACH THOUGHT THERE WAS ONE CAT TOO MANY;
SO THEY FOUGHT AND THEY FIT,
AND THEY SCRATCHED AND THEY BIT,
TILL, EXCEPTING THEIR NAILS,
AND THE TIPS OF THEIR TAILS.
INSTEAD OF TWO CATS, THERE WEREN'T ANY.

—MOTHER GOOSE

Sarah Jane knows as soon as she hears the hissy male voices that the magic is over. She keeps her eyes closed tight so they will not know she is awake. They are talking in quiet, mean voices. "Tell him we got something he wants real bad," one of them says, "and we're willing to sell it. If he asks what we got, you just say this: 'Mooooo!'" The voice wails at the end like a cow in great pain, and they all laugh.

Alarmed, Sarah Jane lets her eyes open a slit, but the tiny hut is empty. The men must be just outside the door. It seems to be her fate to have to listen to men talking about things she doesn't want to hear.

"Now listen, Zippo," says the voice, "if he ain't at this number, you just keep on calling. He'll come a-runnin'. He wants what we got, and he'll pay, so don't give up. You got that?"

Suddenly the blanket covering the door is pushed aside and two men enter. They are bent over because the hut is so low. Sarah Jane squeezes her eyes shut, but not before she sees who the two men are: Squint and Roylee.

She has fallen from the frying pan right into the fire. It is amazing how much trouble you can get into just by being alive.

"So where the fuck is she?"

Sarah Jane feels spittle and hot stinking breath on her face. She lies very still.

"You're not sleeping, you old bum-cunt. Where'd she go to?"

A sudden sharp blow to her ribs makes her eyes fly open. Roylee's there with a gun, and he's about to hit her with it again. "Don't!" she squeals, trying to roll away, but she is already pressed up against the wall.

"Where is she?" Squint brings his face in close.

"Who?" she wails. "Where's who?"

"The crazy nigger bitch that lives here," says Squint. "Who do you think?"

"I don't know," Sarah Jane cries. "I been sick!"

Squint glares down at her, his tiny eyes like sparks under his jutting brows. Sarah Jane feels sure he can see better than he lets on. "Now you listen up, Cow Lady. I'm gonna teach you a real important lesson."

Sarah Jane wishes she were unconscious again, floating on her magic carpet, escaping this. It occurs to her that all her life she has been wishing to escape from whatever was happening, and that usually she has found a way. She is an escape artist, so maybe she can figure how to escape this.

Squint says, "You got asked a question, cunt, and you gonna answer it." He nudges Roylee, who puts the muzzle of the gun on her stomach and starts to press it down.

Sarah Jane lets out a gasp.

"Where did she go to?" Squint asks.

"You just woke me up," she says. "She's gone. I don't *know* where."

"She have a hot date, maybe?" Squint says, and Roylee laughs like a hyena. "No? Well, then maybe she went to church. It's Sunday, ain't it?"

Sunday, Sarah Jane thinks. Good. There's still time before Monday.

"Give the cunt some help, Roylee," Squint says.

Roylee shoves the gun into her gut so hard that Sarah Jane gags. She tries to talk but can't catch her breath. She holds a hand up to get them to stop.

"Oh," says Squint, "Look, Roylee, she got the white flag up. She's gonna answer our questions." He puts his face even closer to Sarah Jane's so she can smell the beer and rotting meat on his breath. "Now you gonna tell us where the nigger went. And I want to know how an old bum like you got so *popular* all of a sudden. What does that big Kraut want with you, Cow Lady? My eyesight is none too good." He glances at Roylee. "Is she a total dog or what, Roylee?"

"I seen worse," Roylee says and then laughs like a maniac, "but I sure can't recall when."

Squint takes the revolver from Roylee. He holds it against Sarah Jane's temple. "Now you gonna tell Papa Squint all about it. When's the nigger coming back? See, Roylee and me might need to plan a welcome home party for her to show we ain't prejudiced. Right, Roylee?"

Sarah Jane wishes she were brave enough to resist this, but she knows from past experience that she isn't.

26

CACKLE, CACKLE, MOTHER GOOSE,
HAVE YOU ANY FEATHERS LOOSE?
—*MOTHER GOOSE*

As she walked in the door the phone was ringing. Usually she let the machine take it, but on an impulse she made a dash for it and answered before the fourth ring.

"You are Missus Molly Cates?" The voice was high and lilting.

"Yes?"

"The Cow Lady say she need you to come to her please."

Molly braced herself against the counter. The police had been looking everywhere for Sarah Jane Hurley, and Molly was eager to talk to her too. She tried to keep her voice calm. "Where is she?"

"She sick, got a fever."

"Who are you?"

"I am Mother Teresa."

Oh, oh. This was going to be delicate. "Where *is* Cow Lady?" Molly asked. "What can I do to help?"

"She want you to come to her now please. Very important she say. Tell Molly Cates, life and death."

"Maybe we should call 911, for an ambulance."

"Ooh, noooo. That you cannot do, missus."

"Why not?"

"It would defeat the miracle, which you are to behold."

"Miracle?"

"Yes, missus. You will write about it, she say. You will make me famous, like the other Mother Teresa, that one in India. You will write in a magazine about the miracle."

"Well, I'd sure like to hear about that. But I'm worried she might need medical attention."

"She be much better now. You will see. Come right now and I will show you."

Molly pulled her notebook out of her bag. "Where shall I come?"

"You know where the two roads Barton Springs and Lamar come together?"

"Yes."

"Stand on the corner that is to the south and the west, where there is paintings on cloth. I will come to get you and together we will walk to her."

"All right. But it will take me about fifteen minutes to get there. How will I know you?"

The woman chuckled, a light musical riff. "You will know me. I am Mother Teresa."

"Just in case I don't, what are you wearing?"

"A robe of many colors. You *will* know me." The woman hung up.

Oh, boy.

Molly put the phone down. She should call Calvin Shawcross, who had the Emily Bickerstaff murder, and let him decide how to handle this, but he was likely to be too heavy-handed. And she had a hunch this Mother Teresa might provide some grist for her homeless article. Anyway, she could call Shawcross later, after she'd had a chance to talk to Cow Lady.

And there was no real risk to this. It was broad daylight on a Sunday afternoon. They were meeting at one of the busiest intersections in town. And she'd be willing to bet this Mother Teresa woman was squirrelly, but not dangerous. But just to be on the safe side, she stuck her cellular phone in her bag, and after a few seconds of thought, she left the revolver where it was in the secret compartment. It had proved itself highly useful last night. She was beginning to see why people got devoted to their handguns.

She drove south on Lamar in the sparse Sunday traffic, thinking about Parnell. She'd vowed she would talk to him today. And she would. She had to, but it was a relief to have this excuse to delay it. Strange that, just as she was getting close to answering the most compelling question of her life, she seemed to be losing momentum.

She turned onto Barton Springs Road and parked behind a hippie coffeehouse that had somehow survived intact from the sixties.

She walked the three blocks to the intersection, which had been developed in the past year into a multilaned traffic nightmare. Two corners sported fast food places, the third corner, a Texaco station. At the fourth, a self-serve car wash was surrounded by a chain link fence covered today by a display of tie-dye fabrics. Austin was the kind of place where a tie-dye artist might still eke out a living. It was also the kind of place where an intersection like this could coexist a few blocks from a spring-fed pool and a beautiful park.

She stood on the corner and looked around. The rain had stopped, but the sky was dark and the trees were still dripping. The air was so thickly humid that breathing took a conscious effort.

Molly leaned against a utility pole and waited for the woman who called herself Mother Teresa. The accent was Caribbean; she would probably be black. There was not much foot traffic here, so she shouldn't be too hard to spot.

A minute later she saw her walking from the west on Barton Springs—a tall, extremely thin, mahogany-colored woman wearing layers of colorful, patched dresses that hung to her boots. Her posture was as upright as if she were carrying a basket of fruit on her head. As she drew closer, Molly saw that the turban she wore was made of silk scarfs of many different patterns braided together.

She walked up to Molly and looked her over quickly.

"Follow me, missus." She turned and headed back the way she'd come.

Molly fell into step with her. "Where are we going?"

"Why, to where I live. That is where the Cow Lady be. Someday a shrine will be erected there to mark the place of the first miracle and healing. People will call it the Lourdes of Texas, and they will come from far and wide to be healed. You will be part of this."

"Is it far?" Molly asked. "We could drive there. My truck's right nearby."

"Oooh, nooo. It is in the wood. To walk is the only way."

"Okay. Tell me how Sarah Jane is."

"Sarah Jane?"

"Cow Lady."

"Oh, she is very good indeed." The woman turned her small, elegant, wrinkled face toward Molly. "For a person who come back from the dead only one day ago."

"Back from the dead?" Molly affected a neutral tone.

"Yes, missus, she was laying cold, no sign of life in her at all, out in the rain. At the roots of my sacred tree she was waiting for the miracle."

As they walked, the woman continued to talk nonstop about finding Cow Lady in the rain and bringing her back to life and healing her. Just past a decrepit service station, she turned into what looked like an ancient parking lot with patchy, cracked asphalt. Uncut grasses and weeds nearly obscured a NO DUMPING sign that stood on the corner. At the rear, a driveway of crumbly cement led back to a wild overgrown area that looked more like the Amazon jungle than South Austin. They stepped over a low cable meant to keep cars out and followed the driveway to where it ended in a dirt path. Molly looked back and was amazed to see that civilization had disappeared. They might have been miles from the city, instead of a few hundred yards from a busy urban intersection.

"Come," said Mother Teresa. "It is not good for the Cow Lady to be alone after such an experience."

The path, after the heavy rains, was a mud rut and Molly's

favorite black suede loafers were sinking deep into the muck. She winced and trudged on.

They entered a densely wooded area where the path was so covered by the undergrowth they had to push their way through. Molly was getting scratched by briars. She waved away a swarm of gnats that swirled around her and stuck to her sweaty face. Ahead of her, Mother Teresa moved serenely, seemingly unbothered by gnats or mud or humidity. She seemed to live on some higher plane of existence.

Finally she came to a stop in a small grassy clearing, in front of something that could have been a chicken coop or a clubhouse slapped together by six-year-olds. It was a box made of some old charred wooden boards, with rags and newspaper stuck into the cracks. A sheet of crumpled, rusted tin rested on the top, weighted down by rocks.

Molly stared at the structure. This couldn't be where the woman lived; no one could live here.

Mother Teresa turned and smiled widely. "This is where the miracle happened. This is where the Cow Lady was healed." She bent over and lifted a filthy blanket covering the opening. Molly pulled out her shirttail and used it to wipe her sweaty face. She wouldn't go inside that box on a bet. Just looking at it made her claustrophobic. She'd have to bend over double to get in and there were probably lice, and God knows what else, inside.

"Come." The woman held the blanket higher and beckoned to her. "Here she be."

"Thanks," Molly said. "I'll wait out here. Ask her to come out, please."

"She be sick, in bed. You come, missus."

Molly shook her head. She squatted down and tried to peer inside the dark box. "Cow Lady," she called in a low voice, "are you there?"

A shaky voice answered. "Yes. Come in."

Mother Teresa bent down and entered, letting the blanket fall back over the opening. Molly straightened up, but she stayed where she was.

As she stood there waiting, she felt a prickling on the back of her neck. The sensation was so intense, she was afraid to move. The only sound was the steady dripping of the trees and the faint whir of insects, but she knew someone was standing behind her. The presence was like a ripple in the humid air.

She turned her head slowly. Just a few feet behind her stood a man with a gun pointed at her back. He was built like a fireplug and had tattoos up and down his thick, hairless arms. "Slow," he said, "real slow now."

Molly turned around. His hard, blunt features had the blankness of a stone carving and his dead brown eyes seemed not to reflect light. It had been foolish to come here alone, but all her life she had done foolhardy things like this and she had gotten away with them. Not this time, it appeared.

The man nodded toward the hut. "In there."

"No." She shook her head. She would take her chances out here in the open.

The man took a step toward her and, before she could even react, something smashed into her chin, snapping her head back and blurring her vision. She stayed standing for a long moment, reeling, as galaxies of stars whirled past her.

Molly Cates finds herself on her hands and knees in the mud. Tears are spurting from her eyes. She can't remember how she got to the ground. She can't remember starting to cry either. Her jaw is screaming in pain and she can't see straight.

"Get inside. You say no to me again, you dumb cunt, and I'll rip your head off." He lifts his muddy boot to her forehead and gives her a push with it.

Feeling broken and dazed, Molly crawls through the mud to the entrance. The man pulls the blanket back and she drags herself inside.

The only light comes from one candle and the cracks in the wall that let in a few rays of dingy daylight. It smells of sweat and decay. Against the wall is a mattress and on it Sarah Jane Hurley lies. Her hands and feet are tied with rags, her eyes are wide with fear. Mother Teresa is hunched into the corner and, right next to her, a man with long black hair has his arm wrapped tight around her neck, his hand covering her mouth.

The man with the gun squeezes his thick body inside, so there are five of them now, packed inside a wooden box barely large enough for two.

"Golly, Roylee," says the black-haired man, "we got us more than we bargained for—a harem, but I don't know. Two crazy old scum-bums and"—he lets go of Mother Teresa's head and leans close to Molly so he can look at her face from about a foot away with his tiny deep-set eyes—"this one here might of been okay, but it looks like you done broke her chin off."

Molly raises a hand to her chin. Blood is dripping and it feels like raw hamburger. Her lower lip is split and hugely swollen already. She groans without intending to.

"Don't whine now," says the black-haired man. "We just got to sit tight till our customer comes. Roylee, you and me got to figure out what to do with these two extras. You think we could sell them all to the Kraut, give him some group discount? Let him do whatever sick-oo Kraut thing he's got in mind?"

Roylee taps the gun muzzle on Molly's head, sending ripples of pain to her jaw. "Nah, Squint. Who'd want 'em?"

Squint points at Molly. "Let's see what she's got in that bag."

Molly has forgotten all about her purse. It is still hanging from her shoulder. Roylee jerks it away from her and tosses it to Squint, who dumps the contents onto the mud floor: the cell phone, her notebook, wallet, lipstick, comb, keys, checkbook, a couple of pens. He is about to toss the bag away when he stops and hefts it in one hand. Then he squeezes it and his eyes light up. He finds the secret compartment right away and pulls the gun out. "Lawdalmighty!" he cackles. "Lookee here, Roylee. She was *armed.*" He sticks the pistol in his pocket and says to Molly, "Don't do you no good, you dumb bitch, if you don't *use* it."

Molly tries to speak. She wants to say that her policeman

boyfriend knows where she is and he's on his way here right now, but when she tries to speak, her lip and chin won't obey her will. Her jaw might be broken, she thinks.

Squint picks up her wallet. He takes the bills out and stuffs them in his pocket. Then he pulls out her driver's license and holds it about an inch from his eyes. "Molly Cates," he reads, glancing up at her with his slitlike eyes barely visible under the jutting brows. "Expires 5, '99." He grins. "Might be sooner than that, Molly Cates. You just never know." He tosses the wallet into the corner. "Let's go outside, Roylee, so's we can talk."

"We ought to tie 'em up," Roylee says, pointing the gun at Molly and Mother Teresa.

"Yeah. Throw me them rags over there," Squint says. He pulls Mother Teresa's skinny arms behind her back and ties her wrists, then her ankles. As he's doing it, she says, "It is a wrong thing to stop a healing miracle when it is in progress."

Roylee snorts. "Nutty as a fruitcake."

Then Squint turns to Molly. She knows she should make a break for it. Once you are tied up, you are as good as dead—it is the lesson taught in all self-defense courses, and she believes it. She has seen these men up close and heard their names. They have to kill her now, and the other two women too. It might be better to get shot right now, while making a run for it.

"Hands behind you," says Squint.

Molly hesitates. She glances toward the door.

But Roylee is fast. Before she can move, he's on her. This time he smashes the gun into the side of her head and she crumples. This time she doesn't see stars. This time she doesn't see anything at all, for a long time.

When she awakes, her hands and feet are tied, her head is cracking open, her brains spilling out. A person could die from such a headache. She doesn't know where she is or if it is day or night. Her cheek is stuck to a pool of dried blood on the dirt floor. She moans. She's cold and she has to pee.

"Poor Little Bopeep," a voice whispers in her ear, *"has lost her sheep.* How're you feeling?"

"Cow Lady," Molly murmurs through swollen lips. It is hard to form the words. Painfully Molly focuses on Sarah Jane Hurley's face, which is only a few inches from hers. It seems to be dark outside, but the candle is still burning.

Now she becomes aware of a faint voice droning: "Lying at the foot of the sacred tree, her life flown away, and that is when I am working the first miracle and returning her to life." Molly hasn't the strength to lift her head and look and, anyway, her cheek is still stuck to the floor.

"I'm sorry," Sarah Jane says. "I didn't mean for you to walk into this. I didn't know these dudes were coming when I got Mother Teresa to call you."

"Why are they doing this?" Molly's words are barely understandable, even to her.

"They're waiting for this *really* bad dude—Billy Goat Gruff, a big German guy, to come. He wants to kill me. He'll probably kill us all. He's the one killed Tin Can and he's gonna wipe out everyone in the Senate with a poison gas. So killing a few more is nothing to him."

Molly is trying to take this in, but her head is so thick and woolly. In the corner Mother Teresa continues to drone on about the miracle of the Cow Lady. Both stories—the one about killing everyone in the Senate and the one about bringing Cow Lady back to life—sound like fairy tales to Molly; she isn't sure which one is more fantastic.

"How do you know this? About the Senate?" she whispers to Sarah Jane, each word an agony to get out, but she needs to know.

"I heard him and another man talking about it when I was under the deck, where I used to sleep. He killed Tin Can 'cause they thought she heard them, and saw them, but it was me that heard."

"What happened at the library?" Molly asks.

"He found me there and tried to kill me—Billy Goat did. These assholes told him where to find me."

It is making some terrible sense to Molly now. Tin Can

murdered. The book on poison gas stolen from the library. The fight at the library. The FBI agent worried about a plot in the Capitol. It fits together. If she'd been paying attention, she might have seen this picture. But she wasn't paying attention. She was wrapped up in her own little world, looking at all the wrong things, as usual.

From the corner comes the crooning voice, "And I carried her to my place of healing just as God commanded me to do."

"When?" Molly asks in a whisper.

"Huh?" Sarah Jane says.

"The poison gas in the Senate," Molly says, every word an agony.

"Monday."

"How long have I been out?"

"Hours. Lots of hours. I've lost track."

"I've got to pee."

"Me too."

"They'll have to let us go outside to pee," Molly says. "I'm going to—"

"No! Don't call them," Sarah Jane says, her eyes wide with alarm. "Don't. But listen, maybe you could reach—"

Molly is so exhausted by the problem, she drifts back to semiconsciousness. When she wakes again, she is shivering, cold and wet, and a dirty gray is seeping through the cracks in the hut. Can it possibly be dawn?

Mother Teresa is asleep, snoring gently.

Sarah Jane Hurley is lying there, watching Molly. "Gramma," Sarah Jane says, "what big eyes you have."

It is a madhouse, Molly thinks. She is going to die right here on the dirt floor of a madhouse. "I peed in my pants," she moans.

"Me too," Sarah Jane says. "Feels good to say 'What the hell' and just let it go."

"I don't know. I was asleep," Molly says.

"No," Sarah Jane whispers, "you were passed out, all night. I think Roylee gave you a concussion."

"Is it morning?" Molly asks.

"Monday morning, I think," Sarah Jane says. "Listen, my

bag is in the corner there, behind Mother Teresa. They didn't notice it. There's a knife inside."

Molly lifts her head to look, but the shooting pain in her skull stops her halfway.

"I can't reach it," Sarah Jane says, "but you're closer."

Molly tries to sit up but she can't—her arms are tied behind her and her ankles are tied so tight her feet have gone to sleep.

"Mother Teresa." Sarah Jane raises her voice just above the whisper she's been talking in. "You awake?"

"They will be punished," says Mother Teresa, "for stopping the miracle."

"We can't let that happen," Sarah Jane tells her. "We've come too far. Listen, Mother T, can you get your hands into that bag behind you and get something for me?"

"The miracle is ruined. They have stopped the miracle and they will know the wrath of God who gave me the mission to—" Mother Teresa stops talking and they all freeze at the sound of footsteps and male voices talking right outside. Someone new has come.

"Zippo, my man," Squint says. "What's the word? You sure was long enough about it, keeping us waiting here all night with our thumbs up our butts."

"Not my fault, Squint. Couldn't get him to answer his fuckin' phone till now."

"He's buying, ain't he?"

"Yeah. But he can't come right now. You do her, he says, and he'll pay. He'll meet you at the Plasma Center tomorrow where you met him before."

"Two grand?"

"Yup. He said he'll pay."

"Okay, Zippo. You done real good. You go on now and I'll give you yours tomorrow when I get paid. That's my man."

There is a pause as Zippo leaves. Then Squint says, "We gotta do 'em all, Roylee. Right now."

"I'll do 'em."

"Just make sure they don't get found no time soon. Not that anyone'll be looking for this bunch."

"The dump, over yonder," Roylee says. "I'll bury the bitches in garbage."

Molly is shivering. Her brain is still thick, but she knows a death sentence when she hears one.

Suddenly the blanket is jerked aside; Roylee pushes in. "Peew, smells like some pigsty." He grins at them. "What've you been doing in here, you bad gals?"

"Come on," Squint calls from outside, his voice tense. "Let's get this done before someone comes and sees them here."

"Okay. Get up!" Roylee says.

Sarah Jane says, "How can we? You got our feet tied."

Roylee pulls a jackknife from his pocket. He opens it and bends down to cut the rag binding Mother Teresa's ankles. He does it with one upward thrust. She gets up, adopting the bent-over posture the low roof requires.

Roylee leans down to Molly's feet and cuts the bonds. Then he taps the gun against her bloody chin. "Get up, you cunt. We're gonna take a walk." Molly doesn't think she has the strength. It would be easier just to stay put and let Roylee shoot her right here. She tries to stand up, but her head whirls and her legs are rubber. She collapses back down.

"Help her," Roylee tells Sarah Jane.

Sarah Jane holds her feet up so he can cut her bonds. He does it with one swipe. Then she offers her bound hands up to him and explains, "So I can help her up." He hesitates, then takes the knife and slashes through the rag binding Sarah Jane's hands. "Get her up," he says, pointing the gun at Molly.

Sarah Jane Hurley puts an arm around Molly and tries to lift her up. "Come on," she says, "you gotta help."

"I can't," Molly says.

"You can." She gets a better hold on Molly, under her arms, and, with an amazing burst of energy, hauls her up to her knees. Then, as Molly is struggling to get on her feet, Sarah Jane does something that convinces Molly the woman is crazy: she puts her shoulder against Molly and shoves her down into the corner Mother Teresa has just vacated.

"She fell," Sarah Jane says quickly. "Wait. I'll get her

up." She leans over Molly and reaches her arms all the way around her. She takes a few seconds and then leans in closer so she is nearly lying on top of Molly.

"I told you to get her up," Roylee says, "not fuck her."

"Okay, okay," Sarah Jane says. "Take it easy." She backs away and hoists Molly to her feet as if she is a sack of meal.

Molly's head pounds and her legs wobble. But somehow she manages to keep her feet underneath her.

"That's right," coos Sarah Jane.

Squint holds the blanket aside for them as they stagger outside, first Mother Teresa, then Molly and Sarah Jane, then Roylee with the gun pointed at them.

Squint comes close and looks them over. "Do it so they don't never get found," he says.

"Don't worry," says Roylee. "There's enough trash down there in that old dump to bury an army in."

"Wait!" says Squint, grabbing Molly's arm. "A watch."

Roylee looks down at Molly's wrist and smiles. "Gold, looks like. Shame to waste it on the dump." He reaches out and tries to pull it off, but he can't figure out how the catch works. Molly fumbles with it and finally manages to get it off. She hands it to Roylee meekly and feels a wave of self-disgust wash over her. She is a chicken plucking herself for the slaughter, offering up her neck to the knife. She has always thought of herself as a fighter, a self-sufficient survivor, who would never go down without putting up a hell of a struggle, but she hadn't understood that by the time they get you to the slaughterhouse you're so beaten and exhausted by the trip, you don't have the strength to resist.

She glances up at the dirty gray overcast sky. It is so humid and her skin is so wet and she's shivering so hard, she can't tell if it is raining or not. All she knows is that she has wandered into the wrong place at the wrong time and is about to be shot dead and buried in a trash heap for her foolishness.

Or maybe this is her just deserts. She's made bad karma for herself, violent karma. When she used force against Olin Crocker, she broke all her rules of moral behavior and now she's paying for it. Violence begets violence.

SHE HEAVED A SIGH AND WIPED HER EYE
AND OVER THE HILLOCKS SHE RACED;
AND TRIED WHAT SHE COULD, AS A SHEPHERDESS
    SHOULD,
THAT EACH TAIL SHOULD BE PROPERLY PLACED.
                            —"LITTLE BOPEEP," LAST VERSE,
                                        MOTHER GOOSE

If she could just clear her head and think straight, she might come up with some plan, some resistance. But her hands are tied behind her and her legs are so weak and her head is splitting. Without Sarah Jane Hurley holding her up she wouldn't even be able to walk.

Roylee points the way, jabbing the gun in the air. "That way," he says, indicating the far side of the small clearing. Molly is so disoriented she doesn't know if it is the way they arrived yesterday or not. She looks around, trying to get her bearings.

Squint is standing next to the hut with his hands on his hips, his slitlike eyes glinting in their direction.

"Move!" Roylee barks at the three women.

Mother Teresa starts walking. She makes a low moaning in her throat, a noise that reflects perfectly the despair and fear Molly feels. Sarah Jane keeps a good hold on Molly, her arm wrapped around Molly's back and under her arms. Together they move haltingly in the direction Roylee has pointed.

Molly's mind churns. There are only two of these weasels—Squint and Roylee, and Squint can barely see. She and Sarah Jane and Mother Teresa are three, but a pathetic three. She is not sure that Mother Teresa knows what's going on and she, Molly, can barely walk and her hands are tied. Sarah Jane Hurley seems alert, but she might well be crazy. Together they don't add up to even one normal person.

"Come on, cunts, move it," Roylee says.

Hot panic washes over her.

She doesn't want to die, doesn't want to die like this. She doesn't want to die so much that she would do anything to avoid it—beg, kill, debase herself—anything to buy some time.

With each step, it grows—her desire not to die. It is inflaming her, squeezing her guts. She slows her feet. When they get to that dump, it is the end. Delaying it is the only thing. She drags down on Sarah Jane's arm, to slow her. Sarah Jane is puffing, staggering to support Molly, who is trying to drag her to a halt.

Why should they cooperate? He'll just kill them anyway. Why should they walk there? Why should they do what he says?

Now her blood is boiling, her body taken over by fear.

Why shouldn't they just go wild?

They are almost to the tree line where the clearing ends. Too fast. This is going too fast.

It is intolerable.

Ahead of them, through the trees, Molly can see what appears to be a drop-off. The dump. No. She stops moving her legs. She will not do it. Not another step. She pulls back on Sarah Jane, drags her to a halt.

"Move," Roylee says. He raises a foot and kicks Sarah Jane in the back. "Get."

Sarah Jane tries to haul Molly forward. But Molly goes limp. She refuses to budge.

Sarah Jane grunts with the effort of trying to hold her up.

Molly turns her head and whispers in Sarah Jane's ear, "Let me go."

Sarah Jane turns and looks down into Molly's eyes. She holds the gaze for a few long seconds, then, slowly, she lets her sink down.

The ground is soft from all the rain, and cool. Molly

doesn't know she is going to throw a fit until the first scream forms in her throat. She lies on her back, her arms still tied behind her, and opens her mouth. It comes out a wail. She does it again, louder—a real scream. She kicks her legs. Her heels drum on the ground, then she starts to jerk her body. She screams and kicks and jerks, picturing the fat girl in elementary school who used to have epileptic seizures in the cafeteria. Molly wants to foam at the mouth and have her eyes roll back in her head the way that girl used to do.

Once she gets going, she gathers momentum. It is the most natural thing in the world—to kick and scream. A reasonable response. She shouts louder, kicks harder. She bucks and shrieks. The fit takes on its own life. She couldn't stop if she wanted to.

Roylee is standing over her with the gun, furious. He kicks at her, but she is jerking around so much he can't land a good one. "Get up, you bitch!" he yells, but Molly keeps on screaming, drowning him out.

"She's having a fit," Sarah Jane says. "You gotta wait till it's over."

Mother Teresa kneels on the ground. *"I am the one who has been called to take care of the sick and dying,"* she says, unwrapping her turban. "We will put something in her mouth so she does not bite her tongue."

"Jesus Fucking Christ!" Roylee shouts. "Get *up!"* He kicks Mother Teresa so hard he sends her sprawling.

Sarah Jane leans down to Molly and says into her face, "Keep going."

"Squint!" Roylee wails. "Come here."

"Get this done, Roylee, you fuck-up," Squint calls back. "Just shoot them. We'll drag them to the dump."

Molly screams louder. Her throat burns. Her jaw and head pulse with pain. Her arms and legs are getting scraped from all the thrashing, but she keeps on going. The pain just eggs her on. She embraces it. It feels so good to be doing something.

Then suddenly she hears a new voice. She lifts her head to see what is happening.

Across the clearing is an apparition—a tall, skinny man

with long beard, black with streaks of gray. A biblical prophet, Father Time, the Grim Reaper, Molly is not sure. He is limping toward them, calling something, but it is hard to make out what with all the noise Molly is making. She stops screaming to hear.

"What's going on?" he calls out. "Fair lady, I—"

"Lufkin!" Sarah Jane shouts. "Stop! He's got a gun."

"Hey," he says, stopping in his tracks, catching sight of Roylee holding the gun. "What the—?"

Roylee is moving his gun frantically from one to the other, first pointing it at Molly, then at Sarah Jane, then at the bearded man at the other side of the clearing, then back at Molly.

The bearded man is holding his hands up. "Hey, wait a minute there, Roylee. It's just me—Lufkin. Let's talk about this, man," he says.

Molly resumes her screaming, her throat raw now. She wants to divert attention from Lufkin. Maybe he can help them; God knows, they need help.

Squint, still standing next to the hut, calls out to the bearded man. "Lufkin, that you? Hold on a minute, man." He walks toward him with his head raised as if he is sniffing the air. "I can explain this."

"No," Sarah Jane yells. "Run!"

But Squint is only a foot away from Lufkin now. From his pocket he pulls the gun he took from Molly. Lufkin just gapes in surprise. Then he opens his mouth to speak, but Squint sticks the gun right in Lufkin's stomach and fires. It happens that fast.

"No!" Sarah Jane shrieks.

Molly lets out a real scream.

Lufkin staggers and falls.

Squint kneels down, puts the gun to the fallen man's head and fires again.

"No!" Sarah Jane screams. "Oh, God, no!"

"We're going," Roylee says. He lands a kick on Molly's ribs. "You! Get the fuck up!"

Mother Teresa has gotten to her knees. She is crawling back toward the hut, moaning, her unwrapped turban trailing behind her like a banner. "I must return to the place of the miracle."

"You! Stop!" Roylee calls out to her.

Mother Teresa keeps on crawling.

Roylee points the gun at her back and fires. Mother Teresa makes a little cry and crumples to the ground. Then he turns the gun on Molly. She gasps and stops her thrashing. She is next.

Sarah Jane whirls around, tears running down her face. She slams both her arms up into Roylee's raised arm. The impact sends the gun flying. Then she bends down and grabs Molly by the collar. "Come on!" She jerks her up.

Molly is on her feet.

"Run!" Sarah Jane screams, letting go of Molly's collar.

Molly is shaky, but she is up and moving on her own, first stumbling, then walking, then she is running. Sarah Jane leads the way. She is surprisingly fast.

Molly expects at each second to feel a bullet in her back. She is tensed for it, ready. As they hit the tree line, she glances back. Roylee is scrambling in the weeds for the gun. Squint, still on the far side of the clearing, is running toward them, gun in hand.

She turns to look at what lies in front of them.

A weedy bank descends to a flat dirt ditch, a bulldozed gouge in the earth the size of a large swimming pool with a steeper bank on the far side. Inside the ditch are several huge piles of trash—the dump. There are no trees or bushes, no cover, but it is the only place to go.

They can't go back—Roylee and Squint are there. But Molly is terrified at the idea of getting trapped in the ditch and being unable to get up the far bank.

"Come on." Sarah Jane starts down the bank into the ditch.

Molly hesitates on the edge.

Sarah Jane looks back at her. "We'll hide! Come on."

Molly looks back and she can see through the trees Roylee running toward them. He's found the gun.

Molly turns and starts down the bank, picking up speed as

she goes. With her arms tied behind her back, she pitches forward, barely able to keep her balance.

At the bottom rises a trash heap taller than Molly, made of rotted plywood and rusted plumbing fixtures, chicken wire, mattresses, paint cans, grass cuttings, cans, bottles, and plastic garbage bags. Beyond that are three more heaps of similar trash.

Sarah Jane heads toward the second pile, half of which is composed of huge plastic bags with grass cuttings bursting out of them. She circles the pile and says, "Here."

Molly looks up at the bank. Roylee hasn't got there yet. If they hide quick he might not see where they've gone.

To Molly's amazement, Sarah Jane pulls a knife from her pocket and uses it to cut the rag binding Molly's wrists. Then she points to a narrow space between two bulging green garbage bags near the bottom of the heap. "Get in there," she commands. "As far as you can. I'll be behind you."

Panting, Molly falls to her knees. She crawls into the dark hole, squeezing herself inside, underneath the huge soft bags. It is dark and smells of mown grass and rotted lettuce. Something sharp snags her sleeve, but she keeps pushing herself farther in. Terror propels her on. As she worms a few more inches, and then a few more, she feels Sarah Jane burrowing in right behind her.

Her knee lands on something sharp and jagged. She feels the skin break. It hurts fiercely, but she keeps moving.

Finally she comes up against a solid barrier that won't give way. She stops. Behind her, Sarah Jane bumps against her feet. In the semidarkness Molly tries to feel what's blocking the way. It's a piece of wood furniture, she thinks—a dresser maybe. But they should be close to the center of the heap now anyway. She pulls her legs in and curls up small to make room for Sarah Jane.

It is silent, the world muffled, and for just a moment, here in the middle of this dark heap, with the weight of the trash bags on top of her and the decaying vegetable smells in her nose, with Sarah Jane curled next to her like a twin fetus, Molly feels safe. She closes her eyes and hears her breath echoing deep inside her body, slowing down, quieting. This is what it must feel like for hunted animals that go to earth after being chased, this moment of feeling safe inside a burrow.

It doesn't last long. The thud of running feet breaks the silence. She can imagine Roylee's short, thick thighs pounding down the bank. Her body clenches up. He is heading right this way. He's seen them crawling in here. Or he's seen the pile moving as they burrowed in. He's on his way to get them. They've made it easy for him; they've already buried themselves. All he'll have to do is shoot them. And she will just lie here, curled up, and let it happen. It's over now.

"Okay, you cunts." His voice is so close she nearly gasps. "You are dead meat." There is a crash of glass smashing and the thud of something heavy being slung to the ground. He is starting to dig in the trash.

"Roylee!" a distant voice calls. "You got 'em?"

"Not yet."

"Shit, Roylee. I *told* you to shoot 'em. Damn you."

"I'll get 'em. They're here, got to be."

"You finish 'em off. I'm gonna drag these two up here down there before someone comes along and sees them. It's Grand Central–fucking–station up here. Goddamn that Lufkin sticking his nose in. I didn't wanna do that, but he was just begging for it."

Molly feels a flicker of hope. Someone might come along and save them. People must come here sometimes because someone dumped all this stuff here. But it's illegal, so they probably do it at night.

Curled up, she can see her knee where the jeans are torn and a dark stain is spreading. It feels as if there's a piece of glass in the knee, but she can't move her arms down to explore it.

Molly looks to Sarah Jane, hoping for comfort. In the semidarkness the woman's large dark eyes are wide open, alert, fierce. She has managed to hold on to the knife while squeezing in here. It occurs to Molly now that that's what she was doing in the hut when she knocked Molly down in the corner. She was getting the knife out of her bag. It was quick thinking, but it's not going to do them a hell of a lot of good against two guns.

Now the sounds of Roylee throwing trash around are coming fast and furious—thuds and crashes and grunts and oaths. "I'm gonna find you. Come out now. Make it easier on yourselves. You make me keep looking, I'm gonna torture you before I kill you. I swear I will. I'm gonna cut your noses off and your eyelids and your nipples and stuff 'em in your mouths so you can't scream when I shoot you."

Molly curls up tighter and tells herself there's still a chance, they are so close to civilization. She tries to picture the restaurants and telephones and police cars that are just a quarter mile away on Barton Springs; all they need is to stay alive and make it that quarter mile to get help. She has fallen through a crack in the city into this stinking ditch, this violent, brutal place where Roylee and Squint rule, where they do what they please and no one cares enough to stop them, where a sweet, gentle nut like Mother Teresa is shot as casually as flicking a fly off, where the man with the beard—Lufkin—is murdered simply for trying to help them. And down here she is as expendable as they are, no more valuable than the garbage she's lying on. She glances at Sarah Jane and it occurs to her that this is where this woman lives all the time, where Tin Can lived, where the other homeless women she is writing about live—inside this crack in the world where you become invisible, where the default mode is brutality and eventually a mean death.

Well, she's had enough. She wants to call it off right now, to go back to her real world up there. She wants to go home and soak in a hot bath, and wrap up in her clean terry cloth robe and drink tea and call Jo Beth and Grady and tell them she cherishes them. She wants out of this stinking heap of garbage. She wants to call an ambulance and warn the police about the poison gas in the Senate.

Roylee is getting closer now. The thumps and grunts and crashes are very close. He is going to find them. It is just a matter of time.

Suddenly Molly feels a sharp sting on her ankle, then another on the top of her foot. Goddamn. Something is biting her. It feels like fire ants, but if she reaches down to brush them away, she will move the bags on top of her and Roylee will see it or hear it. Again she feels a sting, then another, and another. It hurts so much it brings tears to her eyes. In the half-light she watches Sarah Jane Hurley's face. Every few seconds her cheek flinches; she is getting bitten, too, but she isn't crying. She's used to pain, Molly thinks.

Sarah Jane looks back intently at Molly. She seems to be sending her a message. She is trying to get Molly ready for something, trying to enlist her cooperation. The gleam in her eyes and the tension in her hunched shoulders is saying, Use the pain, reinterpret it, brace yourself, get ready to fight back.

"I'm gonna find you if I have to take every piece of stinking garbage off every stinking pile." Roylee sounds so close now she could reach out and touch him.

Suddenly Molly feels the bags above her shifting. Roylee has started on this trash heap now; he's pulled off some of the bags above them. She hears them thump to the ground.

A distant voice calls, "Okay. I'm gonna bring the other stiff over. Then you get up here and help me get them down the bank."

Molly is watching Sarah Jane's face register this. When Squint gets down here their odds will be worse than they are now. Now is the time.

She can hear Roylee's labored breathing. She feels bags being moved around above her.

Some new light filters in from above. He's nearly down to their level.

Sarah Jane's face is tensing. Her right fist tightens around the knife. She takes in a long breath, then with a burst of energy that makes Molly gasp, she thrusts herself upward, shoving the bag on top of her out of the way.

Molly braces for the sound of a gunshot.

Sarah Jane's feet scramble up and disappear. She's out.

Molly holds her breath, then pushes the bag off her and rises.

Sarah Jane and Roylee are down on the ground, struggling and grunting. He's got hold of her wrist, but she's still clutching the knife. He doesn't have the gun. Molly clambers over the bags and looks around desperately for it, but the ground is so strewn with loose trash she can't find it.

Roylee has Sarah Jane's hands pinned now and he's managed to get a leg over on top of her.

Molly is frantic, sweating, looking around desperately for a weapon.

Roylee is prevailing. He gets his whole body on top of Sarah Jane's and he sits up, still holding her hands down.

Molly spots what looks like the porcelain lid of a toilet tank. She grabs it up. Roylee is banging Sarah Jane's arm against the ground, trying to get her to drop the knife. Molly hefts the heavy lid and smashes it down on the back of his head.

The noise is a resounding thwunk.

Roylee falls face forward on top of Sarah Jane. A trickle of blood runs from his hairline down his face. She's killed him, but she doesn't care. She feels nothing but the urge to run. She drops the lid on the garbage heap. "Let's go," she says. "Let's go."

Sarah Jane shoves Roylee's limp body off her, turns him over on his back, and straddles his chest. She puts her knife to his throat. His head is back, his mouth hanging open. There is blood on his face but he is breathing. Molly watches, unable to make a sound.

Sarah Jane hesitates with the knife pressing against Roylee's thick neck and glances up at Molly. Her chest is heaving and her face is flushed and dripping with sweat. There's a smear of blood on her cheek. She asks Molly the question with her eyes.

Molly puts a hand to her jaw and touches her split lip. She hates him. He is an animal. He shot Mother Teresa in the back. He needs to die. If Sarah Jane goes ahead and slits his throat Molly will say it was self-defense and she will do it under oath. But she can't give a nod to this.

She shakes her head. "Leave him."

Sarah Jane turns back to Roylee and hesitates, the knife pressed so tight against his throat it is drawing blood.

"No," Molly says, "don't. Bad karma. Let's go."

Sarah Jane stands up. "Where's his gun?"

"I can't find it," Molly says, "but we don't need it. Let's get the hell out of here."

Together they take off running. When they get to the high dirt bank they use their hands to scramble up. Halfway to the top, they hear a shout from the other side. Molly glances behind her. Squint is standing there on the edge calling, "Roylee! Where the fuck are you?" She prays he is too far away to see them.

They scramble up the rest of the way and start running, not knowing where they are or what direction they are heading.

In spite of everything that's happened, she feels an ecstatic rush of pleasure as they run. It is heaven just to be alive.

HARK, HARK! THE DOGS DO BARK!
BEGGARS ARE COMING TO TOWN:
SOME IN JAGS, AND SOME IN RAGS,
AND SOME IN VELVET GOWN.

—MOTHER GOOSE

Molly slows to a jog when she catches sight of a road and
cars—civilization, safety. Behind her, Sarah Jane Hurley
throws her head back and gasps for air.

Molly is so turned around, she doesn't know until she sees
the old filling station that it is Barton Springs Road they
have come to. Somehow she has come nearly full circle, back
to the place where she met Mother Teresa yesterday. Yesterday! This whole ordeal has probably taken place in less than
twenty hours, but it feels like a century.

She has no idea what time it is. Her watch is gone and it's
too overcast to see the sun. She needs to send the police and
an ambulance to Mother Teresa's hut right away. But the first
thing is to get a warning to the Senate. It might be too late.
Or the whole thing might be a hoax, but she's not taking any
chances. She has a hunch it's the real thing.

If only she had her cellular phone she could call 911 right
now. Well, they're back to civilization now. They'll find a
phone.

Molly leads the way now. She runs to the old service station next to the parking lot. When she opens the door the
man at the cash register reacts immediately. He charges

toward her. "Now I told you people a hundred times not to come in here no more. What've I got to do to—"

"This is an emergency," Molly says. "I need to use the phone."

A German shepherd who has been lying under the counter stands up and starts barking.

"It's always an emergency with you people, isn't it?" He's a burly man with "Burt" sewn on his pocket. He stands in front of her, blocking her way to the phone that hangs on the wall. "I'm sick of you deadbeats bringing a mess in here. I just mopped this floor." He looks at her with such distaste that Molly glances down at herself. She is covered with mud and blood and garbage. Her pants are torn, so badly on one leg that an entire bloody knee is exposed. Her shoes are caked with mud. She has left a trail of mud clods behind her.

She pushes past him. "It's a matter of life and death. I *have* to use your phone."

"No, you don't." The man beats her to the phone and clamps a hand on it to stop her. "Now get out of here. And get a job."

Molly is breathless with outrage. "Call the police yourself," she shouts, "and deliver a message for me."

"What message?"

"There's a bomb in the Capitol. They need to clear everyone out of the building."

"You drunks disgust me."

Sarah Jane is standing at the door, puffing and red-faced. "That's a public phone," she says. "We have every right to—"

"You stay out of here," he yells at her. "I seen *you* before."

Now the dog is barking nonstop; it is pandemonium.

Molly has never felt like this before, furious and powerless and demeaned all at the same time. Who does he think he is? He can't do this to her. Time is crucial. She tries to wrench the phone away from him, but he is too strong for her.

This is just wasting time. She has a better idea.

She picks up a can of motor oil from the shelf next to the cash register. Pleased to feel how heavy it is, she calls out to Sarah Jane: "Stand back." Then she takes aim and heaves the can at the big plate-glass window. This'll get him to call the cops right quick. But the can bounces off the glass and thuds to the floor.

The dog whimpers and slinks back under the counter.

The man tries to grab Molly but she ducks and runs out. She calls back over her shoulder, "Call the police, for God's sake! *Call them!*"

She grabs Sarah Jane as she runs past. "Come on," she says, "let's try over here."

They dash across the street through the traffic to a restaurant with a red awning over the door. The door is locked. A sign says the hours are 11 A.M. to midnight. "Oh, shit," Molly says. "It must not be eleven yet." She looks around frantically. Time is flying away. And once she gets to a phone it's going to take awhile to get the message through.

She remembers that only two blocks away, behind the coffeehouse, her truck is parked, with a phone in it. But then she remembers that she doesn't have her keys.

"We should get a ride to the Capitol," Sarah Jane says, huffing. "It'll be faster."

"After we call," Molly insists. "Have you got any money?"

Sarah Jane shakes her head.

The coffeehouse two blocks away is probably the closest phone. She heads in that direction with Sarah Jane following.

Four women turn the corner, laughing and talking. They are in business clothes and look like the sorts who carry phones with them. "Excuse me, please," Molly says. "Does one of you have a cell phone I might borrow for a minute? It's an emergency."

Three of them cast their eyes down at the sidewalk and keep walking, giving Molly wide berth. The fourth glances at her and murmurs, "Sorry. We don't."

Molly can't believe it's this difficult to make a phone call right here in the middle of the city. This is an area she has frequented in the past and she has always seen it as laid back and funky and friendly. Suddenly it looks like an enclave for the privileged.

They get to the coffeehouse and Molly pushes in ahead of two men. "Where's the phone?" she asks.

The girl behind the counter takes her time in answering. "Over there." She nods her head toward the back. Molly hurries back. The phone is next to the men's room. A skinny teenager is using it, leaning against the wall, twisting the cord around his arm as he talks. Molly taps him on the shoulder and says, "I've got an emergency call to make. Sorry."

The boy shrugs away from her and says, "Hey!"

"Hang up, please. I've got an emergency."

"Wait a sec." He turns around to face the wall. He continues to talk into the phone.

Molly takes hold of the phone, jerks it away from him, and unwinds the cord from his arm.

"Hey!" he says.

She presses the switch hook to end his call.

She wants to ask him for a quarter, but she can tell by his expression that she would have to mug him for it. She doesn't know if you can call 911 without a quarter, so she tries it and it works.

"This is an emergency. I'm Molly Cates from *Lone Star Monthly* magazine. I need you to call over to the Capitol, the Senate chamber. There's a poison gas bomb set to go off there any minute. In the Senate. Call them. Tell them to evacuate. Send some cars over there. Everyone needs to get out now. If they don't they'll all be killed." She finds herself gasping for air at the end of this.

"How do you know there's a bomb, ma'am?"

"That will take too long. I'll tell the police when they come for me. I'm at Flipnotics on Barton Springs Road. Send a car to get me."

"Yes, ma'am. I'll dispatch one of our units."

"How long will it take?"

"We've got lots of calls right now. Probably ten minutes."

"Listen, this is a Code 3. Top priority."

"Yes, ma'am."

Molly is not sure she is being taken seriously. "Also, I need an ambulance. Connect me with Lieutenant Traynor in homicide, please."

"I can't transfer you, ma'am. Are you reporting a crime in progress right now?"

"No. Listen, time is wasting here. Call over to the Senate. Then when the car comes, I'll show them where the bodies are." She knows she is not being as coherent as she'd like.

"Ma'am, you will have to give me an address—"

"Flipnotics on Barton Springs is where I am. There's no address for where the homicides were committed. They're in the woods behind here and at a dump back there. I'll—"

"Come on!" Sarah Jane is shouting to Molly from the door. "I got us a ride. Come *on!*"

Molly says into the phone, "Notify the Senate *now.*" She slams the phone down and runs to the door. Sarah Jane is standing in the street next to a green Volkswagen beetle, talking to the driver. She has unbuttoned her shirt and is unpinning something from inside it. She holds it out to the driver. "See. A hundred bucks."

The driver, a young man with a long greasy pony tail, studies the bill. Then he glances over at Molly and frowns. He says to Sarah Jane, "She the other one?"

Sarah Jane nods.

"She's gonna get my car all dirty."

"You can clean it," Sarah Jane says, holding the bill right under his nose so he can smell it.

He grabs it. "Get in," he says. "Back seat."

Molly is torn with indecision. She knows how long the police response time can be. Standing here waiting will drive her crazy. This driver is a bird in the hand. They are no more than five minutes from the Capitol. She is desperate to get over there. She has to be sure the message got through. "What time is it?" she asks the driver.

He glances at his watch. "Ten forty-five."

"Okay," she says and struggles into the back seat. "But fast. This is an emergency. Go up Lamar to First. Take First to Congress, and go up Congress to the Capitol. If you get us to the front door of the Capitol in five minutes, I'll send you a five-hundred-dollar bonus."

"Oh, sure you will," he grumbles, glancing at her in the rearview mirror. "Lady Bountiful."

Sarah Jane slides in next to her and the driver takes off. The car is ancient and makes lots of noise when he guns the motor.

Molly leans forward. "You have a cellular phone?"

"Nope."

They are stopped at a light. "Go right through the red light here. Don't worry about cops. We'd *like* to pick up a police escort."

He runs the light. His eyes in the mirror are wide open with surprise at what he's doing.

Molly sits back and tries to catch her breath. "You said you didn't have any money," she says to Sarah Jane.

"I meant no quarters."

"But you had a hundred-dollar bill."

"It was my ... sort of good luck charm. I was planning to give it back to Ellie."

"Ellie?"

"My daughter. To show her I'm serious about turning my life around."

"But you spent it on this ride," Molly says.

"Seemed more important."

Frustrated by the slow progress they are making, Molly leans forward again and says to the driver, "Pass these creeps. Just honk and pass them."

"Jesus," he says, but he does it.

Molly can barely sit still. She is second-guessing her handling of this. "You know what we should have done?" she says with a sudden insight. "We should have called it in as a bomb *threat*."

Sarah Jane looks at her. "Yeah. That might get some attention."

"The second man on the deck," Molly said, "not the Kraut, the other one. Did you actually *see* him?"

"No. Tin Can did, not me. I didn't see the big one, the Kraut, until the library. But I recognized his voice."

"You think you'd recognize the other guy's voice?"

"Maybe."

"Why were you stealing the book?"

"I *wasn't* stealing it. I was borrowing it to help me show I was telling the truth about what I heard. Now I won't be able to go back there anymore. And it's my favorite place."

"We'll figure something out," Molly says. "Did you ever remember the second verse?"

"What?"

"Little Bopeep. What it was she dreamt."

"Oh. *Little Bopeep fell fast asleep and dreamt she heard them bleating.* That's what she dreamt, that she heard them bleating."

"Then what?"

"Let's see. *When she awoke, it was a joke, for still they all were fleeting.* Something like that."

"What you did back there——" Molly says, "I could never have done it. You were just amazing."

Sarah Jane shrugs. "You're the one knocked him out. And throwing a fit like you did—that was real good."

Molly studies Sarah Jane Hurley, really looking at her for the first time. Her frizzy gray and brown hair stands out from her head like electrified Brillo. Her cheeks are flushed red from exertion, and her large dark eyes glitter with life force. She hasn't remembered to button up her plaid shirt and her dirty undershirt shows.

Molly reaches out and buttons her shirt for her.

Sarah Jane smiles. It is the first time Molly has seen her smile. Maybe she isn't crazy.

Molly leans forward again and asks the driver, "What's your name?"

"Fred."

"Well, Fred, let's see how fast you can do this open stretch of First Street."

"Cesar Chavez," he says, accelerating. "They changed the name."

Sarah Jane taps her on the shoulder. "Why didn't you call me back when I left you that message?"

"I was out of town. As soon as I got it, I did try to call you at HOBO. But you weren't there."

"Oh. I saw a cop go in, so I was afraid to go back in."

"What did he look like?" Molly sees the turn coming. "Fred, here's your left. You can make it. Don't stop. Go right through."

"White hair," Sarah Jane says, "mustache. Fifty maybe. Pretty thin."

Molly smiles. "He thinks he doesn't look like a cop. You've got a good eye."

"There's a warrant out for me in Houston."

"I know."

Sarah Jane is silent for a moment. Then she looks back at Molly. "How are you? You took such a hard knock back there I wasn't sure you'd ever wake up from it."

"I think I've got a permanent headache. And my knee got cut at the dump, and I've got these ant bites all over my feet. How about you?"

"Me? I've never been better. I was brought back to life and healed, you know."

Molly studies her, trying to decide whether she's crazy or not. She says, "That must be pretty...exciting—being brought back to life."

"Yeah, it is. I feel really bad about bringing all that shit down on Mother Teresa. And Lufkin too. He kept his word. He was coming to help me get out of town."

"Not your fault," Molly says. "None of it. There'll be time to think about it later."

Sarah Jane leans forward and says to the driver, "Now just lay on your horn, Freddie, all the way up Congress, like you're an ambulance. Step on it."

He does step on it, and pedestrians scatter before them as the Capitol dome gets closer. "Fred," Molly says, "what time is it now?"

He glances at his watch, then back at the road. "Ten forty-nine."

The session must be under way, unless they've evacuated. Surely, Molly thinks, they have to take a call like hers seriously. She hopes to see lots of flashing lights and a crowd of people out front on the Capitol grounds. But there is just one police unit and the usual foot traffic walking in and out. Something has gone wrong, she is sure of it. "Here's the plan," Molly says. "We're going to run right up the big stairs to the Senate. We won't stop to talk to anyone. If they're still in there, we'll make them get out. We'll yell 'Fire' if we have to."

The Volkswagen screeches to a halt at the front steps. "Ladies," Fred says, "four and a half minutes." As Molly climbs out of the back seat, he hands her a slip of paper. "My address."

They scramble out. They run up the steps with Molly in the lead. She pulls open the big door. A tour group is standing in the rotunda looking up at the dome. A guard stands next to the Sam Houston statue and several men in suits are walking through the foyer.

The guard alerts when he sees them. Molly calls out to him, "There's a bomb in the Senate! Evacuate the building. Sound an alarm. Call up there on your radio and tell them to get everyone out. Right now!"

He puts his hand on his gun and looks at her from under his big Stetson. "Come over here, please, ma'am," he says, moving toward them the way you'd approach a snarling dog.

"You aren't listening!" Molly is screaming at him now. "Use your radio to call up there." She runs toward the stairs, giving the guard a wide berth.

Every face in the tour group is turned toward them now, staring. "Get outside," Molly calls back to them. "We're going to evacuate the building. Hurry!"

The staircase, which is wide enough for an entire cavalry to ride up, is empty. Molly takes the steps two at a time. Sarah Jane is behind her and the guard is following them, talking into his radio and keeping them in sight as he climbs. Molly slows at the top so Sarah Jane can catch up with her. "Listen," she says, panting, "they're not taking this seriously. We need to do it ourselves. I'm going to go first to distract them. You go right through the Senate door and yell up a storm. Tell them there's a bomb and they all have to get out. Keep yelling till they're all out."

Sarah Jane looks panicked. But she nods.

They turn the corner and there's the reception committee waiting for them, of course, in the lobby, standing in front of the closed door into the Senate chamber—two Austin policemen, a DPS security officer, and a man in a dark suit.

"Go ahead," Molly whispers to Sarah Jane.

"There's a bomb in there," Molly says, approaching the

men, talking fast and loud. "It's a poison gas bomb and it will kill everybody in there. Tell Special Agent Heller from the FBI."

The man in the dark suit starts talking into his radio.

"Listen! You can't take a chance on this. I'm Molly Cates from—"

"Ma'am, are you the one that called 911?" asks one of the cops.

Molly sees Sarah Jane walking with her head down, trying not to attract attention. "Yes, sir. I'm Molly Cates. An editor at *Lone Star Monthly.*" She decides to try dropping some names and keep the talk going so they'll all be looking at her. "I'm Senator Morrisey's godchild. Go ask him. Get him out here so he can tell you. Why haven't you evacuated? I called more than ten minutes ago. Do it now. If you don't, you'll be held responsible when—"

"Ma'am, ma'am, will you come in here a minute, please?" He beckons her to a side office. "We need some more information from you, ma'am. Could we talk in here?" He motions toward the little room off to the side of the door.

She follows him. "We're wasting time here. You need to get people out and do a search."

One of the cops sees Sarah Jane opening the door and he sprints to intercept her, but she's already slipped in and closed the door behind her. He rushes in after her.

Molly breaks away and hurries to the door. She's not sure Sarah Jane is up to the job, so she wants to be there to back her up.

Sarah Jane is standing in the middle of the chamber. Looking up at the gallery, she shouts in a firm voice, "It's a poison gas bomb and it will kill everybody in here when it goes off. So y'all need to move out of here *right now.*"

Several guards are heading her way fast and the lieutenant governor is pounding his gavel. "Madam!" he shouts into his microphone. "If you have something to say, please—"

Sarah Jane pays no attention to him, and neither does anyone else. "Keep it orderly, folks," she shouts up to the gallery. "I see a school group up there. Let those children out first, and the wheelchair people. Stand back and let them through the door." Her voice has real carrying power and the authority of a drill instructor.

On the floor, senators and aides are all standing, gathering papers, moving toward the doors. Thank God. They believe us. Molly catches a glimpse of Parnell and his aide and Garland Rauther as they leave with the rest.

Up in the gallery, pandemonium is breaking loose. Guards are running around trying to direct the traffic. There are only two doors and everyone is trying to push through at the same time. The noise level is rising by the second. The lieutenant governor is screaming into his microphone. "Calmly, calmly, ladies and gentlemen! This is just a drill! We'll reconvene this afternoon at one o'clock. Please keep calm! Everyone out of the building for this routine drill. Keep calm!"

An alarm starts to blare out in the halls. It sounds like an air raid and is music to Molly's ears. Finally someone in power is taking this seriously. The alarm should alert the whole building.

Two guards are holding Sarah Jane's arms and trying to get her to leave, but she is refusing to budge. Molly, still standing at the door, is torn. She wants to get out with the rest of the people evacuating. The panic is contagious. But she can't leave unless Sarah Jane does. She walks into the chamber, which is easy since most of the senators have cleared out.

There is too much noise now for Sarah Jane to be heard, so she stops yelling. Everyone is on the move anyway. One of the guards holding Sarah Jane's arm shouts, "Come on!" Sarah Jane wrenches away from him. "I'm gonna wait till everyone's out," she insists.

A young woman guard takes Molly by the arm and tries to move her out. Molly shakes her head and stays put. "You go on," she shouts into the woman's ear.

Agent Heller bursts through the door. He is wearing his usual fatigues and yellow beret and Molly feels a wave of relief at the sight of him. "Is that you, Miss Cates?" he demands. "What in bloody *hell* is all this?"

"Heller! There's a poison gas bomb in here. We'll tell you about it outside. Make sure everyone gets out."

"Where is this bomb?" he asks.

Sarah Jane says, "I think in a camera or other stuff they use to take pictures. I think that's what they said."

"And it's gas?" he asks.

"Soman," she says.

"Holy shit!" He looks up at the gallery and calls out to the man in the dark suit, who is looking down on them. "Brinker! Is everyone up there out?"

"Yes, sir."

"Good. Look for cameras and flash equipment. Be careful. It's nerve gas."

Then he turns to the guards. "I'm Special Agent Heller. FBI. Move out to the hall now and help with traffic. It's chaos. I'll take over in here."

The guards let go of Molly and Sarah Jane and leave quickly. Heller says, "Go on, ladies. I'll join you outside in a few minutes. We've got *lots* to talk about."

Molly and Sarah Jane look at one another and nod. They've done their job. There's no reason now not to get the hell out.

"You get out too, Heller," Molly says over her shoulder. He is the last one remaining, except for two guards, who are walking around the chamber talking into their radios, and the FBI agent in the suit up in the gallery.

"Move," Heller says.

Molly and Sarah Jane walk through the lobby. They find the halls packed wall to wall, with people still pouring out of the offices and meeting rooms. The entire building is clearing out. The staircase, broad as it is, is the logjam. It is packed and the progress is very slow. A group of panicky children are crying and one has fallen on the stairs. The teacher is trying to get back to him. The noise, bouncing off the terrazzo floors, is deafening.

Molly has a sudden stab of worry. People are getting hurt and it might turn out to be for nothing if this is a false alarm.

They wait at the top of the stairs until everyone in the hall has gotten into the traffic on the stairs. It feels as though they are the hosts at a party and need to let all their guests go first.

Molly is sure Sarah Jane feels that way too, because she is standing aside and ushering people along.

As they finally start down, Heller joins them. "Boy, do I ever want to hear what you two have to say," he says as they follow the crowd down. The progress is one step at a time, but the traffic is moving steadily and behind them are only a few stragglers.

From the top of the stairs a guard, red-faced and agitated, calls out to Heller. "Agent! Come up here, please. ASAP."

"I'll see you ladies outside," Heller tells them. He runs back up the stairs.

Molly and Sarah Jane finally make it down the stairs and through the rotunda to the south door. Four guards and an Austin policeman are moving people out the door, saying, "Keep the drive clear, folks. Move way back to the grass, please. Keep the drive clear."

As they descend the steps, three police cars wail up the drive with their lights flashing. Four more are barreling up Congress. One of the cops who jumps out says, "Bomb squad's on the way. Keep that driveway clear. Out of the drive, folks. Move way back. Quickly now. *Way* back."

Now Molly is aware of sirens screaming from all directions.

The cops park on the lawn, jump out, and set about moving people back and stringing up yellow tape to keep the drive and the area at the front door clear.

By the time Molly and Sarah Jane reach the south lawn, hundreds of people are there, milling around, excited, buzzing, everyone trying to get information.

Two white vans screech up the driveway. The vans aren't marked, but Molly thinks it's the bomb unit.

A big Austin cop who was in the reception group earlier spots them and walks over to them. "After all this," he says, "you two ladies better have something good."

Agent Heller appears on the steps, talking with a policeman, who then shouts out, "Everyone get back! Back! We got some ambulances coming. Folks, this is not a drill. This is the real thing. We need you to cooperate."

Heller surveys the crowd. Molly waves her arms to get his attention. He sprints down the steps and across the grass toward them. When he reaches Molly and Sarah Jane, he says in a low voice, "Jesus Christ, there *is* a bomb. Just went off. Whole room's full of gas. We got three men in there. Dead, I think. But we can't go in for them until we get some masks. The doors are closed but we don't know if this stuff is going to travel." Looking up, he shouts to a group of Austin policemen, who are just standing around, "Get that crowd farther back! Move the perimeter way back!"

He looks back at Molly and Sarah Jane. "How did you two know about this? I want to hear *everything,* right from the start."

Molly is about to speak up when Sarah Jane steps forward and says, "I can tell you all that, but first I want to say I did not attack that guy at the library. He attacked *me.* He was trying to kill me and I don't think it's fair to keep me out of a *public* library."

Agent Heller nods, as though it all makes sense to him. Then he says, "I agree. I can take care of that for you, ma'am. Now tell me how on earth you knew about this poison gas."

> THERE'S NOTHING WRONG WITH SHOOTING,
> AS LONG AS THE RIGHT PEOPLE GET SHOT.
> —"DIRTY HARRY" CALLAHAN

Grady Traynor didn't show up until late afternoon. By then Molly Cates had spent four long hours in the suite the FBI had commandeered in the Reagan Office Building next to the Capitol. She had already told and retold her little part of the story to Agent Heller, five other FBI agents, two Austin cops from the bomb unit, and three from homicide. When Grady finally arrived, she'd been sitting in the outer office for a half hour watching the receptionist answer a constant barrage of phone calls.

Grady showed his badge to the receptionist and came in. He sat down next to Molly and looked her over——her bandaged chin and scabby, swollen lip, her stitched-up and bandaged knee braced on the table in front of her. She was wearing the green scrub suit the EMS medic had given her after he'd tended to her wounds.

"I'd kiss you," Grady said, "but I can't find a place that looks like it wouldn't hurt."

"Oh, I'm sure you can," she said. "We'll work on that later."

He took hold of her hand. "Molly, I leave you sleeping peacefully and a few hours later you've been kidnapped and pistol-whipped, you've witnessed two homicides, you've fractured the skull of a homeless man, you've tried to break the window in a service station, and you've saved the state legislature from a poison gas attack."

"Just the Senate. Anyway, Sarah Jane did the saving; I was just along for the ride."

"Well." He sat back and looked her over again.

"So his skull is fractured." Molly still felt in her elbows the jarring impact when she smashed the toilet lid down on his head. "I'm amazed anyone could live through that."

"Hardheaded. He's already regained consciousness."

"I'm relieved to hear I didn't kill him."

"I thought you might be. But you would've saved the state some trouble; they'll bring a capital murder charge against him."

"Good."

"We haven't picked Squint up yet, but we will."

"Oh, Grady, Mother Teresa was this sweet nut case and Lufkin was trying valiantly to help us.... The wrong people got shot out there."

"You wouldn't believe how often I see that in my work, Molly." He smiled at her, that rueful, ironic smile of his that never failed to snag her heart.

She squeezed his hand in both of hers. "I'm so glad to see you. I need a few favors."

"Uh-huh."

"Please see what you can do to help Sarah Jane Hurley."

"She needs help. The Houston warrant is for aggravated assault—stabbing a woman in a downtown shelter and fleeing to avoid arrest. The woman was badly injured, but she was stealing from Hurley and also had a knife, so I think there are extenuating circumstances. I don't know how serious they are about pursuing her. It was more than a year ago. I'll check."

"Good."

"There's also this matter—she and a friend, this Lufkin who got shot, apparently found Emily Bickerstaff's body first and didn't report it."

"But she's cooperating now, Grady, and she's a hero. Surely that counts for something."

"Well, she may be a hero, Molly, but she sure waited long enough to do something about the gas plot. Five more minutes and it would have been too late."

"Would you have listened to her, Grady? If she'd come to you—a bag lady, a drunk, a woman with a warrant for assault. Would you have bought her story?"

He sat looking pensive for a few long moments. Molly loved him for that: he was man who, from time to time, was actually willing to look honestly and critically at himself. "I'll work on both those matters," he said. "What else?"

"The library. She's worried about that."

He rolled his eyes upward. "Jesus, Molly. Can't this wait?"

"It's important to her, Grady. She likes libraries. Now that she's a hero maybe they could give her an honorary lifetime card or something. At the very least they need to let her back in."

"I'll check."

"And, Grady, would you get her daughter's phone number for me? Her name is Ellie—I don't know the last name—and she lives in Brenham."

Grady nodded.

"And one more favor. The guy at the service station—the one who says I tried to break his window? Burt."

"Yeah?"

"I want you to use the rubber hose on him. Break his fingers."

"That bad, huh?"

"He treats the homeless like insects."

"I wish there were a law against it."

"Me too." She lowered her voice and glanced over at the receptionist, who was still on the phone. "What's the scuttlebutt here?"

He shrugged. "How should I know?"

"Oh, come on, Grady."

"Well, Cullen Shoemaker and his mother are on their way back from New Orleans in FBI custody."

"His *mother?*"

"Uh-huh."

"She wasn't involved, was she?"

"I don't know, but two of the McNelly Posse members are being questioned downstairs right now. Of course, they're swearing the posse is a *service fraternity* and they are just clean-cut college boys, but they *have* suggested that both Cullen Shoemaker and his mother may have planned this."

"Oh, *no.*" Molly pictured the sensible gray-haired grand-mother in the Senate hearing room, leaning forward in her seat, listening to her son's diatribe. "She couldn't have supported a plot that would kill children and innocent people. After what she's suffered, she couldn't *do* that. It would be doing the same thing to other people as what happened to her."

"Molly! Haven't you learned *anything?* This gun business is one of those wildly irrational issues. People do lunatic things when they believe the very basis of their freedom is under attack. We have a long history of that in this country."

Molly could hear Cullen Shoemaker ranting to the Senate committee. *If we let them disarm us, pardners, the same thing that happened to those folks in Waco will happen to us— coldblooded massacre. Don't think it won't. If we let those jackbooted thugs from the ATF get us on their list, then we are up shit creek with no paddle. That will be the end of our free-doms, pardners,* the *end.*

Elizabeth Shoemaker, Molly recalled, had been listening earnestly, nodding even. "Maybe you're right," she admitted.

"The problem is, you have this idea women are more civi-lized than—"

"We are!"

He looked at her coolly, his pale eyes calm and sure. "Bull-shit."

Molly leaned back on the sofa, picturing Elizabeth Shoemaker, saintly, in her sensible shoes. "Well, I've been wrong about nearly everything else. I might as well add this to the list."

Grady's eyes opened wide with interest. "Really? What else have you been wrong about?"

"The list is endless. I'll fill you in later. What about the actual bomber? The German, the one Sarah Jane calls Billy Goat Gruff?"

"Our artist is working on a composite right now with a man called Rhyming Rudy and the maître d' at Creekside Grill and Sarah Jane."

"What else?" she said. "There's something else, Grady. I can see it in your eyes."

He leaned forward and said quietly, "A print. They lifted one perfect thumbprint from the fake camera that launched the gas."

"Oh, good. One more favor, Grady. The last one."

"Uh-huh."

"Get me out of here. They told me to wait, but I have an appointment with Parnell Morrisey in twenty minutes. Will you vouch for me?"

"Sure." He leaned over and kissed her on the cheek. "You know, Molly, you missed getting gassed by three and a half minutes."

"That close?"

"That's what Heller says."

She felt a twinge of anxiety, not about the close call with the gas, but about what Heller might have told Grady. "You've talked with Agent Heller?"

"Yes."

"Did he tell you he came to see me the other night?"

"Yes. He said you had Cullen Shoemaker spotted from the get-go. Says he should have listened to you, Molly, instead of focusing on Wanda Lavoy. *There's* something you were right about."

She studied his face to see if Heller had told him anything else. Even if he had, it was unlikely Grady knew about the Olin Crocker incident. And if he did know, he'd decided not to let her know he knew. Secrecy sure made for complications—too much to remember. She vowed to avoid it in the future and live her life like an open book.

30

> NEEDLES AND PINS, NEEDLES AND PINS,
> WHEN A MAN MARRIES HIS TROUBLE BEGINS.
> —MOTHER GOOSE

Molly Cates sat waiting on the cool granite base of the Confederate soldiers monument. It had been her favorite statue on the Capitol grounds ever since she and her daddy had first visited Austin the summer her mother died. After they had taken the usual visitors' tour of the Capitol, they had walked the grounds and stopped here to read the inscription and talk about the Civil War. This afternoon, when she'd called Parnell from the FBI office and told him to meet her, this was the first place that came to mind. Over the phone her godfather's voice had sounded unsurprised and weary, resigned to the inevitable, as though he'd been waiting all his life for that very call and, now it had come, he might not be able to muster the energy to go through with it.

She was exhausted too. Every inch of her body ached right down to the bone, her lip hurt every time she opened her mouth, her knee was throbbing, and the bites on her feet itched with a vengeance. This was probably the worst possible time to confront him, but she was not going to put off the reckoning any longer.

It was five hours since the gas had been released in the Senate chamber, and the Capitol itself was still sealed off to everyone except the bomb squad and FBI agents. At each of the entrances two DPS troopers stood on guard. But the grounds and the several surrounding blocks were a madhouse, swarming with media and cops and curiosity seekers. Scores of media vans were parked outside the grounds and a steady stream of cars with gawkers looking out the windows crawled by. Just outside the police perimeter, TV reporters were setting up to broadcast the evening news from the Capitol grounds.

Now she caught sight of Parnell. He stood at the yellow police tape, talking with two of the bomb squad officers who were still suited up like spacemen. He glanced toward her, then headed across the grass, walking very slowly. His shoulders were stooped, his feet looked heavy, like a man with barely enough energy to resist gravity's pull. When he reached the monument, he didn't speak to her or even look at her. Instead, he stood close to where she was sitting and studied the inscription carved into the marble, underneath the four bronze Confederate soldiers posted at each corner. *"Died for states rights guaranteed under the Constitution,"* he read. "I bet that's not how they teach the story up in New York City."

Molly recited the next line from memory: *"The South, against overwhelming numbers and resources, fought until exhausted.* That's certainly the story they taught at Lubbock High."

"But you can see it now from a Yankee perspective too," he said.

"Sure."

"Do you think it's possible to understand almost any act if you can get yourself into the right perspective?"

"No." Molly shook her head for emphasis. "Some things are unforgivable, beyond understanding. Like what Cullen Shoemaker tried to do here today—sacrificing innocent lives for a political idea. I will never understand that."

"Your capacity to understand and forgive has its limits, then."

"Oh, yes."

He looked directly at her for the first time. He was squinting against the sun, which had finally come out just in time to set. The bags under his eyes were so swollen, they seemed to be dragging his whole face downward. He said, "You look terrible, sweetheart."

She studied his ravaged face. "You look pretty bad yourself."

He seemed to be trying for a smile, but gravity was too much for him and he couldn't manage it. "Didn't sleep much last night. I hear you were held hostage and nearly killed."

She nodded. "*Very* nearly. Parnell, I've always wondered why people say someone who survives an ordeal is brave. I wasn't brave at all. I didn't know it was possible to be so scared. I nearly burned myself up with fear. I would have done anything not to die." She was surprised that, in spite of what she was about to do, she still expected sympathy from him, and reassurance. She had pulled up the leg of her pants to check the bandage on her knee and now she smoothed down the edges of it. Parnell looked down at it and winced. "I'd sure like to hear the story," he said.

"Not today. It's your turn to tell *me* a story."

"But you think you already know it, don't you?"

"Yes."

"I hear you threatened to kill Olin Crocker," he said.

"No. I threatened to blow his balls into raw hamburger. I don't think that would have killed him."

"Would you have done it?"

"Of course not."

"He thought you were dead serious."

"He called you?"

"Uh-huh. Got me out of bed Sunday morning. What would you have done if he'd refused to tell you?"

"I'd've slunk off, probably, and never known."

"But now you know."

She looked him in the eye. "I know you paid Crocker sixty thousand dollars to call my daddy's death a suicide."

His expression didn't change. "Well, that's true. I did pay him to call it a suicide. Because it was a suicide."

"No, Parnell. It wasn't."

He shook his head and the smile he'd been trying for finally came. "God save us, Molly, when you get ahold of an idea."

"Parnell, I *know.*"

"What is it you know?"

She lowered her eyes, unable to bring herself to look at him when she said it. "I know Rose was having an affair with my father. For more than twenty years."

"How do you know that?" His voice was steady.

"Old letters between Harriet and Daddy. I went to the family archives yesterday."

He nodded slowly. "You've been mighty busy, Molly."

"Yes, I have."

"And you think you've put it all together, at long last. You finally have your truth."

"Yes, I think so."

"So it's a country and western song, Miss Molly? That old honky-tonk theme." In his twangiest West Texas voice, he drawled, "My woman, she done me wrong with my best friend, so I done the sucker in." The mournfulness of his voice and the slump of his shoulders belied the flipness of the words. "Is that what happened?"

"It must have been terrible, Parnell, to find out that they were having an affair, deceiving you all those years."

"Yes, it was worse than terrible, Molly. But tell me, why did I just kill *him,* then? Why not her?"

"Because you loved her too much to kill her."

"So . . . our country song gets more melodramatic yet. That cheatin' woman of mine, she done me wrong," he twanged, "but her blue eyes cryin' in the rain begged me to spare her life. Is that what happened, Molly?"

"Yes."

"And why did I do it just then, when Vern was about to get married?"

"Because you finally found out about the affair."

"I see."

"Where's Rose?" Molly asked.

"She's over yonder on the west lawn." He turned his face

in that direction. "Sittin' on the bench feeding the squirrels. Damned rodents."

"Does she know about Crocker's call?"

"No. I didn't see any reason to upset her with that."

Molly's eyes were stinging with the effort to hold back tears. "No one will ever love me the way you love Rose."

"I don't know, Molly. I've never seen a man love anyone more than your daddy loved you. Vern thought the sun rose and set in your eyes."

"I loved him too. So much. But he wasn't the man I thought he was."

"Oh, now, Molly. Who of us can stand up to the scrutiny you've been giving your daddy of late? Vern had a soft spot for the ladies, there's no denying it. And God knows"—he closed his eyes—"the ladies had a soft spot for him."

"Oh, Parnell. It's much more than that. He never really succeeded at anything. He was a failed rancher, an unfaithful husband. He couldn't manage money. He drank too much, got depressed, depended on his older sister to bail him out like she was his nursemaid." She found herself hugging her knees into her chest and rocking slightly.

Parnell reached down and patted her shoulder. "Molly, Molly."

"And he wasn't even a very good writer." She pressed her forehead against her knees, completing the circle, making her body into a cocoon.

"Sounds to me like a real human being, with lots of flaws. Can I tell you a story, Molly?"

Molly picked her head up and looked at him, amazed. Here was a man who would be telling stories even as he was standing on the gallows with a rope around his neck. "Sure. Tell me a story."

He put a foot up on the monument's base and leaned forward, resting his arm on his knee, the storyteller's classic pose. "Remember the day you got tossed by Jocko? It looked for a while like you might bleed to death. He'd caught an artery, old Jocko, and I never saw anyone as small as you lose so much blood so fast. Your daddy went in to donate blood 'cause they were running short. You and he had the same type. It was a valiant thing for him to do because you remember how he was scared to death of needles." He looked to her for a response and she nodded. She did remember.

"Well, sure enough," Parnell continued, "Vern fainted dead away while they were taking it. I was there, and Rose was there, when he came to. He opened his eyes and asked us if you had died while he'd been out. No, we said. As a matter of fact they had the bleeding stopped and it looked like you were out of danger.

"Molly, he was so relieved and happy he bawled like a baby, and, while he was crying, he said, "Parnell, did you see the way the kid handled that horse? She damn near made it. If that horse hadn't been so goddamned old and slow, I believe she would have counted her coup on Jocko. Isn't she something else?'"

Parnell closed his eyes, remembering back. "He never let on to you he felt that way 'cause he was supposed to be angry with you for breaking the rules, but really he was so proud of your courage and daring, your defiance and your pigheadedness. I believe if he was here right now he'd be unhappy you found out all his peccadilloes and weaknesses, but he'd be so proud that you're the same swashbuckler you were then."

Molly had never heard this. She had vowed she wouldn't cry at this meeting, and she didn't, but she wished she had a tissue to blot her nose.

"I feel sort of the same way right now, Molly. I didn't want the story of how Vern died to come out, but I always knew that, if it did, you would be the one to drag it out into the light. I can't help but feel a little proud. But you aren't quite there yet, sweetheart."

"No?"

"No." He turned back to the inscription on the monument and moved his fingers slowly along the carved letters like a man reading Braille. "You have in mind my making a confession? You want to send your police lieutenant to take my statement? Nice fella you got there, by the way—that Grady Traynor. I believe I'd hold on to him this time."

"I do want a confession, Parnell. I want you to tell me about it."

"Oh, Molly, sweetheart, I didn't kill Vern."

"Then Rose did." She watched his face closely for a reaction, but his expression didn't change.

"Ah, now we've got a *real* country and western song going," he said. "She loved that man so much she couldn't stand to see him love another, so she shot him dead just before his wedding day. Even though she was married to his best friend, a true-blue fella who worshiped her." He looked down at Molly. "Now that's a *real* sad one, isn't it?"

"Yes, it is."

"The problem is, Miss Molly, you're thinking Jimmie Dale Gilmore when you should be thinking Shakespeare."

"Huh?"

"Romeo and Juliet."

"What do you mean?"

"Well, you've got some of the story right, but you're handicapped. See, you're so sure of your assumption that it keeps you from seeing the truth. This is a bad problem for a writer, honey," he said gently, "and for a human being who's almost forty-five. You might need to work on that some."

"What assumption?"

"That Vern was murdered. It's gotten in your way." He stood up straight. "Let's do this together, Molly. You tell me what you've reconstructed and I'll steer you back on track when you go astray."

She thought about it. "Okay. Daddy gave Harriet the dirty work of breaking the news to Rose, the news that he was in love with Franny and he was going to marry her. He had decided he could never see Rose alone again. It was over. It was finally over. He was too weak to tell her himself, so he had his sister do it for him."

She looked up at Parnell for confirmation. He nodded.

"Rose must have been devastated," Molly continued. "She told Harriet she was going to go see Daddy at Lake

Travis and make him change his mind. Harriet called her brother to warn him Rose was coming. That would be the phone call that Franny remembers, the one that changed him so much, that sent him into a tailspin."

Parnell was nodding, his face expressionless. But suddenly Molly saw something she had missed over the years, probably because it had happened so gradually: the downward sagging of his eyes, his cheeks, his mouth had molded his face into a permanent expression of extreme grief—a mask of tragedy. Parnell was a man in perpetual mourning.

She looked away from him. "I suppose when Rose got there she pleaded with him to run away with her, or she said she'd tell you about it and get a divorce—something like that. She couldn't stand for it to be over because she loved him." She looked at Parnell for confirmation.

He cleared his throat. "You aren't being sufficiently melodramatic, sweetheart. Your version is too rational and restrained."

"Oh?"

He leaned forward and rested his forehead against the polished granite of the monument. After a moment, he spoke. "Rose said she couldn't live without him—*literally*. She said if he went ahead with his plan to marry Franny and break with her she'd kill herself. And he had to take it seriously, Molly, because she'd made two attempts before, when he'd tried to break it off."

"Suicide attempts? Rose? I never knew about any suicide attempts."

"Well, it's not the sort of thing one shares with children. Rose was hospitalized both times. I believe one time we called it a miscarriage, and another time we called it pneumonia. At the time I didn't understand why she was doing it. I thought it was depression. I didn't know it was her response to Vern's attempts to end their affair."

Molly looked at him, amazed. "No wonder he was so anguished that week. He was torn between Franny and Rose. He'd broken off the engagement, but Franny wouldn't accept that, and Rose was threatening to kill herself. He was in torment. He didn't know what to do. Even Harriet couldn't help him."

"And you know where I was?"

She shook her head.

"I was right here in Austin, working. The legislature was in session," he said through tight lips. "I was busy carrying on the affairs of state, all puffed up and self-important. I had no idea—*no idea*—this drama was unfolding. I didn't know it was about to slide downhill into tragedy. I didn't know all this passion was loose in the world. I didn't know it would kill your father and blight all our lives forever. I thought Rose was in Lubbock tending to her sick mother. There is no end to the things I didn't know." He took a deep breath. "Might as well go on with your story, Molly."

"Well, as Franny describes it, this agony went on for a week. There were calls to Harriet and attempts to get him to a doctor. Then, on the last day—" Molly stopped, unable to go any further.

"Now, Molly, open your mind. Let go of those preconceptions." Parnell was staring straight ahead, as if in a trance. "Close your eyes, sweetheart, and you'll see what happens next."

Molly closed her eyes, but she couldn't see anything at all.

"Come on, Molly, you're a writer and you've been trying to write this scene for twenty-eight years. Here's your chance. Use what you've found out and what I've told you. Trust me—I've told you nothing that isn't true. Use it. Tell me what you see happening."

Molly pictured the old houseboat, tied up at the rickety dock at Old Gun Hollow. She smelled the slightly fishy, oily smell of the lake and heard the water lapping around the hull. On the deck sat the two aluminum folding chairs and the plastic table that always had a coffee cup on it. Inside was his office, the most wonderful, romantic office she'd ever seen— a houseboat office full of books and photographs, his old Underwood typewriter, his coin collection. She could picture Vernon Cates in there drinking bourbon and trying to figure out how to save himself from the mess he'd gotten into. But that was as far as she could go; she couldn't see what happened next.

She shook her head.

"Think Romeo and Juliet," Parnell said. "An aging Romeo and Juliet, to be sure, but they had been lovers even back then, you know, when they were teenagers."

She had been visualizing murder as part of this scene for so long, she couldn't picture anything else. "I can't."

He took a deep breath. "Rose has been staying nearby at a motel for six days. She hasn't gone to the house because you're there, Molly, and they are determined to keep this from you. She comes to the houseboat every day, arguing with him, begging him to change his mind and go away with her. She swears she'll kill herself if he abandons her, and this time she'll do it right. Vern is a wreck. Franny is coming by and calling every day too. His women are driving him crazy. He's always been fragile, Molly, and now he is breaking down."

He paused. Even with her eyes closed Molly could tell he was having trouble catching his breath. "Okay, Molly. You take it from here. Vern arrives at the houseboat that last day to try to get some work done. Can't you just see him in his work clothes—his old jeans and boots—driving up in that battered white Chevy pickup? But when he gets there, someone's already at the boat. Who is it?"

"Rose?"

"Yes. Rose. Describe the scene for me."

"He pulls up to the dock," Molly said, seeing his long legs in the faded jeans as he slides down from his truck, hearing his boot heels strike the wooden dock. "He's been drinking steadily all week and he has a flask of bourbon in his pocket. He walks out to the boat. He finds Rose there."

"Yes. And what has Rose done?"

"I don't know."

"Romeo and Juliet, honey."

Molly saw it now: Rose's slender body crumpled on the deck, her shining dark hair loose and spilling over her pale face. "She's tried to kill herself."

"Yes. She's done it. She's taken sleeping pills again, just as she threatened, and she's lying dead on his deck. Can you see it?"

She could see it now, all too well. In a hot panic Vern runs to her—his longtime lover, the wife of his best friend. He kneels down over her and he lifts that delicate wrist of hers, the perfectly manicured hand, but her skin is cool and he can't find any pulse at all. It's too late. He is sure she is dead.

"How does he feel, sweetheart?" Parnell asked.

Molly heard his moaning, saw him bent down over the body, sobbing. "He feels he's killed her. The worst thing in the world has happened. He's to blame and he can't stand it."

"That's right. He can't live with it, can't face what's to come. So what does he do now?"

She saw her father stand up, tears streaming down his face. He pulls the flask from his shirt pocket and takes a drink, then another. He wants out of this horror. He can't take it, can't bear it. "But," Molly said, breaking out of her concentration, looking up at Parnell, "there's no gun."

"Oh, yes, there is. Rose brought the gun with her from her mother's house. Waving pills around is not nearly as dramatic as waving a gun around, so she brought it with her from Lubbock. She'd been carrying it around with her in her purse. Of course she didn't use it; she was far too fond of her own beauty to do that. Even if she were going to die, and I don't think she ever really intended it, Rose wanted to die beautiful. Especially if Vern would see her."

He paused, breathing heavily, before going on. "So describe it to me, Molly. You wanted the truth at all costs. Let's look at it. What happens next?"

Molly's heart was hammering. She felt it all—her father's guilt and panic and hopelessness. "He takes another drink from the flask. He feels his life is over. He puts the gun to his head."

"Yes. Then what?"

Molly barely had the strength to speak. The two words come out in a whisper: "He fires."

"Yes, Molly, he does. But Rose isn't dead, we know that. She wakes up, just like Juliet, and finds her lover dead. Then what does she do?"

"She calls you, Parnell."

"Of course. And you know what I do, don't you? Mr. Fix-it. I drive out there. And when I get there, I find my world has ended."

Molly hugged her knees tighter. She started to rock again. She was as exhausted as if she had lived through the scene herself.

"Oh, Molly, sweetheart, you look wiped out. Shall I take it from here?"

She nodded. A lump had grown in her throat which prevented her from speaking.

"I drive her away from there"—Parnell's voice was emotionless—"back to Austin, but when I get there I think of all the problems. We've brought the gun with us because it might be traced back to Rose's mother, but I get to thinking about what else might be on that houseboat to link Rose to what happened there. If the truth comes out, it would ruin my political career"—his voice was raspy with self-loathing—"and we couldn't have that, could we? So I hire this man who has been known to do dirty work before, and I get him to go out there that night and put the body in the lake. I also get him to sink the houseboat."

"To destroy any evidence Rose might have left," Molly said.

"Of course. Fingerprints, letters, whatever."

"But the man you hired," Molly said, "he couldn't resist stealing Daddy's coin collection that was lying right out in the open."

"But I didn't know that then," Parnell said. "Not until four years later when he pawned them, and you found out."

"You were still worried enough to pay Crocker off, though."

"Sure. If Crocker'd done any investigating at all, he'd have found out Rose was there that week. So I paid him to call it suicide and let it rest. He was happy to oblige."

Molly sighed again and shook her head, thinking about Olin Crocker. How her futile efforts to get information from him had affected her life.

"Amazing, isn't it, Molly," Parnell said as though he were reading her thoughts, "how destructive and far-reaching a lie can be—like a poison that spreads out and blights everything it touches."

Molly was tired beyond anything she'd ever felt before. "How do I know you're telling the truth now?"

"Look at me, Molly."

She glanced up. His face was turned toward her, his cheeks wet with tears she hadn't known he'd been shedding. Pain and regret were etched into every crease, every pore. "Am I telling the truth?" he whispered.

She nodded. "But this *isn't* Romeo and Juliet. Because in this story Juliet ends up living happily ever after with her rich and successful husband."

"Molly!" Parnell shook his head. "You know better than that. This is not a melodrama, it's a tragedy. No one lives happily ever after in a tragedy. Not after something like this. Maybe they *looked* happy, but they weren't."

"Why not?"

He put his palms flat against the side of the monument and leaned forward until his forehead rested against the smooth granite again. Molly knew how cool and comforting that cold stone must feel to him. "Why not?" he repeated into the stone. "Do you really think he could forgive her?"

"I don't know."

"Do you really think she could forgive herself? Don't you think that every time they tried to make love the body of that man—his best friend, her lover—was lying there between them? Don't you think she woke every morning sorry she hadn't really died of those sleeping pills? Don't you think he mourned every waking moment for his friend and the uncomplicated love he once felt for his wife? Don't you think a secret like the one they shared was a poison eating them up from the inside, corroding her joints, weakening his heart?"

Molly felt hot nausea rising in her throat. "I don't think

this song would sell, Parnell. A downer even by C and W standards."

"Too much truth for you, sweetheart?"

Molly sighed. "Did Harriet know?"

"I never told her and I know Rose didn't, but I think she figured it out."

Molly glanced around and was surprised to see that everything looked the same—the grass, the pink granite Capitol, the clouds overhead. Her whole history had suddenly shifted. Her father, the man she had idolized all her life, had killed himself rather than face up to the consequences of his acts. He was not the man she had believed him to be. Her history, her heredity, was different from what she'd thought. Which must mean that she was not who she thought she was. She'd been so sure of things, so sure she knew, but she'd been wrong about everything.

She would have to rethink everything in the light of this. But not now. Not right now.

After a long silence, Parnell spoke. "Let me ask you something, Molly. You've gone to a great deal of trouble and sacrifice to figure this out. Are you happier now that you know?"

"Happier? No."

"Well, was it worth it, then?"

"You talk as though I had a choice."

He nodded, conceding her point. "So what are you going to do now?"

There was a silence while Molly considered it. "I think what I'm going to do is this: I'm going home now and take a long bath and some pain pills 'cause my knee hurts like fury. I'll put some ammonia on my bites and go to bed. Tomorrow I'm going to sleep late. Then I'll go to the florist and buy a huge pot of daisies. Remember how much he loved the ones that grew along the road at the ranch? I'll go pick Jo Beth up from work and we'll drive out to Lake Travis to the Tech cemetery. We'll find the grave. You know, I've never been there, Parnell, not once in all these years. I'll introduce him to his granddaughter and we'll put the daisies on his grave and we'll say good-bye to him. And I'll come home and go back to work. I'm *way* behind."

Parnell squatted down in front of her. He took hold of her hands. "That sounds like a real good plan, sweetheart. Say hey to Jo Beth for me. And to Vern too."

"I'll do that."

His eyes were wet. "Now. May I ask you a favor? A hard one, one I have no right to ask."

Molly nodded.

"Rose is sitting over there, probably wondering what we're gabbing about over here. Do you think you could go over there and say hey to *her* and show her you survived your ordeal mostly intact? When she saw you all bunged up and covered with mud this morning, she was real worried."

Molly was stunned by the request. He was asking her to perform an act of forgiveness that was light-years beyond her.

He leaned his head down and kissed the bandage on her knee. "Remember, Molly, when you were little, how you'd go around getting everybody to kiss your boo-boos to make them better? Well, I wish I could kiss this terrible wound of yours and make it go away. But I can't. You have to heal it yourself."

During all the twenty-eight years she had searched for the real story of her daddy's death, Molly Cates had been certain that at the end there would be justice, punishment, and revenge. Never for a moment had she considered the possibility that forgiveness might be what was waiting at the end of the journey.

But now, as she thought about Rose and Parnell living all these years with the poisonous aftermath of her father's death, she found her anger melting away, her bitterness drying up. What she had really needed was an ending to the story. And now she had one. It was an ugly, painful ending, and she hated it, but she could feel already that in time she would come to accept it.

When she had mustered the energy, she stood up. "Tell you what, Parnell." She took hold of his arm. "Let's walk over there and see if Rose needs some help feeding the squirrels. That okay with you?"

OLD ROGER IS DEAD AND LAID IN HIS GRAVE,
LAID IN HIS GRAVE, LAID IN HIS GRAVE;
OLD ROGER IS DEAD AND LAID IN HIS GRAVE,
HUM HA! LAID IN HIS GRAVE.

—MOTHER GOOSE

"We didn't even need to bring the daisies." Jo Beth settled the pot amid the long grasses next to the headstone.

Molly looked around the small cemetery. Everywhere clusters of radiant white daisies had sprung wild out of the scrubby soil. "He's growing his own," she said.

"Aunt Harriet picked this place, didn't she?" Jo Beth stood on tiptoe, shading her eyes against the bright sunlight. "You can even see the lake. It's perfect."

Molly hunkered down at the grave. "It *is* perfect." The pink granite stone was simple but finely carved—Harriet's understated good taste. Just his name and his birth and death dates.

"You still haven't explained why now," Jo Beth said, squatting down next to Molly. "I've been bugging you to do this for years, but you wouldn't. Then you kidnap me from work to come here today. Something's happened."

"I've decided to end my period of mourning."

"No more vigils?"

"No. I've done my last one."

"Really? You mean it? You're finished?" Jo Beth's voice was excited and barbed with incredulity.

"Yes."

"Wow. What's happened?"

"It's a long story. I'll tell it to you at lunch."

Jo Beth stood up and brushed the dirt off her skirt. "About time."

Molly reached out and put a finger on the V in his name. She closed her eyes and traced the sharp edges of the carved letter slowly; it was like a small arrow pointing down at the earth where he was buried. "Rose and Parnell say hello," she said.

"Tell them hello back," said Jo Beth, thinking Molly was talking to her.

"I will." Molly stood up. "Jo Beth?"

"Hmm?"

"He was a man who loved and suffered a great deal, your grandfather. He loved me with no reservations and he taught me how to enjoy life. Not a perfect man by a long shot, but I miss him every day."

"I wish I'd known him."

"Me too, baby. Me too."

THERE WAS AN OLD WOMAN WHO LIVED NEAR A
    CREEK.
SHE HAD SO MANY MEMORIES IT MADE HER KNEES
    WEAK.
SHE FLOATED THE SKY ON A BOTTLE OF WINE.
SHE FORGOT ALL HER TROUBLES AND FELT, OH, SO
    FINE.

—SARAH JANE HURLEY

Sarah Jane Hurley is sitting in the quiet parlor of the boardinghouse on San Gabriel, paging through magazines. She likes staying here because the shabby oak furniture is big—her size—and comfortable, and because there are stacks of old *National Geographic* and *Life* and *Redbook* magazines.

A young woman sticks her head in and looks around. Sarah Jane hopes she isn't going to come in and turn on the television. Having to listen to all that racket pisses her off.

"Ma? Is that you?"

Startled, Sarah Jane looks up. "Ellie!" she says, pressing her hands to her chest. Her heart is bounding right through her ribs.

Sarah Jane stands up and the magazines that were in her lap scatter to the floor. "Ellie. How are you?"

"I'm good, real good. How about you, Ma?"

"Well, I'm just fine." Sarah Jane feels suddenly compelled to speak the truth: there are days when she feels like she's going to smother under all the details, the reality and the remembering. "I mean, I'm fine *today*, right this minute. You know, one day at a time."

Ellie walks over, wraps her arms around Sarah Jane, and

gives her a long hug. When Sarah Jane recovers from the shock of it, she hugs her back, desperately, savoring the wonderful solid feel of her daughter, her broad back and billowy bosom, just like her own. It's a dream, of course. Sarah Jane has never been good at separating fantasy from reality, and during the past few years she's been hopeless at it.

They let go of each other, finally. Sarah Jane stands back and looks at her daughter. Ellie has cut her hair. It is short now and curly all over her head. She's stopped trying to straighten it. She looks . . . dreamy.

"You look just beautiful, Ellie. I like your hair that way."

Ellie runs a hand through her curls. "Oh. It's been like this for more than two years, Ma."

"Two years? Really?" Sarah Jane is overwhelmed by how much they've missed of one another's lives, too much to ever catch up on. Anyway, she's not sure catching up is a good idea: there's so much about the life she's led the past three years that she doesn't want Ellie to know, ever. She is embarrassed to tell this, even at her meetings, but she really feels that she was brought kicking and screaming back to life, and has become a new woman. She doesn't want Ellie to know about that other person, Cow Lady, although there are moments when Sarah Jane misses her—her freedom and her numbness.

"I kept that hundred you gave me, Ellie," Sarah Jane says. "I was planning to give it back to you—the exact same hundred-dollar bill. Remember you were so mad and you said I'd go right out and spend it on booze, but I didn't. I kept it pinned inside my shirt—sort of a good luck charm—till last month. I used it for an emergency, to get a ride to the Capitol."

"I read about it in the paper. They say you saved all those people."

"I came awfully close to *not* doing it, Ellie." Her voice shakes as she says this because only she knows how really close she came to not doing it.

"But you did, and I'm real proud of you."

"Well, thanks. How did you know where to find me?"

"The lady who called told me."

"What lady's that?"

"Oh, the one from some magazine. I forget her name. Said she thought you'd like to see me."

"Well, I do, yes, but I thought you were still mad."

"I was before, but I'm not now. You know?"

"Sure. Sure I do. I'm not easy to put up with, the drinking and all." Sarah Jane chokes back tears; crying is too cheap a way out. She has cried plenty the last month, though, and she has let herself remember it all—the neglect, the violent rages, the drunken fights with Harold, the lost jobs, the forgotten birthdays, the fire—and she has even stood up in front of other people at her meetings and told about it. "I'm awful sorry, Ellie, but it's past now."

"Oh, Ma."

To give herself a minute to collect herself, Sarah Jane bends over and picks up the magazines she spilled on the floor.

Then Ellie says, "I was thinking maybe we could go out for lunch."

"Oh, I'd love that, Ellie, but I can't."

"Oh."

"See, I've got my meeting at noon. You know, my...AA meeting. And after that I have this little, oh, it's not really a job—I don't get paid—but it's something I do on Monday, Wednesday, and Friday at two."

"What's that?"

"I read to kids at the library, at the little branch right next door to where my meeting is. I was just hanging out there and they said why not make myself useful." She shrugs.

"That sounds so good, Ma. Remember when you used to read to me and Tom? You were so patient reading those same rhymes, over and over. I still know them all by heart."

Sarah Jane smiles. "So do I."

"Well, Ma, you're busy and I don't want to interfere. But maybe we could have dinner instead. I took the whole day off, so"—she give a little laugh—"I might as well stay and live it up."

"Yes. Sure. That would be so good, Ellie."

There is an awkward silence when the two women look at

one another and Sarah Jane thinks that Ellie must be think-ing what an old wreck her mother has become, with her skin so wrinkled and weathered and her hair gone so gray and out of control.

"I talked with Tom yesterday," Ellie says.

Sarah Jane feels herself clench up, preparing for the pain that is sure to come. "How is your brother?"

"He's pretty good, living back in Houston again. He read about you in the paper. Says to tell you you did good."

Sarah Jane is stunned by this, overwhelmed. Tom has re-fused to see her or talk with her since he was seventeen. She has not seen him for twelve years. This is the first message he has sent her. "He said that? To tell me I did good?"

"Listen, Ma," Ellie says, "I've got my car outside. I could drop you at your meeting. Is there anywhere you'd like to go before?"

Sarah Jane looks at her daughter's hair. "You know, I'd like to get my hair cut, Ellie. Maybe we could find a place that would take me without an appointment." Since this is just a dream, she figures, all things are possible.

Ellie looks at her mother's hair and smiles. "We can try," she says.

Epilogue

On Molly Cates's computer screen:

My birthday has come and gone.

I am now the same age as my father. We are contemporaries, he and I.

I know more about him than I did when I began writing this essay. Much more. I know he experienced his share of failure and mediocrity. So have I. I know he made some mistakes that caused great suffering to himself and the people he loved. So have I. I know he committed adultery. So have I. I know he kept dark and dangerous secrets all his life. So have I. I know now that he died by his own hand. In my darker hours, I have considered that path too.

So here I am in my forty-sixth year with this as part of my paternal heritage. But in a few months I will be older than he ever was. I will enter brand-new territory that he never trod. Maybe I will feel like a racehorse then, pushing my nose out in front of the pack, breaking away, moving on, setting my own pace. Maybe I have outlived and outgrown whatever pattern my father set for me. Maybe I can show my daughter—and myself— that when we make mistakes, even terrible ones, it is possible to acknowledge them and move on. Maybe it is also possible to forgive ourselves and one another.

When I was eleven and foolhardy, I broke Daddy's strictest rule and rode my horse into the pasture where Jocko the bull lived. Jocko attacked, goring my leg and tossing me across the pasture. Then he badly gored Scout, my old quarter horse.

I lost gallons of blood and nearly died, they tell me. Weeks later, when Daddy was driving me home from the hospital, he told me he was very sorry, but that while I'd been ill, Scout's wounds had gotten infected and they'd had to put him down.

I was devastated.

"It was all my fault," I said, sobbing. "I killed him."

Daddy patted me on the knee and kept on driving.

"This is the worst thing that could ever happen," I wailed. "I broke the rules and I killed Scout."

"This is a hard one," he agreed.

"You must hate me," I sobbed.

Daddy pulled the truck over to the side of the road. "Sweetheart," he said, wrapping his arms around me, "there is nothing you could do that would make me hate you—absolutely nothing in this world."

I continued to weep into his shoulder, gasping for breath.

"We're family, you and I," he whispered into my ear, "we can understand and forgive everything."

That is the voice that has remained with me, the voice I hear reverberating when fear and self-doubt threaten to overwhelm me.

My father was grievously flawed. He is closer and dearer to me now than when I chose to believe him perfect.

About the Author

MARY WILLIS WALKER is the author of *Zero at the Bone*, which won both the Agatha and Macavity awards and was nominated for an Edgar; *The Red Scream*, winner of the Edgar Award; and *Under the Beetle's Cellar*, recipient of the Hammett Prize, the Anthony Award, and the Macavity Award. She lives in Austin, Texas, where she is now at work on her fifth novel.

MARY WILLIS WALKER

"One of the creepiest killers since Hannibal Lecter meets a plot and heroine worthy of Patricia Cornwell. Welcome to the big time, Mary Willis Walker." —*Kirkus Reviews*

Edgar Winner: Best Novel!
The Red Scream
____57172–9 $6.50/$8.99 in Canada

Under the Beetle's Cellar
____57173-7 $6.50/$9.99

Zero at the Bone
____57505-8 $6.50/$8.99

All the Dead Lie Down
____57822-7 $6.50/$9.99